KING DAVID'S LEGACY

31.32° N, 35.35° E
MASADA, JUDAEAN DESERT, ISRAEL

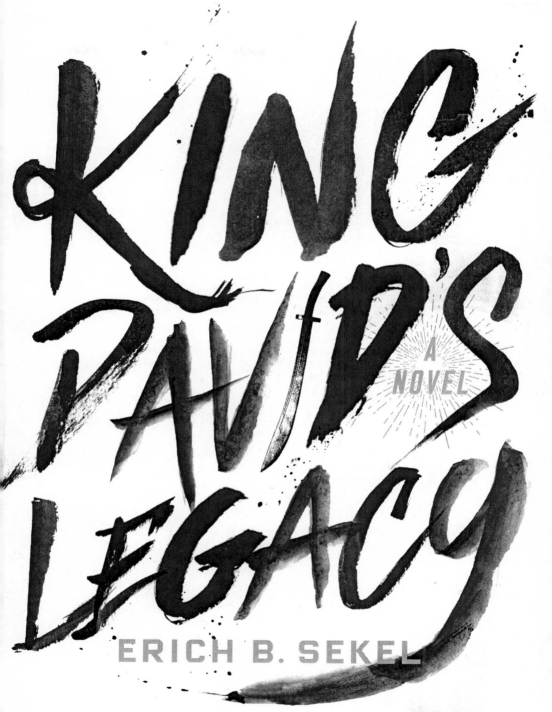

King David's Legacy

A Novel

Erich B. Sekel

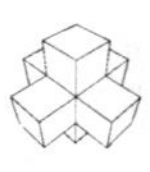

Rubicon Publications

RUBICON PUBLICATIONS
New Jersey Limassol, Cyprus

ISBN 978-0-9861218-0-7 (paperback)
ISBN 978-0-9861218-1-4 (epub)
ISBN 978-0-9861218-2-1 (mobi)

Rubicon Publications are printed on permanent and durable acid-free paper.
This book is printed on paper with recycled content.
Printed in the United States of America.

10 9 8 7 6 5 4 3 2 1

FRONTISPIECE PHOTOGRAPH *Masada in Israel* by Robert Hoetink
COVER PHOTOGRAPH *David in Stone* by Lorae Thompson
COVER DESIGN/BOOK DESIGN/TYPESETTING Vin Dang

WHETHER THEY LIKE what they read or not in the coming pages, a thanks to my family, friends, colleagues, and students who inspired this book. But a special thanks to Edward Daniel, Joseph Deodato, and Karolina Lempert for proofreading; Catherine Weening for editing; and Vin Dang, for everything design-related in this book.

1

IT HAD BEEN YEARS since he knew a morning where he could stomach the thought of the day ahead. As he reached for his cell phone to reset the alarm for a later time, he contemplated excuses for why he might not make it to work that day. He had already used the "dishwasher flooding his kitchen" excuse, and figured not even his friend, Liam Barry, a tough Irish principal, yet understanding with Frenchy, would believe he could have such bad luck as to have that happen twice in one week.

"Maybe I will just tell the truth. There's lots of sympathy these days for people with depression," he thought confidently.

But he knew that saying such an excuse would be admitting something he, himself, refused to believe.

"I'm not depressed," he calmly rebutted, "My life just sucks, that's all."

He rolled over in his bed and gripped his pillow.

Since his surgery, he had more pillows than he knew what to do with, so he had become accustomed to spooning one of the particularly soft pillows that were scattered around him, while he contemplated a way out from the workday.

As his mind shot from one excuse to another, he thought back to the second day of his rehab after surgery. He had undergone surgery to fix his deviated septum, an easy and relatively painless procedure. But the second part, having his throat shaved so he would have a wider passage to breathe and, thus, not snore, was his wife's idea, and quite the opposite of a pain-free procedure.

Ironically, she left him two days into his rehab, tired of seven years of depression, and constant excuses for why he drank so much. He reminisced for a moment about how, through his Percocet haze, her leaving didn't seem real. She had threatened to leave many times before, but he was always able to convince her to stay, convince her that he would change. When she announced her most recent departure, he believed that he could draw on his charm, charisma, and the fact that he was incoherent and recovering from surgery to cancel her threat. He felt confident enough that he could prevent her consistently amended departure date, something he firmly believed she would never follow through on.

But when she showed up two weeks later with her father, ready to take her belongings, the reality of her threat began to sink in.

Her father's face flashed in his mind: a man who looked much like an elderly Magnum P.I. giving him a hug on that gloomy moving day, and saying he was sorry things turned out the way they did. Though trying to show no emotion, Frenchy cried in the faux 80's TV hero's arms.

After they drove off, Francis returned to his apartment, bitter, and determined to make this her mistake, her fault.

"I don't need her," he thought at first, recalling always being able to flirt and succeed with the opposite sex in college and assuming his newly found freedom would be no different.

He could get his "ladies' man" voice back and woo the girls as he did before.

But his defiant spirit soon faded as he realized he wasn't the person he was when they started going out, or in college for that matter, and that he had truly been in love and lost not just his wife, but also his best friend.

He shook his head, trying to dismiss the memories. He rolled over, muttering to himself and cursing his life, trying to remind himself that he didn't care about anything, an easy way of shunning his thoughts. His recent thoughts quickly solidified his decision to skip work, assuring himself he had the right to take a personal day, his seventh that year. His love for his job seemed no match for his unpleasant thoughts and fear of dealing with his issues.

But, as with most days, when he resolved to avoid work, the only thing that could make him budge from his bed and ignore his feelings of regret and self-pity burst into his room with a graceful, yet forceful gait, determined for his attention and immediate relief. He opened his eyes to her familiar face that greeted him each morning.

"What the fuck do you want?" he asked, staring into her eyes, angered by her persistence. She pushed her nose against his lips, causing him to scream in disgust.

"Jesus, fuckin' Jackson! Goddamn you, every time!"

He wiped his clenched lips and looked at her semi-cocked head and her mildly retarded look of confusion, not understanding his problem.

"Well, shit, at least you waited until it was close to when I should be up this time." He mumbled to himself as he threw the spooning pillow from his arms.

"Do you have to go out?" he asked, accenting his voice so he sounded like the people he always despised when he would hear them as he walked down the street. He sneered recalling the sight of said people baby-talking an animal who probably either had no idea what they were saying, or was smart enough to recognize that humans are a bunch of idiot food dispensers who throw biscuits when they crap outside the apartment.

She put her paws up on the bed, not pleased with his slow movement, and started scratching at his arm. She had gotten him halfway, but she needed to push the issue.

While the desire to fall back in bed and hide for the day was strong, the prospect of finding a puddle on his precious rugs or a turd in his closet proved enough to completely stir him.

Reluctantly, he stood up on his valued imitation Persian rug, finally acquiescing to her doggedness. Whenever he looked at his rugs, he always went over his response if a guest ever called him out on having a machine made replica as opposed to the real thing.

"I have a taste for fine things, just not the money."

That phrase always seemed to make it okay that the rug came from Home Depot.

As he stumbled to put on his half-chewed flip-flops, he reached for his pack of cigarettes and plopped one in his mouth. He reminded himself that, at age thirty, it was no longer acceptable to smoke . . . But he had a year, two months and three days, so he was currently still in the clear. He put the leash around the chain collar of his Pit Bull/English Pointer mix, the breed he chose to call her depended on the company. When he was buying Guinness from the liquor store across the street from his apartment, the type of liquor store that has everything behind bulletproof glass, he chose to mention to his fellow patrons, who seemed to never not be in the store no matter what time he went in, that he had a pit bull. When at barbecues where he was a friend of a friend's girlfriend, it was best to mention the English Pointer traits so as not to be asked to leave again because, as one host once said, "There are children around; I can't have a dog like that here."

As she jerked him forward, he noticed the many beer bottles on the kitchen counter. He said aloud, as he did each day, prior to his wife moving in, "No more drinking. Tonight, I will come home and relax with no beer. Today, I will really do it; I am too tired to continue like this."

She pulled him closer to the door, his calf hitting into two large brown boxes, obstructing his clear path to the yard. He gritted his teeth at the daily pain, glaring at the hindrance. He pulled at the leash, bringing Cleo back to his side. Unlike most days, he stopped Cleo's continued drive to the outside. He removed a book from the box and wiped the dust from the cover. He ran his fingers over his name, prominently displayed at the bottom. He sighed sadly.

"God dammit why didn't I listen to everyone? Fuck. If I'd just done what everyone said. 'Take your time, research every angle, don't rush.' Whatever. Fits my life."

He dropped the book into the box, kicking it apathetically. He looked down at Cleo, sitting anxiously, her tail wagging on the linoleum producing clumps of her own tumbleweed.

"You're the only one who doesn't judge or criticize me. Well, maybe you do, but you sure as shit know how to keep it to yourself. Come on, go!"

As Cleo slammed into the partially attached screen door and entered the backyard, he immediately enjoyed the carbon monoxide air from his cigarette. The cool breeze quickly reminded him that he was in the yard in his boxer briefs again, nothing more.

"I wonder if this is legal," he muttered to himself, knowing full well that he asked himself that same question each day, but never had the energy to actually put on a pair of shorts to put an end to the recurring cosmic question. He chuckled as he thought about what his nature oriented friend once asked him: "Isn't it liberating, and kind of exciting? Being publically nude that is." This statement had made Frenchy and his other friend smile awkwardly in agreement. He chuckled for a moment, recalling the strange traits his closest friends possessed.

As he had hoped, after being outside in his small but feces filled backyard, Cleo, his perverted dog, pooped and peed, thus making his day one worth participating in, despite physically hitting his professional failure. Perverted because, though fixed, she never seemed to get past the humping-of-the leg phase that so many adolescents are able to progress past. Frenchy's wonderful grandmother who consistently called his dog a "whore," once introduced herself to a girl Frenchy brought home by blurting out "you know his dog has sex with him all the time" upon their first meeting.

After that phrase, it was too late to explain what she was talking about and while he liked the girl, Frenchy saw no real chance of their relationship going anywhere after such a blunt and disturbing statement.

Frenchy returned to his apartment from the day's defecation with a vivacious spirit. Though he was wildly depressed and convinced he could not handle the day only seven minutes prior, his simple bi-polar attitude and the fact that it was forty-one degrees outside had him feeling invigorated. He threw Cleopatra a dog biscuit and dropped his underwear, instantly running towards the bathroom mimicking a teenage coed after a long night of drinking.

As he stepped into the shower, his thoughts turned quickly to the day he would eventually die. As with all his rituals, no matter how hard he tried, he could not shake such a disheartening reflection. Along with so many other quirks and oddities he possessed, another was the belief that if he thought about dying, he would never die, because he would have taken the surprise element away from death.

"I drink, smoke and eat fast food; I'm just waiting for the day it actually happens."

Though a simple change in lifestyle would help postpone the eventuality, he still felt this odd practice to be his best preventive measure. Nevertheless, though aware of his vices, and the reasonable path to change them, he quickly raced through possibilities, trying to preempt any for that day. He had seen and heard too many stories of people who died alone in the shower, or getting dressed, or perched on a toilet. As his eye caught his framed Elvis Presley picture above his medicine cabinet, he appreciated how the King had preserved his fame, despite his inauspicious end. However, Francis was confident that he would not be so fortunate, if death took him in a similar manner.

When he stepped out of the shower, he felt cleansed and renewed. He vowed to change his lifestyle. He recalled the path to healthiness, and resolved to quit drinking and smoking and be the man he knew he always wanted to be, the man he should be, the man he always fantasized he could be. The kind of guy who was smart, funny, but in a unique, you told a bad joke, but you're so great, it's funny, guy. He wanted to be the man Maggie had always loved.

He dried himself, placing the towel on a hook on the door. He wiped away the condensation from the mirror above his sink and stared at himself. He tugged gently at the added weight he had put on that unfortunately manifested itself as the beginning of a second chin.

"Son of a bitch, I look like Seth Rogen before he lost the weight."

He shook his head and completed his hygienic prep and opened the bathroom door, peering out towards the window to his backyard. Quickly darting naked passed the window, he ran into his bedroom. He began to get dressed, his thoughts returning once again to his ex-wife. He recalled her face the day they met on the T in Boston.

Frenchy, being his obsessive self, noticed immediately her flaws. There was one small hair near the chin, not enough for anyone to notice except someone as meticulous as himself. She wore beat-up black sneakers that made her cuter to him, but not appropriate to wear when bringing her home to Mommy. Her fingertips seemed calloused which he would find out later had to do with testing for her diabetes. At first he thought she was a tough carpenter on the side, but he quickly found that thought odd and inappropriate.

Yet in all her flaws, he could not help but be in awe at how he felt at that moment. His ears immediately turned a moderate shade of blood red, and he began to feel the beginnings of sweat forming on his brow and above his lip. He fiddled with his hat and said hello. She smiled kindly and said that he looked familiar. When she figured out she had seen him when he had delivered a mattress to someone on her dorm floor, he began to explain that he worked for the Office of Housing at Boston University. They smiled at each other, and talked the rest of the way to Harvard Avenue, with both of their stops terminating in Allston, Mass.

"Waste of fucking time," he quickly muttered, signaling to his brain it was time to move on from this thought before he ran to his bed and clutched his pillow as a child might in fear of going to school.

He switched to his familiar fantasy of Frenchy, the cool guy. He briefly smiled, but his expression returned again to dismay, as his daydream was interrupted by reality once again. He thought about how when he had been that guy, Frenchy the "cool guy," it was usually twelve beers into his night and his audience of friends had enjoyed plenty of overpriced drinks at a bar with a theme of eight dollar beers.

Yet, as he dissected his thoughts, he returned to what he knew was a catch-22. When drunk and surrounded by drunks, he was the man he always dreamt of. He smiled as he heard his roommate's voice saying, "You are the funniest guy I've ever met French."

But when sober he had no confidence and no faith in who he was as a person. Moreover, he often felt embarrassed and ashamed the next morning at how he had acted during nights of debauchery, which seemed to exacerbate the situation. No drinking meant the true Francis Degnan, but drinking was the only way to be the cool guy he wanted to be. He paused and sighed, reaching the ultimate question he arrived at every day, but could neither answer nor handle.

He groaned again as he looked at himself in his bedroom mirror. Despite these unhappy thoughts and the major crossroad he had reached once again, he tried to encourage himself.

"This is going to be a good day, a new day," he thought, attempting to bury the negative feelings he had just arrived upon.

He glanced over at Cleopatra, her head buried in her crotch as it often seemed to be for hours each day.

"I need to get you a boyfriend, or girlfriend. Whatever you want."

As he finished dressing, a set of bagpipes caught his eye. They were displayed behind his TV, because it seemed that was the best use for them after he ordered them from Minnesota on the internet, because he was convinced he could teach himself how to play. Now they were a staunch reminder of one of his many drunken ideas that never played out in sobriety. He cursed the Internet for not giving a breathalyzer before purchase.

He refocused and ignored the multiple depressing reminders in his room and began to harness his attention to the pending day. He thought about his three classes of U.S. History I and one of World Civilizations he had to teach today.

"I'll wing it," he thought, having a modicum of faith in his abilities, "but tonight, I will actually prepare the lessons for tomorrow."

He returned to his kitchen and methodically picked up his wallet, keys, cigarettes and cell phone before spraying cologne on every inch of his body. Once, when he was sixteen, he had been told by his mother that he smelled a bit "ripe." Since then, it was eleven swipes of Old Spice deodorant and anti-perspirant on each armpit, and twenty-two sprits of cologne.

"It's a weak cologne, and I smoke, so it balances out," he reassured himself.

He grabbed a Red Bull from his refrigerator and the iPod Maggie had given him that replaced his antiquated Walkman. He moved quickly through his living room and towards the door. He ritualistically looked over at his lovely Cleopatra, who had upgraded her surroundings for her daily cleaning to the couch he tried to keep her from, and reminded her to make good choices while he was gone, something he had gotten used to saying which he had stolen from a movie he had long since forgotten.

He left his apartment and his eventful OCD beginnings to the day, to start his journey to school. He attempted to ignore the fact that there was garbage on his street and in his driveway, despite having swept both, twice a day. Though he knew living in a city meant being surrounded by garbage, he had always hoped that the community would step up and begin taking care of its hometown. Since he was a child he always believed in civic duty, and respect for the dignity of your home. Sadly, like so much in his life, his belief was not shared by all. He recalled the student from the local public school who walked past him one day as he swept up the sidewalks, and dropped an empty bag of chips on his dust pan in some idiotic attempt at solidarity, despite the fact that the student passed the open garbage can that Francis was putting the trash in.

As he stepped into his car and began his commute, his zeal for the day built more and more as he left the sad reminders of his life in his home. As he made a left onto Kennedy Boulevard, he began to fantasize about driving around Jersey City like a mob boss or at least like a political boss, knowing tons of people in his city, being the cool guy everyone knows and loves and waves to, getting high fives and generic compliments from all who he passed. He smiled and reclined coolly in his seat, and began to attempt his dream role. He waved at the crossing guard he had never met as he turned onto Astor place; she always waved back so it made the effort worthwhile. Frenchy often wished that people he wanted to impress could see him drive to work. Though it was insufficient for his ego, he often saw many of his former students and their parents as he drove the three miles to work, making him feel valuable.

He lit his third cigarette of the day, as per the usual, as he approached Grand Street, .75 miles away but perfectly timed to give him two drags after he got out of his car in his parking spot, five blocks away from school.

At every turn, he noticed how downtown Jersey City had changed. The moment he crossed under an elevated section of the New Jersey Turnpike, the world of garbage, crackheads, and drug dealers where he lived disappeared, and the new world of finance, money, and "yuppies" began.

In his years as a student at St. Ignatius Prep, he had been robbed at knife point and beaten severely on his ventures home. Now, the city was populated not with felons, but with pretty white women walking small, puffy dogs, or pushing baby-carriages.

"I bet she wouldn't jump me . . . that is the violent jump me, or the hot jump me for that matter," he thought to himself as he attempted to avert a direct stare at a young woman with her dog, who seemed to have just rolled out of bed and put on anything that happened to be near her bed, which made her twice as beautiful in his eyes.

Seeing her made him recall back to his last few attempts at linking up with the opposite sex. He sneered as he pondered a profound question:

"Why don't girls make the moves on guys? Liberated my ass," he remarked to himself, as he remembered never being asked out by a woman, but failing consistently when he fulfilled his gender duties.

After parking in the lot, he flicked his cigarette as he headed towards Grand Street. He looked towards the front door of the school which was roughly two hundred feet away. He smiled in thanksgiving, as he had learned from the maintenance staff that he could bypass seeing his superiors, by entering though the much closer door that led to an elevator taking him directly to his office. This came in handy on the days when he debated his ridiculous philosophical question, "to get out of bed, or to not get out of bed," which inevitably led to a late start to the day.

He crossed Grand towards his secret entrance. He began to feel fatigue. Though he had accomplished nothing but arriving to school late, he was tired from all the mental battles that took place. He started to think about the moment he got off from work and was able to grab a six pack to celebrate a hard day's work. He briefly acknowledged his 180° from the morning's resolution of "no drinking" to the usual inebriation celebration.

Yet, as with every day, the fact that he arrived at work was enough to convince him that he deserved a few drinks; not too many, but just a few. He quietly entered Ogden Hall and rushed into the ancient, but efficient, elevator.

As the elevator bounced to a halt at the third floor, he exited and walked towards his office. He heard the voices of his "flock," as he called them. His flock was made up of students who, whether Frenchy understood it or not, took a liking to him, and decided they needed to spend every free moment in his office, which he left open to all students throughout the day, a move he learned from his mentor, Father Tony Azzarto S.J, a close friend to his family for many years and a legend at Saint Ignatius Prep.

"Where you been Doc? It's 7:45; we thought you were going to be absent again," one of them remarked, showing teenage concern for the possibility of losing his hangout.

"I'm always here," Frenchy stated as per his usual response, hoping the kids would believe him and that he would convince himself as well.

"Yeah, whatever Doc, you're always sick," Daryl frustratingly rebutted.

Frenchy often forgot that he made up so many excuses for missing a day's work, that his students viewed him as having the immune system of an eighty-year-old crack addict.

"Did you read the paper this morning?" Ricky asked, interrupting Frenchy's moment of enjoyment for internally using the crack addict reference that often offended many when he used it in casual conversation.

"So, did you check *The New York Times*," Ricky pushed, enthusiastically.

Ricky was a tall, lanky, African-American boy who seemed more excited this morning than usual to wax poetic with his teacher.

"No, I didn't. If this has to do with government shit, I don't want to know," Frenchy replied as he fumbled with his keys and thought about how much he disliked the decision makers and, more pointedly, their decisions.

"Not that, the new shit about ol' Adolf," Ricky responded, becoming more excited as he realized that Frenchy had not read the paper and he would be the first to share the good news.

"Am I supposed to guess the punch line to that joke or are you gonna tell me?"

Ricky ignored the sarcastic remark and focused.

"Some soldier from WWII just released a letter he had received from Hitler about a secret mission. A Nazi nigga. I guess the dude was dying and wanted to get it out. It was in regards to . . ."

"Regarding," Frenchy interrupted, "remember give my regards to Broadway, but regarding all els . . ."

"What?" Ricky asked, staring blankly at Frenchy.

"You said regards to; it should be regarding."

Ricky vacantly stared at his teacher, unsure of what was going on. His eyes slowly looked around and returned to his look at Frenchy.

"Are you waiting for me to say something?"

Frenchy realized there was no winning the grammatical debate.

"Forget it, what was it in regards to? And don't use the n-word."

"Oh yeah, the letter was in regards to a search for the Sword of Goliath." Ricky anxiously awaited a response.

Frenchy froze, a feeling of excitement and anxiety suddenly engaged in battle in his stomach.

"The Sword of Goliath, huh?" he asked, looking back towards his office door and attempting to hide his response.

"Yeah, the thing you're always talking about? The one you said has spiritual and intrinsic value?"

"I am impressed that you have been listening," he remarked negatively.

"Yo Dizzle, we listen," Ricky said, hoping to combat his mentor's negativity.

"Sure," Frenchy remarked, feeling the excitement slowly fade as he began to dismiss the veracity of the news.

"So why is this being discussed, what does it matter, it doesn't exist, remember?"

"Treasure hunters are going nuts. Well, not nuts; let's just say they are talking about it. They've been saying it's not entirely impossible that it exists. Although most are saying it doesn't. But at least some are saying that, because, according to the news, Hitler wanted a search to be started in Jerusalem. Doc, they said it's like the bastard child of the Holy Grail, I mean they didn't say that; I am saying bastard child, but think about it, man, to have Goliath's sword, I bet it would be worth a shitload of money. Anyway, I figured you would be the first person who would get calls from anyone interested in finding it since you wrote that book on it."

Ricky ended, hoping to make his mentor happy.

"Yeah, but apparently, no one read my book or, if they did, they laughed at it, so I am not worried about an increase in phone messages, just probably the usual excuses for not handing in assignments. But why debate. Let's find out shall we?"

As Frenchy turned from hanging his jacket behind his door, he had a flash of hope that his phone would be lit up with messages from all the scholars and individuals who had called him a poor excuse for a historian, as one newspaper quoted in his review of his book, *The Power of Goliath.*

He eyed his phone and was surprised that it read twenty-seven missed calls.

"See, I told you, playa, they need the info, Doc," Ricky said, feeling validated for his report.

As he fumbled to enter his voicemail code, he heard the sweet sound of "You have twelve new messages." He hit the number one on the phone to get started on what he suddenly believed would be the rejuvenation of all his hopes and dreams.

"Francis, give me a buzz when you get in, I have a question about something I received in the mail today, from PSE&G. It seems they need to read the meter, and they won't accept our meter readings anymore, which I don't . . ."

"Message deleted. Next message," the automated system said.

"Francis, you're never gonna believe who I just spoke to, my cousin Bern . . ."

"Message deleted, next message."

"Hi, Francis, I'm gonna try you on your cell . . ."

"Message deleted."

He paused to check the missed calls.

"I thought as much," he scoffed in disappointment.

"They're all from your grandmother, aren't they?" Daryl asked, as Frenchy returned to looking at his cell phone, attempting to contain himself from bursting into laughter.

"Yup, all from Grambo."

"Well, whatever, sorry to get your hopes up. You know, I did read some of your book," Ricky stated, hoping to cheer him up.

"Yeah, me too, it was good," Daryl added, hoping to support Ricky's consolation.

"You read the part where I acknowledged my students by name," Frenchy said sarcastically turning towards his computer.

"Yeah, but it had a page number at the bottom, so I did read some of it," Ricky said, laughing.

"Cheer up, Doc, it's Alfredo day at the Gotham."

"Granted, I appreciate your consolation, but you know I have never eaten at that deli."

"Yeah, but at least you always know what they're serving each day."

Voices from the hall began to get louder as the rest of the crew arrived.

"Who's absent? I need a free today to sleep," Munchies asked.

"Let me check," Frenchy said as he logged into his computer.

"Ms. Lopera, Messrs Mernar and Contreras, and . . . . Ol' Teddy Daniels is here after third period."

"Fuck," Muchies yelled in his usual disappointment.

"Hey, your mouth, watch the language when the door is open," Francis exclaimed, knowing full well that he and the kids knew he was a hypocrite for chastising his flock for the language. He had once told a freshman who was caught in a lie about an assignment "If you ever bullshit me again, I'll toss your ass out the fuckin' window."

"So Doc, did you hear about the . . ." Munchies started before being interrupted.

"Yes, I heard about it, and no, no one has called me," Frenchy responded with disdain.

"Whatever, Doc it's Alfredo day," he said moving on. The look on Frenchy's face strongly dictated a not interested vibe.

"You know, despite the reviews of your book, I bet you will see an increase in sales because of this Hitler letter shit," Munchies asserted, his nickname because he enjoyed the occasional snack now and then.

"Thank you, Munch, but my mother can only buy so many copies," Frenchy responded, irritated that his failure seemed to be known to even his students. "The bell already rang; get to homeroom," he remarked at his motley crew of students. As they filed out, they shouted when they would be back.

"I have first free, I have third and fourth free . . ." the students shouted, signaling that he would have a large group during the periods he needed to get work done.

Francis looked up and noticed the quietest of his flock, Alex Lupo exiting slowly. Though he often fell into the backdrop of the office conversation, Francis knew his father had been diagnosed with pancreatic cancer. Attempting to remind himself that life was not all about himself, Frenchy called to the morose young man.

"Hey, Alex, how's your dad doing?"

Alex's face turned red and he dropped his head.

"Not too good; he's lost a lot of weight. His hair is gone too." Alex's eyes began to fill up with tears."I don't know what to do. It's not fair, Doc, he's only forty-four. And my mom never stops crying. I found her in the kitchen with the lights off sobbing."

Frenchy scrambled to think of what he could say to comfort the boy, but knew that any speech on "it being in God's hand's" would be a sham and not who he was.

"That sucks, my brother. I don't know. Just do your best to be there for your mom and take care of yourself. I assume Oscar is helping you through this."

"Yeah, he keeps my mind off of it best he can."

"Good, that's all you can do right now. Try to focus on the positive."

"I will Doc, I will."

As Alex left, his face reminded Frenchy of how unequipped he was to help his students with their problems.

"What the fuck kind of advice is 'Try to focus on the positive?' Whatever. What do they expect from me?" he thought, "I have my own shit, too, I can't help them with theirs. I can't even help myself; how could I do anything for them?"

He sat back in his chair and sighed. For a moment, he fantasized about what it would be like to be a wise good-advice giving teacher who solved problems by uttering a few sentences.

At that moment, the loudspeaker came on and the call for Morning Prayer was announced by the chaplain. As per his usual custom, he did not stand as requested for Morning Prayer, and continued with his work for his second period history class.

The idea of prayer had stopped being important to him, as it seemed none of his prayers were ever answered. He rarely asked anything for himself and the few things he did were not only ignored, but also taken in the opposite direction. Things he asked for others never happened either. Frenchy knew he wasn't an atheist, but he certainly didn't believe that there were rewards for the good and the just.

The Morning Prayer reminded him of how he had prayed so hard for the success of his book. Yet, all he received was mockery for his work.

Still, as he sat ignoring the prayer and preparing the quiz for his second period class, he could not help but wonder about what Ricky had said. Had Hitler really tried to find the Sword of Goliath? Frenchy laughed aloud, realizing Hitler's letter couldn't be worth much. If Hitler was trying to find it, that put himself and Hitler as the only two who believed it could be found.

"Not exactly the company I would like to be associated with," he said aloud.

He continued to stare at his lesson book, trying to fight his curiosity. But he could not help himself. Why would Hitler believe it was still out there? He grabbed at his hair, attempting to steer himself back to work. His mind continued to race with questions. This was the subject he had been ridiculed for writing about, and now it was front page? He gritted his teeth in irritation. He knew he had no time to check, but he couldn't shun his curiosity. He jumped out of his seat, running down the staircase and towards the principal's office.

As he landed awkwardly in front of the chapel at the foot of the staircase, he composed himself and walked down the long corridor of Wallace Hall. He approached the faculty mailroom, stopping suddenly in front of the door. He realized he had not checked his mailbox. He couldn't resist the possibility of finding letters of requests to head up archaeological hunts for the sword from private donors, willing to pay anything for his help and expertise, despite the unlikelihood that such letters could have arrived so quickly.

He fumbled with his keys for a moment trying to find the correct key to get into the mail room. As he put the key to the lock, the door opened quickly, hitting him square in the head.

"Oh shit, I am so sorry, Francis," the woman exclaimed. They really should have a window so you can see into and out of this room."

Though dazed, he didn't need to see who it was who tattooed his forehead. Her sweet voice made his stomach tighten.

"No, it's my fault, I should have knocked. Definitely should have knocked, or at least tapped the door to let someone know I was coming in . . . you know, it seems I just, you know, I forgot to knock."

Despite the blow to his head, he was keenly aware that he was already babbling like an idiot.

"No really, let me get some ice it looks . . ."

"No, I am fine. Hey, at least they invested in solid wood doors, eh?"

Frenchy knocked his fist against the door, foolishly smiling, fully knowing the awkwardness of his joke.

"So, you look very happy today," he said, scratching his head, as he visualized the words forever leaving his mouth.

"What!" he muttered to himself quickly looking away. He knew the blow to the head had knocked him off his game, but even that statement had him questioning his skills. He immediately regained consciousness and realized that he must retreat and start his offensive when he was not injured.

"Yes, thank you, I am happy," she graciously responded to his asinine comment.

"Well, I better go, got a second period class, you know how that is," he said, as he smiled, hoping to end this disaster without her having to fake knowing what he was talking about.

"Yeah, me too, AP English second period."

"Well, good luck with your English, Nikki," he said quickly.

"Thanks," she said, hesitantly smiling and walking away.

He momentarily paused and realized that if he was going to get up the nerve to ask her out, he would have to do much better than, "Good luck with your English."

"Jesus, her first language is Spanish, now she's gonna think I was making fun of her. God dammit why do you suck at this so much?"

As he watched her walk away, he reached for his keys again.

"After all that shit, I still didn't get into the goddamn mailroom."

As he finally opened the door, he saw his best friend, Larry, standing in the mailroom, coffee cup in hand, smiling.

"What the fuck was that? You got tourettes or something?" Larry blurted out in his unique way.

"Shut your shit up, Lar, I'm not in the mood."

"You know, French, there are guys who can help you with this woman problem. You know, guys like Hitch, in that movie with Will Smith and the hot Puerto Rican."

"Here is an itemized response to that statement. Her name is Eva Mendes; not all Hispanic women are Puerto Rican. You're a douchebag and an asshole, and I don't need help; I was dazed from the assault on my forehead. I was unprepared; I will get her next time," Frenchy firmly stated, hoping to convince Larry, as well as himself.

"Suit yourself, guy, but you're not gonna have forever with a girl like that; she'll be dating some hot tight t-shirt wearing meathead by next month. Shit, man, we live in Jersey."

"It's February twenty-eigth," Frenchy uttered in reluctant agreement.

"Hey leap year, son, you got one more day," Larry said with a huge grin on his face.

"Hey on a rational note, what the fuck are you doing in here, alone?" Frenchy asked hoping to move on from his Rico Suave debacle.

"Hiding from Sid; he wants me to cover his second period. So I figure since he already checked his mail, if I hang in here long enough, he will never find me in time."

"That is pathetic, Lar," Frenchy uttered, hoping to put Larry down for once.

"Not pathetic, my brother, smart."

Frenchy reached into his empty mailbox and sighed.

"So lunch today, huh," he asked, realizing after all that transpired, there were no lucrative requests to fulfill his dream.

"5A lunch, you know it, bitch. Hey by the way, did you hear about that Hitler shit . . ."

"Yes, and I really don't care," Frenchy snapped, wanting to move on from the last seven minutes.

"Touchy little Nancy huh?" Larry remarked sarcastically. "Well, whatever, see you at lunch," Larry grinned as he resumed his exaggerated position of looking like he was checking his mail in the event someone walked in.

As Frenchy closed the door, he clenched his fists. Despite his joking with his friend, his anger at who he was and his failure as an author overwhelmed him. He rubbed his eyes in frustration, cursing himself for writing his book. It had given him nothing. Yet now he began to believe that someone would find the sword he was supposed to find, and his life would still be shitty and he would not benefit from any of it. He stood in the hall staring towards the main lobby. Despite his self-resentment and despair at the entire situation, his interest could not be quelled. He continued towards the principal's office on the far side of the lobby, heading directly towards *The New York Times* on the front desk.

"Hey Sid," He remarked at the chairman of the Math department as he walked by.

"Hey French, how's it going?"

"Good. Hey I think I saw something in your mailbox a second ago, better check it out."

"Thanks, I will," Sid responded as he began to get his key out to open the mailroom door.

"That may have made my day," Frenchy remarked to himself as he heard Sid greet Larry and mention how he had been looking all over for him.

Still, Frenchy's focus remained on *The New York Times.*

As he entered the principal's office, he greeted Grace and Cecilia, the principal's secretaries, quickly laying his eyes on the front page of *The New York Times.*

"'Fighting increases in Palestine.' Apparently, *The New York Times* doesn't see the news of the Sword as front page worthy," he said to himself.

As he searched for the article, his eyes were satisfied by the headline on the sixth page: "Long lost information points to Hitler's search for Old Testament mythical artifact."

"Unbelievable, even now, they still think it is a myth," Frenchy remarked to himself with disdain.

As he intently read the article, he dismissed the search starting points proposed by Hitler's letter.

"Fuck that. They've got it all wrong," he uttered in disbelief. As he continued, the article mocked the treasure hunters who now discussed possible expeditions to the Levant hoping to find the Sword.

As he finished reading the article and began to fold the paper back to its original form, a minor headline caught his eye: "World renowned biblical historian, Rabbi Daniel Tannen, dies after battle with cancer."

Frenchy stopped. He had spent months with Rabbi Tannen discussing the Talmud searching for any references to Goliath and his sword.

"Jesus Christ. I had no idea he was that bad. Shit, of course he had to die yesterday," Frenchy lamented to himself.

"I'll have to make the viewing," he quietly mouthed to himself.

He reminisced about his first encounter with Rabbi Daniel Tannen and how the well-respected Rabbi had raised an eyebrow as to why he wanted to research the Sword of Goliath. Frenchy cracked a sad smile in appreciation for all the help he had given. Despite Frenchy's crazy claim that the Sword of Goliath could still be recovered, Rabbi Tannen had nurtured his dream that one day he would be able to find his sought after prize. As he sighed in sadness, the second period warning bell rang.

"Oh shit," he blurted loudly, "I'm not prepared for class."

He ran out of the office towards his second period classroom. He didn't have a permanent classroom, so he bounced from classroom to classroom, thus being referred to as a floater, which always made him laugh as he recalled his enjoyment for potty humor.

As he slowed his run to a disciplinary serious walk, his students greeted him with choruses of questions.

"Hey Doc, did you hear about the . . ."

"Yes, let's get seated," he forcefully asserted as he walked into his classroom acutely aware of that fact that he had no books or papers with him. He waited nervously as he attempted to create a lesson before the second bell.

"Good morning, gentlemen," he said, hoping filler would come to him that would last forty-five minutes.

As he looked at their faces, he realized that they were his best class, and since he was in no position to provide a faux lesson, he resorted to his best option, an attempt at the truth.

"Gentlemen, I have a splitting headache and I left your quiz upstairs in my office. I can go get it, but why not give you guys a free period, and we can take the quiz tomorrow?"

The classroom erupted and they began to grab their things and head for the door.

"Shut up, you tryin' to get me busted? And this is a one-time thing," he said, as he immediately recalled the last time he said that phrase, three weeks earlier.

"You the man, Doc," some of the students remarked.

"Yeah, I'm quite the man, now shut up and quietly get the hell out of here."

"I need a drink," he said as he rubbed his face and watched the last student exit the classroom.

"That quitting drinking thing lasted real long," he sarcastically muttered to himself.

As he stood in the empty classroom, Marie, the woman from the switchboard entered the room.

"You are quite the popular teacher," she sweetly, remarked. Marie was a wonderful person. A woman in her forties who never stopped smiling. She had to be wonderful, to sit at a desk alone from 8 a.m. to 3 p.m. answering calls, and receiving packages.

"I got this for you yesterday and I was instructed to give it to you this morning by eight a.m. I'm sorry it's late. They overloaded me with office supplies this morning. I couldn't find it," she said, as she walked out of the room.

"Have a good day."

"Yeah, thanks, you too," Frenchy remarked happily, suddenly realizing that no class meant a cigarette break.

He closed the door, looking to his left and right, hoping not to be seen leaving the empty classroom.

As he walked towards the basement door that led out to his secret cigarette hideout, he glanced at the return address on the small box.

"Rabbi Daniel Tannen, East ninety-fourth street, NY, NY 10128. That's weird, and coincidental," Frenchy remarked to himself. "I must have left some shit at his house. Not sure what eight a.m. has to do with it, but whatever."

He shrugged off the thought and pushed the door open, as he heard, the principal Liam Barry, come over the loudspeaker.

"Dr. Degnan, please come to the principal's office at your earliest convenience."

Frenchy immediately felt the anxiety you get when you have been blatantly caught doing something wrong. He knew full well that it was against school policy to let students out early or to give them a free period.

"Shit. I knew I would get busted eventually, but dammit, that was pretty fuckin' quick," he remarked to himself.

"I'm down here already, so smoke'em if you got em' before I face the music."

2

A LINCOLN TOWN CAR PULLED UP to the front of the Sinai funeral home. The driver rushed to open the passenger door, but the old man was already on his way to the funeral home's main entrance. He wore a black suit and carried a fedora in his right hand, his left hand gripping a wooden, slightly warped cane. His wrinkled face told the story of a difficult life, filled with tough decisions and struggles.

As he approached the funeral home, he paused to reflect on his surroundings. It had been but a week since he was last in New York. His commitments had him traveling frequently; some desired travel, some not what he always wanted. He tentatively smiled at his surroundings as he momentarily thought about this trip possibly being his last. His good friend and colleague Rabbi Daniel Tannen was dead. But it was not to pay his respects that he had traveled 4,000 miles to the upper east side of Manhattan.

The driver opened the door to the funeral home and the old man gradually made his way to the desk, located to the right of the entrance.

"Is Sarah Tannen here?" the old man asked the funeral director. "Please tell her it is Rabbi Judah, to see her."

"One moment, Rabbi," the director remarked, turning and walking towards the first mourning area.

As the rabbi turned to look out of the front window at the city, a city he had spent much of his life in, his thoughts returned to the last time he and Rabbi Tannen had met. It had been his most recent trip when they last spoke, and their meeting was far from laid-back. He anxiously removed a handkerchief from his pocket and wiped his mouth. Despite an arduous life of difficult moments and experiences, this present moment caused him to tremble with trepidation.

"Rabbi Judah, what an honor to have you come here," a young woman said, rushing over to the aged man.

Sarah, a woman in her late twenties was the youngest daughter of Rabbi Tannen. The sight of the old man brought pride into her heart. His presence seemed to honor, and confirm her beloved father's passing.

"It is good to see you, Sarah," the rabbi said, embracing his old friend's child. He looked kindly at her and smiled.

"You know, it was not too long ago, I held you in these frail old hands," He said, presenting her with his slightly trembling hands. "Now, you have grown into a fine young woman; your father was fortunate to have such a loyal daughter."

"I wish you had phoned to let us know what flight you were on, we would have come and picked you up," she said, appreciating his presence at such a sad time.

"You have plenty on your mind right now, my dear. I did not want to be a burden."

"Well, please, the coffin has not been sealed; we are still able to see my father. You were his closest friend," she stated, taking his arm and leading him into the main room. She glanced over at the *shomer*, a watchman over the corpse. Despite accepting her father's passing, this aspect of the Jewish tradition made her uneasy.

"How is Zion?" Sarah asked, using the name her father always used when he talked about Israel.

The rabbi dropped his head slightly and sighed.

"It seems there will never be peace in our promised land," he remarked. "Hatred on both sides seems to dominate daily life. Men, women, children, killed daily in markets, neighborhood blocks, and all other places. To some extent, Sarah, I envy your father. At least he is at peace with the Lord."

Sarah paused as the Rabbi seemed to be overwhelmed.

"Though he lived in New York, his heart always rested in Zion. He talked frequently of his time there, of the day he would return. Unfortunately, he never made it back," she said, suddenly reciprocating his emotion. She attempted to repress her tears.

"His spirit and his heart live on in you, my dear, and he will always live in Zion," Judah said, putting his wrinkled hand on her cheek to console her.

As they moved forward slowly, they approached the open casket. Rabbi Judah began to utter a prayer in Hebrew. Sarah, who had stayed by her father's side for the last six months, began to tear and move off to the side. Though he had been sick for many months, she still had never prepared herself for the inevitable.

She recalled back to the morning her father's doctor and close friend Nabil El Deri told her that her father had passed away. Nabil is a Muslim, a fact that caused her father much grief from his other friends. Nabil refused to allow her to enter the room to see her dead father.

"Wait until the viewing, he had a very difficult end, I do not want you to see him like this."

Though at the time she wanted to embrace her father, she knew that Nabil, far from being the cautious type, would not have kept her from her father if it wasn't in her best interest.

She had struggled during his last few months, witnessing him fight his illness, so she acquiesced to his recommendation.

As Judah finished, she returned from her memories to the present. Judah turned to Sarah, recognizing her sorrow.

"I know how difficult this time has been for you and your family. I pray each day for you and your sisters." The old man looked down at his friend, his thoughts again recalling momentarily, their last conversation. The pain of that memory caused him to drop his cane. Sarah quickly picked it up and handed it to the Rabbi. He smiled at her and looked down at his wrinkled hands and remembered his responsibility.

"Sarah," he softly said to her, taking her arm and leading her towards a paisley covered couch near the coffin.

"I wonder if you could help me with one last thing. An old man's meticulous nature is hard to defeat."

"Of course, Rabbi Judah, anything for my father's closest friend," she said, attempting to compose herself.

"Tell me, my dear, there was a package I had sent to your father roughly two days ago, to be passed on to a friend of his—was it ever sent forward?"

Sarah wiped the tears from her eyes and regained her focus, not expecting that to be the help he needed.

"Uh, yes, I believe it was sent two days ago, same day. To a Francis Degnan, correct?" Though her father's death had been difficult to handle, the last two days had been the most trying, as she spent much of her time "tying up loose ends" for her father and preparing to lay him to rest.

As she looked into the aged eyes of the rabbi, she began to recall all the errands she had done for her father.

"That was the man who should have received it. Tell me, did your father open the original package?"

The rabbi was a cautious man; he knew it was a tough time for Sarah and somewhat of an odd request given that fact, but he needed to confirm the real reason he had come to New York.

"No, I believe he left it to be sent as it had arrived. Why? Is there something wrong?"

Sarah now became suspicious, as her father had also been very meticulous regarding this package, ensuring that all was done exactly as he asked.

She quickly felt uncomfortable at Rabbi Judah's inquiry into the same errand.

"No, my dear, I just wanted to make sure it was sent to Mr. Degnan. It was a final favor your father did for me. He was truly a man of honor and dignity. You should be proud of your father, he has made Zion proud."

Sarah's eyes began to well up with tears again as she thought about her father. His last words to her earlier that week when he took a turn for the worst, echoed in her mind.

"Know that no matter what anyone says, I fulfilled my duty to God," he said, through labored breathing. She regained her composure and strength and focused on Rabbi Judah.

"Thank you for your kind words, Rabbi Judah, I shall not forget them."

"And I shall never forget your father, nor what he did for Israel," the Rabbi remarked as he kissed her cheek and struggled to his feet. He began walking towards the door.

"You won't be staying?" Sarah asked, shocked at how quickly he planned to leave after his odd line of questioning.

"I am sorry, my dear," as he turned back towards her, "I must return to Zion; there is much in need of my attention."

As he looked at the young girl he had known for many years, he lamented leaving her in such a manner.

"I will be back very soon. I promise to honor your father appropriately," he said, consoling Sarah.

"You have already honored him with your presence and your love. He would be very grateful," she said, feeling more and more uneasy about this visit with the Rabbi.

"The righteous shall receive all the rewards in heaven," Rabbi Judah said quietly, kissing Sarah's forehead again, before walking quickly towards the funeral home's door.

"And the realist is saddled with the burden on earth," he said quietly, as he exited the home.

He pulled a cell phone from his overcoat and hit send, recalling the most recently dialed number.

"The package was sent," he uttered, seeming exhausted by his words. Silence from the other end signaled skepticism.

"She sent the package?" the voice asked.

"As expected and planned," the aged man replied, hoping to reassure his colleague. "I will be going to my apartment to pick up the Map. We can recover the Sword and use it to unite our people for the coming war. It will be our great unifier as we move forward. Tell the Prime Minister we are one step closer, thanks to Tannen"

"The full map is at your apartment?" the deep voice asked.

"Yes, Assaf, Tannen gave me his half and I stored it in my apartment after meeting with him last week. Do not worry, it is safe."

"Please return immediately with the map. The Prime Minister desires a speedy completion to this aspect of the process."

"Of course," the rabbi said, closing the cell phone with a shaky hand.

"God reward all who toil in your name," he said as he moved towards the limousine, looking up at the cloudy sky." That is my only hope."

"Where will you be staying, sir?" the driver asked as he opened the door for the rabbi.

"Ninety-sixth and Park, my good man, but only for a brief stop, and then onto Newark Liberty."

"Yes, sir," the driver responded.

As the limo pulled away from the curb, Judah thought of his last conversation with his dear old friend during their last encounter in New York, not three blocks from this funeral home, and not a week to the date.

"I don't think it should become known to the world. It should not be possessed by one country, by one leader. Our world is filled with greedy people with ruthless ambition. It doesn't matter if you believe it has power or not. It is how people respond to symbols. Look at the Romans and the standards for each legion. They were willing to die, to protect nothing more than a staff with an image on it. Think about what would happen if our people rallied behind it. There would be no peace. We should burn the map and forget about its existence," Tannen said vehemently, quickly sitting down to catch his breath.

Judah gestured towards his sick friend, unsure as how to help.

"I have always agreed with you, but times have changed."

Judah paused, understanding his friend's position.

"You have always been a good man, but this is not about being good; it is about survival, not just for you and me, but also for your daughters, for our people. I am sorry I broke our agreement and I revealed our find. I made a mistake and for that I plead for forgiveness. But what is done is done. Still they believe this could be the advantage we need. Please, Daniel. Think of what they do to our people each day. Think of the hate that they have for us. Do not let the notion of equality or fair play cloud your judgment. This is a war that we must win. We will win! It is not an issue of right or wrong. This belongs to us."

Judah's words seemed to touch the ailing Rabbi.

"And what of Dr. Degnan? He is innocent, he must not be hurt. I don't care what irrational fears our government may have, especially that Assaf. Degnan is harmless," Tannen pushed, aware that Degnan's interest in the artifact brought him in the path of those determined to possess it.

"Assaf Greene has promised to handle him in partnership with the FBI. He will not be harmed. They will just . . . ensure his cooperation. We just don't want any interference with our acquiring it. All you have to do is forward whatever is sent to you and all will be as it should. We have put together a package offer for your friend. Believe me, he will be satisfied with our proposal for his assistance. But it is imperative that it comes from you. So please, pass it on. It will be dropped off to you soon."

Tannen stared confused at his friend.

"FBI? I don't understand, why must I send it? I want no part in that."

"If you send the package, then he will see that you support our proposal. He is more likely to accept."

Tannen put his hand on his chest, thinking about the circumstances. His mind recalled the violence he had witnessed during the time he spent living in Israel. Judah shifted anxiously on the bench.

"Daniel. We are both old men. You are very ill. In your final days, we could do something amazing. We could save our people forever. What greater way to be remembered?" Judah said, putting his arm on his friend's shoulder.

"I suppose you are right," Tannen said. His body seemed to relax as he rendered his decision.

"I only ask that you do not retrieve it until I am in my grave. As much good as it may do, as you say, I do not want to see the bad that may come along with it. And Degnan is not to be hurt."

Judah nodded in agreement. "You have always been a man of reason. You have made Israel very proud with your decision."

Tannen scoffed quietly, looking over at his friend.

"Old Friend, it is not my country I am worried will not be proud."

3

AS JUDAH'S LIMOUSINE DROVE UP LEXINGTON, Sarah walked out to the curb and watched his departure. She reached down into her purse and removed a letter that Dr. El Deri, her father's physician, had left her on her night stand the morning her father died. Rabbi Judah's visit had left her feeling uneasy and unsure about what his visit had really been about. She opened the envelope and began to read the letter. A letter she had been too distraught to read before. She opened the envelope only to find a second envelope enclosed with a note. She opened the note and began to read.

> My Dear Sarah,
>
> I know how difficult these last few weeks have been on you. You have been nothing but a loyal and loving daughter. However, in these last days, I believe I have been betrayed by a close friend. Unfortunately, the package you sent is not the last request that I have for you. I have realized now that I was a fool to trust certain people in my life. In retrospect, I almost wish I had not uncovered their treachery before I take my last breath. Still, I must put my faith in you and in a close friend. As soon as you read this, please contact and meet with a Dr. Francis Degnan. He is a teacher in Jersey City at Saint Ignatius Prep. You briefly met him once when I was working with him on a book he wrote. It is difficult to explain, but believe what I say. It is as severe as it will sound. I believe the governments of Israel and the U.S. are threatened by him. I do not wish to go into any further detail. I have bought him some time, but it is imperative that you take this note to him. He should understand and be able to avoid them. Just please make sure you get this message to him. Then, please, leave him. Go and stay with your cousins. I have no desire that you be involved in this. I am sorry for this being my last letter to you, but know I cannot allow this to occur. Love always.

Sarah stood shocked staring at the note. In no way did she expect this to be the last words she would have of her father's. She shook her head in disbelief. She began to dissect her father's words. She had done what he asked of her, the day before he died, by sending the package out. Now she began to wonder what her father had been involved in. She returned to the letter, rereading, attempting to process its obscure message. She looked back at the door of the funeral home and blindly walked towards the door.

She stopped in the lobby and looked over towards her father's casket. He had made it clear that when she read the letter to find Degnan. But she could not leave him now. Yet, his words echoed in her mind. What did he mean betrayed? Was this related to Rabbi Judah? She dismissed the notion that Judah would have betrayed her father. They had been classmates, they had worked together on archaeological digs, and they had studied together for years.

Sarah stared at her father's almost unrecognizable body. She gripped the note and held the second envelope in her hand. Suddenly, she called to the funeral director.

"Mr. Cohen."

The funeral director rushed over, concerned by her tone.

"Would you get me a cab?" she asked shoving the envelope and note into her purse.

"You are leaving Sarah? You will not sit . . ."

"My sister will be here very soon. I must go," she interrupted him.

The director looked at Sarah's frantic expression and chose not to oppose her demand.

"As you wish."

The director signaled to another gentleman standing near the mourning room.

"Please get Ms. Tannen a cab."

"Right away sir," the young man said, opening the door and moving towards the street. Sarah walked immediately behind him and stepped into the first cab that stopped, her heart rate increased as the words of her father's letter began to give her a feeling of panic.

"Where to?" the driver asked.

"Jersey City, Grand Street," she said quickly, securing her seatbelt.

The driver began to explain the cost of traveling into New Jersey.

"To Jersey, there is a fee of . . ."

"I'll pay, just go please," she said firmly.

As the cab sped off, she nervously looked at her cell phone, becoming keenly aware that she should have opened the letter sooner. She looked back at the funeral home. Her mind raced as she recounted the last half hour and her change in emotions moving from extreme sorrow, to confusion, and now panic.

"I just hope I am not too late," she muttered as the cab headed towards the Holland Tunnel.

AGENT CARL ESPINOZA rushed into the deputy director's office with a manila envelope. He had been monitoring the case his boss had given him intensely for the last week. Problems arose, but he astutely and proudly handled them without having to present to an impatient boss. But this time, a problem on the job had come up that he could not and would not handle without his Director's advice. He quickly interrupted the director's secretary.

"Sir, I need a moment; it's urgent."

"Will you excuse me, Julie, Carl and I have some time-sensitive material to discuss," the director stated, never taking his piercing eyes off Carl and the file he looked unpromisingly at.

"Of course, sir, I will type these notes up," Julie said, looking curiously at Carl, wondering what was so time-sensitive.

"Thank you, Julie, would you get the door on the way out?"

As the door closed, Al Jensen's demeanor turned hostile. A senior member of the FBI, he had seen many agents come into his office frantic and panicked. It was usually nothing to get worried over, but for every young agent it was the be all and end all of importance. Though he was always able to handle these "emergencies" with ease, he seemed particularly irritated at the sight of Espinoza, frazzled and anxious.

"Why the hell are you here? I specifically told you what I wanted handled, which means you handle it, and when it's done, you come into my office and nod, signaling it is done, so I can do the same to my boss. That's how this shit works. That's how I expect you to complete your assignments."

"I am sorry, sir, but there may be a problem," Carl said urgently.

"What problem? I was told the old man's daughter mailed it, you saw it mailed, we know it arrived because we delivered it—all should be done, we just need to wait What's the problem?" Jensen felt affirmed in his ability to resolve the panic in one sentence.

"Sir, it seems Tannen sent a decoy," Carl stated, pushing the urgency element in his timid voice.

"A decoy? Come on, you've got to be joking. This is ridiculous. There are no decoys in cases like this."

Jensen mocked Espinoza for attempting to sound important with his word choice. Espinoza stared blankly at his superior.

"Fine, Carl, if that's the case, then how did we not detect and intercept? And why do you believe this now? Huh? Where is this decoy? Give me the freakin' file."

Espinoza handed the manila folder to him. Jensen opened it removing picture scans and dropping them on his desk spreading them quickly.

"You see, you scanned it. What's that in the box? C4. You confirmed it. What's the problem?" the director asked confidently.

"Sir, that is C4. And yes I confirmed it. But there must be something wrong. Tannen must have tampered with the original set-up."

"Carl, he couldn't have opened it. If he did he would be dead . . . in a different way from the present, not from illness. And what's this not delivered correctly?" Jensen stumbled over his point.

"Sir the problem is . . . ," he began, pausing to regain strength.

"You didn't answer my question, how do we know it wasn't sent correctly?"

Jensen's irritation grew as Espinoza seemed flustered.

"Jesus Christ, now is not the time for a petulant Oliver Twist moment, out with it."

"First off sir, it is eight oh five a.m., and we have no calls about a bomb going off in Jersey City. If all had been done properly, the bomb should have taken him out and only him, maybe a few students, but still by now it should be done. Second, we searched Tannen's apartment after his death, and found the original box. Therefore, he must have opened the original and changed the packaging. It must not have tripped when he opened it. In addition, we have found nothing in his apartment, so he must have gotten rid of the detonator."

Jensen looked down at his desk, realizing Espinoza's point.

"So then, what, the one sent to Degnan is just C4? This is incompetency at the wrong time. This was a simple task and you have failed." Jensen momentarily glared at Espinoza, eventually looking down at the scattered photos. "Fine, then we need to change our plans. Bring Degnan in, we can still work through this, make something up as to why we need him. You know what, even better: tell him we need his help with a state matter. He'll buy that horseshit. Then bring him in and I'll find out what they want to do with him."

"I'm on it, but what about the detonator?" Espinoza said. Despite his boss' attacks on his capability, he was a meticulous and determined investigator.

"Forget about the detonator, it's useless without C4, it's nothing more than a piece of wire. You just get Degnan. Go, now!" Jensen shouted, picking up the phone.

As Espinoza quickly moved towards the door, the director of the FBI, New York division, slammed into the office.

"There's been an explosion on the Upper East Side, Ninety-sixth and Park, a few minutes ago. There is not much info right now, but it looks like this was no accident. NYPD is there now, but we need to be there as well."

The FBI director stared angrily at Jensen. Jensen snapped back at his director not fully comprehending what was being said.

"So what does this have to do with me? Send someone up there then," Jensen said, brushing off what seemed to be something another agent could deal with given the crisis he was trying to handle.

"It was an Israeli's NYC apartment. A Rabbi Judah, and this has everything to do with you," the Director stated sharply at Jensen.

Jensen paused from dialing as the information began to sink in. He remembered Espinoza's words about no bomb going off in New Jersey. He looked at Espinoza in irritation. Espinoza looked down humbly. Though a blunder this large was never cause for celebration, he was quietly pleased that he was vindicated from his superior's claim that Tannen had not tampered with the package.

"This changes nothing, Carl, stick with your task, I'll handle this," Jensen said grabbing his jacket from the adjacent coat stand. Espinoza quickly left the room, looking down as he walked past his superiors. The director grabbed Jensen's arm as he moved passed him.

"This assignment is very important. To sound cliché, 'this came from the top.' You better get your shit in order; I can't cover for you or your people on this one."

"Everything will be in order, there is no problem," Jensen said, determined that he could control any problem that arose.

The Director put his hand up to Jensen, gesturing for him to pause.

"I suppose what I just said is a result of anger and tension. I know you don't know all the details of this 'situation' but the most important part for us is to ensure that this agreement is not jeopardized. We are on the verge of the most profitable treaty the U.S. has ever been involved in. The Vice President expects us to handle any possible roadblocks. So, you handle them. I want to be kept up to date consistently from here on out. Find out why our plan has been disturbed."

Jensen nodded in agreement.

"Our objective is clear and we will complete it. I'll find out what happened up on Park."

5

AS FRENCHY STEPPED OUTSIDE to have his cigarette, he smirked to himself nervously, knowing he was in for a stern lashing from his boss for releasing his second period class. He paused from his anxiety and looked down at the many cigarette butts scattered around his feet.

"Shit, I smoke a lot," he thought to himself, fully aware he was not planning on changing at that moment.

"I need to get an ash tray from maintenance."

He stared into the faculty parking lot and thought about the many times he had come out to smoke in the last four years. The happy cigarettes he smoked when he was first engaged to Maggie; the hung-over cigarettes which sadly seemed to be every cigarette he had smoked in the last four years before noon. The humiliated cigarettes when the faculty got word of the reviews of his book and found it necessary to remind him of it, each and every time they saw him. The sad cigarettes when Maggie left him and he would come out and think about all the moments and years he had spent with her, now gone, and the need to "start a new life" as his best friend once advised him.

As he thought about the Guinness he knew would make everything better, if he just got through the school day, he smiled, reaching for his vibrating cell phone in his pocket.

"Ricky" flashed on his cell phone screen.

"What's up, Ricky?" he happily answered.

"Doc, there are some lame guys in black suits in the main office, they look like narcs."

"Anyone who is different and in a suit, you guys think is a cop," Frenchy said, irritated that this garnered a phone call.

"Just kidding, Doc, but I think they are waiting for you, they might be interested in hiring you to find the Sword."

Even Frenchy found this a plausible possibility, considering he had just been called to the principal's office, and this was the day the news on the sword had been released . . . and he was the leading scholar on the topic, even if he was the only scholar on the topic.

"You may be right, Ricky, I'll be there in a few, where are you?"

"In your office, where else?" Ricky responded in puzzlement.

"I'll let you know how it turns out," Frenchy said, closing the phone and feeling the hourly swing from the depressed and "life sucks" mood, to "things may not be so bad."

He stamped his cigarette out and headed towards the door, swiping his key fob to gain access.

He looked back at his cigarette station.

"Shit, that looks bad. I wonder if they know how many times I come out here to smoke on a given day," he thought to himself, shunning negative thoughts and returning to the prospect of finally becoming the Indiana Jones he always dreamt of.

As he emerged from his subterranean cig-hideout, his excitement reminded him of the first time he dreamt of moments like this, just before his book was released. He strolled towards the Ogden Hall doors, and adjusted his posture, holding his head high. He wanted everyone to see him walk to glory. Even if it turned out to be false, he couldn't resist the moment.

He strolled down to the greetings of the students waiting for their next class lining the hallway. He enjoyed the greetings of his students, for he was proud to be himself for the first time in a long time.

"I can't wait to celebrate with a few pints tonight," he happily remarked to himself as he looked straight towards the principal's office and his hopeful glowing future.

He fixed his eyes on the first gentleman he saw. Though he wasn't sure why they would send law enforcement men or whatever they were, to ask for his services, he smiled and calmly waved his right hand towards Principal Barry speaking to the suited guest.

"Morning, Liam," he said confidently. "I heard the call, and came as soon as possible. How can I be of service," Frenchy said, attempting to control his smirk.

"Francis, this is Agent Espinoza of the FBI. He would like a few words with you."

"Of course, I am always at the government's service," he said shaking Espinoza's hand.

"Shall we meet in the conference room?" Frenchy said, gesturing towards the main conference room; one everyone could see into and wonder what is taking place. Frenchy wanted to make sure all his faculty friends who mocked him could get a glimpse of him metaphorically flipping them off.

"I would like to meet with Dr. Degnan alone, if you don't mind," Espinoza said firmly.

"Nonsense, Liam is one of my close friends and I would like him to be here to give his input in on the situation," Frenchy pushed, hoping to augment the spectacle while also recalling Liam's joke about Frenchy in search of a "Jew's Excalibur" at a faculty meeting a year earlier.

"I insist," Frenchy said putting his arm around Espinoza and Liam and ushering them into the conference room.

"Is your associate going to join us?" he asked, gesturing towards the second agent who had not spoken since Frenchy's arrival.

"No, Agent Forester will wait outside."

"I get it, no worries. Good luck with the trees my brother," he laughed, enjoying his joke. "I'm just jiggling your balls bud, have a seat here," Frenchy gestured to a wooden bench outside of the conference room.

Forester seemed to show some emotion for the first time since arriving by twitching in irritation.

As the three men sat down at the round mahogany conference table, Espinoza reached for a letter in his right pocket.

"I won't waste time, Doctor, the government is in need of your professional expertise in the recovery of the . . ."

"Sword of Goliath, yes I know."

Espinoza smiled to himself recalling his director's words about how Frenchy would buy into the fact that they would want his help. Espinoza began to enjoy his role, as he took Frenchy to be smug and pompous.

"You are the only man we can turn to. Tell me, Doctor, can you help us, will you help your government?" he asked, reveling in his acting skills.

"I am always ready to fulfill my civic duty, Agent Espinoza. You know, I taught seventh grade Social Studies for two years before my time here at Saint Ignatius, and I always reminded my students that a true citizen is one who puts the needs of his country and fellow person above all . . ."

"Excellent," Espinoza said, interrupting the pretentious parade of crap his target was marching.

"We need you to come with us immediately, for there are treasure hunters scattered across the globe looking for this object. Time is of the essence. Principal Barry, would you grant Dr. Degnan a sabbatical?"

Frenchy's eyes widened, reveling in the formality of the word.

"Yes, will you Mr. Principal? I'm in need of a sabbatical." Frenchy smiled at his boss, oddly batting his eyelashes, which seemed to confuse both Espinoza and Barry.

"Of course, I will make arrangements immediately," Liam said, confused and surprised that all of this was happening.

"So, if you give me a few days to get my affairs in order, I will fly down to Washington so we can begin."

"No, you must leave with us now to be briefed at our offices in New York," Espinoza said sternly.

"I can't leave now, I have to get my files and papers to begin the search. Believe me, we may need them," Frenchy said, in disbelief that he would be needed literally at that moment. He also was not going to allow this opportunity to gloat to pass by.

"I am sorry, but we do not have time for that, you need to come with us now, we can get your things later. The only thing you need right now is the package that was sent to you by Rabbi Tannen."

Frenchy wrinkled his brow suspiciously.

"How do you know I got a package?"

Espinoza paused, his thoughts racing for an answer.

"Because we're the FBI. It's what we do. We make sure we know everything about important people."

Frenchy's suspicion quickly fled after the disingenuous compliment.

"Besides, maybe it contains research that you had completed with him."

Espinoza began to grow impatient with the game he was playing.

"Well, that may be true," Frenchy said, returning to wondering why there was a rush for him to leave. "But furthermore, that information is not enough; I have got notes, charts, maps, ancient documents at my house . . . or scans of ancient documents. Shit, my dog is at my house; I have to make sure someone takes care of her."

Espinoza tried to halt Frenchy's spontaneous tantrum. He knew he had lost his advantage with Degnan.

Espinoza decided to handle things the way he should have from the beginning. "You're right; you can return home and we can meet later this week. Perhaps, Forester can help you get the things you need from your office."

"Okay, that seems more reasonable. I just need to go up to my office to get my package and my laptop, and I'll get things from home, and be ready say, tomorrow, noon?" Frenchy said, feeling victorious that for once he had stood his ground.

"That sounds fair," Espinoza said, opening the door and walking out. "Agent Forester, please help Dr. Degnan with his things."

"It is really not necessary; I can get my things . . ."

"I insist, it is the least I can do for being rude and frantic. I have a director on my ass and he said that he needed you to be briefed immediately. I am sorry for my pushiness," Espinoza said hoping he could coax him to come immediately without using force.

"Well, I suppose I could call my mother to get my dog, but we have to stop by my apartment on our way because I need to get my shit," Frenchy said, feeling more important than he had ever felt in his life.

"Sure, and we can bring your dog as well. Please show Agent Forester to your office and he will get your things."

"Well, that seems fair," Frenchy said, won over by the coddling. "Let's go, my woodland friend," he said, putting his arm around the unamused agent.

As he walked towards the stairwell leading to his office, he turned and gave a thumb's up to his principal, and returned to his giddy joy. "I always knew people would see that my theory on the sword was more than just plausible," he said to the silent agent. "I am just surprised that it took this long. You know, for someone to see the value in my book."

The agent quietly walked up the stairs behind Frenchy, uninterested in entertaining Frenchy's gloating.

"You know, I first got the inspiration for the book when I was attending Boston University in a series of classes called Core Curriculum. We had to read the first five books of the Old Testament, or the Torah, or Pentateuch in Greek, if you prefer, and I knew I had found something special . . ."

"Is your office close sir?" Forester said, interrupting his chatty companion.

"Yes, right up here. Anyway, I was sitting in my Core discussion class, and I realized that this was an artifact that no one had ever looked for or thought could be real. So I set out to research and find it. Unfortunately it took a long time to research and I never had the money to get an expedition up without private funding. Here we are," He said, stopping his practice answers for his dream interview on *Larry King*.

He reached down to open his office door, surprised to find it closed.

"Like I was saying, Funding was the only thing that was holding me back from . . . Hey Ricky!" Frenchy gestured welcomingly at Forester. "You were right. The government needs my help. This is an FBI agent . . ." Frenchy ushered the agent in to greet his student.

Frenchy looked at Ricky's face. Though mostly a cool character, Ricky could not hide showing his thoughts and emotions on his face. Thus, his look of, "don't yell at me," mixed with "I did nothing," confused Frenchy. At that moment, Frenchy saw a quick flash of motion, a woman emerging from behind the door holding his Micky Mantle baseball bat standing over Forester, the FBI agent dropping to the ground.

"What the hell are you doing woman?" Frenchy exclaimed looking at the unconscious agent.

"Chill Doc this is . . ."

"I don't care who it is. Woman, you just knocked out my meal ticket, my ticket to fame and popularity, to prestige, awards . . ."

The woman struck Forester again.

"Shut up Dr. Degnan," she said firmly, reaching for Forester's gun and rounds.

"Are you robbing him? Is that what this is about? Well, let me tell you, bitch, you will not screw up my . . ."

"I am not robbing him; I am getting his gun."

She threw the gun and clip under an adjacent couch in the office. She turned towards Frenchy quickly.

"You don't remember me, do you?" she said, slamming Frenchy against the wall.

"No, I don't, because I like women who don't assault me," He said, not fighting back because he was actually intimidated by her forceful behavior.

"My name is Sarah Tannen, Daniel Tannen's daughter. We met once when you were working on your book with my father."

Through his hazy emotional movement from pride, to anger, to fear of being killed by a random woman, he realized who she was.

"What the fuck are you doing here, and why did you hit Forester? And Ricky, you knew about this shit? And you know you can't close my office door without me in here. And don't eat on my desk . . . God dammit! This is anarchy."

"Let's go," Sarah shouted grabbing Frenchy by the shirt and pushing him out into the hallway.

"Grab my package, Ricky, this bitch is crazy," Frenchy shouted as he was ushered out into the main hall.

Ricky ran behind them and shut the door, locking Forester in. Frenchy had always complained about having a door in which he could be locked in, but maintenance never fixed it, despite Frenchy's persistence and claim that he could not work knowing he could be trapped. For once, someone ignoring his claim paid off.

"Alright stop, fin! I am not going anywhere; my dream life is waiting for me downstairs. By the way, like I was saying before being interrupted by the Jew version of Barry Bonds on estrogen, Ricky you were right. The agents were here for me and the government wants my help to find the Sword of Goliath," he blurted out in excitement.

"The what?" Sarah exclaimed stopping and turning sharply at Frenchy.

"The Sword of Goliath, the artifact I researched with your father, the subject of my book, the thing I have spent my life working on because it is the only damn artifact in this world that has not been found or made into a fucking movie. I will finally be like Indiana Jones, or Nicholas Cage in *National Treasure*, or any other douchebag in a movie searching for historical shit. Sorry, children, but I am going to finally get a chance to live my dream and find it. I'm not going anywhere."

"Well, I hate to shatter your ego, but they don't want you; they want to kill you," Sarah said, taking Frenchy's package from Ricky and shoving it into his chest.

"You opened it!" he exclaimed, irritated that someone would go through his things.

"You left it on the hood of a car in the parking lot annex, you dumb shit. You know, where you smoke your cigarettes."

Frenchy looked astonished that someone knew his secret hiding spot.

"You know this place?" he asked, racing through what he had said or done in his not-so-secret hiding place.

"My bad Doc," Ricky said confessing to his sin. "We all know where you go to smoke, and she said it was a matter of life and death that she find you, so I told her."

"Well, Judas, last time I go anywhere without looking over my shoulder."

"Let's go," Sarah insisted.

"No, they want me to find the Sword of Goliath, and I am going to find it for my country. You will not spoil this day for me, despite the fact that you just knocked a guy out who didn't seem to like me anyway. Fuck, I'm sure he will love me now. Just leave me alone, will you? Ricky, go back to class."

"You are as stubborn as you are oblivious. Read this!" Sarah exclaimed pulling out her father's letter from her purse.

"What's this?" Frenchy asked, irritated at this delay.

"My father left it for me before he died. He also instructed me to send this package to you yesterday to arrive today. For God's sake, look in the package first."

Sarah stared him down.

Frenchy fumbled to open the box and look in. As he finally opened the flaps of the box, he pulled out what looked to him to be two tubes of silly putty and a cable TV wire.

"Why would you send this to me? What the fuck is it?" he said, looking confused.

"I think it's an explosive and I didn't know what was in it when I sent it, but clearly my father did not send it armed, so he was not trying to hurt you."

"Yeah right, bullshit, you ever see *The Last Boy Scout* with Bruce Willis and one of the Wayan brothers? The motherfucker exploded when he pushed it onto a bar sticking out from his trunk. I could have been smoking a cig and boom! Dead."

"C4 does not explode from being around cigarettes, you idiot, and he obviously wanted you to be okay, hence why he sent me with this letter. Now open and read this letter he told me to bring to you, so we can figure out what's going on."

As he paused and stared at Sarah's exasperated face, he was momentarily struck by how pretty she was. Frenchy eyed her dark brown hair, a few slightly lighter streaks accenting it. His gaze fell upon her neck, immediately wanting to lean in and kiss it. He slowly moved up to her eyes, becoming fixed on their subtle beauty. He smiled at her shyly. He felt a hand come across his face.

"Open the damn thing, you daft prick, what's wrong with you?" she said, furious at his thirty second delay.

"What the hell? I was, but I suddenly got caught up in the thought that you tried to kill me."

"Bullshit you were smiling like a creeper. And I didn't try to kill you; I sent the package that my dying father asked me to. Maybe I should have armed it myself." Sarah's anxiety at her day and Frenchy's lack of cooperation began to take a toll on her patience.

Ricky looked on and wondered when he should step in and refocus the group, but he felt it not his place.

"Well, that would be about right, from a woman who thinks it's okay to assault federal agents and unsuspecting men . . ." Frenchy was interrupted by the PA announcement.

"Dr. Degnan, would you and your guest please come to the principal's office. We are waiting; thank you."

"Forget that, we need to get out of here" Sarah shouted running towards the stairwell. "Any ideas?"

Frenchy stared blankly, trying to process all that was said.

"We can go to Global, Doc, no one would check there. It's an old trucking depot by the Hudson River." Ricky exclaimed.

"That would be great if Global were the next office over, but we need to get out of here first," Sarah exclaimed, rolling her eyes at such an unhelpful response. She looked back and forth through the halls, aware that it was a matter of time before Forester's partner came looking for them.

"Well, if you can promise to shut up and not insult me, I can get us out of here," Frenchy sarcastically stated, still reeling from the entire change in his day.

Sarah looked at him with daggers, about to rip into him. Her anger was quickly cut off by Ricky.

"She will; let's go, Doc."

Frenchy shoved the letter into his pocket and looked down the hallway. His eyes met Espinoza's at the far end of the hall. The agent stopped trying to make sense of what he was seeing.

"Dr. Degnan, please we really must go," he called out trying to avoid scaring him off. Espinoza began to briskly walk towards Degnan.

Sarah, trying to mask her words, quietly said, "Let's go."

Espinoza looked at Sarah, sensing she was not a fellow teacher as he approached. "Dr. Degnan we cannot waste anymore time."

"I'm ready, my brother, I'm just waiting on your partner. He's checking his email on my computer. And don't mind my bitchy colleague. She's on her period," Frenchy whispered, leaning into the agent.

Espinoza squinted at Frenchy's statement and started towards his office. He stared at Sarah, still curious at her presence.

"Let's go," Frenchy mouthed to his companions as they waited for the agent to turn the corner into the little alcove leading to Degnan's office. They quickly, but quietly, bolted towards the staircase leading to the fourth floor, the old Jesuit residence.

"I hope you know where you're going, Doc," Ricky said, trying to keep pace.

"No worries, I used to play on this floor when my uncle lived here; he showed me everything."

"I hope so," Ricky quietly muttered to himself, as they ran up the stairs to the sound of Espinoza shouting in anger after them.

"Not to be that nigga, but going up usually doesn't lead out," Ricky yelled in panic.

6

AS THE BLACK CROWN VICTORIA MADE ITS WAY through the traffic of police cars and fire trucks, Al Jensen's thoughts recounted his earlier conversation with his young agent. He shook his head in irritation at his recollections. What had gone wrong? He was convinced that he had planned well and all had gone as intended. The package destined for Dr. Degnan's place of work was sent by Tannen's daughter, intercepted by agents, scanned, confirming that there was C4 explosive in the package, and resent to its original destination. In addition, Tannen's actions had been carefully monitored by his agents. Still, something must have been overlooked.

Jensen continued towards the heart of the chaos on ninety-sixth street. Despite the problems with his case, his thoughts honed in on the goal of his case. Eliminate Francis Degnan. Suddenly, alone with his thoughts on this case, he began to speculate on what it was that Degnan had done, to garner such punishment.

Though Jensen, a devout Catholic, often disagreed personally with certain orders, he carried them out with swift efficiency. While aiding in the killing of an American citizen was not what he originally envisioned as an ordinary assignment when he became an FBI agent, his loyalty remained to the many, not the individual.

He gripped at his chest, feeling beneath his shirt. He rubbed his fingers over the chain, triggering a nervous tick. He suddenly began to gag. He rolled his car window down to spit. As he fumbled to gain composure and control his breathing, his eyes rested on his hands, lying on his lap. He coughed again gasping for air

"It's irrelevant if he is with them. He has their blood in his veins, and, moreover, the capability to alert them of what we now know. Detention is not an option."

Jensen shook, trying to force the words of his former commander out of his head. During his time in the military, Jensen had served in a covert operation in Zimbabwe in the late 1970s during the Rhodesian Bush War. As the Cold War slowly thawed, his unit remained focused on the arming of the

Zimbabwe African National Union, and the disarming of their Soviet backed countryman.

Jensen cleared his throat loudly, returning to his flashback.

"Sir he's just some villager. He got us what we needed. He's absolutely no threat to us. For God's sake he just shit himself."

"I don't give a shit if he's the fucking pope. He showed his true colors as he immediately turned on his people when we caught him. He'd flip and welch in a second when they catch him."

"If that's the case, then let his people kill him."

Jensen's muscles tensed, reliving the anger he felt when he defended the young man.

He looked beyond the first fire truck to the entrance of the corner apartment building. Regardless of why things had gone wrong and what he and his men had missed, the present scene confirmed the fact that things were not going as expected. Had there been C4 and a detonator in another package? Why would Tannen have interfered? Jensen shook his head in disbelief. He knew that there would be no reason for the Rabbi to have interfered. Moreover, if this explosion was related, Jensen could not believe Tannen would try to cause any harm to his colleague, friend, and confidant. Though Jensen knew little about Tannen, he was aware that the two men were lifelong friends.

As his eyes scanned Rabbi Judah's building, he saw everything he had wished by some wild chance wouldn't be there. Camera crews from every station, trying to get a glimpse into the nightmare on ninety-sixth street. Onlookers, some confused as to what had happened, others offering their own interpretation and explanation of the events. Finally, he saw the paramedics working on the injured.

He reached to open the door and was greeted by the chaos of the scene.

"Officer, get everyone the hell back to ninety-third street,, set up a new perimeter, and move them out of visual range!" Jensen shouted, replacing his contemplative thoughts with more forceful commands.

A younger agent who had arrived at the scene earlier approached him.

"Sir, there is one confirmed dead, and one other person injured," the agent said to Jensen as they moved towards the entrance to the Carreira-Paul apartment building.

"It seems from the doorman, that the bomb was in a package delivered to the front desk by an elderly man."

"What man? Was he Muslim?" Jensen asked attempting to gain more information. 9/11 now warranted a question about the person's religious affiliation.

"The doorman could not say much about the man, except that he dropped the package off at around eight a.m. today during his shift. He works mornings from six a.m. to two p.m."

Jensen looked sharply at the young agent, irritated at the lack of concrete information. Various thoughts began to run through his mind. It was more than possible that this was done by a Muslim extremist, angered still over the conflict between Palestine and Israel. Jensen's processing jumped to the increase in White Supremacist groups over the last ten years and entertained the chance that this may have been a random target in a generally Jewish neighborhood. Early in his career with the FBI, he had monitored many of these groups and their growing strength and influence. His thoughts temporarily comforted him as they offered an alternate to this being related to Degnan.

"Who opened the package," Jensen asked, returning to the conversation.

"The deceased opened the package in the vestibule, rather than taking it to his apartment. It seems he picked it up from the front desk. Our witness says that he began to walk towards the elevators while attempting to open the package. He stopped there, waiting for the elevator. A few seconds later, there was a small explosion. The area caught fire quickly so the body was burned. We got here about thirty minutes after the police and fire departments. The explosion was contained. Thankfully, it seems it only took out the victim and some shards of debris hit the doorman Mr. Hall. There has been no identification on the body because he had never seen the resident before."

"I thought you said the package was picked up from the front desk?" Jensen said attempting to make sense of how the doorman of a moderately sized building did not know the residents.

"Hall said he knows that he had never seen him before. Hall started working here six months ago. He is familiar with the residents and is sure he had never seen this man before."

"Why did he let him up?" Jensen persisted.

"Sir, he had a mail key to his box and had a package at the desk. Hall assumed he was a resident. Plus, he said he was hardly the suspicious type, claims he was very old."

Jensen paused, feeling increasingly sure that this was no random act.

"Don't worry about the identification. I am pretty sure the deceased is Rabbi Judah," Jensen said, irritated at his own words.

"How do you know, sir? Forensics said they are not sure they will be able to get a positive identification for some time," the young agent questioned.

"Son, don't ask me about my business. Now find out which apartment is his."

"Sir, I am sure that the fire department will not allow us into the building until it has been cleared by the . . ."

"Where is the fire chief? I'll speak to him," Jensen snarled.

"He is right over there sir," the young agent said, pointing to a white haired man standing near the curb of the main entrance to the Carreira-Paul.

As Jensen walked towards the fire chief, he thought about how he would explain this tragedy to his director and, in turn, to the Vice President.

"Excuse me, Chief, Al Jensen, FBI. I need to get into Rabbi Judah's apartment, he lived in this building. I believe we may find in his apartment information that may explain what happened here today."

"FBI?" the fire chief asked.

Jensen looked intently at the fire chief.

"Well, regardless, no one can enter. I am sorry, Agent Jensen, but I cannot allow anyone into the building until it has been cleared. It shouldn't be long."

The chief resumed his previous discussion.

"Unfortunately, I do not have that luxury, Chief. Either you let me in or I am going in myself. This is a matter of national security and I will not wait for engineers to deem this building okay for families to return to their Upper East Side apartments. I am not a resident, and I don't give a shit about engineers." Jensen gritted his teeth, almost daring the fire chief to oppose him. "Or perhaps we wait and another bomb goes off in the city?"

"Let him in. At your own risk, Mr. Jensen," the fire chief said, sizing up the belligerent agent. He gestured to his men to allow Jensen into the building.

He walked through the entrance of the Carreira-Paul, peering around the corner towards the elevator bay. A fireman continued to spray the section with water.

As he took in the scene, he continued to inventory and analyze the events of the morning in his head. The failed package to Degnan. The expected outcome for Degnan hitting Judah. Jensen inspected a shard of metal lodged in the plaster near the front desk. He recalled the words of his director who had met with Rabbi Judah the previous week in Israel. Judah had guaranteed that Tannen agreed with their plan and would follow through on his task. At the time, Jensen refused to trust Judah implicitly and intercepted the package to be thorough and ensure Tannen honored the agreement.

"Guess Judah was wrong," Jensen said, snickering in disgust at his own statement as he stared at the controlled carnage that seemed to provide a clear answer. Jensen turned towards the vestibule that housed the residents' mailboxes. He took his cell phone out of his pocket and called his director.

"The bombing seems to have killed Rabbi Judah."

Jensen's statement was met with silence at the other end of the phone.

"Are you sure?" the director said unsympathetically, breaking in unexpectedly.

"Well, put it to you this way, unless we hear otherwise, we should assume that he's dead. The body hasn't been identified. But the explosion has all the characteristics of the package intended for Degnan. We should assume there was a second package from Tannen, for whatever reason. Still this is a manageable situation."

While still heated from his discussion with the fire chief and his agent, Jensen decided to move forward with the case.

"I'm meeting with the Secretary of Defense in an hour; explain how we can 'manage this,'" the director said, eager to hear Jensen's assessment.

"Sir, Espinoza is detaining Degnan as we speak. From what you told me, the only one who matters is Degnan and we will have him in custody. Assuming Judah is the unfortunate loss here, nothing has changed. Our job was to get Degnan out of the way, and he will be. Whatever the fuck up, we achieved the outcome. In fact, the loss of Judah could be an advantage if we spin it properly."

Jensen, felt he had made sense of all that had taken place and even found a bright spot in the morning's set-back.

Jensen's explanation was met with silence once again. Finally, the director broke through,

"You may be right. I will ensure there is the proper coverage on the bombing and I will explain things to the Secretary. I need you to make sure Degnan is detained and formerly charged. I'll handle the rest."

"It will be done. I'm on my way up to Judah's apartment . . ." Jensen said, as the director interrupted.

"Don't worry about that now; just make sure Degnan is detained. We can worry about the apartment later. Come back to headquarters. We'll meet after I speak with Secretary Hansen."

Jensen pulled the phone from his ear, realizing the Director had already hung up. He started to scroll through his phone, selecting Espinoza's number. Espinoza answered immediately.

"Bring Degnan back to headquarters and we will formerly charge him there . . ."

"Sir, he's gone," Espinoza said, hyperventilating. "I'm chasing him down now,"

Jensen listened in disbelief, slowly becoming angry that all he had done to run damage control could be foiled by the inability of his agents.

"Listen to me, you find him and get him to headquarters. If you have to, you fuckin' shoot him. But don't come back until you have him."

Jensen slammed the phone shut and pushed past a camera crew that had broken through the police barrier. He jogged towards his car, fuming at the newest problem. He jumped into his car looking back at the scene. He shook his head and sped away.

7

"THIS HAS GOT TO BE THE DUMBEST IDEA! Why are we going *up* to lose them?" Sarah shouted, as she tried to keep up with Frenchy.

"We go up to go down; that's how it is, that's the way it's gonna be, now shut it," Frenchy shouted, gasping for breath. His thoughts returned to earlier reflections on how he should quit smoking so he wouldn't get so winded.

The three ran up the narrow stairs of Ogden Hall until they reached the old Jesuit residence.

"I have never been up here before," Ricky shouted, realizing he had a new tidbit of info to tell his comrades. "I never knew this existed."

"You never looked outside and saw that there were 6 floors to this building?" Frenchy gasped in irritation.

"Would you shut up and move," Sarah shouted, hearing Espinoza not too far behind.

"It's right here," Frenchy shouted, pointing to a small door on the side wall, near one of the Jesuit bedrooms.

"What is it?" Ricky asked, confused by the fact that the door seemed much smaller than it should be.

"It leads to the church."

"That leads to the church?" Sarah said skeptically, as Frenchy opened the prehistoric, semi-hidden door.

"The priests had their own passage to the church. Come on."

"Why would priests need their own passage to the church?" Sarah asked, irritated at Frenchy's assumption that this apparent door to Narnia would make any sense to anyone else.

"Because they needed to get there quick. Batman has his fuckin' slide, priests have theirs, just it's not a slide."

Frenchy quietly shut the door behind them and followed Ricky and Sarah.

"Just keep going," he softly directed.

"No shit, Doc, but I can't see anything," Ricky said, attempting to highlight the lack of light.

"Just go, here, use this," he said, handing Ricky his Zippo.

Ricky lit the Zippo and started forward at a quietly quickened pace. The smell of dry wood and dust pushed them faster on their escape. As Ricky quickly moved, a step buckled and he grabbed for the non-existent railing.

"Be careful," Sarah shouted, realizing the peril Frenchy had put them in attempting to escape.

"Yeah, sure, I'll be careful. Fuckin' termites and busted wood, but me, I need to be careful," Ricky retorted as Sarah took the Zippo and the lead from him.

"That's a great idea," Frenchy blurted out, after looking around at the passageway, failing to let anyone in on his plan.

"Give me the lighter," he shouted, snapping his fingers at Sarah.

"Don't snap at me," she said, irritated at Frenchy's rudeness.

"Jesus, may I please have the blessed lighter, you barking lunatic," Frenchy shouted, exasperated.

Sarah handed him the lighter firmly and Frenchy took the Zippo and turned around towards the previous steps. He slowly put the lighter under one of the steps, trying to light the old wood.

"Don't do that . . ."

"Easy lil' Kim," Frenchy interrupted, proud of his attempt at pop culture humor. The step quickly went up in flames and some of the wall as well.

"See, now they can't follow us, and we have a diversion: We can use the fire trucks to distract them as we escape." Frenchy smiled as the steps began to crack. "Oh shit," he exclaimed looking down, surprised at how quickly the step caught.

"Run!" Sarah exclaimed, pushing Ricky forward.

The three ran down the rickety stairs and towards the door at the end. Frenchy started pushing Sarah and shouting.

"I'm asmatic, I can't breathe, too much smoke, losing consciousness."

Sarah pushed past Ricky and slammed into the door, entering the sacristy of Saint Ignatius Church. Frenchy gasped for breath, holding his knees.

He looked over at the fire alarm switch and pulled it.

"Nice idea, jack-off, you could have killed us!" Sarah exclaimed, furious at Frenchy's attempt to "burn their tracks."

The trio paused as they listened to the fire alarm echo through the church.

"Nice language in front of my student, crazy lady," Frenchy chastised, attempting to shift attention from his moment of arson.

"Shit, Doc, you're asthmatic? Why the fuck do you smoke then?" Ricky asked, finally releasing his shock at the revelation from his cigarette-smoking mentor.

"Not really, just then I was asthmatic," Frenchy said, seeming to satisfy Ricky's query.

“So, now what?” Sarah asked, hoping to move on from the idle chat.

“Let me think.”

Frenchy nervously looked around the sacristy. He looked over towards the only window in the room and peered out at the faculty parking lot. He knew his car was too far away in the other parking lot for them to be able to make it undetected. As his eyes scanned the lot for the agents, his gaze fellow upon an old beat-up Ford cargo van.

“I know; we can take the Red Menace.” Frenchy said, looking eagerly at Sarah.

“Is that a joke?” she asked, honestly wondering if he were serious or just suffering the effects of stupidity as a result of his “Asthma.”

“Sweet, the Red Menace; fuckin’ nice, Doc, and the keys are in here.”

Ricky reached for the drawer near the chalices for the spare set of keys. Sarah looked up towards the wall of the sacristy noticing the smoke filling the room.

“What is the ‘Red Menace,’” Sarah asked, confused by what seemed to have been an inside revelation between her two comrades.

“That is the Red Menace.” Frenchy smiled, putting his arm around Sarah and ushering her over to the window to see a majestic, beat-up old red van parked in the corner of the faculty parking lot. As he smiled, the smoke alarm in the church sacristy went off. He looked back at their earlier escape route. Smoke bellowed, leading flames out with it

“Okay, time to go, children. Ricky, they didn’t see you so you take the keys and get in the van. We’ll hide under the van gripping the undercarriage. You start out towards York Street and make a left onto Montgomery. Once you are clear of any agents, stop and we’ll get in.” Frenchy stood up, proud because he came up with this scheme himself. He felt he was already acting the part of Indiana Jones, and now he would get to use the tactic he always thought of when people in movies would try to escape undetected . . . Hide under the car and hold on to the pipes. Ricky looked satisfied and ready to try this new adventure; but Sarah halted the two men.

“The undercarriage of a van? That’s your plan?” Sarah said, shocked that both seemed okay with their strategy.

“Yeah, no one ever thinks to look under a car when people are trying to escape. Ricky, remember in the movie *The Negotiator* with Samuel Jackson and Kevin Spacey? Jackson’s trying to escape and Spacey is helping him and the only place they look for Jackson at the checkpoint is in the back and the trunk. If he had been under the car, they would have never checked.” Frenchy slapped his hands together feeling he was on a roll. After a few shaky moments, he felt supremely confident of his plan.

"Wasn't Samuel Jackson not in the car anyway?" Ricky asked, recalling the movie's scene. Frenchy turned towards Ricky gesturing with his face to let it go and to agree. Sarah rolled her eyes, tired of the constant movie references.

"Yes, but he would have made it out under the car if he wanted to. Either way we got to go, through the window or we can burn."

Frenchy opened the window and began to make his way out into the parking lot. Ricky and Sarah followed.

"Ladies first doesn't work for you guys huh?" Sarah asked, staring at Frenchy.

"I needed to get down to help you guys when you dropped down. I was thinking of your safety," Frenchy said not really caring about her statement.

"Chivalry is dead that's for sure."

"It's not dead, just not practical at this moment, now shut up and let's go," Frenchy shouted, interrupting Sarah's lament. Ricky jumped into the driver's seat and Frenchy dove under the van. Sarah reluctantly followed behind, despite her disapproval.

She stared at Frenchy as he tried to pull himself up and situate himself under the van. She appreciated his attempt, but also realized that he was no small man, and she doubted he could hold his weight for much more than a few feet.

"Francis, it's not going to work. And it looks clear at the exit from the parking lot. Let's just go."

"Doc, she's right we're clear," Ricky exclaimed, anxious to get moving. Frenchy fell from his herniated perch and quietly got into the cargo section of the van.

"It would have worked, you know," he jeered, quickly climbing into the back of the van and laying flat on the floor. Ricky turned the key and the aged van gave a loud clue as to why it earned such a name as the Red Menace. Ricky slowly pulled the bellowing beast towards the exit gate.

Around them, the sirens of fire engines echoed in the near distant. He slowly exited the parking lot and made the right on York Street, stopping at the intersection.

"Are we clear?" Frenchy asked from the belly of the beast.

"I think we may be," Ricky cautiously responded. "There is nobody out yet. So much for fire drills." He said remarking at the slow evacuation. "Not to complain but a skinny black kid driving a beat-up old van may draw attention. This ain't LAPD land but just sayin', maybe not a good idea."

"Jesus Christ anyone who sees you will think you are picking up scrap metal, now shut up and drive this fuckin' van."

Ricky shook his head, slowly accelerating through the intersection.

"For the record, that was fucked up on multiple levels. But whatever, I'm just sayin'. Where do I go now?"

"Make a left and another left and head uptown."

"To your apartment?" Ricky asked, shocked that he might be taking them into the hands of the authorities.

"No, head up to Kennedy Boulevard; we need a good hideout and I may know a friend who will help us."

Frenchy paused to verify in his mind a place where they could hide out. He knew he didn't have much time, but he needed a place to read the letter. He knew anyone related to him would be getting a visit from his new best friends, so he needed a place where no one would think to look for him.

"We're headed to Ali's," Frenchy stated. "It's maybe the one place they won't look for me, and he sure as hell doesn't care much for the U.S. government."

"I'm not so sure that is a good idea. Based on his name he is probably under surveillance all the time. And why would he help us, and can he be trusted?" Sarah asked. Her look seemed to indicate that Frenchy's confidence was not being felt by all.

"It will be fine. I worked with him on a few projects. Interfaith shit, Muslims, Jews, Christians learning to get along, getting in touch with their feelings, dancing, some shit like that. He's a good friend. And like I said, he is no fan of the government; at least not since 9/11."

"What do you mean?" Sarah said, her original skepticism of what kind of man this Ali was seemed confirmed.

"No, not like that," Frenchy answered realizing from the look on Sarah's face. She was not understanding what he was saying, despite the fact that Frenchy was using all the appropriate cryptic language he hoped would make him sound in control.

"I mean, since 9/11 he has advocated for better treatment of Muslims; no profiling. He himself has been a victim of all sorts of paranoia by the government. For Christ sake, they gave him a cavity search at Newark airport. Yeah, fingers in the ass. So I doubt he is going to be calling any feds to come and get us. And if anyone had read my book," he said loudly, glancing towards Ricky, "they would know that he is the only man in this world, aside from your father, who believes or believed in my claim that the Sword of Goliath exists and can be found."

Sarah looked at Frenchy's momentary maddened demeanor and oddly saw the man her father had so appreciated as a friend. In all the chaos and shifting emotions of the day, she had missed the chance to speak or listen without yelling and screaming. At that moment she admired his passion and determination. Sarah smiled and patted him on the back.

"Let's hope that fire idea was a fluke when it comes to your decision-making."

Frenchy smiled back, appreciating that an attractive woman had touched his back and also that he seemed in control and, for once, he was not drinking and was not desiring it.

"You can just call me Indiana Jones Jr.," he proudly said, smiling and putting his Irish cap on. Sarah playfully rolled her eyes.

"I thought Indiana Jones was already a junior because his father was the first?" Ricky interjected, confused by an inconsistent storyline and unaware of his mentor's attempt to gently flirt with Sarah.

Frenchy glared up at Ricky, attempting to convey to his young student that the question was killing his courting attempt.

"Really, fucker?" Frenchy asked.

"Sorry, Doc," Ricky said, realizing it was not the time for an inquiry on Indiana Jones's genealogy.

"Sorry, that was inappropriate language. Shit, who knows, maybe you will be my Short Round," Frenchy said, smiling and rolling onto his back in the debris and dust that filled the back of the cargo area. Sarah watched as he closed his eyes and sighed.

Ricky cocked his head, confused by any reference to the Indian Jones movies prior to *Indiana Jones and the Last Crusade.*

"What the fuck did you call me?"

JENSEN'S CELL PHONE WENT OFF AGAIN as he sped back to the office. His ring, the *Hawaii Five-o* theme from the eighties which usually made him smile, irritated him, fearing what news he might receive now. He answered quickly.

"You better be about to give me the best fucking news ever," he stated, not looking at the caller ID and assuming it to be Espinoza.

"Sir, it's Espinoza. It's chaos here, sir, the school is on fire and we lost Degnan."

Jensen grinded his teeth and felt the urge to defenestrate his mobile, forget about this entire fiasco, and head for a nice round of golf.

"What do you mean the school is on fire? What the fuck did you do? Did the bomb go off?"

"Espinoza paused, knowing no matter what response he gave, he was going to get an unpleasant reminder of his present failure.

"The bomb didn't go off sir, I believe Degnan still has the package."

"Where is he?" Jensen snarled, barely composing himself enough to spit out the three words.

"I don't know where he went. We had him but he went down a shaft or something. It took me some time to find it and when I went to pursue, he must have lit the thing on fire. Next thing I know the school's smoke alarms are going off and the building is being evacuated. Forester was knocked out by some lady with him. It looked a bit like the Rabbi's daughter, sir. I thought she looked familiar but I didn't realize it until after they got away."

Jensen's anger was quelled by this new aspect of the ordeal.

"She was at the funeral home. Our director confirmed that she was there. Judah confirmed with her that all had gone according to plan. Not to mention the fact that her father is dead. You're telling me that she left her own father's funeral to join Degnan? And why?"

Jensen's mind raced wondering what else he had missed in his ascertaining the situation moments earlier.

"I think it was her. Can only go on the photos I saw. Degnan didn't know anything was wrong. He believed everything I said, and was ready to come with us. But something happened when he went with Forester to get his belongings. I went up shortly after looking for them, but they took off running when I went to get Forester."

While all that Espinoza was saying made sense, Jensen returned to struggling with how such a simple task went wrong.

"What do you want me to do?" Espinoza asked, unsure of his next course of action.

"Start searching Jersey City for him. Call headquarters and have them compile a list of everyone he is related to and knows. Where did you say is the package?" He asked, attempting to recount the earlier information.

"He took it with him sir," he answered, afraid of what else would set his boss off.

"Good. Put the word out to all law enforcement. Francis Degnan is a fugitive and is in possession of a large quantity of explosives. He is also wanted in connection with the fire at the school. He won't be able to get far with that following him. Find him and bring him to headquarters. You understand?"

Jensen's practical problem-solving emerged quickly, calming Espinoza. He appreciated Espinoza's silent acquiescence. Jensen cracked his neck, his confidence returning. Despite his two failed marriages that ended in ugly divorces and left him convinced women were incapable of rational thought, his no-nonsense attitude garnered admiration from his superiors and underlings.

"Consider it done sir," Espinoza responded quickly.

"Carl," Jensen sighed and said calmly. He paused again, realizing this case was hitting a breaking point.

Immediately, Espinoza felt a feeling of extreme anxiety. Getting chewed out by his boss was not his favorite thing. However, his fiery boss calmly calling him by his first name seemed to give him a feeling far worse than the usual verbal lashing. He recalled back to when he felt this feeling as a boy when his teacher, a woman who only yelled and screamed at he and his fellow classmates, suddenly began to calmly speak. It scared them more than any high pitched rant. He expected Jensen to lunge through the phone and gently bite is head off.

"Yes, sir?" he said tentatively waiting.

"There's a lot riding on this. I don't mean like how you do on your next performance review. I mean this is a very sensitive case, and we have to handle this swiftly, but extremely carefully. We need to find Degnan and we have to find him now."

Jensen paused realizing for the first time he couldn't just shout orders and expect his young agent to feel invested in a case he knew little about.

"I know I haven't told you everything about this case. I don't know all the details myself, but fortunately or unfortunately I am getting more as things go wrong. You know that this was a case with very simple objectives. But the issue seems to be far more complex. The Vice President and the Secretary of Defense are all involved in this. I don't know what it's about, but it is something linked to a treaty for the country. Whatever the details are of this treaty, it supposedly could boost our economy, and truly solidify the United States as the dominant world power, across the board—militarily, economically—all categories."

"Who is this treaty with?" Espinoza said interrupting, tired of fluffy nothingness that told him little about what was actually going on.

"From what I have figured, given the people we have been dealing with, it is either with Israel or insert the next largest country with Jews in it."

Jensen had not been told formerly, but he assumed Israel to be the rational choice.

"Why Israel?" Espinoza asked, attempting to process.

"If you are asking my opinion? I would assume control of the Middle East. Think about it: Our friendship with the state of Israel has always been one of support in their struggles over their supposed homeland. It has been in our interest to ensure that the Israelis have the upper hand. But it has been motivated by our desire to put a check on the Arab nations in the surrounding area as well as have an ally in the region."

"And we want the oil in the region," Espinoza stated, attempting to hurry to the meat of the case.

"Oil may not just be the only thing that we want, but that sure as hell wouldn't be a bad product of this. Our economy, our way of life, is firmly rooted in this sought-after natural resource."

"But why the hell does a damn high school teacher from Jersey pose any threat to the government, to any of that?"

Jensen wiped his brow feeling Espinoza's frustration at not understanding the correlation. He pinched the area between his eyes, pausing to share in that question. What did Degnan have to do with this? His director had given him more information about the case than Jensen had given Espinoza, yet he, too, began to wonder what threat the young author posed.

"Honestly, Carl, I really don't know. But I do know that there are some men in high places of our government who made it clear that he was to be eliminated from the scene. Maybe it's a vendetta. I have no idea, but we were to ensure that the explosives were sent to him and that detonation took place. Regardless of the reason, I was told he was a threat to national security and to this treaty. That may give you a bad taste in your mouth, but you better get used to it. That is the way this job works. You may not want to do everything you are told and you may not understand why you have to do it, but if you want to go anywhere in this job, you have to learn to ask less and forget more."

Espinoza remained silent, irritated with a generic answer.

Jensen pushed his own questions about the case to the back of his mind, reverting back to his responsibility as Espinoza's boss. He paused, hoping Espinoza understood what he was saying. Though a difficult boss, and not always the most pleasant to his men, he recognized in Espinoza the sudden desire to understand the very dangerous "why" in their chosen profession.

"Trust me," he said calmly. "Find Degnan, that's our job and our only concern at this point."

Espinoza held the phone firmly and stared at the section of the school being dealt with by a crowd of firefighters. His posture changed as he stood militantly regaining his composure. His mind left the questions that he had just posed and snapped into his usual position as an executer of tasks, regardless of what they were.

"I'll handle it," he said confidently.

"I know you will; that's why I picked you and Forester for this."

9

THE POLYCOM CONFERENCE PHONE sat silent on the mahogany desk of the aged Prime Minister Gershom, prime minister of Israel. He looked wearily at his watch as he reclined in a leather-clad arm chair adjacent to his desk. Though he knew his present work would result in a treaty that would ensure the survival and prosperity of his people, he could not relax until he knew that all had been done and the treaty secured. He had expected a call earlier in the day from his counter-parts in Washington, assuring him that their part of the agreement had been upheld. He became uneasy when a few hours passed and he had heard nothing. He became panicked when he heard from his aide, Assaf Greene, that things had not been completed. Now he sat awaiting a status report on the safety of his people's precious artifact.

He stared at the phone and continuously checked his watch. He stood and walked towards a table near the entrance. He reached for an ornate glass pitcher and poured a few ounces of whisky into an equally decorative glass. He had never been in the habit of drinking, particularly whiskey, but he had received a case of the finest Kentucky mash from his American equivalent. He quickly downed the glass and his slightly trembling hands seemed to stop for a moment as he allowed the whiskey to flow through his body and temporarily subdue his anxiety. He turned slowly and looked towards a man sitting in the chair facing his desk. The man sat casually busily working on his iPhone.

"It has been too long," Gershom said to his seated guest, allowing his frustration to break the silence.

"There must be something wrong. Judah has never failed to come through, nor has Tannen. Things are not as they should be. It is not right; perhaps we should cancel this entire plan. We have the resources to protect our land . . ."

His distracted friend snapped up from his work and looked over at Gershom. He swiftly attempted to calm Gershom.

"Nothing is incorrect and all will be fine. You worry too much, Yitzach. What do the Americans say, hiccups in the road? No big deal? Just relax," he said, putting his iPhone in his pocket, assuming any sign of work at this moment would only augment his friend's desire to end their present dealings. He walked over towards Gershom.

"Though you are anxious now, that will all pass. Remember, soon we will be allied, truly allied with the most powerful nation in the world, and our people will be destined to dominate this region, as we were anointed to and as we were promised."

He paused and sighed, looking at Gershom

"My friend, have another glass of American whiskey."

He put his hand on the Prime Minister's shoulder and lifted the flask to pour his restless superior a new glass. He smiled and looked into the old man's eyes. He sensed weakness in Gershom but ignored that feeling for the moment. He recognized that there was a problem with his friends in the U.S. but he knew his superior was too quick to abandon the established plan.

"Assaf, you know I trust you, but perhaps this has gone too far," Gershom said, hoping to encourage his closest advisor to agree with his suggestion. "I mean we do not even know if he could have ever found it. Just because he had interest in it does not mean he would have ever even pursued it or found it." He took a sip of his whiskey, wiping his fingers across his lips. "Think about what we have done."

Assaf stared sternly at Gershom. While he felt the feeling of irritation gaining strength, he composed himself.

"It was, and is, necessary that we eliminate anyone who could possibly be a threat. There can be no room for possibilities. Doubt is not an option. That man and his letter were certainly going to garner Degnan's attention and either he or someone he would help would present us with a problem."

Gershom shook his head and turned to put his glass on the table, Greene's eyes fixed on him.

"If they have failed, I want to end this. We do not need to continue. Judah knows all that is needed and he has all the information to find it; we do not need to pursue this American."

Assaf looked away from Gershom in anger and stared blankly towards the window. He reached into his pocket and produced a worn photo. He looked down at the photo of a young woman and smiled. He slowly turned back towards his superior, raising the photo to his eyes.

"Would she want you to take a chance? Would she want you to cancel because the plan has not gone perfectly?"

Gershom stared at the photo and looked beyond the photo into Assaf's eyes. He looked down, away from the photo. Though he thought about his daughter each day, the sight of her always brought her voice back into his mind, restoring the sadness he constantly fought to keep at bay.

Greene persisted.

"Please stop and reflect. Soon, we will hold the true power of our people. We will be in control of the most powerful artifact in the world. No more middle men, no more protectors. We will have it here. Not even the Christians' supposed Holy Grail can rival what we will have. And we will have power over all in the region. We will defeat all in our way, we will expand the land God gave to our father Abraham, and we will take back all that has been stripped from us since our first ancestors first fought for the land that God promised! Gone will be the days of losing children to suicide bombers!"

Assaf's passion and patriotism filled the distraught and uncertain Prime Minister with life. Assaf had spent many years in the Israeli army fighting against Palestinian extremists. The atrocities he had witnessed and participated in fueled his anger towards the neighboring Muslim nations. He was a strong supporter of expanding Israel's borders and, regardless of the consequences, was not afraid to express his belief that Israel should dominate the Middle East, not just simply exist. There were many who considered him a radical and felt he should not have been selected as Gershom's top advisor. When he was appointed, there was an overwhelming sense of shock, from many who had labored for peace between Israelis and Palestinians. For them, Assaf's rise signaled a regression in their work to bridge the gap between the warring peoples.

Gershom took Assaf's hand.

"You were always so good to my daughter. I was always proud to call you my son. I know how you feel, truly I do. Each day, I think about her."

He paused and looked at the phone on his desk.

"Let's wait and see what has transpired. I appreciate your words. Perhaps I am acting prematurely."

Assaf regained his composure and smiled at Gershom.

"Thank you, sir. I believe it to be the best for all."

10

"WHERE TO, DOC?" Ricky asked, as he drove the large red cargo van to a red light at the intersection of Montgomery Street and Kennedy Boulevard.

"I told you a left at the light and a right onto Belmont. Shit!" he shouted; he now had sheetrock dust on his pants. "These were brand new God dammit," he said, looking over discreetly at the fact that Sarah was on the only clean section of the van.

"Do you want to switch positions," Sarah said with an air of sarcasm, smiling at Frenchy's irritation at not being in a more luxurious vehicle.

"It's fine, I'm good," he said humbly, realizing his idols would never have complained about the dust. Ricky made a right onto Belmont and slowed down.

"Is that it, Doc?" he said, pointing at the one building with writing he could not read.

"How'd you guess? Of course that's it. Pull in the small lot beyond it; I don't want to take any chances of people seeing us get out."

Ricky made the left into the lot and drove to the back of the lot.

"You know what, pull behind the dumpster. It isn't the best hiding spot, but it should put us out of plain site."

"Are you sure this is a good idea?" Sarah said, remaining steadfast to her concern for their current location.

"Trust me, Ali is the man, he will be able to help us out. Besides, I really don't think we have much of a choice. We need a respite from all this. Today went from kind of good to generally shitty very quickly."

"Why didn't you read the letter in the van?"

Ricky swung the chainlinked van key, aware of the lost time.

"Fuck yourself, that's why."

Frenchy turned away, recognizing his student's point.

"Sorry, that was wrong. And yes, I should have. If you are gonna be my sidekick, please pull your weight. I have always told you kids I'm not that smart."

Frenchy and Ricky nodded in reconciliation. Frenchy shook his head at his frustration and began to awkwardly crab walk towards the rear exit of the van to avoid getting anymore debris on his pants.

"I really hope you're right," Sarah said.

"I am," Frenchy said, straining to hold himself up.

"Hey Ricky, open the goddamn door."

Ricky moved to the back of the van and opened the rear door. Frenchy got out quickly, brushing off his pants and attempting to compose his outfit.

"I'm fine, you don't have to help me," Sarah said, irritated that she had to struggle out of the back without any assistance from the two gentlemen.

"Let's knock on the back door; I don't think we should go in through the front."

Frenchy began to cunningly creep over to the back door beyond the cargo van. Sarah watched shaking her head, and struck by how silly it was that he was creeping through a parking lot open to multiple views. As he continued his spy-like behavior, a loud bang sounded from the exhaust pipe of the Red Menace. Frenchy jumped and shrieked in surprise.

"Holy shit," Frenchy bellowed. "Well, that was fun," he said, gripping his chest.

"Nice job on making sure no one sees us," Sarah commented, walking past Frenchy towards the door.

"It's important that we move quietly and in a stealthy manner," he said, irritated that she did not see the importance of his actions.

"Then in the future, commandeer a vehicle without a hole in the floor and in the exhaust system of a tank, now, let's go!"

Sarah annoyingly gestured towards the door. Frenchy, not willing to take her on over this issue, slapped his leather jacket and headed towards the door.

He stared at Sarah as he approached the back door. He was struck again by her beauty, particularly her eyes. They melted him to his core, destroying the facade he hoped would display bravado and confidence. Frenchy knocked loudly. Sarah looked forward as she heard noise from beyond the door.

"By the way, you scream like a little girl."

Ricky laughed and covered his mouth as Sarah sarcastically smiled at Frenchy.

"Damn, son, she called you a lil' bitch."

Frenchy turned and stared at Ricky and then returned his gaze towards Sarah. He mockingly forced a laugh.

The lock on the door clicked into an open position and the knob turned.

Frenchy muttered under his breath as the door opened. "Don't remember Dr. Jones having to deal with this bullshit."

A young man stood in the door, staring at the trio.

"Mr. Degnan. Good to see you. Unexpected, but you are always welcome to visit. Please come in," he said, recognizing his visitor.

"Greetings, Mohammad, good to see you, too, and sorry for the random visit. Is Ali here? Please tell him it's urgent. My student and I found this crazy homeless woman loitering in front of the center and felt we should notify the . . . proper . . . authorities," Frenchy said gesturing to Sarah.

He realized that his joke was not being taken well by Sarah and it seemed to have confused Mohammad.

"Just kidding, brother, please just let him know I'm here."

"Of course, please have a seat," Mohammad said, gesturing to two chairs off to the left of the corridor. He walked down the hall, switching on a second light.

"I've never been back here before," Frenchy said, attempting to make idle chat to avoid the verbal lashing he assumed was on its way from Sarah.

She sat down and looked up at him.

"Not bad Francis, not bad," she said, smirking at how confused Mohammad had looked.

"I know, I know, I have always been told I am quite funny."

Frenchy sat down and removed his hat, spinning it briefly on his finger. He stopped his playful twirl, looking grimly at Ricky.

In all the excitement, commotion, and his attempt to flirt with Sarah, he had forgotten that he was being chased by FBI agents and he had a high school student with him.

"Ricky, I think you should get out of here. Go to the corner on the Boulevard and take the Number 10 bus and get home. They don't know who exactly was with us. Your parents would kill me if they knew I allowed you to get involved in this."

"He's right, you know, you should go," Sarah said, cutting in to agree with Frenchy as she too began to allow things to sink in. "Who the hell knows what's going on, but you shouldn't be involved."

Ricky rolled his eyes in frustration, tired of being treated appropriately, as a teenager. Despite almost being trapped and burned alive and driving a vehicle he shouldn't have, Ricky was enjoying the thrill. Like his mentor, he, too, thirsted for a little action and adventure. Now that he was almost eighteen, he was ready to experience firsthand what he saw in movies.

"Doc, I'm almost eighteen; I can make decisions on my own. My parents would never want me to leave you in distress."

Ricky paused, hoping that if he said it passionately it would make sense.

"Not to be 'that guy,' but your parents are Italian, and, well, you're black. They're way more protective of you."

"What the fuck does being adopted have to do with this?"

"Alright, that came out wrong. I'm simply saying they are so much more protective of you than your older siblings. You're their baby boy."

Ricky rolled his eyes.

"True, but they need to cut the cord eventually. Plus, you need me. Everyone is looking for the two of you. But not me. I can be your transportation. And let's face it, you need a sidekick. All the great explorers and adventurers had sidekicks. Lewis and Clarke, Holmes and Watson, Shrek and Donkey. Think about it."

Frenchy laughed for a moment at his student's well-chosen, flattering words.

Sarah looked at Frenchy.

"You're kidding right?" Sarah didn't share Frenchy's appreciation for Ricky's point. "Shrek and donkey? You're both crazy. Ricky, you can't come with us. We don't even know what we are doing or why they are chasing us. And flattery aside, Francis, he has to go home."

Sarah stared sharply at Frenchy. He knew he couldn't let Ricky stay, but he also knew that, as strange as it sounded, he thought this might be a good thing if Ricky stayed. He paused for a moment, putting his finger up to his lips. He could use Ricky's help, and he did bring up a good point that Frenchy couldn't be driving around in plain sight in the driver's seat. Convinced he would regret the decision of allowing him to stay, he couldn't bear the thought of his student resenting him. He smiled at Ricky and nodded.

"Alright, Short Round, you're in."

Ricky smiled and went for the high five moment he often waited for.

Sarah threw her hands up in the air and returned angrily to her seat.

"Unbelievable!" she exclaimed.

Frenchy looked down at Sarah.

"What? He brings up a good point, and he is connected. He has family members from here to Bayonne, don't you?"

Ricky quickly nodded in agreement.

"Besides, how can I resist the chance to teach my student real-life lessons on history and human relations and things that are mysterious and difficult to explain?"

Frenchy looked away, realizing he genuinely had stopped trying and had no idea what he was saying.

"Well, when he is arrested for harboring fugitives, he will learn a great lesson then."

As the trio seemed to be at a breaking point, the door at the end of the hall opened and a man emerged. He wore the traditional white tunic that many Muslim men wore. As he approached, his bearded face smiled at Frenchy and he extended his hand to shake Frenchy's.

"It is always a pleasure to see you my old friend."

The Imam embraced Frenchy and they exchanged a greeting in Arabic. Ali turned to Ricky and extended his hand.

"You must be one of the many students Dr. Degnan has spoken of. I hope you know how proud he is of you and your classmates, even if he is incapable of admitting such a sentiment." Frenchy put his hands up in pause.

"Let's not let him get a big head here, he and his friends can be a pain in my ass, too."

Ali smiled and winked at Ricky.

"Of course, they are, they are boys."

Ali turned towards Sarah. He bowed his head slightly towards her.

"This must be the homeless woman Mohammad mentioned," he said, smiling at Frenchy who did not expect that part of the message to be relayed by the messenger.

"Well, you know Dr. Degnan, always looking out for others," Sarah said, folding her arms and sarcastically smiling at Frenchy.

"Please, let us go to the library to speak."

"Let's," Frenchy blurted out, happy to move forward.

"It has been some time since you have visited, and last time you used the front door. I hope everything is alright."

Ali opened the door to the main lobby of the mosque, allowing Sarah and Ricky to enter. He looked suspiciously at Frenchy, raising his bushy eyebrow to his friend, hoping to coax him into an explanation.

"It's a long story, but it's the reason I'm here. And yes, the backdoor entrance does have something to do with it."

He paused, looking at his Muslim friend.

"I may be in a wee bit of trouble and need your help sorting things out. I hope I am not imposing?"

Ali smiled.

"By imposing, do you mean asking me to aid and abet fugitives?"

Frenchy winced and bounced his head from side to side.

"Maybe not so much aiding and abetting, more like not knowingly helping individuals who the FBI would like to talk to. No one has called us fugitives yet."

Ali raised his arm gesturing the group to make their way up the stairs.

"Instead of the library, let us go upstairs. You can explain everything. You can tell me what it is like to burn down a school."

Frenchy stopped in his tracks.

"What?"

"It seems you are quite famous today, the way you always dreamt, only for a slightly different reason."

"Great," Frenchy said walking up the stairs.

Sarah leaned against the banister and stared at him as he moved past her on the stairs.

"Well, so much for keeping a low profile."

Frenchy put his hand on Sarah's back to move her along up the stairs.

"It will be fine, trust me," he said, unsure himself if it were true.

"Anyway, I am not worried about being accused of burning the school down. I am worried about being chased by FBI agents."

Ali smiled.

"Nothing's ever dull with you—except doing research with you on your book," he said, grinning.

"Oh, how I love the jokes from everyone today. And trust me, ain't nothing dull about this."

11

GROUPS OF FIREFIGHTERS swarmed Saint Ignatius Prep on Grand Street. The old building burned strongly as the firefighters fought the blaze. Students watched from beyond the perimeter, pointing, some smiling at the passing rumor that they would have no school for months. Espinoza crossed away from the blaze towards his partner, Forester, leaning against the black Crown Victoria.

"What's next?" Forester said, keenly aware of the time that had elapsed since they last saw Degnan.

"We put it out that it was Degnan who started the fire. He is considered armed and dangerous and that he is in possession of explosives. That should buy us some time to find him and it ensures that he won't get far."

"Maybe he's still in the building. You know, he might be dead," Forester stated, recognizing the possibility that Degnan failed his escape attempt, aware that they never saw him after the fire began.

"No, he's gone mobile. Him, Tannen's daughter, and some kid."

Espinoza looked back at the fire, recounting the day's events.

"If that was Tannen's daughter, then what the fuck was she doing with him?" Forester said as he rubbed the bruise on his head.

"Something's wrong. She was there to get him out and away from us. She must know way more than expected."

Forester's posture changed as he folded his arms at his colleague's statement.

"Well, if we get these three, we're set: objective complete. Think about it. Originally Degnan was to receive the package from Tannen. That got botched so we had to convince him that we needed him to go on a mission."

Espinoza continued to look back at the school, irritated that he had failed to get Degnan and allowed him to escape.

"Go check with the principal and ask if there are any vehicles missing. He is either on foot, or he was able to slip past us during the fire. Let's pay a visit to his apartment. I have a feeling he may have returned home."

"Did you just hear what I said? And really? He would go to his apartment? Granted, he seems dumb as shit, but really?" Forester questioned, assuming there was no chance Degnan would play that easily into their hands.

"He was dead set on his dog and his research. That probably hasn't changed. Headquarters is sending over a list of family, but we should start with his home."

"I hope you're right; that would work out nicely for us."

Forester headed towards a group clustered together at the end of the block. Among them was the principal busily checking with the approaching faculty members on the student head count from each year.

Espinoza watched his partner walk away from the car. His mind began to race with the information he had received from his boss, and his thoughts on his present dilemma. He knew that this was an issue of great importance and somehow led to a possible treaty between the U.S. and Israel. He also felt strongly about completing his assignments without debating or questioning them. He knew that part of being an agent was trusting in the bosses who passed it down. But despite his willingness to follow through and find Degnan, a part of him began to struggle with his objectives.

"Why the fuck should I be helping kill an American?" he mumbled to himself.

He laughed at the thought of this entire ordeal being exclusively about oil. He himself drove a Ford Escalade, and knew how important oil was to the economy and to the country. The last time he had filled the tank, gas was $3.59 a gallon and he remembered cursing the gas companies. Still, his mind continued to wrestle with the thought that people's lives were expendable if it benefitted the greater good. In this case, he wasn't sure it would be for the greater good, or perhaps simply for the oil companies. He believed in the protection and care of all the citizens of the United States, not just some of them. He didn't care personally about Degnan or the other two, but they represented, in his mind, a crisis. He began to regret being told more of the details of the case he was dealing with. Before, he could just do his job. But now his assignment conflicted with his conscience. To make matters worse, his own boss didn't know what the relationship was between Degnan and "a threat to national security," something Espinoza doubted plausible, having met Degnan in person.

As his mind pulsed with questions and thoughts, his cell phone rang.

"Yes," he said, irritated at the interruption of his present thoughts.

"Carl, it's me. There are no vehicles missing according to the principal, but he is not positive. But Degnan's car is still here. He must be on foot."

Espinoza tried to focus. No matter his belief in right or wrong, he now had to move on Degnan.

"Fine, that's better, get back here and let's go."

"Already behind you," Forester said running up to the car. Espinoza nodded. He immediately was caught up in the energy that Forester was exuding.

"I don't waste any time," Forester said, throwing the door open and jumping into the car. "Are you ready to do this?" Forester said, riding the adrenaline of having a small lead on Degnan. Espinoza slammed the car into gear.

"Always, my brother. Always."

12

GERSHOM SNAPPED TOWARDS HIS ADVISOR as the phone rang loudly. He slowly made his way towards his desk, unsure if he wanted to answer and hear the awaiting news. Before, he could not wait to hear reports on the day's events. Now, he feared the news more than the unknown. He slowly picked up the receiver.

"Yes," he said quietly.

"Gershom? It's Cristy. I have some interesting news about your favorite person. Degnan has escaped, supposedly helped by Rabbi Tannen's daughter."

"Tannen?" Gershom interrupted. He sat down in his chair and looked across at Assaf, who sat down in the opposing chair.

"Yes, his daughter. It would seem the good rabbi either changed his mind or his daughter is batshit crazy. He apparently did not share your desire to secure your sought-after cutlery and move forward with the treaty. He must have told his daughter something because the original package to be sent to Degnan was tampered with and we're not sure what Degnan received. But there was a second package sent. It was sent to Rabbi Judah. He's dead. The bomb took him out when he picked it up at his apartment."

Gershom sat stunned at the news. He looked over at Assaf, and repeated Judah's fate to his attentive companion.

"Why would Tannen have done that? They were the closest of friends. In his last days, he finally agreed to turn over the map that he possessed revealing the location. I know he had struggled with the idea, but he agreed."

"It would seem he changed his mind. Did he know about our plans for Degnan?" the Vice President pressed on, attempting to find out exactly what triggered the entire mess.

"He could not have discovered that. Judah promised that he would not be hurt; only we knew what was transpiring. He must not have believed Judah. What about the map? Judah was traveling to his apartment to get the map, his half and Tannen's."

Though Judah's death was a tragedy, Gershom moved forward, realizing it was imperative that the map be recovered.

"I didn't know he had it in his apartment. That information would have been helpful. I thought he had given it to you."

The Vice President became irritated. As far as he was concerned, he had fulfilled the U.S.'s part of the deal. Degnan would be taken care of one way or another. As a very realistic man, Cristy found the entire matter to be silly and superstitious. That he had FBI agents running around trying to apprehend Degnan, so he couldn't threaten the location of a silly artifact that Gershom believed to be mystical, contradicted his reason. Still, his desire to gain land and resources in the Middle East had him on the phone doing his best to care.

"The map is at Judah's. It must be recovered immediately. In truth, once we have that, we can recover the sword. Degnan is less of a worry now, knowing that you are working to apprehend him. But the map is crucial."

Gershom's earlier desire to cancel their plans to eliminate Degnan returned as he realized it was no longer necessary to eliminate him as he could not launch a recovery expedition while a fugitive. The Vice President paused, listening to how focused the Prime Minister was on the ancient artifact.

"Fine, I'll have my men get the map. But you need to tell me what is so goddamn important about this artifact. At first I didn't care, but this entire request is costing us time and effort."

The Prime Minister stood up and moved towards the window.

"The supposed artifact we want is the sword of the Philistine Warrior, Goliath, killed by King David. Though it was found by Judah and Tannen over sixty years ago, I was only told about their discovery recently. Still, they agreed on their find. Unfortunately, rather than recovering it for their people, they chose to conceal its whereabouts. Rabbi Judah was finally able to convince Tannen in his last days to allow the location be known to the Israeli government. He agreed to provide his half of the map. They had split the map to ensure neither would betray their agreement. Though it was simply symbolic, they both knew where it was. Nevertheless, Judah revealed this to me three weeks ago."

Gershom walked over to a pole displaying the Israeli flag. He tenderly caressed the flag, a proud smile appearing on his face.

"While this may mean nothing to you, this sword is a symbol for our people, of our first triumph over the peoples who took, and now are trying again to take, our homeland away from us. And whether true or not, we believe it holds mystical powers. He who possesses the sword, we believe, holds the power to rule Palestine."

The Vice President interrupted.

"What would a map do? Why wouldn't your two intelligent Rabbis remember where it was?"

"As I stated earlier, they knew where it was. Their gesture was symbolic, a pact between the two men. They swore they would never reveal its location, but I am quite sure they did not want to risk the possibility of it never being found again. The map assured its location would be preserved, but not revealed unless both agreed.

Cristy's interest in the response faded immediately.

"Anyway, Degnan needed to be taken care of because he knew the location of the sword?"

"In all probability, yes. And when recent interest in the artifact emerged, we knew that it was only a matter of time before someone actually looked to him to find it. We had to make sure this did not occur. Perhaps we were a bit ruthless in trying to eliminate him, as opposed to simply preventing him from having the chance to find it. But then again, my advisors are very thorough."

He smiled at Assaf, comfortable speaking of Degnan's elimination now that things worked out without any need for loss of life.

"The irony of the entire ordeal is Degnan worked with Tannen on his book about Goliath's sword, and was mocked for it being farfetched and ridiculous to believe it could be found. All along he was working with one of two men who actually knew where the sword was hidden."

Gershom chuckled to himself.

"So, what do you want done with Degnan?" Cristy pushed, annoyed at the comical moment.

"Please detain him until we have the sword, then let him go, provided he has no information that would jeopardize our success."

Cristy's patience finally ran out. He was tired of allowing the Israeli Prime Minister to dictate the steps towards the treaty.

"We need to move forward with the signing of the treaty, now. No more conditions," the Vice President said, pushing his agenda forcefully.

Gershom paused and looked at Assaf. He knew that Cristy's request was evenhanded. While passionate in his belief in the importance of this sacred artifact, he was keenly aware of how it could look from an outsider's perspective.

"That is fair. Let us meet here soon. I assume the President is aware of this treaty?"

Cristy scoffed at the question.

"He knows enough. The Secretary of Defense and I will be there tomorrow; I don't do soon. I want this done now. I will let you know about Degnan's status. Regarding the map, I will have agents pick it up and we will bring it to our meeting tomorrow. Your artifact will be found by your men and our special friendship will be even stronger." Cristy gritted his teeth attempting to be polite.

"I look forward to your arrival," Gershom said confidently, hanging up the receiver and sitting down in his desk chair.

"Despite all that has happened, we will have the map tomorrow."

Assaf nodded in agreement, looking at his watch.

"Our interests are satisfied, and the U.S. receives what they desire. With the might of the U.S. supporting us, we will soon dominate the Middle East. And without any death, I might add."

Assaf smiled cautiously, walking over to the table with the whiskey flask, and filled two glasses, bringing one to Gershom.

"To Israel," Assaf said, raising his glass.

"To Rabbis Judah and Tannen. I will not let this last action smear his lifelong dedication to his people."

The two men smiled and sipped their glasses.

"Americans do produce good whiskey."

The pair laughed at the welcomed moment of levity.

"Come, this day has a positive end . . . despite its obstacles. Let us rest."

13

"AGAIN, THE MAN IN THIS PICTURE is Francis Degnan, a teacher and resident of Jersey City. Wanted in connection with the bombing of an apartment on ninety-sixth street and the recent fire at Saint Ignatius Prep in Jersey City. Authorities have stated that he may be in possession of weapons as well as explosives. He is being accompanied by a senior at Saint Ignatius prep, Ricky Badaracco. The student's involvement in these crimes is unknown. The police and the FBI have instructed anyone with information on his whereabouts to call . . ."

The Imam hit the power button on the TV. He sat behind his desk in the center's library, awaiting his company's reaction.

Frenchy stood in the middle of the room, his mouth slightly open. His eyes began to fill with tears. Ali raised his hand to gently bring his friend out of astonishment.

"Francis, I am not going to turn you in. It will be fine," Ali said, hoping to comfort him.

"I cannot believe what I just saw. I'm a fugitive. I'm a fuckin' OJ Simpson. They think I tried to burn down my school."

" Well, you kind of did, Doc, not that you were trying to hurt the school or anyone in it, but, well."

Sarah assessed the situation and interrupted Ricky, putting her hand on his shoulder, shaking her head to discourage him from continuing.

"This is not what I planned when I started this day."

Frenchy walked to the couch near the TV, and sat down, still stunned.

Despite knowing the FBI was "interested" in speaking with him, he was appalled that his family, friends, neighbors, and students, would now believe that he was a terrorist, a criminal.

"Look, forget about what they said on the TV, we need to figure out what's going on. Where's the letter from my father? We need to read it now."

Sarah knelt down in front of Frenchy, holding his shoulders and hoping to move him beyond the recent news bulletin.

"What exactly has taken place?" Ali asked, hoping for clarification.

Sarah looked at Frenchy and stood up facing Ali.

"I'm sorry, we went from bad jokes to very serious in a few minutes. My name is Sarah Tannen, Rabbi Tannen's daughter. He passed away yesterday. He was a friend of Francis'."

"Of course, Rabbi Daniel; I have met him before. He helped Francis with his research." Sarah nodded in agreement.

"Two days ago he asked me to send a package to Francis. I did. It turns out what I sent him was this."

She grabbed the box next to Frenchy and displayed the inside of the box for Ali.

"Without sounding like an expert, I do believe that is C4 explosives? Why would you send this to him?"

Ali momentarily became concerned with his female guest.

"I didn't know what was in it. But there is nothing to make it go off. This is a cable wire, probably from my father's bedroom TV. My father obviously didn't intend to hurt him. Especially since he left me this note."

She reached into Frenchy's pocket as he sat with his head in his hands. He gestured in irritation.

"Don't touch me."

"Oh, please," she said, smiling at him and happy to see him returning to his usual self.

She handed the note to Ali. The three stared at Ali as he read the letter.

"Well, clearly your father knew what was taking place and why the FBI are presently pursuing Francis. It would seem he would prefer that you stay out of it," he said, looking over his glasses at Sarah, implying she should not be accompanying Francis.

"I couldn't just leave him to this fate. I sent the package. I feel somewhat responsible," Sarah explained.

Ricky leaned over to Frenchy and muttered.

"Doc, she wants you."

Frenchy looked up, his cheeks turning red.

While what Ricky said gave him a momentary high, he had no time to think about that at the present instant.

"Whatever, I'd take my celibate life over being a fugitive any day."

He looked away, aware that he had just said celibate to a student regarding his own life.

Ali looked at Frenchy.

"Well, what does the letter say?"

Frenchy mocked Ali's urgency, unable to move beyond the news report. He took the letter and began to carefully open it. While he always longed for a life of excitement and adventure, his present situation made him less than thrilled to be opening the letter, fearful of what might be next on a turbulent and tumultuous day.

Frenchy removed the letter from the envelope and began to read.

"Out loud, please," Sarah said, unable to wait her turn.

Frenchy rolled his eyes and began to read aloud:

> Dear Francis,
>
> Normally a letter that one receives after another's death is viewed as a positive gesture, because they usually indicate an inheritance. Unfortunately, you are becoming heir to something you may not want, and for this I apologize. It has been over sixty years since we found the Philistine Goliath's sword.

Frenchy began the next word and froze.

"Bullshit," he shouted aloud. He stared at the letter and began to quickly read ahead. "This has got to be a joke. Is this all a joke?" Frenchy asked frantically, looking at his companions. "Seriously if this is a prank, it's not fuckin' funny anymore. I started crying before."

Frenchy's eyes darted from one person to the next, awaiting some sort of acknowledgment of his proclamation.

"This isn't a joke," Sarah said, curious as to what spurred on the question.

Frenchy's eyes widened as he realized the possibility of the situation's veracity.

He returned to reading the letter furiously to himself.

Sarah and Ricky simultaneously yelled at Frenchy, using different names, hoping to force him to return to sharing the information with the rest of them.

"I've got to read that part again," Frenchy said, standing up to read.

"It has been sixty years since I found the Philistine Goliath's sword. I know this might give you pause and make you wonder if I am experiencing dementia, but it is true. In 1946, Rabbi Judah and I, while working on an archaeological dig outside of Jerusalem, discovered a sword. We thought little of the discovery except that it seemed to be Iron Age work. However, our other previous finds authenticated it. We had found references to its location, but we were skeptical of their legitimacy. At the time, we both agreed that no one should possess it, particularly after the horrors of the Second World War. We mapped the location and left it to remain hidden. While Judah never fully agreed with the concealing of its discovery, he honored our agreement. Recently, as my health faded, he asked that the Sword be given to Israel. He had told the Prime Minster of Israel without my consent. The Prime Minister and his closest advisor believe it is the key to rally all of Judaism to protect and expand the Holy Land. They pushed for me to give my half of the map, despite the fact that both Judah and I could never forget its resting place. I am not proud, but I agreed. However, the Prime Minister and his pugnacious advisor viewed you as a competitor, a threat. Still, they agreed to leave you alone. Unfortunately, they changed their position. I sensed that they would not honor their promise to leave you be. So, I ensured that you would not be hurt, by altering the package intended to kill you. I am sorry that I have put you into harm's way. Know that it was never my intention to have you harmed. But what I saw taking place is not what being Jewish is about.

"Regardless of what has transpired since my impending passing, I imagine you are still a target of their interest. And obviously if you are reading this, my daughter has found you. Two years ago when we researched and discussed your book, you told me that you believed you could find this lost artifact. Now is your time to do just that. Worry not of the map. I could not take a chance. If they had the full map, they would have found it immediately, with or without my trusted friend. But this will not deter them from still searching. It is up to you to find the sword before they do, and if you locate it, I trust you will know what to do it. Or of course, do not seek. It is your choice. You can remain hidden for some time and take your chances that they find it before they find you. Given your ties to your hometown, that may be the best course. If you choose that, know that once they have it, you as a threat will disappear. But again, you have the chance to seek what has been such a part of your life. Know that I firmly believe that no artifact or symbol should be possessed by any one person or people, particularly those who would use it for their own gain.

"You have a good heart. I believe you will do the right thing. But no matter your decision, know that what you believe in does exist.

"Sincerely, . . . Daniel Tannen."

There was silence among the group as they attempted to process what had just been revealed. Ali reclined in his chair, putting his hand on his shoulder. Frenchy continued to stare at the letter, re-reading sections, trying to make sense of Tannen's words. Ricky stared at Frenchy. While the words did not seem to fully make sense, he believed it to be a pinnacle moment for his mentor.

"Fuck! Why are we quiet? This is the shit, Doc! This is what you've been waiting for. Hard evidence stating that you were right. It does exist. And this is your chance to find it."

Frenchy looked over at Ricky, and returned to reading the letter.

"What did he mean you'll know what to do with it?" Sarah asked, stuck on what she thought was an odd statement.

"Well, hell yeah, he would know what to do with it. Sell it and get rich, bitch."

Frenchy smiled, appreciating Ricky's enthusiasm and his moment of levity in a tense situation.

"I imagine that's not what my father meant."

"I know, I know. He was joking. I just . . . I don't understand. All along he knew I was right. Now he dies and tells me I was right, but if I want to find it, I have to compete with a country and the FBI, with no map. Who the fuck does that? If only he had just told me this before God dammit. My life would be so different today."

Frenchy stood up, placing the letter on his seat. He walked towards the window behind the couch. He stared out at the parking lot, looking at the red van, thinking about all that had transpired since he woke up in the morning.

He suddenly felt betrayed by his friend. While Tannen's desire to keep it from people who may abuse its alleged power made sense to him, it did not sit well that he was in his present position.

Sarah walked over to him and put her hand on his shoulder. From her limited time with Frenchy, she easily deduced that this was a significant topic in his life, one of extreme passion that had produced little positive.

"I know what you are feeling. I get it. But I don't think you should feel betrayed. My father obviously believes in you since it is you he chose to send this letter to. In his last actions, he went against his closest friend, and his country, his people. And he reached out to you. To do the right thing as he said. You should be proud."

Ricky nodded, turning and looking at Sarah.

"She's right," Ali said. "You have been given a great responsibility, if you choose to accept it. If Israel has this symbol, and if its importance is true, then the Palestinians will be completely moved out of the Holy Land. They will come under attack."

"You don't know that," Frenchy said, becoming irritated with the talk of responsibility. Ali looked down, recognizing Frenchy's volatile state.

"Either way, Francis, you must decide what you will do. Let's not forget that it was your research that speculated that it had mystical powers."

Frenchy held his hand up, attempting to stop Ali from continuing.

"Come on, you and I know that's bullshit. I wrote it because how could it not be important, and why not mystical powers? Shit, look at the fuckin' Blarney Stone. But it's not true."

"Fine," Ali said, continuing, "but, it was you who linked the battle of David and Goliath as the first major conflict between Israeli's and Palestinians to the present day battles. If that's true, then maybe the Sword's powers can be true."

"I don't understand," Sarah said, cutting in. "What does that have to do with today's conflict?"

"Some speculate that the Philistines are the distant ancestors of today's Palestinians. In fact, Palestine, the name, is derived from the word 'philistine,'" Frenchy explained. "My thesis of the book was that the Sword represented the power of Palestine. Whoever possessed it would dominate the region. But let's not forget that this was just a theory. And if Rabbi Tannen is correct, then my theory is incorrect. If the sword does have power, it has nothing to do with who controls the Levant."

"How so?" Ali asked. "Well, remember I traced the history of the Sword and who possessed it from Goliath to present day. Every person or group that controlled it happened to also control Palestine. But it's been missing for years. There have been rulers of Palestine long after it disappeared. So maybe I was wrong: no power, no mystical funny shit."

"Wait, before we get into this, are you going to search for it?" Sarah decided that any discussion on his research would be mute unless he decided to actually take on the responsibility of finding the Sword.

Ricky looked at Frenchy, his face encouraging him to agree.

"I guess, but I don't know how we can do this. Remember the FBI is after us, we have no map, and we are basing this on your father's letter written when he was dying. I don't know, this all seems a little shady if you ask me."

Sarah processed Frenchy's points. Her father's words, however cryptic and confusing, seemed to clearly express his desire for Frenchy to find the Sword.

"My father made it clear that he wanted you to find the Sword and, well, protect it. He put his faith in you that you would believe it could be found, and that you could find it. To me, it doesn't matter the circumstances; you have a job to do."

"Why are you pushing so hard?" Ali asked, curious as to why she was insisting so. "Your father did not even want you involved in this. You should be with your sisters."

Sarah shook her head in irritation and looked at Frenchy.

"I already said, I will not just leave you with this fate. I am here to help. Besides, if this was so important to my father, I want to help in any way I can."

Frenchy smiled at Sarah's willingness to help, and her dedication to her father.

"Alright, we will do it, but just so we are on the same page, there is a good chance we won't find it. In truth, I would put my money on us getting arrested before we ever really get started."

"So? They will not hurt us. They have nothing against us."

Frenchy shook his head at Sarah's firm belief in liberty and justice.

"Well, great; I feel better. You're right. Oh, and I'll see you in Gitmo."

"Let's not worry about that yet," Sarah said, trying to ignore Frenchy's comment.

"Are we in agreement, we will do this together?"

Frenchy looked at Ricky and then panned over to Ali.

"You guys shouldn't . . ."

Ricky interrupted.

"Don't even, nigga, you know I'm in."

"N-word, inappropriate."

Frenchy and Ricky smiled.

"I suppose I could help you out. After all, I would certainly prefer that you find it rather than anyone else. And while I appreciate your faith in justice, Ms. Tannen, my life is proof that you can detain anyone, no matter their innocence," Ali said, sitting down and crossing his legs.

"Thank you for that report. So, all good?" Sarah said, ensuring each of her companions nodded. "Now, what the hell have you been babbling about?"

Frenchy cocked his head and winced. "Babbling? Sit back and get ready for some real bullshit."

14

ESPINOZA LOOKED CAUTIOUSLY as he pulled up across the driveway of 47 Boyd Avenue. He looked to his left where there were a group of teenagers sitting on the steps of the opposite house. They suspiciously peered towards the black vehicle and casually got up and began to walk down the block. Espinoza stared as they cautiously looked back at the car.

"You want to circle back and talk to them?" Forester asked, aware of the attention his partner gave to the group.

"Forget it. They think we're here for them. This section of Jersey City is a cesspool. Shithead drug dealers and crack heads on every corner. Liquor stores everywhere look like beacons in these neighborhoods."

"You know Jersey City?" Forester asked, curious as to how Espinoza was familiar with the conditions of their present environment.

"No, I'm from Baltimore. But some things are the same no matter where you go."

Espinoza pointed to the corner liquor store, lit up like a Las Vegas attraction. Forester shook his head, disgusted at the site of men hanging out in front of the liquor store in the middle of the day, brown bagged beverages in their hands.

Espinoza looked though Forester's window and stared up at the front porch of Degnan's house.

An old woman sat in a plastic blue chair, a gray cane in hand and a black pocketbook hanging from the cane. She stared suspiciously at the car blocking her driveway.

"We can go through the back," Forester said, eyeing an alleyway he assumed led to a backyard.

"I got a better idea: let's go talk to her. The house is registered to a Mary Berkowitz which is Degnan's mother's name, so it must be his grandmother or some relative."

"He's a fuckin' Jew?"

Espinoza laughed.

"Doubtful, by the way he drinks. And he's a private schoolteacher so small salary, probably not a Jew."

The two shared a hearty laugh.

Forester wiped his face and looked up at the old woman.

"You sure she won't tip him off."

Forester's faith in his partner was rock solid, but his concern focused on avoiding divulging info to Degnan on their movement.

"She's old, look at her. She probably lived through the Depression. I doubt she will remember our conversation anyway," Espinoza said, gesturing his belief in her dementia.

He opened the door and stepped into the street, carefully combing his surroundings with his eyes. Forester got out and met him at the curb.

"You better be right," he said taking off his sunglasses. Espinoza gently slapped him on the back and began walking up the brick steps.

"Trust me, she probably has no idea where she is," He smiled and waved to her.

"Excuse me, ma'am, good afternoon . . . ?"

"You know, my grandson will be home soon and he will need to get in the driveway," the old woman said, pointing below her porch with her cane.

"Of course, ma'am, we just need to ask you a few questions and we will be out of your hair."

The old woman rolled her eyes and pointed her cane at the agents.

"I don't want to talk about Jesus. You people never stop. Did you call me last night? I know all I need to know about Jesus. My brother was a bishop, you know, in Bergen County. I have a picture of him with the Pope; you don't believe me? Hang on, I'll get it."

The elderly woman did not seem pleased with her guests desire to talk with her. Forester looked at Espinoza and rolled his eyes.

"That won't be necessary, ma'am. Are you Mrs. Berkowitz?"

The old lady stopped moving towards the front door and turned slowly and stared through squinted eyes at her guests, wondering how they knew her name. She became concerned that they weren't her original assumption.

"I am the homeowner."

"Well, ma'am, my name is Carl. We are looking for Francis Degnan; he is helping us and we were trying to meet up with him."

Forester looked at Espinoza questioning his approach.

The old lady seemed relieved.

"Oh, Francis is not home. I could call him; you know, he has a cell phone, but he never answers the damn thing. My daughter has a cell phone, too, but she answers the phone, do you want me to call her?"

Forester sighed, realizing that Espinoza was right that the old woman was batty, but failing to see how this was a better idea than his alleyway entrance.

"No, ma'am, we were just wondering if you talked to him today. He told us to meet him here."

"He didn't call me today. I called him but he . . ."

"Never answers his phone, yes, I understand," Espinoza said, attempting to avoid a repeat.

"You know, that reminds me of a song. Here I am, waiting by the telephone, all alone, waiting for someone to call . . ."

The old woman began to sing, looking at the two men, expecting them to recognize the song.

"Do you know that one? I never really liked Sinatra until I got older, but you know, he used to rent an apartment above my friend's garage over on Armstrong Avenue. Rita Houke. She was in love with William Ryan, and he should have married her, but he liked to drink and gamble and . . ."

"Thank you, ma'am, I think we are all set," Espinoza said, cutting off the long perplexing string of nonsense. "Have a good day," Espinoza said, walking down the stairs, rolling his eyes, and shaking his head at Forester. The old woman continued to talk as they walked away and began to sing another song she was temporarily reminded of.

"Alleyway?" Forester asked.

"Yeah, that was painful. Shoot me if I ever begin to babble like that," Espinoza said, shaking his head in amusement.

The old woman watched the two men enter their car and drive away. She sat quietly for a moment chewing on her right thumbnail. She looked down the street and began to stand and move towards the first steps. A mini-van driven by a middle-aged woman pulled up across the driveway. Mrs. Berkowitz walked over to the passenger side door of the van, opening it and throwing her pocketbook in.

"Jesus, Mom, do you have to throw things every time?"

"Shut up, Rose," she said, pulling her leg slowly into the car and slamming the door shut with her cane.

"What's the matter?" her daughter asked.

"Nothing. Everything is fine; stop always asking me if there is something wrong. If there is, I'll tell you."

Her daughter threw her hands up slightly in the air in frustration.

"Let's go to the bank, I need to deposit a few checks."

They pulled away and drove towards the red light at the top of the block.

"Anything good on TV today, Ma?" her daughter asked.

"No, not much. Did you talk to Francis today?"

Mrs. Berkowitz looked back at her house as her daughter made the left onto Kennedy Boulevard.

"I haven't; why?"

The old woman winced as she settled herself back in her seat. She raised her eyebrows and looked straight ahead.

"No reason, I just have a feeling he would have found today's news very interesting."

15

JENSEN STEPPED OUT OF HIS VEHICLE, locking it with a click of the handheld remote. He moved towards the elevator in the parking garage under the FBI headquarters. The uneasy feeling that resided in the pit of his stomach continued to remind him that there continued to be a delay on the completion of his case. He pushed his suit jacket sleeve back to look at his watch. His assignment should have been completed by nine o'clock. Instead, it was 2:05 p.m. and Degnan was still at-large.

As he pushed the elevator button, he eyed the ring on his right hand. His ring, a crucifix fused to the gold band, often helped center him during days of tumult. His belief that his work protected and cared for all people in the world was called into question at times. Yet, the sight of Jesus' suffering often gave him comfort as he understood that others, too, may have to suffer as Jesus did to ensure the safety of all. Unfortunately, gazing at the ring currently gave him no calm. He rubbed the ring, turning it on his finger.

Jensen stepped into the elevator and scanned his ID card, allowing him to access his floor. He looked down again at his ring. The symbol of Christ gave him a feeling of guilt. As his case had developed over the last four hours, he had lost the feeling of impartiality. He rarely struggled to separate himself from a task or case. Yet, he feared his present assignment, was about power and money. He shook his head as he thought about Degnan, laughing that his first feelings of guilt on the job were over an imbecile from Jersey.

As the elevator arrived on the twenty-second floor, he stepped out and moved quickly towards his office, agents busily moving throughout the office. He nodded at his secretary and entered his office.

"I don't want to be disturbed for ten minutes, Julie," he said, closing his office door.

He removed his black jacket, placing it over the visitor's chair, and sat informally in his chair, sighing. He looked at the pictures that adorned his wall.

His gaze fell on a picture of a young boy sitting on his desk. He took the picture and examined it closely. He smiled as he thought about how young his son was when the photo was taken. His expression shifted from happy contemplation to a panicked look. He suddenly imagined his son being the man the government wanted to kill. He gazed out of the floor-to-ceiling window, wondering where Degnan was at that moment. He imagined that Degnan's family undoubtedly had heard the reports that their son, brother, uncle, was wanted for terrorist acts. He looked back at his son's photo. It had been years since he had updated the photo. Though he was often busy and rarely saw his son, he often thought about him, presently about to graduate from a Catholic high school in Cleveland. Jensen began to envision what his son would think of him if he knew that his father was handling a case that included the murder of a Catholic high school teacher. What if it was his teacher?

He reached into his drawer and removed a manila folder. He began to read Degnan's profile. Jensen looked over his resume. He stood up and walked over to his bookshelf, removing a green covered book with a picture of a sword spanning the cover of the book diagonally. Though a government agent, his passion always remained with classical history, his major during his time at Dayton University. He walked towards his desk reading the title, *The Power of Goliath*. He sat down, opening to the first chapter.

Based on Degnan's resume, this was the only real accomplishment he had in his life. Though Jensen had dismissed the book as far-fetched, his review of Degnan's file showed only one possible connection to any dealings with Israel. Degnan's writings on an Old Testament artifact were the only association with Israel.

Yet, even this link made no sense to Jensen. Perhaps, this was a vendetta, he thought to himself. He recalled a section of Degnan's book, in which he spoke about the conflict between Israel and Palestine, sharply criticizing Israel's treatment of Palestinians.

Jensen opened to the chapter. Degnan had said Israel had no right to claim the land solely for Jews. Could this be the key to why he was to be eliminated? Jensen continued to read.

Despite Degnan's opinion being the only plausible connection, Jensen could not imagine said claim being distinctive enough for Degnan to be singled out. His analysis was interrupted by a knock on the door.

The FBI Director entered the room followed by a well-dressed man carrying a leather briefcase.

"Al, this is Secretary Hansen. I was bringing him up to speed on the occurrences of the day."

"It's an honor, Mr. Secretary. I had the privilege of attending a lecture you gave on anti-terrorist tactics a few years ago."

Jensen shook Hansen's hand.

Hansen showed little emotion. A man in his sixties, he had heard similar statements so frequently so it no longer elicited a response from him.

"Al, we need to go back to Judah's apartment. Secretary Hansen has been advised by the Vice President that there is something important in his apartment that is needed in order to move forward with the treaty."

Jensen snickered in his mind, irritated that he had been on his way to Judah's apartment when the Director stopped him, requesting him to return to headquarters.

"I'll call our agents at the scene and have them bring it in," Jensen said, picking up the office phone.

"We want you to go."

Hansen stared at Jensen sharply.

"Fine," Jensen said, placing the phone back on its base. "What am I looking for?"

The Secretary reached into his briefcase and produced a printed image of a box.

"This is what we need," he said, holding it up to Jensen.

"What is it?" Jensen asked, not expecting what he regarded as a decaying wood box to be the goal of his assigned task.

"It's not important what it is, truthfully; I don't give a damn about it, but the Prime Minister of Israel specifically requested that this be recovered from Judah's apartment."

The Defense Secretary's irritation in the deed hinted at his overall attitude towards the entire state of affairs in the case. A sentiment that made Jensen feel somewhat relieved that his frustration was shared.

"Just get it, and return. I am leaving for the Middle East this evening."

Jensen fixed his eyes on the picture of the box. He took the print-out from Hansen.

"I'll get it," he said, moving over to his desk and laying it on Degnan's book.

"I would like it now," Hansen said, irritated that Jensen did not jump to his task immediately.

"Of course, Mr. Secretary, I will leave immediately."

Hansen nodded and opened the door, exiting the room with the Director following. Jensen stood as the men left, sitting down again once they had departed.

He held the picture in his right hand, inspecting it again. He momentarily felt a rush of adrenaline, feeling closer to understanding the case. Though he had wrestled the last hour with whether his actions were right or wrong, each new piece propelled him to continue on course, hoping to understand fully by the end of the ordeal.

He grabbed his jacket, picking up Degnan's file and book, and quickly headed out of the office. He struggled to put his jacket on as he walked past his secretary.

"So much for ten minutes, Julie."

16

"TRY TO FOLLOW ME WHEN I DO THIS because it gets a bit confusing and by that I mean everyone who has heard this thinks it's bullshit, but fuck it, today is already fucked," Frenchy said, standing up as though he was preparing a history lesson for a classroom of unenthused students.

"You may want to sit."

Ricky rolled his eyes and smiled.

"Sounds like I'm back in sophomore year."

Frenchy stared at Ricky, both eyebrows raised.

"You got jokes, huh, squirrely?" he said, pausing to comment, before resuming his stance to begin his lecture. First let me say that, if your father is correct, then everything I am about to tell you is false and, thus, whatever I have been following through the annals of history and what I wrote my book on is not the Sword of Goliath. But as I've said, let's play anyway. There's historical evidence that links the Philistines with the indigenous people of Palestine and, thus, their descendants, the present-day Palestinians. In my book I argued that neither Israelis nor Palestinians had a right to claim the land for themselves exclusively. It should be divided between the two peoples and Jerusalem must be held as an international city, as was supposed to happen according to the UN resolution."

Frenchy's voice filled the room as he exuded passion.

"I think you're getting off target; get back to your sword," Sarah said, appreciating his passion, but wishing to focus her new friend.

"When he beat Goliath, David received his armor, which included his sword, you know, spoils of war shit. Now the Bible talks about David as having the sword and armor at the next battle. Then, nothing: David becomes King and yadda yadda yadda. Now to avoid talking forever, this is where I believe the Sword went. It was kept by the ruler of Israel until the Holy Land was captured by the Assyrian empire, and taken by the Assyrian ruler, Tiglath Pileser III."

"Huh?" Ricky said, confused by the slur of words that came out of his mentor's mouth.

"You idiot; forget it, his name doesn't matter. Look, after Solomon's death, the Assyrians conquered Israel. Your father helped me with the translation of a stone slab written in Akkadian using the cuneiform writing system. It was found in the 1700s by an explorer from Denmark, but that doesn't matter. Many of the slabs were used to decipher the language, but there was this one slab that spoke of a mystical sword that Tiglath possessed, taken when he conquered the northern tribes of Israel. He claimed he held the right to the land because of the sword. Interesting huh? Later it passed to Nebuchadnezzar, after the Babylonians conquered the Assyrians. And, surprise, surprise, found in Mesopotamia, or modern day Iraq, was a declaration from Nebuchadnezzar proclaiming that he possessed the sword of power that gave him dominion over the Holy Land."

Sarah raised her hand and interrupted.

"Couldn't the 'sword of power' simply refer to him as having been a superior military force and thus holding the right?"

"Of course it could, but, again, all of this could be horseshit. Let me tell the story and then we can question it. Just listen. Okay? So next, the sword is given back to the Jews to return to their holy land by Cyrus the Great after the Persians conquered the Babylonians. From there, another gap. No reference to a sword. Not until the Romans led by Pompey the Great conquered Judea in the first century BC. Now, Pompey was fascinated by the Jews. It was he who demanded to be brought into the Holy of Holies in the Temple in Jerusalem."

Frenchy paused looking for some semblance of credit for his statement. Unfortunately, his break elicited no response from his audience, simply assuming he was naturally stopping.

"Anyway, he joined forces with Hyrcanus II, one side of a civil war in Judea taking place at this time, and eventually Jerusalem fell. Pompey eventually returns to Rome, sparking civil war with Caesar. He is chased all around the Mediterranean after his army is defeated at the Battle of Pharsalus, ultimately landing in Alexandria where he was murdered, his head chopped off."

Frenchy paused to regain his breath, having spoken the last phrase without an oxygen break.

Sarah and Ricky smiled at Frenchy. He looked back at them and laughed. He had forgotten how avid he was about history, since losing confidence in himself and his abilities.

"Doc you are stupid smart," Ricky said, shaking his head in admiration.

"I'm not even going to go into how many ways that statement offends me. Anyway, I'm almost there. So, according to Plutarch, who wrote a biography of Pompey, when he returned from the Levant he returned with a sword, given as a gift to him by Hyrcanus II for his help during the Jewish civil war. Interesting no? But Pompey dies, so what happened to this sword? I'll tell you.

He gave it to his close friend, Marcus Flavius Silva, who passes it on to his grandson. And who was his grandson? Only Lucius Flavius Silva."

Frenchy paused again as he reached, for him, the ultimate "a-ha" light bulb turning on moment. His audience of three stared back at him blankly, wondering if that was the end of the story. Ricky's eyes began to look awkwardly from one side of the room to the other, his head not moving.

"Was that a question?" he asked looking over to Ali, hoping he understood.

"Goddammit! You don't know who Lucius Flavius Silva was?" Frenchy said, stunned.

"No, of course I do, I was just wondering what aspect of his life you were asking about." Ricky's attempt to satisfy his mentor seemed to be failing.

"How did you get through freshman World Civilizations class? Lucius Flavius Silva? The governor of Judea during the first century, anno domini, in the year of our Lord, AD?"

"Right, Lucius, I remember, great nigga, sold shoes," Ricky joked, holding his chin and displaying a contemplative look.

"Mother of Jesus . . ."

"Can you just get to it?" Sarah said, interrupting the bickering.

"Silva was the governor who laid siege to the Sicarii at Masada. The Sicarii were one faction of Jews revolting against Rome's control. They all committed suicide at the fortress of Masada, rather than be captured. This is the crucial moment in my story, of the Sword of Goliath's. This is where, I believe, Silva buried the sword, somewhere at Masada, and it is there that it remains."

"Why would he just give it up? I thought you needed it to be the ruler of the Holy Land?" Sarah questioned.

She loved Frenchy's enthusiasm and passion for history and, in this case, his favorite topic. However, as he had narrated his theory on the Sword of Goliath, she had restrained herself from asking any questions that she felt may have poked holes in his theory. Unfortunately, this time, he made a statement for her that she believed could not be ignored.

"Yeah, but I think Silva was so disturbed by the mass suicide, that he decided he wanted nothing to do with the sword. He left it there."

Ali joined the discussion. "But that theory requires the Sicarii to have been after the Sword and I don't remember this part in your writings?" He, too, began to struggle with Frenchy's theory.

"First, of course they were after the sword. It was known that they needed it to control Judea. And two, I wanted to someday go looking for the sword. I'm not gonna put it in my book so some jack-ass can get the glory."

"So, you are saying that your theory after all this is that the Sword of Goliath is at the fortress of Masada?"

Sarah suddenly realized that the last few minutes lecture could have been bypassed by one word. Masada.

"Yes. I believed it was there." Frenchy said, reaching past Ricky to grab the letter from Rabbi Tannen.

"What the hell do you mean 'believed?'" Sarah said, outwardly raising her hands in an expression of frustration.

"I said I believed it was there, only because your father said that I was close. Only he knew my full theory. So, if he said I was close, it can't be Masada, it has to be somewhere else, but close. Of course, what he defines as close could be different from what I believe. Close to me is not at Masada, but in a hole off to the left of the fortress. Your guess is as good as mine."

Ali stood up from his desk and began to look closely at a map of the Arabian Peninsula.

"If Masada is here, than the close surrounding towns are . . ."

Sarah interrupted, losing admiration for Frenchy's passion.

"Wait, you claim the Sword was known by many to have these powers and that it guaranteed that he who possessed it had the power over the Holy Land. Correct?"

"Word, that is correct."

"But many have had power over the Holy Land since the first century. Some for hundreds of years. This would mean the entire theory is false. And you mention these obscure references to swords. That could be anything, it could mean anything."

Sarah noticed Frenchy's face change. His excitement retreated and gave way to shut-down defiance.

"Fine, if I'm wrong, you find it, I don't need to do this."

Frenchy began to put the letter back into the envelope aggressively missing his mark a few times. Sarah put her hand on his and gently took the envelope. Her touch seemed to calm his adolescent outburst, created from many instances of defending his theories from ridiculing audiences.

"I'm sorry; I just got frustrated for a moment. But do you understand why I asked?"

Frenchy raised his hands as he walked towards the window, turning back with exasperation.

"Believe me, I get it. I shouldn't snap. I'm sorry. I get questioned and I throw a bitch-fit. Obviously you see this is a sore subject. Truly, I know there are holes in my theory. I know that my work is not specific enough to convince 'respected historians and archaeologists.'" I get it; I am not so sure I believe it either. But if I've been a little bit off in my theories, I'm okay with it now. For the first time, I'm okay with my shitty book. Because this thing is real and I believe I can find it. Sometimes we get caught up in ideas and don't think them through. That's me in a nutshell. Should I have researched more? Yes. Should I have been objective and not fantasized about mystical powers connected to it? Fuck yeah. More importantly, I shouldn't have written about my fantasies. But as much as it depresses me, everyone was right. I shouldn't have just self-published. I should have screened my work through others. I made an in-your-twenties mistake. Alas, I was very good at marketing so I am reminded of the mistake every day. But whatever happened before is irrelevant. I've got a chance to do something about that mistake. I obviously still hold on to my fantasy, hence my recent exhortation. But I can do this. All my life, I've wanted to be an archeologist, adventurer, or historian, whatever."

Frenchy paused from his delivery. He stared at the envelope.

"I don't know. Sometimes people need things to believe in, to survive, to get through life. Maybe this is mine. You know what? I have waited my whole life to go on a 'quest.' Sure, I'm wanted for murder and for burning down my place of work. Sure, the FBI is after me. Sure, my dog is probably shitting all over my apartment and eating my underwear. But like I said, I'm gonna do this. I'm ready to do this. For myself and for your father."

His three companions stood looking down slightly. Ali began to nod his head. Ricky stood up and gestured to Frenchy.

"Nigga, come in for the real thing. Let the big bear get his paws on you. You know I'm with you, Doc. Let's fuckin' do this" Ricky said, once again providing dialogue from the most recent comedy film he became obsessed with.

The two embraced.

"I'm definitely getting fired for all this."

Ricky laughed.

Sarah stood up as Frenchy and Ricky sighed, feeling mutual support.

Ali approached his two young comrades and joined the embrace.

"I'm with you too," Sarah said, genuinely caring for Frenchy's determination.

"Not a bad speech huh?" Frenchy said, winking.

"And . . . he ruins it.'

"PULL UP HERE, ROSE. I WANT TO USE THE PHONE."

Frenchy's grandmother removed a quarter from a section of her bag. Mrs. Degnan looked over at her mother, confused at her statement. She looked down at Mrs. Berkowitz's open pocketbook.

"Mom, things are falling out of your bag. Hold it upright. Christ do you have to bring everything with you?"

Frenchy and his family often joked that his grandmother carried one of everything in her pocketbook. If you needed a bumper for a '67 Chevy, chances were she had it. Now his mother attempted to pull the car into a spot while catching the assortment of things that fell from her mother's bag.

"Why do you need a screwdriver in your bag, and a flashlight? Dental floss, chocolate covered almonds?"

Mrs. Degnan announced each oddity she picked up from the floor of the front passenger seat.

"Where are you going?" she asked as her mother opened the door to exit.

"Oh, shut up Rose, I don't have to tell you what I'm doing. I'm not a child."

The old woman swiped behind her in defiance and began to make her way to the old pay phone. She placed her quarter into the outdated communication tool. As she punched the number in, her daughter approached her.

"Mom, I have a cell phone. Don't touch that thing; it is covered with germs."

Mrs. Berkowitz raised her cane attempting to create space between her and her progeny.

"Hi Francis, it's me, just wanted to let you know that you had two friends here looking for you. You may want to get home; they are waiting for you."

In her attempt to convey her secret message to her grandson through varying the volume of her voice, her behavior caused her daughter to cock her head in confusion.

"Again, Frenchy, you may want to get home; they're waiting for you."

She stressed every syllable as she bid farewell and hung up the phone. She pushed passed her daughter walking quickly, yet unsteadily, with her cane.

Her daughter stood watching her aged mother.

"What was that about ma?" she asked moving to open the door for her.

"If you would shut up and get in the van, I will explain it to you."

Mrs. Berkowitz slowly stepped into the van, grimacing as she dropped abruptly into the seat

"You want to tell me what's going on, Ma, and why you had to touch that phone? Here, use some hand sanitizer." Mrs. Degnan produced a small bottle of disinfectant.

"Francis is in trouble. Two men came looking for him, they looked suspicious, and I didn't like the Puerto Rican one's attitude."

"Are you sure it wasn't the UPS man, Ma? Or remember, you once ignored the doorbell because when you looked outside you thought it was public school kids selling candy, which we all know irritates you. But remember that? And who was it in fact?"

Mrs. Berkowitz rolled her eyes.

"No, Rose who was it?" She said sarcastically, exaggerating her desire to hear the punch line.

"It was your twin seven year-old granddaughters, locked out of their apartment. They sat out on the porch for two hours until their father came home."

"Can't you for once stop questioning everything I do? These men were not the UPS men. They were FBI. And it makes sense since your son is wanted for murder."

Mrs. Degnan's mocking facial expression changed as she looked over at her mother quickly. Of all the things she expected her mother to say about her son, the word murder was never even in the running. Mrs. Degnan sighed, allowing her head to drop in exasperation.

"Is this about him not watering your plants? I thought you would have let this go by now; he said he will buy you new ones."

"What plants?" Mrs. Berkowitz asked, easily distracted from her train of thought by the mention of new information.

"It doesn't matter, Mom, just don't call him a murderer, he will replace the plants."

"Oh, that's right, murderer, Frenchy. He's a murderer," she said, regaining her train of thought and ignoring the desire to interrogate her daughter about this unknown plant incident.

"Ma, for the last time stop calling my son a murderer," Mrs, Degnan shouted, attempting to express seriousness through her volume and tone.

"No, Rosie, on TV they said that he was a murderer, not me. Didn't you hear about the fire at Prep?"

Mrs. Degnan stared at her mother. Though she found what was being said to be silly and knew that her mother was prone to exaggeration, she felt panicked. Her aged mother once told everyone in her family that her great-granddaughter had brain surgery, describing what sounded like a primitive lobotomy. Fortunately for her great-granddaughter, she had simply begun to take medicine for ADHD, thus leaving the family to wonder what the matriarch of the family had originally heard.

"What! Is he alright? And why would Francis be called a murderer? Are you sure? And what was the call about?"

Mrs. Degnan's hysteria increased as her fears about Frenchy's volatile mental state seemed confirmed. She had for years believed he was an alcoholic and unstable.

"I called him to tell him that there were men after him, FBI, I don't know, but he needed to know they were at the house," Mrs. Berkowitz explained.

"Why not just call him from this phone?" Frenchy's mother lifted her red cell phone attempting to understand her mother's actions.

"Because they would have traced the call. Besides, he doesn't answer calls from you."

Frenchy's mother was suddenly hit with an infrequent feeling that her mother was making sense, and sadly correct about her son's answering deficiency.

"Where did you hear about tracing calls?"

"I saw it on Diagnosis Murder. They can trace calls from anywhere."

Mrs. Degnan shook her head in disbelief at being lectured on law enforcement capabilities by her ninety-three-year-old mother.

"Oh my God, what do we do? He's being called a murderer, he burned down the school. My own son burning down his own school. We have to find him."

"God dammit, Rose, shut the hell up," Mrs. Berkowitz snapped. "I lived through the Great Depression, you know, kids don't know what it was like back then . . ."

"Ma, please," Mrs. Degnan said, in no mood for a story she had heard thousands of times.

"Okay, fine. But there is nothing we can do. If we look for them, then we will lead the cops to them. I say we call Jimmy. He can straighten things out."

"He's just a cop, and what is he going to 'straighten out'? If Frenchy is being chased by the police, then he should turn himself in or we should find him."

Mrs. Berkowitz shook her head in frustration, accepting her daughter's present fears for her son's safety.

"I just think if Jimmy knows, then he may be able to find him and bring him in safely, rather than with everyone calling him a murderer on TV. And he is a lieutenant, not just a cop."

"I need to call him," Mrs. Degnan said as she grabbed her phone and began to dial his number. Frenchy's grandmother grabbed the phone from her daughter's hands and tossed it out of the open passenger side window. The phone cracked as it fell to the ground. Mrs. Berkowitz stared at her daughter, aware that her impulsive move was not the wisest decision.

"Okay, that was wrong, but you deserved it. Call Jimmy."

Mrs. Degnan, still shocked at the quick action of her usually frail mother, stared out of the window, and began to cry. Her mother reached into her purse and produced a quarter and a sheet of paper.

"Here is Jimmy's number and here is a quarter; just let him know what's going on and make sure he finds Francis before anyone else does."

Mrs. Degnan took a deep breath and took the quarter and piece of paper with her nephew's number on it. Her distress and fear for her son choked her. She coughed and got out of the car and moved towards the phone.

"Oh, and Rose," Mrs. Berkowitz said, reaching into her purse. "Use this," she gestured handing her daughter a pair of plastic medical gloves. "The handle may have influenza."

18

"RIGHT IN THE FUCKIN' FACE," Forester shouted, swiping erratically in front of his face.

"Relax, it's an alley between two houses; what'd you expect? Besides, it's the crap I'm stepping in that I'm more worried about."

Espinoza patted Forester on the back, pointing to a layer of composting garbage and leaves lining the alley ground.

"People are slobs. How hard would it be to clean your property?"

Forester didn't seem pleased with his present surroundings, regretting suggesting this approach.

Espinoza paused as the alley began to open to the neighboring backyard.

"Well, from the looks of Degnan's neighbors' backyard, it's not his garbage." Espinoza cautiously looked around the backyard and moved along the fence surrounding Degnan's yard.

"We can hop the fence here; this is the sturdiest spot. Closest to the back door."

Forester gently shook the fence and pointed up towards the back door leading into Degnan's apartment. Espinoza made his way over to Forester, nodding to signal his partner to go first. He stepped up on the fence and in a quick motion swung his body over the top of the ivy-covered chain linked fence and into the backyard, crouching down after his landing.

"Shit," Forester said with a look of disgust.

"What's it now?" Espinoza whispered preparing to jump the fence.

"That's all, just shit. Everywhere."

Espinoza landed with an equally impressive acrobatic handling of the obstacle, landing next to Forester.

"Fuck, you weren't joking. That's a whole lot of shit," Espinoza said, smiling at Forester, enjoying a moment of levity in an otherwise stressful day.

"Come on, just be careful. You step in it; you gotta run alongside the car," Forester grunted as they cautiously avoided the plentiful piles of excrement.

They climbed the five stairs leading to an old porch. Forester opened the storm door, sliding his hand over the lock. He reached into his pocket and removed a small metal tool, a slight curve at the tip.

"I think we can just kick the door in," Espinoza said, unwilling to wait the time it would take to pick the lock.

"Believe me this is a crappy door, give me three seconds and . . ."

Forester closed one eye, focusing on his work. The lock gave off a slight click and the door opened into a small hallway, with three doors within a few feet of each other.

"Okay, well, nevermind."

Espinoza pointed to the right door and nodded to Forester to proceed. As Forester put his hand on the knob and turned, he felt resistance as he pushed, closing the door. He looked at Espinoza and their eyes met, both men smiling, silently agreeing on the cause of the resistance. Forester opened the door forcefully, and Degnan's dog was pushed back momentarily, hurriedly moving towards Forester to jump up in search of affection from the stranger.

"My kind of guard dog," Espinoza said, as Forester patted the dog on her head as she pushed into the agent for a more forceful rub.

"The only kind of dog I want to encounter when we're doing these kinds of jobs," he said, gently pushing her down from his waist.

Forester looked around the kitchen. He looked down the railroad style apartment into the hallway, dining room, and ultimately into the living room.

"Well, like I said, we could never be so lucky that we would stumble upon him," Espinoza said, surveying the kitchen. "Check the other rooms."

Forester shrugged his shoulders, not welcoming the opportunity to search for clues.

"Okay, but I doubt we'll find anything that tells us where he is now. We have a list of his friends and family."

Forester walked towards the hallway as Espinoza continued to cautiously scan the kitchen. He surveyed the beer bottles and empty packs of cigarettes, mixed in with scattered old macaroni noodles and used packets of Velveeta cheese. His guilt for his involvement in the case momentarily faded as he grew disgusted by the state of Degnan's kitchen. He picked up a pile of take-out menus shaking his head.

"Whoever this douche is, I don't think he is going to stop any treaty from being signed," he yelled.

The condition of Frenchy's apartment seemed to confirm his belief that Degnan was no threat. Espinoza began to feel a sense of determination. Based on his findings and personal dealings with Degnan, he did not consider him an astute fugitive. He felt comfort in knowing that he would soon be able to track him down and hopefully avoid having to eliminate what he viewed as the farthest from a threat to national security.

He continued to scan the kitchen, his eyes falling on a postcard on his refrigerator. He removed the card and looked at the picture on the front. He turned the card over and read its description.

"Petra." He began to read the text on the card aloud. Forester entered the room shaking his head. "I'm not looking through his shit. I told you there would be nothing."

Espinoza continued to read, gesturing to his partner to approach.

"Look at this," Espinoza said, handing him the card with the text facing up.

"What is it?" Forester asked, disinterested in reading what he could be told in a quicker fashion.

"It's from a friend of Degnan's, a Muslim, by the sound of his name. But look at the address."

Forester looked at the return address.

"I don't remember him being on Degnan's list of friends," Forester said, intrigued by the postcard's origin.

"I bet Degnan didn't think so either. That Islamic Center is not too far from here. We get to him now, and we'd be done. No bloodshed, and mission complete."

Forester nodded in agreement, handing the card back to his partner.

"I'll call for a car to head over there . . ."

"No, we go," Espinoza said, interrupting.

"I don't want him getting shot because our people think he's dangerous. We will get him and bring him in."

"Well, let's at least get the JCPD to sit on the mosque since he may be there and might move."

Espinoza nodded, placing the card in his pocket.

Suddenly Espinoza felt a punch from behind his thigh. He quickly reached for his gun looking quickly behind him.

Forester let out a cackle as he looked down to see Degnan's dog pleasuring Espinoza's leg.

"What the fuck did you think it was, a person? What person comes up to your waist?" Forester said, laughing at his partner's quick response.

"Midgets and children come up to my waist, jack-ass. You might learn a thing or two on response time."

Espinoza removed his hand from his gun and began to shake his leg, attempting to push his new best friend from his leg. Forester continued to chuckle as he reached down to help shoo the dog away.

Forester began to walk towards the door, pausing and turning around to face Espinoza.

"How was she?" he asked, with a serious look on his face, cracking a smile immediately after.

"That's the kind of cliché statement I would expect, dickhole," Espinoza said walking towards the door, removing his radio, and preparing to contact the JCPD. "Fuckin' hysterical."

"WHY ARE WE LEAVING SO QUICKLY?" Sarah asked, as Frenchy and Ricky ran down the stairs towards the front door with Ali moving steadily behind them. "We don't even know where we're going."

"Let's just get out of here and we can talk on the way," Frenchy said quickly, putting the explosives and the letters into a bag near the door.

"Can I borrow this?" Frenchy asked, raising it to Ali.

"Yes, of course. Now, we have to get out of N.J. . . ." Ali said, before being interrupted by Ricky.

"Jersey? Let's get out of the U.S. The more time we spend here, the harder it will be to get out of the country. Word travels fast when you're 'armed and dangerous'" Ricky said, using air quotes around the media buzz words.

"He's right; if we're going to do this search, we may as well get out of the country now. This thing ain't in the U.S., that's for sure," Frenchy said, pleading to his friend.

Ali nodded and walked towards the sliding doors, leading to a parlor type area. He signaled to Mohammad, sitting in a chair near the door. Ali began to speak in Arabic with his friend.

"Listen Sarah, we can't stay here because eventually they will find us. Jersey City is not that big. Plus, to be honest, I used to suck at manhunt. I could never hide, so the longer we have to hide, the more screwed we will be."

Frenchy settled his outfit, momentarily pleased with his newly found satchel, and prepared for the start of the adventure.

"Okay, fine, I just didn't understand the panicked 'we need to get out of here' feel we had after the whole hugging moment."

"Did this bitch just imply that we're gay?" Ricky asked, chiming in quickly. "I said 'no homo.' Men can hug," he said, throwing his arms up in exasperation, showing his clear sensitivity to the light remark.

Frenchy looked over at Ricky with a perturbed look.

"What the hell is no homo, bitch?" Sarah asked.

"I hate when you guys say that," Frenchy said, shaking his head in disgust.

"Forget it. Right, I somehow look like the weirdo, but you guys are the ones who say it." Frenchy waved his arm in annoyance walking over to speak to Ali.

Ricky strolled over to Sarah and put out his hand.

"You know, we never properly met, Ricky Badaracco."

Sarah laughed at Ricky's comment.

"Sarah Tannen. I suppose if we are going to be fugitives together, we better formally meet."

"So," Ricky said, looking over his shoulder at Frenchy, speaking with Ali and Mohammad. "You know, the Doc is single and, you know, if you're single, that's a good thing to have in common and, well, I've seen the way you have been looking at him and a . . ."

Sarah's hand shot up into the air directly in front of Ricky's face.

"Don't even start. I have not been looking at him in anyway except in shock at his decision making. And just remember, you are a student. If you plant ideas in his head, I will slap the hell out of you. Don't forget, I may be a Rabbi's daughter, but I was raised in Brooklyn."

She made a fist before Ricky's widening eyes, slowly taking it down while staring at her new acquaintance.

Ricky shook off the threat.

"I got you, I'm with you. I just figured I'd mention it."

"Thanks for the tip," Sarah said, walking over to the window to peer out.

"Just one thing, Biggie Smalls," Ricky said, holding up one finger to his lips.

"What?" Sarah snapped, looking back at him.

"So, you aren't saying you're not single?"

Sarah made a gesture to slap Ricky, as Frenchy and Ali walked over, interrupting the somewhat playful quarrel.

"Great, so we're already getting along. Terrific. I have a real good feeling about this team," Frenchy said, widening his eyes in sarcasm.

"Ali says he may have a way for us to get to Egypt. From there we make our way up the coast."

"Shit, Doc, I completely forgot. I've got a way to get us out of the U.S.," Ricky said, hitting himself on the forehead with both hands.

"How?" Frenchy asked, intrigued by what seemed so obvious to his student.

"My dad works at Port Liberty in Bayonne. He could get us on a ship and out of the country no problem."

Frenchy paused, reflecting on the many ways Ricky's suggestion was crazy.

"First of all: No. That requires us to tell your father that you have been with me while I have been wanted for being a terrorist. Second, hell no. I'm not letting your father happily harbor and transport fugitives because I'm your teacher. And third, I don't like ships; I get seasick."

Sarah stepped in front of Frenchy.

"He's right, Ricky; there is no chance your father will be able to help us or want to help us."

Ricky pulled his cell phone out of his pocket.

"I'm gonna ask."

"I really don't think that is a good idea. Besides, Ali says he can get us on a cargo flight out of here," Frenchy said, determined to move forward with Ali's plan.

Ricky's phone immediately began to vibrate. He looked at the number identification and smiled.

"How about 'the speak of the devil' shit old people say," he said, opening his phone and greeting his father.

Frenchy reached for the phone but Ricky quickly moved away speedily going up a few steps, as he assured his father that he was fine.

"Hey, Pop, I need a huge favor," Ricky said, suddenly unsure how to put his situation into words.

"Pop, me and Doc and two other people need to get out of the country."

Frenchy stood frozen, attempting to decipher Ricky's father's reaction by his facial expressions.

"Some of that is true, Pop, but Doc didn't do anything wrong. They're after him, and now me and two others. If they see us, they'll shoot us; we need to get out of here so we can negotiate our surrender."

Frenchy's left eyebrow went up in bewilderment, looking over at Ali and Sarah.

"Pop, I have always been a good son; just believe me on this one. Please, help us get out of here. We need to be on the next ship out of Bayonne. I need to do the right thing on this one."

A silence fell over the entire room as they waited for an answer. Frenchy stared over at Sarah as she looked down at the ground, her hands folded. The temporary break gave Frenchy a chance to look Sarah "up and down." He smiled as he looked at her features. Her dark brown hair seemed to glow as it hung gently over her shoulders. He looked at her lips, pursed at the moment, as he caught a slight hint of her perfume. He felt an overwhelming impulse to jump over and hug and kiss her repeatedly. He fought the overwhelming urge and fixed his eyes on Ricky.

He shook his head attempting to exit his private thoughts. Though aware that escaping from his pursuers would prove to be near impossible, he remembered calling the parent of a student he implicated in a terrorist plot was, hands down, a dumb idea. He looked over to Ali and gestured for him to approach.

"I think we better go with your plan no matter how risky."

"Thanks, Pop, I will never forget this. Don't worry, we'll get there. Okay." Ricky closed the phone, smiling.

His companions stared, unsure if they had heard correctly.

"Let's go, he can get us to Nova Scotia!"

"Seriously? Your father, who thinks I'm a terrorist, is going to help us get on a ship and away from authorities?" Frenchy asked, in disbelief.

"Good thing I tell him how great you are all the time. That, and he didn't think you would ever do anything to hurt a student. Oh, and he saw my name linked to all this shit."

"I gotta tell you, that may be the most reckless, irresponsible parenting I have ever heard. But thank God he's doing it," Frenchy said, becoming conscious of how preposterous it was that things were somewhat working out.

"Oh shit!" Sarah said, peering out the front window.

"There's a police car outside."

The group quickly dropped down attempting to hide below the wainscoting below the window.

"Shit, shit, shit, he's walking towards the door," Sarah whispered. The group clung side by side to the wall next to the door.

"I may piss myself. So much for an adventure. Excitement to I'm on my way to prison," Frenchy said, immediately turning hysterical.

"Where is he now?"

"He's at the door."

A loud knock resonated through the hallway. Frenchy slowly peered over the wainscoting and looked out, attempting to catch a glimpse of the policeman.

"Holy mother of God." He paused looking down at the floor.

"Yes, okay, yes, that might work," Frenchy declared aloud, jumping up and placing his hand on the door knob.

"Doc, what the hell are you doing, he's gonna cap your ass nigga," Ricky loudly whispered.

Frenchy opened the door and stared at the police officer. The officer stared back at Frenchy, sliding his hand around to his weapon.

"You better have a fuckin' glowing excuse for this," the officer said, wiping his olive colored skin on his brow.

"Trust me I do. Now get in here. Anyone with you?" Frenchy asked, peering beyond the officer.

"What the hell is going on?" Sarah asked, slowly rising from her crouched position.

"This is my cousin, Jimmy."

"Your cousin? You guys don't look anything alike," Sarah said, pushing back at the statement.

"Yeah, well, he's half-Irish, half-Italian, and I'm half that, kinda. I can get a sunburn in moonlight, though, there's no Italian in me," Frenchy said, exposing the pasty white skin on his arm.

"What's going on, French? First, word goes out that you are wanted for murder and for burning down Prep, and then I get a call from your mother frantically saying that you're in trouble. Then, I get a call for an officer to wait out front of this mosque until the FBI arrives because you are possibly hiding out there."

Frenchy looked panicked at his cousin.

"Are there other cars coming?"

"Very soon. Tell me what's going on."

Frenchy looked at his companions and anxiously surveyed the outside.

"I'll explain on the way. We gotta go. Please drive us to Bayonne, to the port."

"Are you crazy? I'm here to make sure no one shoots you."

Frenchy grabbed his satchel from the floor.

"Please, if I ever needed you to trust me, it's now." He opened the door and hurried everyone out.

"Thank God, you don't have a cruiser. We would never fit." Frenchy gestured to the police SUV.

Jimmy paused as the quartet cautiously moved towards the police vehicle. He knew he had to protect his cousin, but aiding in his escape seemed to be a quick way of getting himself in trouble. He looked around and sighed.

"Fine, fuck it, everyone in the back and down. If anyone sees me with you, I will claim I'm taking you in. I am not losing my job for this," Frenchy's cousin protested, rushing to get into the driver's seat.

He turned the car on and headed down Belmont towards the Hudson Highway, making a quick right heading past a sign for the highway to Bayonne.

"Alright, French, now talk," Jimmy said, feeling apprehensive about his decision to transport his present cargo.

"To be honest, I'm tired of explaining it," Frenchy said, hoping his cousin would understand.

"I don't give a shit. Out with it and all of you crouch the fuck down," Jimmy said, shaking his head at Frenchy's commentary.

"Okay, well, basically FBI guys came to Prep to ask my help to find the Sword of Goliath, and then she knocked one of them out and sent C4 to me in a package, and then we ran and they chased us and then I set the building on fire trying to hinder their pursuit of us, and then I came here to hide out and I read a letter from her dad asking me to go on a mission to find the said sword, and so we agreed and I think I know where it is, but I have to get out of the country to find it, so now Ricky's dad is gonna get us on a boat, and then I'll find the sword and negotiate so I don't go to jail for anything because I didn't do anything, except maybe set the building on fire, but that could be considered self-defense."

The car remained silent after Frenchy's verbal diarrhea.

"Forget it," Frenchy's cousin uttered, no longer interested in actually knowing the full story, based on the present narrative. "But you don't know why the FBI is chasing you?"

"Nope, I have no clue except that it must be tied to her father and said artifact, and the fact that I know where it is."

Frenchy looked at Sarah, stretched out next him, hoping to receive approval from her for his explanation.

"My father wrote to Francis saying that the FBI and the government of Israel were trying to get rid of him. I came because my father was trying to help Francis and prevent this from happening."

"What's their story?" Jimmy asked gesturing to Ricky and Ali without losing focus on the road.

"Ricky is my student, just happened to get caught up in this, and Ali is an old friend and he is going to help me out."

Frenchy looked up at his cousin hoping he had gained his trust.

"Well, I'll do my best to get you to the port, and I'll try to keep people off of you. You're damn lucky you're my cousin. I'm trusting you. If you lied and I get fired or sent to jail, you're not allowed to come to Easter at my mom's house."

Frenchy smiled; an overwhelming sense of pride came over him, happy that his cousin believed him.

"Deal, but if I am wrong, can we share a jail cell together?"

"No," Jimmy said shunning the last question as he reached for his dispatch communicator.

"All units: suspect Degnan has fled, he is heading north on Kennedy Boulevard in a yellow PT cruiser. Please notify FBI."

The dispatch responded stating cars were in pursuit.

"What the hell is with the car you named? Why that one?" Ricky inquired.

"My ex-wife's. Hey if someone is going to accidentally get shot, I'd rather it be someone who may deserve it." Jimmy laughed as he hit Frenchy's arm, enjoying a chuckle as well.

"Well, if I had known, I would have given you my ex's address as well. You could have told them I was hiding there."

The two enjoyed their disdain for former romances.

"I don't find that funny at all," Sarah loudly proclaimed.

Frenchy and his cousin both stopped immediately, remembering that this was not a guys' night out. An awkward silence fell over the group as the car passed a sign signaling a left off of the highway for the port.

"Sorry, Sarah," Frenchy said breaking the silence. "I don't actually want harm to come to her, neither does Jimmy." Frenchy did his best to sound genuine.

"I was serious . . . Just kidding," Jimmy said, turning the wheel and entering a long road running parallel to the bay. As they moved further along the road, an enormous vessel captured their attention.

"Ricky, call your dad tell him we're almost there; ask him where we should go."

"Will do, Doc."

Frenchy pushed himself up a bit peering through the windshield at the enormous ship.

"You know any place down here where we can get out inconspicuously? The whole area seems wide open."

The SUV approached a small building at the beginning of the wharf.

"I'm not sure, but that's your ultimate hurdle: Getting past the building and all those people onto the ship without anyone stopping you."

Jimmy pointed towards the check-in building and the crowds of cars and people unloading their luggage. He circled around behind the building, and pulled into a vacant parking spot a few rows away from the back of the processing building.

"Doc, my dad said to drive over to the back of the building and stop near the dumpster."

"We are already in the back, Magellan, where is your dad? Tell him to come out and wave to us."

Frenchy looked over towards the building, waiting for Ricky's father to emerge.

"How are we going to get on this ship? We don't have any luggage; we will stick out," Sarah said, feeling she was the only one of the group attentive to key details.

Frenchy pulled at his non-existent beard, pondering her question. A man emerged from a door in the back of the building, waving towards the police car.

"Moment of truth, let's hope he wasn't lying," Sarah commented, worrying that this plan now seemed too good to be true.

"Hey that's my dad, nigga, and he wouldn't lie," Ricky quickly snapped, defending his honor. Jimmy pulled the vehicle up to the door.

Mr. Badaracco walked over to the car and looked in.

"You're helping too?" he asked, eyeing Jimmy.

"Go figure. Let's pray we get through this," Jimmy said

"Ricky, you okay back there?" he asked, concerned for his youngest son.

"Yeah, Pop, all good."

"Fine, now listen, here are your tickets. Disregard the names on the tickets, but just know that it was the best I could do on basically a twenty minute notice."

Mr. Badaracco handed four boarding passes back to the hidden occupants.

"How can this be?" Ali blurted out in surprise, looking at his boarding ticket. "Kevin Smyth? I don't look like a Kevin Smyth."

Ali's statement caused Frenchy to burst into laughter.

"Smyth? Classic. That doesn't scream cavity search," Frenchy said, slowly realizing the possible problem. "You couldn't pick a more . . . ethnic name?" Frenchy asked, trying to arrive upon the least offensive words.

"Look, it's the best I could do. No one told me Osama Bin Laden was one of your companions."

Ricky's father appeared insulted at the displeasure being conveyed.

Ali perked up, anger flooding his mind after hearing his stereotypical comparison.

"Easy big man, he didn't mean it," Frenchy said, calming his Arab friend.

"I can't believe I'm doing this," Mr. Badaracco said finally handing a ticket to his son. "I really can't . . ."

Ricky grabbed his father's hand.

"I'll be fine Pop. As soon as we are clear, we can negotiate our return with people who don't want to kill us. You saw the report. I'm in this as well."

Frenchy and Sarah looked at each other. They had somehow missed the part when Ricky had told his father the death warrant on Frenchy was also out on the rest of the group.

Ricky's father sighed handing him an envelope.

"Here is some money just in case. Degnan, he thinks the world of you. Take care of him. He gets hurt, and you're done."

Frenchy shook his hand.

"I will, and I promise; I swear it. I cannot thank you enough for this. I can't believe you're doing this either."

"Don't remind me. Now, look. Walk up with me to the bay side of the building, and follow my story, look natural, happy, relaxed whatever, just follow behind me. If all goes well, you won't have to show your tickets to anyone."

Mr. Badaracco looked over at Ali, still fuming from the earlier comment. The group nodded in agreement.

"Thanks, Jimmy, I will never forget this, I owe you big time," Frenchy said reaching forward. Jimmy nodded in sarcastic agreement shaking hands with Frenchy.

"You're goddamn right you won't. I'll make sure of that. Just be careful and do what you have to do."

Ricky's father looked around the parking lot.

"Let's go."

JENSEN LOOKED OVER THE PRINTOUT of the object he was to retrieve from Judah's apartment. As he returned to the unpleasant scene on Park Ave, he struggled to focus on the road as his mind continued to race with inquiries as to what the object was and its significance to his work. He put the photo down as he approached Judah's building. Fire trucks and emergency crews remained stationed outside of the building on ninety-sixth street and a section of the southbound Park Avenue lanes had been reopened to traffic. Jensen pulled his car behind the fire truck parked in front of the building.

He turned his vehicle off, looking over at his passenger seat and collecting the photo and the files on Degnan and Degnan's book. He emerged from his car and surveyed the scene. He located the agent he had spoken with earlier in the day when he had first visited the site, who was now speaking to a firefighter near the entrance to the Dumont. He walked towards the building, the agent catching sight of the deputy director.

"Is everything all right sir?" the agent asked, surprised to see Jensen return to the site.

"Fine, Donnelly, everything is fine. I'm on my way up to Rabbi Judah's apartment. Anything new?"

The young agent's eyebrows rose slightly, taken aback by Jensen's changed demeanor, and shocked his superior remembered his name.

"The area has been contained. They're not allowing residents back into the building, but it is clear for investigators. We and the NYPD have been working since you left. And, sir you were right."

Jensen's ears perked up, happy to hear the familiar sounds of validation.

"About what?" he asked, unsure as to why the agent had paused.

"The deceased was a Rabbi Judah. His driver was also slightly injured and taken to the hospital to be treated. He identified Judah as the man who had gone into the building and no one else. A few moments later, the explosion."

Though being correct gave some feeling of satisfaction, he had still held out some hope that he was incorrect about this aspect of the investigation.

Jensen walked over closer to the entrance door, and looked back at a black Lincoln Town car parked near the front of the building.

"Who is the driver?"

Donnelly fumbled with his Blackberry attempting to retrieve the name. "Mr. Basra, Senegal Basra. He had minor injuries. A few cuts and bruises, nothing more. They had taken him to the hospital after we talked to him."

Jensen's interest perked.

"You mean he didn't say that it was Judah when he was first questioned?"

"No sir, he must have been in shock. We got most of the information from Mr. Hall, the doorman. The driver didn't say much."

Jensen walked over to Judah's limo and tapped on the windows.

"So he was injured? How? Look at the car, there is nothing wrong with the car; the explosion was limited to the vestibule and elevator bay."

Jensen paused, pondering this new data. He had not thought about Judah's driver the first time he had arrived on the scene. Now the ambiguous information about the driver, and his mysterious injuries made him break from his original task.

"Maybe he was outside of the car. He probably opened the door for the deceased and remained outside the front door. Again, his injuries were not substantial."

Donnelly felt his earlier anxiety return as he worried that he may have made a mistake and the pleasant and calm deputy director was about to return to the berating supervisor.

"You may be right; no need in trying to figure out just how he was injured. It just struck me as off that's all. Remain here in the front; I will go to Judah's apartment to look around."

The young agent nodded as Jensen began to walk through the main door.

"But I am going to want to talk to that driver. When he is released, bring him to headquarters. He may still remember more as time passes."

"Yes, sir," Donnelly said immediately, moving to call the agents at Metropolitan Hospital.

Jensen walked past the front desk of the Dumont where an NYPD officer carefully looked over the internal section of the desk. Jensen moved beyond the front and opened the door leading to the stairs, observing detectives working in the elevator bay area.

Jensen began the climb to make his way to the fourth floor. He moved quickly, eager to search and find the object so sought after by his superiors. He opened the door leading to the fourth floor hallway. He walked down the corridor, stopping in front of an old door, a mezuzah affixed to the right section of the woodwork around the door. He removed a tool from his pocket and began to pick the lock to the door.

Upon his success, he opened the door and entered the hallway of the apartment. He reached for his flashlight, shining it on the right-hand wall adjacent to the door frame locating the light switch to the main hall light. He looked around at the apartment. The walls were adorned with framed prints, yellowed with age, with Hebrew script on many of them. He removed the picture of the object and walked into the parlor to the left of the main hallway.

He began to search through the bookshelves and cabinets lining the wall. He paused in his search and looked around the apartment. He realized the apartment was much larger than he expected, despite the fact that he knew it to be an affluent neighborhood.

He looked through the hallway into the dining room. A hazel brown box lay on top of a small table on the far wall of the room. He shined his flashlight on the box and began to approach. His heart began to race slightly, hoping he had stumbled upon the object of his search.

He seized the box and examined it. He placed the photo next to it, comparing marks in the photo to that of the box. He smiled to himself as he matched each distinguishing characteristic. He held the box up and looked underneath, still wondering what made the box so important. While he was aware that he shouldn't open the box and, possibly, that he didn't want to fearing that the more he knew, the more he would question his own actions, he slowly opened the delicate box. To his surprise the box was empty.

"Unbelievable," he said aloud, amazed at every turn he had encountered during his dealings.

"Fuckin' empty box; this is what they want. I came all the way up here to get a box."

His excitement at locating the object faded as irritation began to monopolize his mood. He scanned the room, wondering if he had possibly found the wrong box, his eyes returning to the photo. He repeatedly went over the photo and box, hoping that he somehow had made a mistake. He placed the box on the table and removed his cell phone, calling his director's number.

"I have the box in my possession," he said in a monotone voice.

"Excellent, bring it back to headquarters. Hansen is leaving soon for Jerusalem." The director seemed pleased at Jensen's prompt recovery of the object.

"What is so special about this box? Is it what's inside that matters?" Jensen asked, hoping to extract information from his supervisor.

"That is irrelevant; don't worry about that. Just bring it back."

The FBI director seemed irritated at Jensen's queries.

"What is it, God in the box?" Jensen scoffed, recalling watching a documentary on Judaism and how the holiest of holies in the temple in Jerusalem was an empty area, sacred because it was believed that God resided there.

"Just bring it back. It's of no concern to you, or me for that matter. All we need to know is that it matters to someone. Just get back here."

The director hung up the phone abruptly. Jensen returned the phone into his pocket. He picked up the box and walked towards the hallway. His phone began to vibrate. He reached in and answered.

"Sir, it's Donnelly. The driver is missing."

Jensen stopped abruptly, unsure as to how this applied to his enigmatic case.

"What do you mean missing? How?"

"I'm not sure, but the NYPD said he was set to be released and he was going to be taken to headquarters. Next thing they know he's gone."

Jensen's propensity for being correct was beginning to aggravate him. He knew something had sounded odd when Donnelly had described the driver's information, but his disappearance left him completely confused.

"Just hold on, I'm on my way down," he said, ending the call. He moved towards the front door.

Suddenly a sharp pain struck the back of his head, causing him to drop to the floor, the picture and the wooden box dropping to his left.

Jensen lay on the wood floor face down, a small trickle of blood running down the back of his neck. A pipe dropped next to his body, as his attacker bent over to pick up the wooden box. The man's hand was gloved. He carefully picked up the box. He pushed Jensen's body slightly away from the door and exited quietly, pausing in the doorway to look down the corridor. He removed a communicator from his pocket and pressed the button to speak.

"I have it," he said, quickly returning the communicator to his vest pocket and running quickly down the hallway.

21

"YOU KNOW, I JUST WANT TO GO ON RECORD as saying that while I am extremely excited to embark on the adventure of a lifetime, didn't it seem a shitload easier for Indiana Jones to travel than what we are currently experiencing?" Frenchy mumbled, through a permanent smile on his face, as he followed Mr. Badaracco around the side of the processing building towards the wharf leading up to the mammoth ship.

"Would you shut the hell up for one minute," Sarah said, also attempting to look casual as they approached a man checking boarding passes.

The four nervously drew near the front of the line, following their only chance of getting on board.

"Hey Dave, how are you?" Mr. Badaracco, said, putting his hand on the man's shoulder.

"Oh hey, Vic, same old shit."

The young man continued to check people in.

"I'm with you. Same old shit. Listen I got four passengers, I checked them in, turns out we messed up their tickets so I'm trying to be as polite as possible so we don't piss them off. I'm gonna escort them on. The old chicken, Mr. Casio, told me to make sure there are no other hiccups."

Mr. Badaracco quietly spoke to his friend. Frenchy overheard what he was saying and promptly changed his facial expression to match that of a disgruntled traveler.

"Excuse me sir, but is there another problem," Frenchy said, trying to play along.

"No problem, sir, please follow me," Mr. Badaracco said, rolling his eyes at his colleague.

"Enjoy your trip sirs, Miss" the young man said, stepping out of the way to allow the four to walk by.

"Finally a man with manners. I wish we could have dealt with him the whole time. What's your name, sir? I am going to write a letter of thanks to your boss for your politeness."

Sarah smiled at the check-in, pinching Frenchy's side sharply, hoping to halt his performance.

"That won't be necessary, sir, we are just doing our job," the man said, gesturing to include Mr. Badaracco in the praise.

"Come on, honey, let's let this nice man continue," Sarah said, pushing Frenchy up the platform towards the entrance of the ship.

"Would you stop drawing attention to us? What the hell are you thinking?" she said, turning irate.

"Easy there, honey, just wanted to make sure we got on no problem."

The group began to make their way up the ramp. On the side of the ship further down towards the bow, read the ship's name, *Excalibur*.

"Hell's Bells, my children," Frenchy happily declared, realizing the connection between his quest and the ship's title. "That's a sign that things are going to work out," he said, smiling back at his companions.

"Or maybe the name has to do with the fact that this is a damn Disney boat," Sarah said sarcastically.

"Wait, what?" Frenchy asked, suddenly disturbed by the possibility of children running wild on board.

"It's not a Disney boat, it's a new company called Camelot. You know, fantasy shit," Mr. Badaracco said, reaching the top.

"Welcome aboard, sir," a man dressed in the garb of a captain said.

"Ahoy matey, permission to come aboard," Frenchy said shaking hands with the captain who seemed unaffected by the gibberish Frenchy was churning out.

Sarah and the rest of the party made their way onto the ship. Mr. Badaracco turned and gestured for the four to move to the right.

"Have a great trip," he said, attempting to show no emotion. He shook hands firmly with each of the group, lingering a moment when he got to Ricky.

"We hope to see you again very soon," he said as he walked down the chain bridge.

"Right this way. I will take you to your rooms." The attendant led the group down the promenade of the ship.

"Holy shit, I think we may have made it," Frenchy muttered to Sarah as they followed the attendant.

"Save that for when we are moving. For now, you just keep moving."

Frenchy looked to the right observing the skyline of Jersey City. He smiled for a moment, seeing his hometown in a different light, knowing he had a chance to make his fellow Jersey Citians proud. His life had been devoted to the "resurrection of Jersey City," as he often declared. Yet to the present, he never believed he had done enough to better his hometown. The possibility of bringing fame and attention to a city he believed to be the greatest in the world, strengthened his resolve to succeed.

Nevertheless, as he gazed at his home, his eyes caught site of the people below on the wharf.

"Holy shit!" he exclaimed quickly jumping away from the railing and clinging to the wall of the ship.

The attendant jumped unaware of what had just happened behind her.

"Are you alright, sir?" she asked as the group stared at Frenchy, his back and arms flush against the wall. Sarah stared at him. His antics to this point seemed to have pushed her to the boiling point.

Frenchy paused and looked at his companions, visibly struggling to swallow.

"Uh, everything is fine, a bee, real closed, I'm allergic. Had to stay very still, so it wouldn't see me. Everything's okay now, no problem."

The attendant slowly turned around looking at Frenchy's companions as she returned to leading them to their quarters. Frenchy began to inch along, his back still pressed up against the wall. Sarah grabbed his arm and yanked him into a normal walking position, ushering him behind the attendant.

"I'm serious, if you keep doing this shit, I will turn you in myself."

"Chill, chill, not so fast and stay closer to the wall. You know I'm afraid of heights as well as boats; this is a trifecta," Frenchy said, attempting to walk while squirming in her grip.

"That's only two, so it's not a trifecta, you ass."

"No, it is. I'm terrified of you, Ms. I-like-to-assault-Frenchy-and-try-to-kill-him."

The attendant stopped and opened a door leading into one of the hallways heading to a section of the suites.

"These are your two rooms," she said pointing to the left and right doors. "If you like you can get comfortable before you have to come up to the top deck. We will be leaving soon."

The crew member smiled and walked away, leaving the keys to the rooms in the doors.

The group inspected the rooms, pleasantly surprised at the spaciousness and luxury.

"So, Doc, me and Ali will be in here and I guess you and Ms. Tannen in the other . . ."

Ricky smiled as he slowed himself, stopping before finishing his statement.

"You know he's right. I can't be in the same room as a student; it's not appropriate. We are in fact a Catholic school."

Frenchy's banter failed to amuse Sarah.

"Well, as a fugitive from the law, I think all rules are out the window, so thanks but no thanks. Boys in here, I'm in the other room."

Ricky and Frenchy smiled at each other. Ali, somewhat quiet ever since the Bin Laden reference, rolled his eyes and walked into the room.

"It is time for me to pray," he said to Frenchy.

"That's a good idea, everybody take some time to themselves. Let's meet up on deck in forty-five minutes."

"I don't think that's a good idea," Sarah pleaded; weary of having to be the voice of reason. "I think we should spend as much time in here, in the rooms, out of sight, so we decrease the chance of getting identified."

Frenchy waved his hand, dismissing her comment.

"I think we're in the clear. It should be smooth sailings until we get to Nova Scotia. That's when we will have to deal with the next hurdle. For now, let's relax. We can meet on deck when we head out and have dinner. We can plan everything then. We won't be rushed so we can take our time and get things in order. Agreed?"

Ali nodded closing the door behind him.

"Fine, I'll be up in an hour," Sarah said walking into her room and closing the door.

Ricky and Frenchy looked at each other.

"Okay. So I guess we're not going to be in the rooms until then," Ricky remarked, pointing to the two closed doors.

"Come on Ricky, I need a smoke," Frenchy said, opening the door to the promenade and immediately clinging to the wall.

"Yeah, Doc, you've been real good. You haven't had one in like five hours. Not bad," Ricky said, realizing his mentor's achievement.

"Well, being chased by the FBI and fearing for your life will make smoking take a back seat," he said stopping a crew member walking by. "Excuse me, any chance there is a smoking section?"

"Of course, sir, top deck in the rear of the boat," the attendant said, smiling and moving along after pointing to a set of stairs leading to the upper decks.

"Ricky, I see a cigarette and a beer in my future. Come on let's head up top," Frenchy said, suddenly less afraid of the heights and intent on his most recent objective.

"You drink Doc?" Ricky asked, surprised by his mentor's casual speech.

"Rarely, Ricky, very rarely."

ESPINOZA PULLED UP BEHIND THE POLICE CAR on Kennedy Boulevard near Journal Square. He put the car in park and he and Forester stepped out, looking beyond the car at the yellow PT Cruiser. The officer standing near the driver side door of the vehicle began to walk towards them. Espinoza looked towards the back of the vehicle, noticing long blond hair flowing over the driver's side headrest.

"That doesn't look like Degnan or Tannen's daughter," Espinoza remarked to Forester.

"Maybe he's wearing a wig," Forester said, cracking a smile.

"Sorry, Agent Espinoza, but it's not Degnan," the officer said, handing him the woman's driver's license.

"You have excellent investigative skills, Officer, I concur with your assessment," Espinoza said sarcastically, taking the ID and quickly glancing at it.

"Who called it in?" he asked, wondering how a single female passenger could be mistaken for a slightly overweight male in his twenties.

"Detective Calabrese. He called it in," the officer said, tugging on his belt.

"And where is the fine detective now?"

"I'm not sure. But I know he didn't intentionally misdirect us. He must have made a mistake."

The officer sensed the agents moving towards blame for the wrong car being pulled over. He stared at Espinoza attempting to show solidarity with his fellow officer through his posture and demeanor.

"Of course he didn't, Officer, we all make mistakes."

Espinoza's determination to find Degnan waned once again as the multiple dead ends began to affect his resolve.

"You can let her go officer. She's of no use to us," Forester said, turning to walk back to the car.

"Let's check in with Jensen. Maybe he will have some guidance on the issue."

Espinoza followed, taking his cell phone out and dialing his director's number.

"I still want to take a look at that mosque. There is a good chance that he may still be there. You drive."

Espinoza threw the keys to Forester as he walked to the driver's side.

"Who the hell is this?" Espinoza asked sharply, taken aback by a different voice on the phone. "Donnelly, where is Jensen?" he asked as Forester made a U-turn to head south.

"He was attacked as he went through the victim's apartment," Donnelly said quickly, sounding confused and panicked.

"What? How?" Forester looked over at Espinoza, frozen as he listened to the agent's explanation.

"He was attacked from behind with a pipe, as he was exiting the apartment. He's on his way to Metro Hospital now. He should be alright. Looks like a concussion, small lacerations."

Espinoza altered his position attempting to focus on the news.

"Does the Director know about this?"

"Yes, he is on his way down here now." Espinoza waited for a moment, unsure of what his next step should be.

"Keep me informed. When the Director arrives have him call me immediately."

Espinoza ended the phone call, looking over at Forester.

"Jensen was attacked while he was investigating at the bomb site up on ninety-sixth. The guy escaped."

Forester continued to drive.

"So, what the fuck are we suppose to do now?"

Espinoza shrugged, still shocked at yet another aberration from the day.

"I guess we keep trying to find Degnan. We're coming up on the mosque."

Forester turned down Belmont, slowing the vehicle as they approached the mosque. Espinoza scanned the area, looking for an indication that Degnan was there.

"Pull in the back," he said, pointing to the parking lot entrance. Forester pulled up to the dumpster, noticing the bumper of the red van parked behind it.

"St. Ignatius Prep," Forester said, pointing to the faded sticker on the back of the van.

"Looks like he's either here, or was here," Espinoza said, quietly getting out of the car. Forester reached for his gun as they made their way to the front of the mosque.

"Put the gun away. You won't need it," Espinoza said, suddenly fearing Forester's propensity for being "quick on the trigger."

"Hell no, that bitch hit me on the head."

Forester moved over to the door standing slightly off to the side, peering into the mosque through the front window.

A voice from behind the door began to shout. "I will open the door, just don't shoot."

Espinoza nodded at Forester as the door knob turned and Forester pushed his way in. Muhammad stood with his hands raised. Forester pushed him quickly against the wall, holding his gun to his back.

"Where is he?" Forester said, as Espinoza sauntered in slowly, looking around the front section of the mosque.

"He is not here anymore," Muhammad yelled.

Though he agreed to protect Ali and the others, his present position made him divulge information, acknowledging their former presence.

"Where did they go?"

Forester pushed his gun harder into Muhammad's back.

"Easy on him, turn him around," Espinoza declared, attempting to calm Forester's adrenaline rush.

"Sit down, sir," Espinoza said, pointing to a chair near the door, as Forester kept his gun fixed on Muhammad.

"So, where did they go?"

"I swear I don't know. You should know, they left in one of your vehicles." Muhammad had not been aware of all that had transpired during Frenchy's time at the mosque. He had assumed everything was well when the police officer who had arrived didn't arrest them. Though they had left quickly, they had not been detained. Espinoza stared at Forester with skepticism, questioning the veracity of the statement.

"Our vehicles? What did it look like?"

Muhammad looked out at their vehicle.

"Not like that, it was a Jersey City police car."

Muhammad stared at the agent, hoping to end this ordeal with quick straight responses. Espinoza looked at his watch.

"Let's go," he said.

A bewildered look appeared on Forester's face.

"What do you mean 'let's go?'"

"I mean let's go; we got everything we need from him." Espinoza forcefully pushed the door exiting, Forester reluctantly following behind.

"What the fuck man!"

Forester returned his gun to his holster, irritated at not knowing what was taking place.

"Calabrese," Espinoza said rushing around to the parking lot.

"Calabrese. Degnan has a cousin on his mother's side, a cop in Jersey City named . . ." Espinoza opened the passenger side door and grabbed the information on Degnan.

"James Calabrese, Jersey City police officer. Our terrified friend said they left in a police car. I wonder whose car that was?"

Espinoza pointed to the name on the file displaying the full list on the hood of the vehicle.

"Shit, how'd we miss that?"

Forester stepped into the driver's seat and slammed the door.

"It doesn't matter, this whole thing has been a pain in the ass. But all is not lost." Espinoza grabbed the communicator.

"JCPD, JCPD Detective Calabrese, this is FBI Agent Espinoza. We have a possible location on a Francis Degnan. Stand by at the corner of Monticello and Communipaw Ave. and await further instructions."

Calabrese responded quickly.

"On my way; Communipaw and Monticello."

Espinoza replaced the communicator.

"Perhaps we can find out where his wayward cousin has gone."

"YOU SEE, RICKY, there are two types of people in this world: those who are good at life, and those who suck at it. Me, for most of my life, I've been the guy who sucks at it. But my fortune could be changing. All I need is this sword. Not to use of course, I have always thought of myself as a pacifist."

Frenchy took a pull on his cigarette, attempting to display pacifism with awkward body movements.

"But this sword changes everything. You know how they say you can't change your past? Bullshit. This future undertaking will change everything in my past. I won't be the underachieving member of my family. I won't have to hear, you know, your sister's a lawyer and your brother is a pianist."

He and Ricky enjoyed a momentary giggle at his use of the comical sounding word. Frenchy always distorted his pronunciation to increase the chance of someone mistaking the musical profession for the male body part.

"Ah, that shit never gets old. But seriously, it's all my family talks about and then they say, 'but we're proud that you're a teacher.' Bunch of shit. But no more, Ricky, no more." Frenchy raised his glass up and took a sip.

"No more," he muttered looking around the upper level bar of the ship. Though he had a few drinks he was still keenly aware that he was still a fugitive.

"I don't know, Doc. Maybe you shouldn't put so much pressure on yourself to find this thing. You have a great life. You're successful. You're a good teacher and a great mentor to all of us. Why do you think we spend our free time hanging out in your office?" Ricky pleaded to his mentor, hoping to change his negative view of his life.

"You know I enjoy you guys. You make my job tolerable. But in truth, if you're not happy with yourself, no amount of great people can make you happy."

Frenchy stared down at his glass of beer, thinking about how often he spent time talking with his best friend in bars about the present subject.

Noise from the upper deck of the ship signaled the departure from the port. Frenchy grabbed the table, over-reacting to the slight movement.

"You're a jumpy nigga," Ricky remarked.

"Watch your fuckin' mouth, wheezy. And, well, you know what they say."

Ricky stared at Frenchy hesitant about his question.

"Um, what?"

Frenchy took another sip of his beverage, ignoring Ricky's comment and keenly aware he had nothing to say.

"They say, when in doubt, have a drinking buddy."

Though obviously a non sequitur, Ricky's mood changed as he welcomed such a statement by Frenchy. He gestured awkwardly to a passing waitress, missing his chance to get her attention.

"You have to be more aggressive, Doc. Hey, Ms. Thang, my father and I would like another round. Guinness, please."

Ricky smiled as he caught the waitress's attention. Frenchy's eyes opened wide, shocked at the fact that the waitress seemed to accept that he could be Ricky's father.

"Ah, yeah, sounds great, I'm so proud he just turned twenty-one . . . my son . . . I'm a young father . . . of sorts and a black man as well."

Frenchy slurred his words out, smiling at the waitress as she attempted to slip away from the odd duo.

"I'll tell you, I love these European lines; they don't care. They know the drinking age shouldn't be twenty-one. The Europeans know where it's at."

Ricky cocked his head to the side like a confused puppy.

"I think this ship is out of Canada, Doc, not Europe."

Frenchy waved his hands in indifference.

"Same shit. They were all European at some point. This must be exciting. First a fugitive, and now your first beer."

Frenchy raised his glass once again, drinking the last gulp.

"Ah, Doc, I hate to break this to you, but I drink all the time, we all do."

Frenchy gasped, shocked at this revelation.

"What!" he exclaimed, slamming his glass down.

"Doc, we buy beer all the time from the place on your block. All Prep kids do."

"Well, I knew some people did, but never expected it from you guys."

Ricky rolled his eyes, the waitress placing two pints of Guinness down on the table.

"Whatever, grandma; cheers," Ricky said laughing at his own remark, and raising his glass.

"Look, son, I'm your father, you will show me some fuckin' respect," Frenchy said, pointing at himself and suddenly feeling much better.

The two laughed for a moment, Ricky reveling in the future opportunities to brag about what he was experiencing to his friends.

"So, Doc, we're all good. The ship is moving away from the port, and we're on our way, far away, from the bad guys."

"Agreed, my brother, very true."

Ricky took a swig of his beer, proudly. He paused as he looked down at his drink.

"You know, Doc, just between the two of us and I'm not trying to discourage you, but a lot of the shit you were saying when we were back at the mosque and you were explaining your theories . . . It seemed a little . . . off. Are you sure you can find this thing?"

Frenchy's alcohol high came crashing quickly. He lit another cigarette, taking a long pull and slowly blowing the smoke out as he thought. His confidence in himself was so fragile; he had been going back and forth in his head, wondering if his companions' critiques were correct.

"To be honest, and like you said, just between the two of us . . . I don't know. Maybe I'm bipolar. One moment all my theories sound perfect, historically possible, factual, whatever. Then someone says something and, suddenly, even I begin to wonder if I'm crazy."

The ship's horn went off again, signaling a further distance from the shore.

"I mean, you see my passion. I believe I can do this. But to a certain extent, I'm afraid of failing. I wrote that book at the wrong time and with good intentions but not the best research. Actually doing shit terrifies me. Dreams are great but if you actually pursue them there's a good chance they get ruined. That's what I deal with nonstop. Excited to do this, confident, then holy shit I'm about to fail. Not sure what my life would be like without hope in this. If I don't chase it, I can still dream. I guess that's why we're here drinking instead of coming up with more of a plan than 'let's fuckin' do it.'"

Frenchy stamped out his cigarette in the ash tray and finished his beer.

"So, then let's get a plan," Ricky said, realizing he could be a motivator as opposed to a downer.

"Maybe one more," Frenchy said, gesturing to the waitress. Ricky finished his beer and slammed his glass down.

"Hell yeah, Doc. Hell yeah."

The attentive waitress brought the two pints over quickly, aware that the two had already finished. Ricky and Frenchy's glasses came together. Frenchy brought the glass to his lips, suddenly shaking it as he felt a hand slap his shoulder.

"I'm so close to killing you right now," Sarah said, gritting her teeth together in a fake smile, Ali standing next to her, a smirk on his face.

"I almost spilled its glory; don't you know this is the nectar of the Gods?" Frenchy retorted, oblivious to Sarah's anger.

She sat down next to Frenchy, Ali moving to the opposite seat.

"Meet in an hour so we can discuss our plan right? Meet on the top deck? Except you weren't there. Instead we spend almost forty minutes looking for you. Funny thing about this ship, it's not small."

Sarah sat back in her chair, folding her arms.

"But I'm glad to see you found the bar."

She looked down at the two glasses.

"Very nice. Oh, good, underage drinking; way to keep a low profile."

Sarah's sarcasm caused Ali to smile.

"You know, first of all: Nice to see you too. Second, relax, the boat is away from the port, and we're in the clear. We figured we would celebrate our escape."

Frenchy raised his glass once again, staring happily at Sarah.

"Unbelievable. Forget it; I don't know why I bother."

"If you're hungry, let's go eat, I just have to close my tab," Frenchy stood up and guzzled the entire glass down, seemingly in one shot.

He smiled at his companions and walked over to the bar behind him. Sarah looked over at Ricky, staring in disapproval.

"What? Oh, like you wouldn't have taken a chance to drink with your teacher in high school while still in high school."

Sarah's gazed never wavered from Ricky.

"You are not helping the situation. If we are going to be successful, we need him to be on point, aka, not drunk."

Frenchy returned quickly to the table, sliding his credit card into his wallet.

"Who's drunk?" he asked, confused by the fragment he heard as he entered the conversation.

"What's that?" Sarah asked pointing to his wallet.

"It's called a wallet, men carry them. Sometimes they even keep money in them."

Frenchy winked at Ricky, seeking approval for his mocking statement.

"You paid with a credit card? Are you stupid?" Sarah's voice took on a hysterical tone. "They will trace us to the ship, you ass. They'll be here instantly."

Ali's expression changed realizing the mistake his friend had made. Frenchy's spirit slowed as he too grasped his blunder.

"Okay. But it might not go through until later. We are not completely screwed."

Sarah sighed in irritation as she looked down at her watch.

"We need to stay out of sight. Let's go down to our cabins. We are set to arrive in Nova Scotia tomorrow morning, early, around seven o'clock. We need to get off this ship immediately and find a way off this continent.

Frenchy's eyebrows curled in shock. "Seven a.m.? What the hell is that about? That's ridiculously early. And how do you know we arrive at seven?"

Sarah cocked her head to the left staring sharply at him.

"Oh, well, while you were getting drunk. I checked out the itinerary. You know, so we're not aimlessly floating without anything resembling a plan."

He knew she had him again so he chose to nod in agreement.

"But what about dinner? I'm hungry."

Ricky's appreciation for her good planning was interrupted by the absence of nourishment.

"We will order from the room. Maybe Francis can put it on his credit card."

"Oh, ha ha, lick the bar, and seriously, stop calling me Francis; only my mother and grandmother call me that."

Sarah stood up and pushed her chair in.

"Let's go, we've got a lot of work to do before we arrive in Nova Scotia. Work like when they trace your card, people will be waiting for us."

Sarah began walking towards the staircase.

"Boy she is a serious bitch . . ."

Frenchy paused, ensuring she was out of hearing range.

"Seriously, what's wrong with a few drinks?" he asked, turning to Ali.

Frenchy waved at him, dismissing Ali's look of confusion.

"Forget it, straight-edge, you've never had a drink in your life. Let's head down to the rooms. She may be a pain in the ass, but she's right."

The trio followed their irritated companion's path down towards the cabins, the moonlight glimmering on the ocean water.

24

THE FBI VEHICLE SLOWLY PULLED UP behind the Jersey City Police car. Degnan's cousin stood outside, leaning up against the driver's side door. He gestured to the agents as they stopped on the southwest corner of Communipaw and Monticello. He approached as they emerged from their vehicle.

"I've been here for fifteen minutes. I have not seen anything out of the ordinary. You said Degnan was here? Do you mean in one of the buildings? There has been no movement in or out of the buildings on the northeast and west corners. Other than that, you have a church and a café."

Espinoza leaned up against the Crown Victoria cruiser, and folded his arms.

"We were hoping you might know where he is."

Forester's gaze was sharply focused on Jimmy.

"Like I said, since being here there has been no sign of him. I figured you guys knew since you called it in."

Jimmy shrugged gesturing the proverbial ball into the agents' court.

"What made you pick the yellow PT Cruiser?" Espinoza asked, attempting to hide his irritation at his interrogation.

"What are you talking about"?"

"What I said. I'm just curious why you chose to claim Degnan in a yellow cruiser. Did you hope there was one on the road, or did you see it beforehand?"

"You know, I don't know if you think this is amusing, but I'm not in the mood for this shit. My shift is almost over."

Jimmy began to walk towards his car.

"I wouldn't worry so much about the end of your shift."

Forester put his hand up to prevent Jimmy from continuing, his body language conveying a belligerent message.

"Here's the problem, Detective. When we were on our way over to the mosque where we believed Degnan was, the call went out that he was in a yellow PT Cruiser. We found the car, but alas, no Degnan. Just some Jersey broad with a bad attitude and too much make-up."

Jimmy gently grinned. His hope to "stick it" to his ex-wife played out as Espinoza described her to the trait.

"But we still made it to the mosque. And it turns out Degnan had been there, but he left, not in the piece of shit van he arrived in. No. In a cop car. Our Muslim friend at the mosque was a little too scared to keep that tidbit of information from us. And then it struck me, Degnan had a cop for a cousin. Now you tell me, what are the chances that Degnan was in someone else's cop car?"

Espinoza continued his cynical recount, pausing with his culminating question. Jimmy scratched his head, looking away from the agents. Though he knew he could deny the claim, he knew his aiding his cousin had been discovered.

"Okay. I get it; yes I helped my cousin, what would you do? I figured if I were there I could protect him. He needed help, so I helped him."

Jimmy immediately became defensive, aggravated that his actions had been exposed.

"Where is he?" Forester snarled, stepping closer to Jimmy.

"I can't tell you," he said, gaining strength to resist because of Forester's aggressive movement.

Espinoza recognized the escalating situation.

"Look, we don't want to hurt your cousin. We don't care. We are supposed to bring him in for questioning. He won't be hurt. I promise you. You can bring him in yourself, but we go too. But he needs to be found now."

"Sure, he won't be harmed. It's the bureau that's conspiring against him, making up these false charges." Degnan's version differed greatly from the present interpretation.

"They'll kill him if you don't tell us where he is."

"It doesn't matter."

Jimmy shook his head, overwhelmed by the situation.

"He's on a boat leaving the country. I helped him get on a boat, him and his friends. They left an hour ago."

Espinoza looked over at Forester, searching his thoughts for his next move.

"What's the name of the ship . . . forget it."

Espinoza grabbed for his phone in his pocket, turning and opening the passenger side door, realizing his phone was on the dashboard. He searched for the office number, dialing immediately.

"This is Espinoza; I need to speak to Director Hayes, now," he shouted into the phone, pausing as he was connected.

"Sir, we know where Degnan is; he's on a ship, left out near here an hour ago . . ."

He paused, a confused look on his face as he slowly took the phone down, checking to make sure he had dialed the correct number.

"Yes, sir, we'll be there."

He ended his phone call, still looking at his phone.

"We need to head back to headquarters. Director wants us back now."

"What about Degnan?"

Forester did not grasp yet another drastic change in their assignment.

"Director said not to worry."

"What does that mean?"

Jimmy began to worry, assuming something had happened to his cousin, thus calling off the search. Espinoza entered the car, sharing a sense of fear that he had been apprehended and harmed. Forester entered the vehicle and started the engine.

"Wait, what the fuck is going on?"

Jimmy held the door open momentarily.

"You can go." Forester pulled the door shut. Pulling out from the spot quickly.

"Alright, let's go back."

The two sped towards the waterfront heading for the Holland Tunnel. Espinoza remained silent. After a grueling and difficult day, he and his partner were returning without having completed their assignment, and more in the dark then before.

"Maybe someday we'll know what the fuck this whole thing was all about," Espinoza said, putting his hand up to hold the handle above the window.

Forester shook his head and smiled.

"That kind of thinking will mess you up with shit like this. Stick to my father's favorite quote, he told me the day I became an agent: 'Theirs not to reason why, theirs but to do and die . . . minus the dying part."

GERSHOM SMILED as he finished tying his blue striped tie, gazing into his bedroom mirror. Despite the previous day's setbacks, it ended positively. He walked over to a chair positioned in front of a large bay window. He sat down, the early morning sun shining warmly on his face. He looked down at his watch, noting his ability to be ready for his day at 5:30 a.m., exactly, regardless of the previous day's events. He gazed out onto Balfour Street. He was familiar with the neighborhood, spending many years of his life living just a few miles away from Beit Aghion, the current residence of Gershom.

As he observed the sun, hitting the lower section of a large cedar tree to the right of his window, he thought about his daughter, recalling her love for nature. As a child she would spend much of her time examining and collecting anything and everything from around the Cyprus trees in their front yard. He had been proud of her as she nurtured her love for nature, eventually focusing her studies on her passion. Though he had helped her acquire her first job in the Israeli Ministry for Environmental Protection, her determination helped her rise quickly, achieving the title of Project Coordinator at the age of twenty-seven.

His love and protection of her made it difficult when she wed a young up-and-coming politician, who eventually joined his team when he ran for prime minister. Yet her happiness meant everything to Gershom and his new son-in-law worshipped his lovely daughter and he was certain she would be loved and protected with Assaf.

It was this certainty that made her death in the market place, only a mile from the central section of Jerusalem so difficult to bear. She always demanded the freshest vegetables, which had her frequenting the Machane Yehuda, the largest and busiest outdoor market in all of Israel. As fate would have it, many Palestinians were angry after the government began making long term construction plans in the Gaza Strip. One in particular used the market as the target of his anger, killing himself and thirteen others.

As a result of her death, Gershom decided to push forward forcefully with his candidacy for prime minister, convinced that changes had to be made to improve relations between Israelis and Palestinians. Yet as his time as prime minister passed, he gradually began to see no peaceful solution to the crisis. At the urging of his son-in-law and chief advisor, he became increasingly harsh in his treatment and dealings with Palestinians, determined to focus his attention on the preservation of his people, as opposed to the peaceable dealings with the Palestinians. As he sat reflecting, preparing for the day, a knock on the door brought Assaf into the room.

"A beautiful morning isn't it, Assaf?" He asked remembering the positive that would come from the days dealings.

"Beautiful weather wise, but there are better ways to start the day."

Assaf walked over to Gershom, sitting in a neighboring chair to Gershom.

"Is everything alright?" Gershom asked, aware that his advisor did not share the same positive spirit.

"The Vice President and Secretary of Defense are scheduled to arrive at nine a.m. However, I received a fax this morning stating a failure by the Americans to retrieve the box and thus the map of the location of the sword. I received it this morning."

Assaf handed a fax sheet to Gershom, who examined it immediately.

"This agent was attacked after recovering it?"

"It would seem the agent recovered the box and confirmed it with the FBI director. He was returning to their headquarters when he was attacked. By whom, they do not know. But they found him unconscious with the box missing."

Gershom rubbed his hands together, thinking about how to proceed without the map.

"And we are sure he retrieved the box?"

"He confirmed it with his superior. Currently, they do not have any person in custody."

Assaf 's irritation began to show through his tone. He considered this failure by the Americans unacceptable.

Gershom's agreement to go ahead with the treaty agitated Assaf. He felt this would destroy any leverage they had with the U.S.

"Without the map we have no chance of finding our sword. Tannen and Judah are both dead. This is sounding more and more like Tannen sabotaged the entire plan."

Assaf shook his head, aware that Gershom was correct.

"Tannen has ruined everything. In my mind there is only one way we can get the sword now."

Gershom looked over, intrigued by Assaf's statement.

"We need this teacher, Degnan. He is the only one now that may be able to find it."

"You cannot be serious. There is no possibility that he would help us now, and that is if we can find him."

Assaf stood abruptly, pushing his suit jacket back to rest his hand on his hip.

"It does not matter what he wants to do. We will force him to. Leverage his life against his cooperation in this matter."

Gershom's mood turned.

"No, I do not want any more strong-armed tactics or any threat of violence. Enough!?"

Assaf turned away in irritation, angered by Gershom returning to his desire to end the matter rather than do what is necessary to achieve success, no matter how ruthless.

"Fine, maybe we do not force him. Who says we cannot pay him? Sure we wanted to get rid of him, but he is unaware of that. To be safe, we employ a go between to pay him."

Gershom mulled over the plan. He seemed intrigued by the proposal, once again happy it didn't include unjust measures.

"I am sure he will want to know why he was wanted by the FBI. That may be difficult to forget about."

"Again, if we tell the FBI to redact their claim against him and we then approach him to find the artifact, how does that not agree with his desires?"

Gershom agreed with the plan, but began to wonder why this was not part of the original plan.

"Fine, but if it will be that easy, why did we not seek this path from the beginning? It seems like a much more reasonable plan."

Assaf sat down leaning forward with his elbows on his knees.

"Because I leave nothing to chance. Unfortunately, now we have no choice. This is time sensitive. Let us contact the Vice President and make sure Degnan is no longer wanted."

"What about the map?"

After all their discussing and problem solving, the issue of the map had been forgotten.

"Whoever took the map now has the opportunity to find the sword first."

Gershom began to panic, his momentary relief from Assaf's plan suddenly faded.

Assaf reclined back in the chair and reached in his right jacket pocket. He removed a yellowed piece of paper, frayed at the edges.

"The thief only has half the map."

Gershom sat stunned.

"I thought you said Judah had both halves?"

Assaf placed the fragment back into his pocket.

"I took Judah's half. I did not know where the second half was. You can never trust that everything will go smoothly. I took out a little insurance."

Gershom shook his head in disbelief.

"Why would you not tell me? Even in this very conversation you said the map was gone."

Assaf smiled and patted Gershom's knee.

"Does it really matter? I made sure that it was us or no one who would find the sword, except of course Degnan. Regardless, whoever has the other half is as confused as we are. Moreover, it may have been foolish, but I prefer you not know all the details for your own ability to deny it. I hope you can trust that I will do what is best for Israel. Particularly if I need to withhold other aspects."

Gershom shifted in his seat, still reeling from his advisor's revelation.

"I suppose you are right. It matters not, all that matters is that we acquire it."

"Exactly. And after all that, it turns out Tannen helped us."

"How does that apply?" Gershom asked.

"Well, thankfully Tannen saved Degnan's life. I guess eliminating the competition is not always the best idea until you have achieved success. Thanks to Tannen, our competitor will be become our number one employee."

Gershom cracked an uncomfortable smile.

"I told you, peace is better than violence."

Assaf began to dial a number on his phone.

"Perhaps."

26

AGENT DONNELLY CONTINUED TO GLANCE in his rearview mirror, checking on the deputy director as he sat in the back seat, an ice pack pressed against the back of his head, dried blood coated his white collar.

"We're almost there, sir. The Director insisted that I bring you directly to headquarters after the hospital." Donnelly shifted any blame that might be thrown his way, concerned Jensen would not appreciate the medical treatment at the hospital followed by the immediate chauffeuring back to work.

"I'm sure he did. Did we get the assailant?"

"Unfortunately, with the number of exits in that building he must have slipped past us. We found you pretty quickly. We questioned and searched everyone in the building, but there weren't many because of the explosion."

"What about the box?"

Through Jensen's haze, the mention of headquarters jogged his memory.

"Nothing. You mentioned it when we found you but we found nothing. Again, we had nothing to go on. You couldn't describe your attacker when we first got to you."

Jensen switched hands, wincing as the ice pack shifted.

"What time is it?" he asked.

"Eleven p.m."

Jensen shook his head, cognizant of the fact that he had left for Judah's apartment almost six hours before, and on a time sensitive task.

"Where the hell have I been for the last five hours?"

Jensen became irate, realizing he had little recollection of the last few hours.

"I'm sorry, sir, you suffered a serious blow. You have a concussion and they stitched your head."

Donnelly's answer impeded Jensen's escalating anger. Donnelly pulled into the parking garage below the building, quickly driving to a spot close to the elevator. He jumped out of the driver's seat and opened Jensen's door, reaching to help the ailing agent.

"I'm fine. Head back to the scene and canvas the entire neighborhood. Question everyone, search everything."

Donnelly attempted to cut short Jensen's onslaught of orders.

"Sir, all of that has been happening. I think I should help you upstairs."

Donnelly grabbed Jensen's files, a splatter of blood on the cover.

"I'm fine, just find the piece of shit who took the box. Check the cameras."

Jensen grabbed his belongings from Donnelly and began to make his way towards the elevator.

"Alright, sir. I will let you know if we find anything."

Donnelly watched Jensen carefully as he approached the elevator, aware his injury was far more serious than the deputy director realized.

Jensen returned to his anger, recalling his own failure to check the apartment completely before searching.

"Stupid," he muttered to himself, conscious that it is always the unexpected moment when the worst takes place. He slapped the elevator call button in anger, walking in as the car appeared immediately. Jensen knew he was in for a lashing from the disagreeable Secretary of Defense. Still he hoped for a modicum of sympathy given the violent circumstances of his failure to retrieve the object.

Jensen removed the ice pack from the back of his head, recalling that his injury was the result of the empty box he had to retrieve. He wiped his forehead, feeling momentarily dizzy.

The elevator arrived on the headquarters floor. Jensen was greeted by the FBI director standing outside of the elevator, speaking to another agent.

"Are you alright, Al?" the Director asked, showing sympathy for him.

"Could be better. How about some of that Scotch I've seen in your office?"

The Director's sympathy spurred a sarcastic tone from Jensen, feeling he had the upper hand.

"I'll give you the whole bottle," the Director said, shaking Jensen's hand. "Come to my office when you can. Take a moment to collect yourself."

"I'm fine. It takes a hell of a lot more than a crack to the head to stop me."

Jensen encouraged the Director to move towards his office. The two walked to the corner office, weaving through the cubicles and agents busily working around them.

"By the way, any chance for overtime?" Jensen asked, cracking a smile.

"Of course. You know how it is, once you hit 120 hours in a week, you get time and a half," the director said, returning an equally cynical smile.

The two entered the corner office. To Jensen's surprise, Espinoza and Forester sat in two chairs off to the side of the desk. The Director encouraged Jensen to sit in front of his desk.

"Jesus, you're unconscious for a few hours and everything changes. I assume you have captured Degnan?" Jensen inquired, staring gravely at his two agents.

Espinoza and Forester looked over at the Director, hoping he would fill Jensen in on the most recent happenings. Though suffering from a concussion, Jensen was aware something had changed in his case.

The Director raised his hand, searching for the best way to give the current details.

"You should be used to this idea, but our assignment has changed once again, Al. It seems our superiors have decided to renege on the warrant out for Degnan. They have decided that the Bureau is to formally apologize for mistakenly suspecting and accusing Dr. Degnan of murder, terrorist acts, et cetera."

Jensen's shocked look was affirmed by his colleagues.

"I don't know what to tell you, Al. I just got word from Secretary Hansen. Espinoza called knowing you were getting stitched up, so I had him come back to headquarters. They don't want him harmed or pursued in any way."

Jensen pulled the ice pack from his head and slammed it on the desk.

"So, all of it. Everything, just like that, done. What are we, fuckin' puppets? And who is holding the strings? We spend a day running around looking for this guy, and just like that. Let's fuckin' apologize?"

Jensen's fury continued. Director Hayes locked eyes with his deputy.

"Why don't you two gentleman get some sleep. I'll explain the rest of the changes to Agent Jensen alone. We'll get started tomorrow, early."

Espinoza and Forester simultaneously rose from their seats, shaking hands with both men and exiting the office.

"Did that crack to your goddamn skull make you forget who you are? You think I'm enjoying this? We do what we are told and we do not question why. That's the job."

"Cut the shit, Bob. What's going on?"

Jensen picked up his ice pack applying it to his wound.

"We need to monitor Degnan's movements. Nothing more. We need to know where he is. That's our assignment. Espinoza found out that he's on a ship heading for Nova Scotia. We don't approach him, we don't do anything. We just make sure we know where he is. Secretary Hansen made it clear that our only objective is to ensure that he is followed."

Jensen rolled his eyes.

"You're kidding. First we arrange his death, then we try to apprehend, now we have to babysit?"

"I don't give a shit what you do. Just make sure we know where he is at all times. I want you to go with Forester and Espinoza. You trail him. When they want to find him, you better know where he is. Now, he's scheduled to arrive around 7am. We'll have you there by the time he's exiting. That's it. Now I suggest you get some rest."

Hayes stood up walking around to Jensen.

"You may not want to go, but no more mistakes. I want you there with the two of them."

Jensen stood up, glaring at his boss. Though enraged by the day's events, his superior's reminder of their responsibilities quelled his onsluaght. He walked over to the door, stopping to look back. A sarcastic smile surfaced on his face.

"Of course sir. I'll handle it. Nothing I would like better."

"WHAT THE FUCK IS THIS?" Frenchy asked, staring blankly at the flat screen TV in his cabin, with his companions feeling equally shocked.

The reporter for the Channel 7 News continued.

"Francis Degnan, a resident of Jersey City, was wanted in connection to the bombing at the Dumont at ninety-sixth street here in Manhattan, as well as being linked to a fire started at St. Ignatius Prep school, which is his place of work. Well, in a vindicating turn, the FBI and the Jersey City Police have released a statement officially ending their pursuit and apologizing to Degnan. There mistake, the result of false information provided during the investigation, was called by FBI Director Hayes a serious lapse in verifying intelligence. All charges have been dropped against Degnan who the authorities were unable to apprehend . . ."

Sarah shut the TV off and looked at her comrades.

"Nope. Don't get it. That makes no sense. After all they went through to catch us, they just take it all back, like that. Something's not right."

"Well, right or not, this is great news. We don't have to worry about being chased by the feds, and I'm not going to prison or getting killed, which is also a plus."

Sarah paced in front of the television.

"This is great, Doc; we don't have to worry about covert shit anymore. And that's good because you sucked at it anyway. We can do whatever we want, go where we want to go whatever."

Frenchy nodded in rhythm, ignoring Ricky's insult, continuing to bob his head as if to a song.

"Have to say. I agree completely, my brother. I feel so much better. I mean, I didn't mind the excitement of being a fugitive. You know, I'm a rebel, nothing shakes me, but this is so much better. Oh, and Ricky, kiss my ass. Who's up for a little celebration? Drinks on me, except for Ali; I'm not paying four dollars for your seltzer."

Frenchy high-fived his young student. Ali, stroked his beard, unsure what to make of the news.

"I hate to break up your party, but you don't think it's strange that they just decided to apologize? We want to kill you, but, oh wait, never mind, it's fine you can do whatever you want. Our mistake?" Sarah said, aggressively.

Once again, Frenchy's ability to ignore glaring abnormalities in a story frustrated Sarah.

"I'm inclined to agree with Sarah, Francis. We must still be cautious. If there is something I have learned in my time in this country, the FBI doesn't apologize. There must be some motive behind their decision."

Frenchy shook his head, smiling as though Ali's mistrust was absurd.

"Normally, I would agree with you, but in this case, they know I didn't do anything. So they let it go. Besides, I'm sure they found out that we were out of the country. Nothing they could do anyway."

Ali continued to stroke his beard, not convinced by Frenchy's explanation.

"Tell you what: we will still stay out of sight. We'll play it safe, pretend we are still fugitives. Okay? Does that make you two feel better?"

Frenchy darted his stare between Sarah and Ali, hoping his compromise would appease his skeptical friends. Sarah and Ali nodded in agreement.

"I still don't like it," Sarah sneered, sitting down in the lounge chair next to the TV.

"Okay you don't like it, blah blah blah. But let's plan this out. When we get to Nova Scotia, we need to find a way to get to the Middle East, specifically Masada; Masada baby!" Frenchy yelled, once again amending one of his favorite movie scenes.

"Ali, you're Muslim and therefore sketchy, can you get us to the Middle East from Nova Scotia?"

Ali stared emotionless, accustomed to Frenchy's teasing.

"I will see what I can do. But no promises. My limited knowledge of our destination tells me there is not a large Muslim population in Halifax."

"I knew I could count on you."

Frenchy winked at Ricky, jokingly jabbing at his young student.

"Francis, what about when we get there, how do we locate it?"

Sarah was not satisfied with simply getting to Israel.

Frenchy sat down on the edge of the bed and hunched over.

"Well, I've been thinking. Your dad said I was not far off. Now I had told him that I believed Lucius Silva left the Sword there at Masada, because he was so appalled at the mass suicide, wanting nothing to do with the Jewish people and their shit. Now I had told him I believed it to be in the old Roman fortress on the top, up snake's path. Maybe he is telling me that it's just not there, on the top. It could be at the base. I don't know."

Sarah smiled, getting swept up in Frenchy's excitement about the pursuit and the recent rescinding of his arrest warrant.

"I don't know; again, that's pretty tough. My father could have meant you were close, i.e., in Asia as you said before."

Frenchy scrunched his face together jokingly responding to her negative response.

"Well, how about this, let's go and check. If it's not there, we reassess. Deal? I mean shit, we have all the time in the world now. Nobody chasing us. We can spend the next few months searching."

"Not to piss on your parade again, but I'm not spending months doing this and he has to go back to school."

Frenchy grinned, enjoying her comment.

"It's okay, I'd let you piss on my parade any day," Frenchy said, winking.

Though usually irritated by Frenchy's comments, Sarah's overwhelming disgust for his lewd comment left her speechless.

"Come on, Ms. Tannen, you can't mess with the Doc," Ricky said, hoping to break what seemed to be her beginning heaves of regurgitation.

Sarah paused, composing herself. She glared at Frenchy, shaking her head.

"Well, if Ali can get us there, fine. But you make a comment like that again and I won't kill you; I'll make sure I find everything that terrifies you and put together a montage of your destruction."

Frenchy tried to swallow. He realized his comment brought out a side of Sarah that he now wished had remained hidden.

"Yup. Not gonna do that again."

Sarah looked over at Ali, sitting quietly.

"Like I said, I will do my best."

Frenchy clapped his hands together, posting a positive thumb to his companions.

"I'll be in my room; we have to be up early so no late night swapping stories boys," Sarah said, picking up her purse and walking out, smiling. Frenchy waited until he heard her door close.

"Okay, Ali, seriously; can you get us there or are we screwed?"

"We'll get there. I may know someone who can get us to Europe. From there, we worry about the next hurdle."

Ali stood up and walked over to the lounge chair.

"Why can't we just fly now? We don't have to worry about anything. You're not wanted anymore," Ricky asked, realizing slow travel seemed unnecessary.

"We have no passports, Ricky, we need a connection."

Ricky nodded, realizing the drawback to his plan. Frenchy walked over to the small refrigerator near the TV stand. He opened the door and removed a bottle of champagne.

"It ain't Guinness but this shit will work."

Ricky and Ali watched him intently.

"We have to rise early, Francis," Ali cautioned.

"I'll be back in a few; I'm gonna see if I can smooth things over with Sarah. That last comment about her peeing on me may have pushed her into a place . . . um, that I fear. Maybe a drink will cool her down and hopefully I can apologize."

Frenchy opened the door.

"Yeah, Doc, get some . . . go get peed on!" Ricky grinned.

"No. What? Jesus! The shit I have said in front of you. I'm gonna make sure you're expelled. And I was joking about the whole pee thing; it was just a fuckin' . . . whatever I'll be back."

Frenchy closed the door, pausing for a moment to collect himself. Through the entire ordeal, he had gotten the definitive feel that Sarah loathed him. While accustomed to the opposite sex writing him off, he wanted Sarah to like him, to respect him.

He stared at her cabin door, his anxiety trying to convince his attempt to reconcile with her.

"Fuck it. I can't have my love interest on this train wreck of an escapade not be enamored by me," he muttered, inhaling deeply before knocking on the door.

Sarah opened the door, putting her hand on her hip.

"That was quick; you're lost without me already?" Sarah said sarcastically "What'd you do, sell Ricky for a pack of cigarettes?"

"Um, well, I just figured we could talk. I think you have gotten the wrong impression of me. Maybe we could get to know each other better; after all, we are in this together,"

Frenchy held the bottle of champagne up to Sarah, shaking it gently and hoping to entice her.

"I'm sure you don't need any more of that. But, then again, I guess I do need to fill my bladder."

Frenchy looked off, his eyes widening at her comment.

"I'm sorry about that; it was just a nasty joke."

Sarah waved him in.

"And no worries about too much to drink; I'm Irish. I was born with a high tolerance. Back in the day I would chase shots of whiskey with my mom's breast milk."

Sarah shook her head.

"What the hell is wrong with you? Can't you act appropriately for, I don't how, how about thirty seconds?"

She sighed, exasperated, as Frenchy pondered her question.

"Sadly, that one didn't faze me in the same way your invitation to be urinated upon did."

"Seriously, I'm really sorry; that was gross. I'm sorry. Let's forget I said that."

Sarah nodded in agreement, moving to the side to allow him to fully enter the room.

Frenchy walked over to the table, turning over two complimentary glasses. He began to open the bottle of champagne.

"You know, in all of this shit, I never got a chance to tell you how sorry I am at your father's passing. He was a great man and a good mentor for me during my writing."

Sarah looked down at her hands, recalling her departure from the funeral home earlier.

The cork popped on the bottle, startling Sarah. She walked over to two chairs angled towards each other. Frenchy followed, handing her a glass. He poured the champagne properly, the carbonation reaching the very top before retreating. Sarah cocked her head as she looked at him. His sudden improvement from moments earlier made her smile.

"I take it back; if you could stay like this for a bit longer, it might bode well for your future."

"Hey I only act like an idiot when I'm nervous . . . well, maybe not just when I'm nervous, but I really can be serious. I'm like Two Face. Half is acceptable and okay in front of children under thirteen. The other, not so much."

Sarah chuckled, watching Frenchy fill his glass.

"To your father."

Sarah smiled sipping the champagne, leaning back in the chair.

"Did you mean what you said?"

Frenchy definitively nodded sitting in the opposing chair.

"Of course, your father was a great man . . ."

Sarah waved his statement off, realizing she had not given context to her thoughts.

"Sorry, I didn't mean that. I was thinking about what you said today. Did you really mean the Holy Land should be split?"

Frenchy took a large gulp of his champagne and stood up and walked over to refill his glass.

"I know what I think is not popular among Jews. I get it. I also get why Jews believe they deserve to have that land, all to themselves. Trust me, I get that side. But truthfully, it's not right. I know you will hate me for saying that, but it isn't. And this isn't an anti or pro anyone view, and certainly not something I have arrived at quickly."

Frenchy recognized his chance of improving his relationship with Sarah abruptly ending with her question. He walked over and sat down, placing his glass on the table and preparing to defend his viewpoint.

"Look, I view it this way. In world history land has changed hands, often in very unscrupulous ways i.e. the colonists and Native Americans or, close to my heart, Northern Ireland and the British. Is it right that land was taken from people? Of course not. The problem is, time then passes and eventually the people who live there had nothing to do with the way the land was taken. The colonization of Northern Ireland by the British was wrong. But at this point those who live there have a right to the land as well. Land was taken from the Native Americans. But I didn't take it. My grandmother didn't either. Should we be forced to give it back because it once belonged to the Native Americans?"

"But this isn't just land. It is land promised to us by God. It is our sacred land, our Holy Land. It's very different."

"Come on. Get off that shit. If you believe that, then ask yourself this: you really think God would want wars that have cost hundreds of thousands of lives in your promise land? And it's holy to Muslims and Christians too. It's also home to the Palestinians who have lived there for hundreds, thousands of years. Look, I am not saying Jews have no right whatsoever. Actually I may be saying that. But I'm fair. I believe in compromise. I'm certainly aware of the injustices that Jews have suffered for thousands of years. It's just that you can't fix wrongs with more wrongs, to sound cliché. I believe it must be shared. You can't just show up and say 'bitch, this is our land now and we are now a new country and you guys need to move.;"

Frenchy immediately autocorrected himself.

"And sorry about saying bitch, and saying come off this shit. Totally inappropriate."

Despite Sarah's bias towards her own people, she understood Frenchy's point. She shook her head, laughing at his quick apology.

"So what then? How does it get solved?"

"I'm not sure it gets solved, but the first step is to follow through with what the UN declared. Two independent countries: an Israeli State and a Palestinian State. And to ensure no problems, Jerusalem held as an international city, governed by the UN. That's how we start towards ending all of this bloodshed. Plus let's be serious, 9/11 was no random act. It's not like Bin Laden woke up one day and said 'the U.S. is a good place to attack.' He had his reasons to be pissed, something legitimate like the support of Israel by the West. Obviously, no matter how legitimate, it doesn't warrant killing civilians. But to me the hardest thing we can do as a people or as a country is accept culpability. It's easy to say Al Quaeda hates freedom. But in truth they are extremists who are pissed and did what they could to fight back. Still wrong. But I'll put it to you this way, if we look back in history, when people are angry and feel helpless, they turn to any means to fight.

Again, that never makes it right. But dismissing their reasons only keeps it going."

He slammed down the remainder of his glass of champagne and retrieved the bottle, filling up his glass and topping off Sarah's. Frenchy looked at Sarah, concerned that he had angered her.

"In truth, I'm not sure I articulated that last part well, but I'm saying that we must recognize our own mistakes and faults and then work to right things. I get how hard it is to say sorry. But if only someone could start, I swear it may catch on. Palestinians and Jews both need to listen to the opposing side, acknowledge where they were and are wrong, and then discuss how to move forward. Just like all other conflicts. Granted, there ain't a shot in hell this ever happens, but, I don't know, you can hope."

Frenchy squinted, trying to read Sarah's reaction.

"You hate me?"

"Yes, but not for that," Sarah said, playfully. "You're a smart man, Francis. I didn't mean everything I said today. I admire your passion, and I do believe in you, as my father did. There is nothing wrong with dreaming such dreams or having those views."

Frenchy smiled, grateful for the champagne that appeared to soften up his love interest.

"So, if you don't mind me asking, how come you teach in a high school when you have a Ph.D.?"

Frenchy winced at the familiar question, frequently posed by his mother during family gatherings.

"Honestly? It's better to be the well-educated fish in the small pond then in the fuckin' ocean. Of course, in my case, the fact I believe that means I have low self-esteem. And better yet, if you swim around the pond with no balls the smallest fish can overpower you . . . Not sure if this analogy is working, but basically fear keeps me where I am. Very sad, huh?"

"Sad? No. Disappointing? Yes. But who am I to judge? I work with people who deal with issues of self-worth to the most basic issues like how to feed their children. I pass no judgment."

"No judgment? Huh. Will you marry me?"

The two laughed.

"No, but seriously, will you? I'll keep screwing up my life and you can never pass judgment. I smell heaven."

Sarah put her hand on her forehead, hoping to halt Frenchy's strange continuation. She shifted in her seat.

"So, the Sword of Goliath. Passed down as the symbol of power for anyone who ruled Israel, ends up buried at Masada, only to be found by the great Francis Degnan."

"You may continue."

Frenchy lightheartedly coaxed.

The two quietly enjoyed their drinks. Frenchy stopped for a moment, his expression becoming serious.

"What's the matter?" she asked, aware that Frenchy's demeanor had changed.

"Nothing, nothing, just a thought, probably nothing." Frenchy waved off his thought as Sarah leaned forward.

"What is it? What? Don't make a face and then say nothing."

"I don't know why I never thought about it. I guess the things your father told me when I was writing my book, I just assumed he was humoring me. But now that I know he knew the Sword existed, things he said have all new meanings now."

"Well, specifically what? What is it that he said to you that you just realized?"

Sarah grew increasingly interested in his recent revelation.

"Well, it was what you said. He used to joke with me that I would be the great man to discover the Sword. When he would joke he always said he believed I would find much more than just a Sword."

Frenchy shook his head, dismissing his recent flashback.

"I'm sure what he meant was what you do with the Sword, and maybe even how you find it, may impact you. You're a teacher of history. Artifacts can change how we view our world. Perhaps it's not fame that you will find. Perhaps something much more."

Sarah smiled gently, patting Frenchy on his knee.

"I don't know. I don't think I am much for changing the world. What's a drunken Irishmen from Jersey City know about stuff like that?"

"As much as it kills me to say it, particularly after a statement like that, my father believed in you, and I believe my father to have been a very wise man so, again, I believe in you too."

Sarah reclined in her chair, her hazel eyes playfully staring at Frenchy from above her glass.

"Well, maybe you are right; I am the man. Do you know I once saved three children from a burning building?"

Sarah rolled her eyes, stopping mid roll at his statement.

"Really, you did that?"

"No, I can't back that up but I did save their dog."

"Well, that's still somethi—"

"No, I didn't save their dog, but I did call the fire department."

Sarah put her glass down on the table between their chairs.

"Classic. Just when you are redeeming yourself, you go and say dumb shit. Goodnight, Dr. Degnan."

"No, I'm serious; I called the fire department, yup. Me, called the fire department."

She pushed Francis playfully towards the door.

"Hold up. There's a beverage involved," Frenchy squealed, throwing back the last bit of his drink.

"Don't I get a goodnight kiss?" he said as she shut the door.

"Go to bed; we have a long day ahead of us tomorrow."

Sarah laughed as she heard Frenchy continue to shout nonsense about his great call to the firefighters. He knocked again at the door.

"What?" she asked, staring at Frenchy.

"No, but seriously, I appreciate what you said. I just can't be serious when people compliment me."

"All you talk about is fame and praise and here you get it and you can't handle it."

Frenchy nodded sadly.

"Maybe if I come in and you keep heaping praise I can be ready for when others do it."

"Good night Francis," Sarah said, letting out a grunt as she shut the door.

"I need practice!" he yelled.

He stopped in the corridor and smiled, pleased with his late night conversation.

He took a cigarette out of his pack, lighting it as he walked towards the exit to the lower deck.

He looked out at the night sky. He took a pull from his cigarette, his eyes gazing down at the almost glass-like surface of the Atlantic. He shuddered, his fear of heights swiftly returning. He flicked his cigarette into the dark ocean, instantly retreating to the wall, folding his hands to pray.

"I know I'm a fuck-up. I know I don't even believe in you fully. But whatever is the higher power, Zeus, Yahweh, Jesus, Allah, whatever. Help me on this one. This is a pinnacle moment and I am pretty sure I'm screwed. So if there is anyone up there, just let me have this one. Let me succeed. Then, you can go back to shittin' on me. But just this once, help me."

Frenchy began to make the sign of the cross, losing faith midway through the motion. He turned and walked back towards the cabins, quickly spinning and returning to the rail of the ship.

"And for what it's worth, thanks for today, minus being wanted for a crime; but thanks."

"EXACTLY WHAT would you like me to do with this Francis Degnan?" the middle aged man asked, as he sat behind his desk, his hands folded together.

"Very little. Our people will handle everything. I just need you to serve as a buffer between Degnan and Gershom. Jacob will approach Dr. Degnan and offer him one million dollars to assist in the recovery of the artifact whose location can be deciphered using this."

Assaf handed the man a small crinkled piece of aged paper. The man analyzed the piece, running his hand along the right edge of the paper.

"It's only half. This is useless. Maybe if the cut had been horizontal or even vertical we may have been able to recover some information, but it is on a diagonal. The information is fragmented."

The man handed the piece of paper back to Assaf dismissing its significance.

"Agreed, this means nothing to you or me, but maybe he could be able to use it. It may simply confirm what he already knows, but it is important to give this to him. We need to acquire his services. We will make sure he moves on it immediately. However, your presence will make sure that he does not feel threatened. Explain to him that this is a result of new findings about the Sword of Goliath and that you sought him out because of his research and writings."

Eli shifted in his chair, uneasy at his new task.

"How will I know him when he arrives? I have never met this man."

Assaf sneered.

"You'll know him, believe me. I just need you to make him feel comfortable, not threatened. We will make sure his ego is massaged and his interest peaked."

"It is certainly a strange request, Assaf, but I will help my country in any way I can. Particularly when my responsibilities are so limited."

Assaf nodded in satisfaction, standing up and buttoning his suit jacket.

"We will be in communication soon for when to pick him up. When you meet, he will be under the impression that you have provided his transportation here. We will handle that, but do not feel surprised if he mentions that."

"Trust me there will be no problems. All will be taken care of, my friend," Eli said, smiling.

"Would you like more details about this? I feel concerned you have not asked more about my request." Assaf raised his left eyebrow.

"I would much prefer not knowing too much. That continues to be how I remain happy and of sound mind," Eli said, waving off the offer.

The two shook hands and Assaf exited the room crammed with artifacts. He walked down the corridor of Eli's house, exiting and entering a black limousine waiting in front.

"Is everything in order?" Gershom asked.

"Of course. Eli is reliable. But most of all, he has little to do with politics. He is perfect."

Assaf looked at his watch.

"We sent Jacob to meet him in Nova Scotia; the FBI agents will follow his movements. And all shall be dealt with."

"I must admit, Assaf, you have a talent for solving problems. You may make a great prime minister one day.'

Assaf nodded in thanks, flattered by the compliment, despite his initial negative reaction to Gershom using the word "may."

"Sir, it would be difficult to follow in your footsteps after this treaty has been secured and the symbol of our dominance restored. You may be known as a second King David."

Assaf's statement fostered in Gershom a feeling of pride. He, too, had thought of how he would be remembered if he was successful. Though a humble man, the excitement of impending triumph suppressed his usual mindset.

"Perhaps," he said, smiling.

"Perhaps."

THE SMALL FBI PLANE BEGAN ITS DESCENT towards Halifax Airport. The sun slowly began to ascend, shining through Jensen's window. He gazed out, his view seized by the greenish black sea below. He suddenly leaned forward, his attention caught by a ship on the sea. He looked at his watch, attempting to gauge if it was possibly Degnan's. He looked over at Espinoza and Forester, both enjoying a last moment of rest.

Jensen opened Degnan's book, flipping through the pages to the section on the Israeli-Palestinian conflict. He re-read Degnan's support of the two equal states, sharing the land as the UN had originally declared. He removed his glasses and returned to looking out at the approaching land of Nova Scotia. Though tired and still groggy from being attacked, he mulled over his new assignment of following Degnan without being detected.

As he thought about his mark and the previous day's events, he suddenly felt fondness for the unconventional man he sought. Frenchy's escape to Nova Scotia impressed the deputy director. Moreover, Degnan's resilience and refusal to give into the warrant for his arrest spurred on a momentary smile from Jensen. He closed the book and placed it on the seat next to him. He sat back slightly, his gaze returning to the Atlantic. His mind wandered, drifting to the many movies he had watched over the years about adventures and cases involving the FBI. He had grown fond of movies dealing with conspiracy, particularly *The Rock*. Yet the plausibility of a group of Marines taking over Alcatraz seemed closer to reality than his present assignment.

A noise from the belly of the plane indicated the opening of the landing gear. Espinoza and Forester stirred from their slumber abruptly, looking momentarily disorientated.

"Alright, men, time to go play babysitter," Jensen stated sarcastically, leaving his short-lived appreciation for Degnan.

The plane touched the ground, the brakes applied immediately by the pilot until the aircraft had come to a reasonable ground speed.

The three men stood, collecting their belongings and moving towards the side exit of the plane.

"Remember, we have to make sure we are not seen and that we are not known by any Nova Scotians."

Jensen smiled, enjoying the mundane aspect of his case.

"You seem in better spirits, sir," Espinoza said, also enjoying his boss' change in mood.

"Yeah, yesterday I was pissed, as I'm sure you could tell. Today, well, it must have been that hit to my head that jarred the small happiness section of my brain."

The three walked down the stair case onto the runway. They surveyed their surroundings, taking a moment to take pleasure in their casual attire.

"It's six thirty a.m. Let's head over to the dock and we can pick up our mischievous Jersey boy. According to my most recent email, the good doctor and his wayward companions will be getting a visit from another gentleman who will be taking them to Israel."

Espinoza cocked his head, confused by Jensen's statement.

"Don't ask; I'm not. Again our objective: track their movements no matter what."

"So we're headed to Israel, huh?"

Forester shifted his luggage bag to his other hand.

"That's my guess. Consider it an early vacation," Jensen said, spotting the entrance to the terminal. "Let's get ourselves a cab."

The trio made their way through the terminal to the cab stand, stepping into the first available taxi.

"Port of Halifax, sir," Jensen said, removing his Blackberry to work.

"You know, you never told me what happened with Degnan," he remarked to his agents.

"Well, to make a long story short, we would have found him quickly, but his cousin threw us off by sending us after the wrong vehicle and then helped the group onto a ship at the port in Bayonne."

"His cousin?"

Jensen kept his eyes fixed on his Blackberry.

"His cousin is a Jersey City cop. In fact I think he sent us after someone he knew. Maybe an ex-wife. She was quite the bitch."

Jensen laughed, appreciating the move.

"Can't blame him for that. I would have done the same thing; it's just I'm not sure which wife I dislike more."

Jensen looked over for approval of his joke.

"That's right, you're both just married. Give it time; his actions will make sense to you someday."

Espinoza chuckled, fidgeting in his seat.

"Thanks for letting me ride bitch," he sarcastically remarked as he attempted to stretch his legs.

"No problem."

Forester smiled as he stretched his right leg comfortably.

"The two of you better not bicker the whole time."

"So, is the Israeli government going to kill Degnan once he gets there?" Espinoza asked, ignoring Jensen's comment.

"I would imagine they wouldn't go to all this trouble to bring him there only to kill him. I think this whole thing has to do with his research."

Jensen held Degnan's book up to the two agents.

"Either they're pissed at his condemnation of Israel's treatment of Palestinians or they think he knows where this Sword is."

"How did you come to this?" Forester asked, looking over the back part of the book.

"Well, I have spent a lot of time thinking about this. Based on what I was told, the parties' involved, and the fact that I see nothing else that would make him a threat or an asset, it's got to be those two."

"So, all this—the bomb to eliminate him, the chase—all that is over a weapon, a fucking sword?"

Espinoza stressed the object, emphasizing the ridiculousness of that concept.

"It's what I've come up with. But you know what, who gives a shit? At this point, we have the opportunity to watch. I'm sure by the end we will know for sure."

Jensen took the book back from Espinoza.

"Why isn't the CIA doing this? We have no jurisdiction."

Jensen rolled his eyes.

"Who gives a shit? Like jurisdiction even means anything. I'm pretty sure that's become irrelevant . . . as it always has been."

"I've got a twenty that says they kill him," Forester said, patting his wallet.

"I say they don't kill him, but this is not about a sword or his book. I bet it's not Degnan at all. I bet it's Tannen's daughter, I bet she's the target."

Espinoza stared wide eyed, attempting to be serious.

"I'll see both bets. Now both of you shut up. Give an inch and you take it all; I'm nice and you guys get too familiar."

Jensen stared them down.

The agents lost their smiles instantly, attempting to avoid the revisit of an angry boss.

They looked down, submitting to his chastisement. Jensen smiled as he returned to his work.

"That's my kind of commute," he said, looking out at a large ship gliding parallel to their road.

The three looked towards the ship as it moved closer to the port. Jensen smiled.

"As I said before; time to babysit. Bring the popcorn and the porn."

"GOOD MORNING, SWEETHEART! Honey, it's time for school. I have breakfast on the table."

Frenchy gently poked Ricky.

"Housekeeping?"

Ali sat in the chair quietly, reading a passage from the Quran, disinterested in Frenchy's latest goof. Ricky's eyes opened, his body quickly jerking as he took in his masculine mother.

"Come on sweetie, time to get up."

Frenchy laughed and stood upright.

"Chill, chill, nigga; that shit's not funny, Doc. For a second I almost lunged at you. I forgot where I was."

"Watch your mouth."

Frenchy clapped his hands together and walked over to the dresser, grabbing a cigarette from his pack.

"I thought you said you had breakfast?"

Ricky rubbed his eyes and sat up from his bed on the floor.

"Yeah, it's right here; best breakfast ever, and it really gets the bowels moving if it ain't flowin' right."

Ricky recoiled from Frenchy's statement. While happy to share a beer with him, the thought of Frenchy's bowel movements proved to be beyond what he wanted to know about his teacher.

"If you're showering, then you got six minutes to be ready. We dock in about fifteen minutes."

Frenchy walked over to the door and opened it, smiling as it revealed a lethargic Sarah.

"Well, hello, Ms. Thang. I hope you slept well, though the bags under your eyes seem to indicate otherwise."

Frenchy exaggeratedly elbowed the air in front of Sarah, indicating he was joking.

"Yes, and I see you're on your way to pollute the atmosphere and ensure your own permanent bags under your eyes."

Sarah pulled the cigarette from Frenchy's mouth, placing it in his hand.

"Well, as a matter of fact I am on my way topside. I figured I'd get an eye opener before we start the day."

"What is an eye opener?" Ali asked, turning his attention to the conversation before him.

"Oh, just a couple of beers to get the day rolling."

Frenchy saw Sarah's thought process arrive at hostile.

"I'm kidding. Seriously, I am not going to drink; what the hell is wrong with you?"

Frenchy scrunched his face together, disappointed that she believed it plausible that he would drink in the morning.

"Let's get our stuff and head topside. We can scope the scene from there. Ricky, make it quick; we'll be up on the deck where we will exit."

Frenchy moved past Sarah in a hurry to smoke his cigarette.

"Let's stick together; I don't think he should be left down here alone."

Sarah recalled her search for Frenchy the last time they were set to meet on the top deck.

"He's fine; he's eighteen. He can survive while we go upstairs."

Ali stood up and walked towards the perpetually fighting duo.

"I will stay with him and we will meet you above."

"See, problem solved. Let's go."

Frenchy waved Sarah on as he walked out onto the lower deck and towards the stairs leading up. Sarah rolled her eyes and shut the door, following slowly behind him. Frenchy reached the second highest deck and looked out over the railing. He locked his hands around the rail firmly, hoping to prevent any fall. He looked down at the greenish water of the Atlantic.

Among the many fantasies he enjoyed in his life, one was to have been the man to find the Titanic. Though Robert Ballard had made the dream impossible, Frenchy still enjoyed pretending he was the discoverer of the maritime disaster.

Sarah approached the rail, leaning casually and looking out towards the port.

"You seem to be dealing with the heights much better today."

"That's because I know I'm about to get off."

Frenchy lit his cigarette carefully, attempting to keep his firm grip on the rail.

"So what do we do when we get off? We have to get to Israel."

"Not sure. Hopefully Ali can work his Muslim magic and get us there. Otherwise, I've always wanted to see the 'Money Pit,' and when will I ever be in Nova Scotia again?"

Sarah shook her head giggling.

"Do you know all the lost treasures in world history?"

"I do watch too much History Channel. But yes, I do know a lot about lost treasures. Sadly, most have been found. I landed on the Sword of Goliath when I was in college. I watched *Indiana Jones and the Last Crusade* when I was a kid and I wanted to be him. So I started researching the Holy Grail. It was only later on in a class, when we were talking about the battle between David and Goliath, did I ask where the Sword was today. My professor said no one knew. That was pretty much how it all started. I was on and off with research because I was obsessed with an all-new quest."

"What was that?"

Frenchy looked at her, confused as to how she didn't know what he was talking about.

"Women. My new quest was women. I found my first love. And in truth, it was she who encouraged me to go on with my research. So I did. Unfortunately, when I finally wrote my book it was not exactly well-received. I ended up depressed. She left me. And all I had left was my teaching and my dreams of one day proving to everyone that my book and research were right."

Frenchy took a long drag on his cigarette and flicked it over the side of the ship. Sarah looked at Frenchy's face. She did not expect him to open up to her so nonchalantly. She gently bumped her hip into him, getting his attention.

"Like I said, at least three times so far, my father believed in you. So do I. And this is your chance to prove everyone wrong."

"I appreciate that. I will do it." Frenchy fidgeted awkwardly.

"I have to admit it's nice to have you along. You know, you keep me in line. And I guess I should thank you for not killing me."

Sarah looked away, blushing momentarily.

"We had a rocky start to the trip but things are looking up."

Frenchy nodded in agreement.

"Ricky came running up behind Frenchy grabbing his shoulders. Frenchy shrieked in fear.

"Goddamit!"

"You okay, Doc? You're very jumpy."

Frenchy grabbed his chest, momentarily believing this was the end of his life.

"Stop that shit; you're not having a heart attack. I had to get you back for the morning wake-up."

Frenchy calmed himself slowly.

"So, where do we get off this boat?" Ricky looked around, noticing he was late to the disembarkment.

The horn blew loudly as the ship slowly approached the dock. The group moved towards crew members, preparing for the docking.

Frenchy looked out at the port, observing the many people gathered below awaiting the passengers. The crew stepped aside encouraging the first group to depart, shaking hands as they made their way down the ramp.

Frenchy carefully walked across the ramp following his companions. As he neared the end of the ramp, he jumped playfully, happy to land on solid ground.

"Well, we made it. Step one? Bitch-slapped."

"You know, the more I think about it, the more I think we should have stuck around in Jersey. We left so quickly thinking you were being pursued by the feds that we left with really no way of getting anywhere else. No passports, no nothing. Now that we are not in any danger, we are stuck here."

Ricky voiced his reasonable opinion as he looked around, realizing the dilemma they faced.

"Yeah, we already talked about that. So, you are absolutely right, Ricky, and I say go fuck yourself; you're late to the party. Ali, any word on how we can get out of here and head to the East?" Frenchy asked, hoping for a solution.

"There is a man who I called, not much more than an acquaintance. He travels to Nova Scotia frequently. I am hoping he is here now, but he has not called me back."

Ricky tapped Frenchy on the shoulder, as he stared off into the crowd of people.

"What?" Frenchy asked, irritated at his student's sudden repeated assault at his arm. Ricky pointed covertly over towards a man standing with a sign. It read: "Dr. Francis Degnan."

"Hmmm. No shit."

Sarah and Ali looked over, curious to find what sparked his shock. The four stood stunned. They looked at each other, hoping someone would be able to respond to what they saw.

"No way; hell no. I don't think so. We need to get out of here, now."

Frenchy quickly turned, limiting his movements as he began to remove himself from the scene.

"Follow me; we need to get away from here now!"

Sarah grabbed Frenchy's arm, looking down as she processed.

"Maybe not. If the FBI wanted to catch you, they certainly would not put some limo driver with a sign at the dock. Besides, it's clear they know where we are."

"Oh, so I'm the cautious one now. I don't want to take any chances. This is the shit I always encounter."

"What'd mean you always encounter?" Sarah said confused.

"Well, not me but in the movies. Everything seems fine and then a sudden bullshit twist that gets you caught. I've watched too many movies and I know how this shit ends. We are out now."

Ricky scratched his head and took a deep breath, walking over towards the man. Frenchy reached to grab his arm, but was too late.

"Hello, sir, I am Dr. Degnan. Will you get my bags?"

Frenchy looked on with fear, as Ricky spoke to the gentleman.

"I cannot believe he did that. I swear, that stupid shit."

Ricky and the gentleman talked for a moment. Ricky turned and waved for his three companions to approach.

The three walked over slowly, each cautiously scanning the area.

"He's not with the FBI or anyone else. He works for some antique dealer in Israel. He's said he'll take us to Israel to meet with him."

Frenchy raised an eyebrow as he looked the man up and down. He slowly produced his hand to receive the gentleman's.

"My name is Jacob Bakst; I work for Eli Botvinnik, an antiquities collector in Israel. He asked me to provide you with transportation to meet with him. He is in need of your services."

Frenchy made an odd face, arching his nose as though he smelled a rotten piece of cheese.

"Yeah, I heard that yesterday. Not falling for that shit this time. Nice meeting you there, Jacob, and kiss my ass. We're leaving."

Frenchy signaled to his companions to move away.

"Why would Mr. Botvinnik need his services? Are you not aware that Dr. Degnan is a fugitive?"

Sarah stared at Jacob attempting to gauge his reaction.

"I'm sorry, Ms. Neither I, nor Mr. Botvinnik, were aware of that. However, I certainly cannot transport nor harbor a fugitive from the law. Good day."

The man began to walk away, the group stunned by his response to Sarah's bluff.

"Wait!" Frenchy yelled.

Jacob turned, awaiting Frenchy.

"How did you know I was in Nova Scotia?"

Jacob removed his sunglasses, looking carefully at Frenchy.

"Mr. Botvinnik was alerted to your location by a close friend. Let's just say your whereabouts are not unknown to some, including your American law enforcement comrades."

"So you knew they were chasing me? Nope, this douche is suspect."

"As I recall, the warrant for your arrest was rescinded, no? But that does not mean they were not aware of your position. Regarding Mr. Botvinnik, allow me to say that he has a way of finding the people he wishes to assist him."

"That's pretty creepy. Thanks."

Frenchy looked over at Sarah, hoping she could provide guidance on their present situation.

"How are we to know that Mr. Botvinnik is being genuine?"

Ali looked skeptically at Jacob.

"I assure you he only seeks your assistance, nothing more. But you are free to turn down his offer. The choice is yours."

"Give us a second," Frenchy said, ushering his companions away from Jacob.

"Alright, I say we screw this guy and we run," Frenchy quietly whispered as they huddled together.

Ricky shook his head. "I say we go with him; he's giving us a free ride to where we want to go anyway."

"That's exactly what they want us to think. Then we show up in Israel and boom; we're all dead, and I definitely don't trust him. Looks like a pedophile. Plus, there's no way we show up to Canada, and 'oh my God, we need a way to the Middle East' and here is Johnny on the spot, offering a trip. Doesn't happen. No good comes from him. I say we hang out in Canada and find another way. We've got time."

Sarah rolled her eyes.

"Look, this guy doesn't seem to care if we go with him or not. If he's playing us, he's one of the best and I don't think that is the case. Besides, I have family in Israel. I can have them meet us and make sure there is no funny business."

Sarah's reasoning did little to comfort Frenchy.

Ricky and Sarah turned to Ali, hoping his silent contemplation could produce a wise perspective.

"It seems strange that he would be here so quickly, and know exactly where we are. Francis, call your cousin and ask him if our location was known."

Frenchy reluctantly agreed to the suggestion, removing his cell phone, slowly powering up the phone and dialing his cousin's number.

"By the way, how did we all leave our cell phones on the whole time we were being chased? Just driving home the fact that we are all morons and make mistakes. And you thinking this guy is fine could be another one."

Frenchy grabbed the phone holding it close to his face.

"Jimmy? Thank the fuckin' lord. It's me, Frenchy. I don't have much time; did the FBI know where we were?"

The three stared at Frenchy, awaiting some reaction to his cousin's response.

"So you told them. No, that's fine. That helps a lot. Thanks again and I'll be in touch."

Frenchy closed the cell phone.

"He gave up our location. So it's true; they knew where we were."

The group continued to contemplate the best course of action. Frenchy smiled forcefully at Jacob.

"Fuck it, fine, we'll go with him. Let's hope your family will meet us. And like you said, it's a free ride and we don't have too many transportation options right now."

Frenchy broke from the group and walked over to Jacob.

"Alright, skippy dips, we'll go with you, but what exactly does this Mr. Something-ethnic want me to find?"

"The Sword of Goliath, of course. He was under the impression that you would be the best person to uncover it, now that evidence exists that it may actually be attainable."

Frenchy raised his eyebrows, surprised at Jacob's words.

"You seem surprised. What did you expect?"

Frenchy recognized Jacob's point.

"Fair enough; figured it would be more theatrical," he said, shrugging.

"It's just too bad we had to find you here. It would have been easier to acquire your services under better circumstances."

"Very true, sir, very true. So that's it, I find him the Sword and . . ."

Frenchy hinted at an explanation of payment.

"You will be compensated for the find. The artifact itself will be sold to a museum so do not worry about a private collector keeping it. Mr. Botvinnik is a collector, but this artifact will be for all people."

Frenchy nodded in agreement.

"Well-put. But do you have any idea exactly how much he is . . ."

"Please, Dr. Degnan, I am not in a position to negotiate price," Jacob politely interrupted, uninterested in continuing the conversation.

"Fair enough, let's roll my good man. The Sword of Goliath awaits."

Frenchy's confidence in his ticket to the Middle East strengthened.

"Very well, I have a car waiting to take us to the airport. A private plane will take us to Israel to meet with Mr. Botvinnik."

Jacob gestured to a black sedan idling near the passenger drop-off zone. The group followed Jacob, entering the sedan.

"Shotgun nigga," Ricky yelled.

"It is a bit of a tight squeeze, as you say in the U.S.; I did not realize you traveled with so many guests."

"No problem; we can put Ali in the trunk," Frenchy said, laughing and entering the vehicle on the right side.

Ali walked to the opposing side of the car, as Ricky jumped into the front passenger seat. Sarah entered behind Frenchy.

"Wait a second. No fuckin' way; I'm not riding bitch." Frenchy pushed, realizing Ali had pulled a switch by entering on the left side.

"Perhaps you would be more comfortable in the trunk," Ali said sternly.

"Is everything alright, sir?" Jacob asked from the driver's seat.

"Yeah, fine; let's go. But I'm not sitting in a middle seat on the plane."

Sarah gazed over at Frenchy.

"I have a feeling the plane we're going on is a little bit better than the average airliner."

* * *

AS DEGNAN'S VEHICLE DROVE AWAY from the port, Jensen and his men stood off to the side of the check-in building. They cautiously watched the automobile head towards the exit, immediately flagging a cab seemingly waiting for their signal.

They entered the vehicle, speeding off quickly after the black sedan.

"So, what's the deal now, boss?" Espinoza asked, attempting to get a better view from the back seat.

"The Director notified me that we will be following the group back to the airport. Turns out the powers that be know Degnan's moves without our input. Still. We were told to follow Degnan and so we shall. We expected to head to Israel anyway. We sure as hell weren't going to be sailing there. Just a wasted car ride to the dock."

Espinoza looked down at his watch.

"Could've picked him up when they got to us."

"Greater chance we miss him if we didn't come here."

Jensen typed quickly on his Blackberry.

"Our bet's still on right?" he asked his agents, remaining fixed on his work.

"Bet's on," Forester said firmly.

"Well, it would seem that in the next few hours we will have our answer."

"Definitely Israel," Forester asked quickly, uncomfortable with not knowing the latest information on a wager.

Jensen held his phone up to his agents.

"Not just Israel. He's going to meet the Prime Minister."

"**SO IT TURNS OUT** you needed this American after all?" Vice President Cristy said, staring at the Prime Minister from over his glasses.

Cristy reached into his pocket, pulling two cigars out and placing them on the conference table.

"Thankfully it's no longer holding up our agreement."

Cristy slid one cigar across to Prime Minister Gershom.

"Agreed," he said, turning the document in front of him to the second page. Assaf offered him a pen from his pocket. Gershom paused, taking in the moment. He fumbled over the document, attempting to stall. He paused and exhaled sadly, signing the last page of the document. Cristy lit his cigar, billows of smoke coming from his mouth. He passed his matchbox over to Gershom. He lit his cigar, a look of disgust on his face.

"They're strong, aren't they?" Cristy said, reveling in his celebratory smoke.

The Prime Minister sat back, attempting to join his counterpart in commemorating the moment.

"Now, let's talk about how our special friendship will play out.'

Assaf sat down, eager to discuss this aspect of their dealings.

The Secretary of Defense had been sitting quietly to the left of the Vice President. While appreciating the cause for triumph, he wished to move forward immediately with his plans, saving the celebration for another time.

He opened his laptop, connected to a projector on the table, displaying a detailed map of the Middle East.

"With all the money we pump into this country, you'd think you could have a more technologically sound set-up."

The Secretary stared down the Prime Minister.

"Sorry, Mr. Secretary, this is my home, I prefer to work at the office."

Hansen laughed, shaking his head at the meek response.

"As outlined in the treaty, we will establish military bases outside of Eilat, here on the Gulf of Aqaba and here near Nahariyya. These bases will be launching points for joint air strikes against Jordan, Syria, and Lebanon."

"If necessary," Cristy added, carefully completing Hansen's sentence and acutely aware that the Prime Minister had resisted war with neighboring nations.

Assaf sneered at Cristy's politeness, returning to his careful analysis of the details of the Secretary's plan.

"These bases will anger our Muslim neighbors."

"Very true," Hansen said.

"But their consistent terrorist attacks will be our reasoning for the bases. Also their support of numerous terrorist organizations. At least that is what will be said to the world community. Regardless, war with these nations has been a longtime coming."

Gershom shifted in his chair, uncomfortable with the dialogue.

"That should not be our focus when we need to assure the safety of our citizens within Israel. When we discussed the treaty, we agreed the bases are to fortify our position, not to be used to attack."

During the earlier treaty negotiations, each side had held firm on their agendas. For Prime Minister Gershom, the strengthening of Israel was his only goal. With the United States as their ally and a military presence, he believed peace could be achieved in Israel through the relocation of all Palestinians outside of Israel and the monitoring of the borders. Cristy and Hansen, veterans of past relations between the U.S. and Muslim nations, viewed military bases in Israel as the first step in the subjugation of all Muslim nations in the oil-rich Middle East. For years, groups from all over the world attempted to bridge the gap between Christians, Jews, and Muslims. The two American statesmen viewed these efforts as futile. Though proponents of peaceful negotiations with fellow countries, they believed the only way to deal with the nations of the Middle East was force. It was on this point that Assaf saw eye-to-eye with the U.S. While Israel's position in the Middle East remained his primary concern, his life experiences had caused his anger against the neighboring Muslim Nations to swell.

"I assure you, Prime Minister, Israel will be safe, strengthened by the addition of our forces to this region. But make no mistake, Israel is not what we are here for."

Cristy stared the Prime Minister down. Though near the same age, the Vice President exuded an element of ruthlessness and toughness, not shared by his counterpart.

"Well, if you choose to go to war with our neighbors, then there will be no joint air strikes. You will go it alone."

The Prime Minister took a pull of his Monte Cristo, not backing down from Cristy. Hansen glanced over at Assaf, his look enough chastisement to spur Assaf into action.

"If I may interject: Israel's position will grow stronger as the nations who harbor the men who attack us are controlled. We can monitor our borders all we want, but terrorists will still get in because there are nations that support them, finance them, and encourage them. Let us focus on the task at hand. We are in agreement on the military bases. Let us see how our neighbors react. Either way, Israel will be protected."

Gershom's demeanor changed. He smiled at his dependent advisor, comforted by his words.

"I suppose you are right. Perhaps it is best."

Cristy looked back at Assaf, nodding to an unspoken agreement.

"I suppose it is foolish to get ahead of ourselves. We will bring our plans to the President for final authorization and we'll go from there."

Assaf looked down at his watch.

"It has been a long morning gentleman. Perhaps we should break for lunch."

"We will not be staying; we have business to attend to in Washington." Cristy stamped out his cigar, rising from his seat.

Gershom seemed surprised at the abrupt end to their conversation. Hansen disconnected his laptop and shut it quickly, walking towards Cristy who had moved towards the Prime Minister.

"We will brief the President and be in contact with the plans for the military bases." The two men quickly shook hands with Gershom, who fumbled to put his cigar down to acknowledge their departure.

"Assaf, would you walk us out? We can give you the information on our agents who are following Degnan."

"Of course. Prime Minister, I will return shortly with the details."

Assaf nodded at the Americans, walking quickly out of the conference room. The men made their way through the corridor leading towards the front hall. The Vice President placed his hand on Assaf's shoulder, stopping him.

"Let's be clear. Israel's safety is important. But that will come once we control the surrounding countries. The President has made it very clear that he wants this, the U.S. to dominate this region in partnership with Israel. He wants this constant threat from these nations to be eliminated. Once we have our military presence, the Arab nations will protest, and eventually attack. This will give us reason to occupy these nations and suppress the insurgents."

"Do not worry about the Prime Minister. I will ensure he supports our plan. However, I should mention that the UN will not approve of these actions."

Cristy and Assaf chuckled together.

"I am not worried about the UN. They talk and squabble. When they grow a pair of balls, I'll pause before we rip them off. Besides, we've ignored them completely in the past. We've showed them that they have no power without us and what happened? Nothing. Besides, we plan on dissension from other countries. Let them dissent. What can they do? We do what we want to protect our borders, our people, and our way of life. End of discussion."

Despite his agreement with the Vice President, Assaf attempted to hide his disdain for the macho defiant words.

"Now what about this Degnan and this bullshit? Our men are following him and your men will meet his plane. Hopefully, within a few days, he will have it?"

Cristy smiled.

"Ironic that the man you wanted to eliminate turns out to be your best chance to get it."

Assaf looked back towards the conference room, ignoring Cristy's ribbing.

"I will meet you in Washington next week to continue our plans."

Assaf extended his hand and the men shook hands with one another. Cristy and Hansen walked through the entrance door towards their vehicle, a secret service agent opening the door for them. Assaf watched the men depart, an Israeli military jeep escorting their automobile.

Assaf rubbed his hand on his forehead. As the sun shined through the glass windows surrounding the door, a small bird caught his eye. The site of the creature made him smile momentarily. His wife had always reminded him to appreciate the small things in life, something quite contrary to his personality. Yet at this moment, he felt an overwhelming feeling of happiness. His mind drifted to the walks he used to take with his wife around their home, only a few blocks from his present location. He sighed deeply, recalling his favorite moments when she would casually walk passed him to inspect a flower, or a tree branch, a hint of her perfume would fill his nostrils, elevating him to a place of euphoria he had never been able to return to since.

During that time, Assaf smiled more, could enjoy the moments that sustained his wife's love, and care for all of God's creation. Despite knowing all Assaf had been through during his time in the Israeli military, she never stopped encouraging him to love others. When she was killed, the little love and peace Assaf possessed ceased to exist.

Suddenly, he slammed his hand against the front door to Gershom's residence, his anger violently emerging from his momentary respite from his present dealings. He quickly walked down the corridor towards the conference room and Prime Minister Gershom. Gershom watched Assaf sit down and begin to flip through his papers.

"I do not agree with an active offensive against our neighboring nations, Assaf. We are to secure our home, not begin a war."

Assaf, stopped flipping through his documents, his eyes remaining fixed on his papers.

"Prime Minister, what would you have us do? What exactly would you like to come from this treaty?"

Assaf stared at Gershom, angrily awaiting the old man's answer. Gershom paused, searching for his response. His vacillating viewpoints had him unsure as to what he essentially wanted.

"Assaf, I know what you think, but I am simply saying that I am not sure it is wise to launch any attacks against any Arab nations. I know what the U.S. wants. I understand. But I have concerns."

Gershom recognized Assaf's despair and anger, hoping to calmly express his opinion.

"Israel will be safe. These military bases and a campaign against the Muslim world will only strengthen us. The U.S. wants to control these nations. Since 9/11, the U.S. War on Terror has expanded. This will be the final expansion. Let them do what they want. This will only help us."

Gershom put his hands up in submissive acquiescence.

"Alright, Assaf."

Assaf stood up and collected his things.

"Let us focus for now on recovering the Sword. Once that has been located, we can worry about the dealings with U.S."

Assaf's reference to the Sword refocused Gershom.

"Agreed, what is our status?"

"We are right where we should be. Degnan will be brought here so we can plan with him. Then, with negotiation, he should lead us to it."

Gershom nodded in agreement.

"What about compensation for Degnan? I am sure he will not just gift his prize to us."

"He will be compensated. Every man has a price; I wouldn't worry about that."

"YOU KNOW, I GOT ALL SWEPT UP IN THIS SHIT that I forgot to ask; how we're going to get to Israel without passports?"

Frenchy leaned forward from his middle seat position, awaiting a response from the driver.

"Everything is taken care of. Mr. Botvinnik is a very powerful man. He has ensured that there won't be a problem leaving Nova Scotia and entering Israel. Your trip back to the U.S. is a different story. But I am sure he will make arrangements for your return."

Frenchy cocked his head in impressive agreement to Jacob's confidence.

"I'm convinced," he said looking over to Sarah.

"Let's not celebrate until we are safe in Israel."

Frenchy sat back, rolling his eyes at her cautiousness. Sarah reached into her bag and removed her Blackberry. She raised the phone to her head, drawing Frenchy's attention. Sarah shook her head, preempting any questions from Frenchy. He inspected her face intensely, awaiting a change to explain her actions.

"Hadodah hachavivah alay," Sarah said, smiling, as a loud response from the caller caused Frenchy to move back as he had inched closer to her.

"What the fuck is that . . . ? What'd she just say?" Frenchy said to Ali, looking somehow offended by Sarah as she continued to speak.

"It's Hebrew, Frenchy, Modern Hebrew."

"Better be," Frenchy said definitively, adjusting his jacket to assert some sort of dominance.

"Who are you talking to? Who are you talking to? Who are you talking to? Who are you talking to?"

Frenchy continued to repeat his question as he had moved closer to Sarah. She removed the cell phone from her ear and cracked Frenchy on his head, returning immediately to her conversation. Frenchy rubbed his forehead, a look of shock on his face. Ricky, who had been quietly observing the exchange, gestured positively towards his mentor, turning back to resume his sightseeing.

"Keep joking. Laugh it up; enjoy it. I'll drop your ass off at a Jew McDonald's; let you figure out your own way home."

"When will we be arriving in Israel, sir, and which airport?" Sarah asked, pausing her phone conversation momentarily.

"We should arrive early evening, around seven p.m. and I have been instructed to take you to *Beit Aghion* after our arrival. You will not need anyone to meet you at the airport."

"Who dat?" Frenchy asked, confused by Jacob's use of Hebrew.

"It's the residence of the Prime Minister," Sarah said, still irritated at Frenchy for his incessant questioning.

"Wait, I thought they were trying to kill me? Nope, stop the car Sherman." Frenchy panicked.

Sarah rolled her eyes and finished her conversation.

"I'll call again when we land to make sure someone meets us, regardless."

Ali nodded in agreement.

"No, we need to be out now!"

Sarah ignored Frenchy's outburst.

"Oh? So we won't be listening to me and my reasonable statement."

"It's too late for your whining. We're going no matter. Should have thought about that before getting in the car. And my people will watch us."

"Yes, of course. What a great idea; let's invite more of your family. Any of them as nasty as you?"

Frenchy's eyes widened, throwing his head from side to side sarcastically.

"Can I sit in my own section?" Ricky asked the driver. "It's like traveling with my little sister and brother; one ghetto and the other bitchy."

Frenchy and Sarah each produced a shocked and defensive facial expression, preparing to state their case against the other. Ali held his hand up quickly arresting their approaching tantrums.

"Perhaps you could make that two, sir. I would prefer to avoid the chance of catching a stray bullet from their gunfight."

Ricky reached back and encouraged Ali to slap his hand.

"No, no. I invented the high five. Only I may originate said celebration unless you pay me royalties."

Frenchy looked seriously at Ricky, until cracking a smile and winking at his perturbed student.

"But seriously, why'd you hit me? I was just messing around. You have no sense of humor; you're hot and cold. One minute happy with me, next slapping the shit out of me."

He tugged on his ears, attempting to produce a smile from Sarah.

"Please don't do that in front of the Prime Minister. Not just anyone gets your brand of humor; it takes a very, very special person to find your behavior funny."

Sarah sarcastically smiled, patting him on the back and shifting to get comfortable in her seat.

"What a bitch . . ."

"What did you say?" Sarah snapped.

"I said what a serious itch, itch, what did you think I said?" Frenchy stammered, as he scratched furiously at his neck.

"I swear I will . . ."

"Hey look—planes—we must be here."

Sarah reluctantly looked out of the passenger side window at a small airport.

"Halifax Stanfield airport. Isn't this exciting?" Ricky commented.

"Hella good, my brother. Jacob how is this going to work?"

"Relax, Dr. Degnan, all arrangements have been made."

The group assessed the airport as they approached a checkpoint leading to a restricted area.

"Oh shit, check point . . . prison . . . rape."

Sarah grabbed Frenchy's face, covering his mouth.

"Please, just normal Frenchy until we are on the plane."

Sarah released her hand slowly.

Jacob stopped and spoke with the armed guard, presenting his identification and additional papers. The guard casually looked at the forms and waved to the other guard to remove the flimsy barricade that obstructed their path. Frenchy looked back at the guards as their vehicle passed. He waved and smiled at the men, receiving a nod from the disinterested guards.

"Really, that was it? That's how you get past Canadian security. Not sure how I feel about that."

Frenchy shook his head scratching at his neck.

"Is that your serious itch again?" Sarah mockingly asked.

"You know, not that it matters, but again we really didn't think this whole thing through. I mean, seriously, how the hell were we going to get to Israel from Nova Scotia with no passports, no nothing?"

The group paused, seemingly in agreement about their poor planning.

"I mean, granted, it doesn't seem like it was hard to get past security, but we really didn't think that through."

"We would have managed. I told you I have some friends here. We would have made it out somehow," Ali said. Ali did not seem to find it necessary to dwell on a past mistake.

The vehicle made its way onto a section of the runway, approaching a small plane being fueled.

"That, Dr. Degnan, is your plane," Jacob said, pointing ahead.

"It's a bit small; is there anything larger available?"

Jacob turned towards Degnan, unsure if he was joking.

"This plane is reserved for your group only; there will be plenty of space for you. There will only be nine passengers."

"That sounds good. Planes like these are built to cross the Atlantic, correct? I mean they can make it, no problem, right?"

Sarah rolled her eyes.

"You have got to be kidding; you're afraid to fly as well? How exactly did you think you would ever be an adventurer? You're afraid to fly; you're afraid of boats. How's the car ride, everything okay?"

Frenchy sneered.

"One. Your mother. B. I'm being serious, like you asked, and I don't like you anymore. And four, Indiana Jones was afraid of snakes, and D, keep rolling your eyes. Look like you havin' a stroke."

Frenchy rolled his eyes and produced a large exaggerated smile.

"My sister just had a stroke," Sarah said straight faced, as the car stopped near the plane. She grabbed her bag and quickly exited the car. Frenchy rolled his neck creating a few cracking noises.

"Great, she makes fun of me no problem. I do it; I offend her."

Frenchy flopped his way out of the vehicle and towards Sarah.

"Okay, I'm sorry that was wrong, and I didn't know you had a sister who had a stroke; I was just joking."

Sarah dropped her head and slowly nodded in acceptance, putting her left hand on Frenchy's shoulder.

"That means a lot to me; thank you. I'm sorry, too, I didn't mean to make fun of your fears. Is that a fly?"

"Huh?"

Sarah backhanded Frenchy's crotch in one fluid move.

"Gotcha. Well, don't worry; I got the fly."

Sarah smiled and walked towards the stairs of the plane's entrance. Frenchy's ears became red, as he awkwardly hunched over and attempted to repress a squeal. His mind immediately flew to the last time he felt such pain. As a mild-mannered fifth grader, he stood in the playground during recess eating his ice cream as a few other classmates fought one another with umbrellas. Sadly, his preoccupation with his chocolate ice cream cone prevented him from noticing his friend hiding behind him, shielding himself from an oncoming attack. Needless to say, Frenchy unintentionally took the "bullet" for his friend, directly in the testicles. Sadly, the ice cream was also a casualty, as he dropped it upon umbrella impact.

Ricky gently patted him on the back, rescuing him from his memories.

"I know it hurts right now, Doc, and I know you are probably not looking on the bright side of this. But hitting is a sign of affection."

Frenchy looked up from his crouch and heaved a large sigh.

"Ricky, hitting is only affectionate when it is playful and above the belt. That was fuckin' Mike Tyson-style affection. Not cool."

"Well, shake it off, big guy; it's time to go."

Ali followed Ricky towards the plane, stopping to turn back towards Frenchy.

"You two have a very odd way of . . . flirting? Is that the word? Very peculiar courting rituals."

Frenchy pushed off from his knees and returned to a standing position, mockingly repeating Ali's words.

"Is there booze on the plane?" Frenchy asked, as the pilot greeted him.

"There can be, sir, if you would like."

"Good, I'll take all of it and a seat away from the crazy bitch who just got on."

"I will make sure that is arranged, sir," the pilot said, smiling, aware of what had just transpired between them. "But you may sit wherever you would like."

"Good, thank you, and a bag of ice for my balls and tickle tackle."

Frenchy walked up the six steps into the plane. He looked right to the passenger area. Ricky gave a thumbs up as he settled himself on a luxurious seat. He scanned the seats, Sarah's smile catching his eye.

"No hard feelings, Doctor," she said, smiling and patting the seat next to her.

Frenchy cocked his head and branded his middle finger.

"Of course not, no hard feelings," he said loudly, entering the main part of the cabin. "So hot and yet such a barking lunatic," he said, muttering through his teeth.

"THE TWO OF YOU HAVE TO STAY in the back of the plane. Degnan has seen both of you already, so you stay out of sight."

Espinoza and Forester fidgeted in their seats in the flight attendants' section of the small plane.

"This is particularly uncomfortable," Espinoza said.

"How long is the flight?"

"Long enough. Don't worry about that. This is a pretty easy assignment. We are on the exact flight as Degnan."

"It's remarkable what gets put together in such a short time," Espinoza said, alluding to the events of the last thirty-six hours.

"Believe me, if this were coming from me, it would take much longer. I told you when the big boys want something, they make sure things are arranged. Just make sure you guys stay right here and I'll ensure no one makes their way back here."

"So, what's the deal? We're still just tailing him?"

Jensen looked at his watch, peering into the cabin area where their targets were settling themselves.

"That's all. We monitor. Now sit tight; I am going to strike up a conversation with our new friend."

"Is that wise?" Espinoza asked, hinting at his disapproval.

"He has never seen me. I am not worried. Besides, I want to learn more about him."

"That's what I'm talking about. What would you say? We should never get attached or involved in our assignments."

"Trust me, he will not affect my decision-making or my ability to complete this mundane assignment. Besides, the more we know now, the better it serves our job."

Jensen stared back at Espinoza, signaling the end of their discussion.

"Enjoy, boys."

Jensen smiled and made his way into the main area of the cabin, sitting down on one of the seats facing towards the front of the plane. Frenchy's attention was drawn to the man's presence. He looked over at Jensen as he removed his Blackberry from his inside pocket. Frenchy's desire to share his excitement with everyone he met spilled out as he stared eagerly, hoping to solicit a response. Jensen looked up and nodded at Frenchy.

"What brings you on this flight?" Frenchy asked.

"I'm just here for security. The owner likes to make sure all things go smoothly."

"Well, no worries; just a couple of explorers here. We won't be any trouble. Francis Degnan."

Frenchy extended his hand to Jensen.

"Peter Wilcox. And that's always good to hear. You're an explorer?"

Jensen could not let such a comment go without questioning.

"Well, I'm an historian and my services have been retained by an antiquities dealer in Israel. This is my team."

Frenchy gestured to his companions.

Sarah took notice of Degnan's conversation and sternly looked at him, attempting to quiet his waterfall of information.

"Don't mind her; she's a bit of a handful," he said, turning to Jensen, shielding Sarah from his comment.

The engines started as Jacob entered the cabin.

"We should be leaving momentarily."

"So, what exactly have you been hired to do in Israel?"

"Well, did you hear about the new shit about Adolf Hitler's interest in other Judeo-Christian artifacts?"

"Yes, I did read something about that."

Frenchy shifted, preparing to explain his mission, happy to tell someone new about his quest.

"Well, I am the lone authority on the Sword of Goliath, Goliath the Philistine. I have been hired to retrieve the Sword for a private collector. I am told I will be compensated handsomely." Jensen nodded, attempting to show a modicum of interest.

"Where do you believe this artifact is?"

Frenchy smiled and waved his finger in the air.

"I would love to discuss the details but I must protect the location until I have found it. I hope you can identify with my position."

Jensen put his hands up, displaying his appreciation for privacy.

"Say no more. I understand completely."

Jacob walked over to Degnan, carrying a glass and a six pack of beer in his hands.

"Dr. Degnan, as requested. I am sorry we were unable to get you Guinness. We are left with a local amber ale. I hope this will be alright. It is called XV."

"Good ol' Roman numerals. Love it! Just pour it into my mouth," Frenchy joked, leaning back and pointing at his mouth. "No, I'm just kidding, but I won't need the glass. Thanks for getting it. What do I owe you?"

Frenchy knew full well Jacob would not accept any money, but he asked to highlight his importance to Jensen.

"Not necessary, sir. Enjoy."

Jacob placed the six pack on the small table attached to the side of Frenchy's seat. He returned to his own seat, as Frenchy opened his beverage.

"I'm curious, Dr. Degnan, what do you plan on doing with the Sword when you find it?"

"Well, it seems that's not up to me. Mr. Whatever-his-name-is says he's recovering it so it can be sold to a museum. As far as I'm concerned, that's fine by me. If I get money and credit, that's all I could ask for. It's a pretty good deal. You never want items of history to end up in private collector's hands. It robs others of the chance to see them, so this deal is perfect."

Frenchy took a large gulp of his beer, his bloated cheeks serving as a holding cell before he choked it down.

"Wow, that's quite a beer."

Frenchy coughed and looked at the label.

He placed the beer on the table and pulled a cigarette from his pocket.

"I'm sorry but I don't believe you can smoke on any plane." Jensen stared at him, wondering how he could fathom his actions appropriate.

"What? I thought this motherfucker was private. Hey, Jacob, is that true, I can't smoke?"

Frenchy held his cigarette up. Jacob looked over and sighed. He was beginning to grow weary of his travel companion.

"I suppose you could, sir; this is a private plane. But please keep it to a minimum. This will be a long flight."

Frenchy smiled and saluted him.

"No prob, Jake the Snake. I gotcha."

Frenchy lit his cigarette, winking at Jensen.

"When you're important you, get to bend the rules. Hey, when we taking off?"

"Momentarily, Dr. Degnan; we have only been on the plane for thirty minutes."

"True, I'm just excited to get started."

Jacob nodded, returning to the magazine he had begun reading.

"Put that out, what the hell is wrong with you?" Sarah said, becoming aware of Frenchy's recent action. "And don't drink. This is a time to rest, not drink yourself into a stupor."

"Relax there, sweetie; I will rest. And if you think a six pack will get me into a stupor, well then, you've never hung around with an Irishman. We drink until we fight and then fight until we can drink to numb the pain from the fights."

Frenchy smiled and waved his hand, attempting to send Sarah's attention away from him.

The plane began to move slowly. Jensen signaled to Frenchy to buckle his seatbelt. He nodded at him, securing the belt around his waist.

The plane picked up speed before momentarily stopping. The noise of the engines slowly began to roar and the plane launched into full speed. Frenchy gripped his open bottle of beer and reached down to grab the remaining beers, pulling them to his chest. Sarah looked over at him and shook her head in disapproval. Frenchy looked at her, seeing that he had caught her attention.

"What?"

"I hope the pressure pops the bottles and they spill all over you."

Sarah illustrated her hopeful scenario.

"You better hope not. If I don't have my beer, I won't get any sleep and you'll have to talk to me the entire flight and entertain me. Still want them to pop?"

Frenchy smiled, feeling as though he had successfully silenced her.

"You're right, I don't want them to pop, but maybe that poorly decorated gourd on your shoulders."

Sarah smiled sarcastically and turned away from Frenchy.

He faked a lunge at Sarah, returning to clutching his precious beverages.

"I'll pop you. Yeah, I'll pop you."

The plane touched off from the ground, and Frenchy smiled as he thought about how much closer he was to his dream.

"Yeah, buddy."

VICE PRESIDENT CRISTY exited the plane carefully, walking down the steps to the tar mat. He casually saluted the soldiers waiting at the bottom of the stairs. Hansen followed behind Cristy, walking swiftly over to a helicopter located about fifty yards from the plane. The men entered on the right side, settling themselves.

"It's late," Cristy said, wiping his eyes.

"It is, but I think we should brief the president immediately."

"I agree. I was just commenting on the time. Relax."

Cristy glanced out of the helicopter window as the propeller began to rumble.

"Do you think this Degnan will find the . . . shit, what's it called? Whatever it is they want?"

Hansen ran his fingers through his hair, pondering his colleague's question.

"Who gives a shit? It's of no concern for us. Bunch of superstitious bullshit. The treaty has been secured. That's all that matters now."

"I'm aware of that. I'm just curious. Our Jew friends seem to be very serious about it. It makes you wonder."

Hansen dismissed Cristy's curiosity.

"Let me tell you. Things only have meaning if idiots give it meaning. That sword means something only because they want it. Bunch of morons. That they're running around trying to find it, that they have invested money, time, effort into this is ridiculous. It's an old knife."

The helicopter slowly lifted off.

"You're not at all intrigued by their zeal?"

Cristy left his gaze and looked over at Hansen.

"You know, why I am not curious? Because there's always something with these people. They have been nothing but a problem. Who cares about their zeal? They want to chase a religious icon, let them. We always have to deal with the consequences of their actions. The Middle East is a mess because they had to have their Promised Land back. Now we are forced to deal with the terrorists who have been created by their actions. I have not and will not waste any time wondering about whether they'll get their precious steak knife."

Cristy chuckled, appreciating Hansen's humorous take on the situation.

"Well-put. Unfortunately, the world is filled with people who do care about things like this."

Hansen looked over at his companion. He knew that Cristy had much more experience than he did in foreign affairs and feared he was being drawn into a teaching moment.

"Relax, Frank. I am not disagreeing with you. I am simply pointing out that we cannot dismiss things as silly or superstitious. I think the whole thing is absurd. Just remember though, one man's absurdity is another man's passion. But you're right, in the end, it got us the treaty."

Hansen dismissed the brief lesson and looked out at the White House, lit up by flood lights in the distance. Though he did not appreciate being lured into a futile conversation, he recognized the point Cristy had made.

The helicopter slowly made its descent towards the White House, figures around the helipad began to emerge as it drew closer to the landing site. Cristy and Hansen quickly released themselves from their safety belts upon impact and made their way out of the helicopter. A middle aged man stood thirty feet from the helicopter, flanked by Secret Service agents. He wore a green polo shirt, firmly tucked into his blue jeans, his belt buckle prominently displayed. Cristy and Hansen approached the man, Cristy extending his hand.

"How'd everything go with old man Israel?" the President said, smiling, shaking each of their hands.

"Just fine, Billy, just fine; let's get inside and we'll get you up to speed."

"How about you there, Frank? You keeping this old Joe in line?"

The President casually jabbed at Hansen, attempting to humor him.

"Yes, Mr. President."

The trio walked across the South Lawn towards an entrance to the White House. They made their way through the White House towards the oval office, followed by Secret Service agents.

"I figured we should meet up here. I like sitting at my desk when I get good news," the President said, laughing, opening the door to the executive office.

Hansen sat down immediately on the cream colored couch and began sifting through his papers.

"Scotch, Joe?" the President asked, already preparing himself a drink.

"Of course."

"How about you, Frank? You want some good old Kentucky mash?"

"No, thank you."

The President shrugged, surprised anyone would turn down a drink. He took the two drinks and walked over to Cristy, handing him a full glass. He walked over to his desk and sat down, leaning back and sipping his drink.

"So, I assume everything has been settled?"

The President took a swig of his scotch, awaiting Cristy's response.

"Gershom squirmed a little, but he's a soft old man and easily convinced. Aside from that, it went well. Everything else is gravy."

The President took another sip of his drink.

"So, Operation 'My foot Up Your Ass' is a go?"

The President laughed, slapping his desk in appreciation of his joke.

"Yes, although we will have to find a more acceptable name."

Cristy raised his glass in agreement.

"Good, those towel heads killed Americans. It's time we repay them for that. Their hatred of America is despicable. It's time we show them who runs this show."

Hansen motioned for the opportunity to speak.

"It's important that, in the next few weeks, we lay out our evidence for the military bases. Once we have established the bases, I am sure the Jordanians and the Lebanese will provide all we need for an all-out invasion."

"That's the spirit, Frankie," the President said, raising his glass to Hansen, nodding at his interjection.

"What about the Saudis? I'm sure they will protest."

Hansen's thorough nature pushed him forward to ensure the success of the operation.

The President smiled at Cristy.

"The Saudis will have two options: support us or be occupied like the rest of their Muslim people. I have a feeling they will be happy to join us. But it won't matter; they will be occupied. I'm not going to leave anything to chance, no matter our past relationship. Besides, you can't trust an Arab. You can try to work with them but, in the end, they will always sympathize with other Muslims. So don't worry about that. Once we begin to roll through, no one will be able to stop us."

"Let's just make sure that our own people understand that without these bases, another attack is eminent."

Hansen's faith in the Vice President's ability was solid. Unfortunately, he lacked the same conviction for the President.

"Well, Frankie, that's where I have been doing a little thinking. There is no better way to show the need for these actions then with a little reminder of what could happen without them. Correct me if I'm wrong, but we have a burnt school and a bombed Jew's apartment."

Hansen nodded in agreement, uncertain of what the President was moving towards.

"And I believe the first attack on the World Trade Center came from men who were based in Jersey City? Well, that sounds like the makings of a good story. 'Muslim terrorists bomb Upper West Side apartment building and burn school.'"

Cristy sat up, intrigued by the president's suggestion.

"That's not bad, Billy. I also got word that Degnan is traveling with a Muslim cleric from Jersey City. Perhaps he is apprehended on his way back to the states."

The President took another sip of his drink.

"You know, Joe, that ain't bad. But let's include Degnan—a home grown terrorist who supports Muslims—now that's a gift that keeps on giving. Hell, we'll have people so worried about another attack that they'll be begging us to set up those bases. Where are these people, anyway?"

The President became increasingly excited as they formulated their plan.

"They are being trailed by FBI agents. They should be in Israel soon."

"Perfect. When they're done running around, our boys will apprehend them and bring them back and we will have ourselves our terrorists."

Hansen raised his hand, hoping to pause the planning.

"We were told that he is with a woman and a student? What about them?"

Hansen's question seemed to stump the president.

"Hell, I don't know, include them in the whole thing, too. Whatever, that's not that big of a deal. We can iron this out. You guys figure this out and we can move forward. We have time on this one."

The possible hiccup in the plan seemed to frustrate the simple-minded president.

"We will, Billy; we can get this together."

"Good, well, that's all for now; I'm tired. Let's plan everything out tomorrow. Just remember we keep this between the three of us. I don't want everyone in on this until it's a done deal."

The President took a last quick gulp of his drink and placed it on the tray to the right of his desk. He turned quickly and walked towards the door. He was joined by Cristy and Hansen, fumbling to get their things together after the abrupt end to their meeting. The three parted ways, the President stumbling momentarily as he walked down the corridor. Cristy turned to Hansen.

"Never challenge him when he's on a roll."

He smiled at Hansen and winked.

"I didn't expect such a quick end to our meeting," Hansen said, placing his papers in his briefcase.

"I know, but President Harris is . . . he's special. I've known him for years. He's a good man. But ride out his enthusiasm. Next time, don't question. Just go with it."

THE THREE MEN SAT QUIETLY at the small table, a few feet away from an old refrigerator. The silence was broken by the antiquated refrigerator turning over. Smoke filled the air as the men looked down at the table, each smoking a Turkish blend cigarette. One man quickly stood, walking over to a dirty window, above the kitchen sink. He looked at his watch and sighed, returning to his outward gaze.

"Why have we not heard from him? He should have contacted us by now."

A second man shifted in his seat, removing another cigarette from his pack.

"It is not always easy to communicate without worrying about possible wire taps. I am confident Balsam is taking all precautions to ensure privacy?" The man finished speaking, lighting his cigarette with a silver lighter.

"But what if he has been taken? Amir, you know that was a possibility. We should not remain here for much longer."

Amir took a long drag from his cigarette and looked over at his other companion, looking for aid with his present conversation.

"Ishmael, please remain calm. Samir and I share your concerns. But Balsam's propensity for caution has no doubt slowed his communication. We can move to the West as soon as we hear from him."

Ishmael looked at his watch again, not satisfied with his comrade's response. Amir stared at Ishmael, his eyes signaling to Ishmael to return to the table.

The lone cell phone on the table began to vibrate, each man jumping to reach for the phone. Samir picked up the phone and answered in Arabic. The two men stared intently at him, hoping to deduce the conversation's content from his facial expression. Amir took a final pull on his cigarette, stamping it out. The silence continued as Samir listened carefully.

"Understood. We will make the appropriate arrangements."

Samir closed the phone, placing it on the table. His companions stared impatiently, waiting for him to explain the long anticipated conversation. He lit a cigarette and wiped his brow.

"Balsam could not confirm Ali's information. There was no map in the box. It was empty."

The men sat motionless, attempting to understand their situation. Ishmael stood once again and walked over to the refrigerator, placing his hands on the top of the appliance.

"So, what does this mean?"

Ishmael's anxiety now turned to confusion, uncertain what their next step would be.

"I believe we continue with the operation. Regardless of the map confirming our information, we are already invested in the work. We must continue. We will not have much time after today."

Amir had been part of many plots and schemes during his life. He understood the time constraints and knew they must continue with their plan.

"But this could be all for nothing," Ishmael pressed, irritated at his companions ease with their decision.

Amir angrily stamped his cigarette out.

"Are you telling me that you doubt his information? He told us where to begin our excavations. I do not believe he would lead us astray. We must continue. In addition, as we come closer to possible interference, we have to be ready. Let's focus on that for now. Once he arrives, he may have new information but, more importantly, he will have the man who can give us the information we need."

Samir nodded in agreement, looking to Ishmael for a similar response. He deferred to his older colleagues and bowed his head to them.

"We need to increase our supplies and make our way out to Masada. We will have the rest of today and this evening to work before any chance of resistance."

The three began to collect their cigarette packs and cell phones before walking through the doorway of the kitchen and down the staircase to the first floor. They were greeted by a cluster of men, anxiously staring at them as they emerged from the last stair. Amir waved the men towards him and began to speak in Arabic.

"The time has arrived. We must ensure the protection of the dig site. Collect the weapons, all we can, and place them into the vehicles. Our duty to Allah, peace be upon him, is to protect the men working at Masada. We must ensure that we, not the infidel hoards that are trying to drive us from our homes, are successful. Submit to Allah's will."

The men nodded, evidently aware of the possible perils that they may face. The men walked towards the front door of the small house and exited, some men rushing to a small shed to the right. The group quickly removed from the shed various weapons and began to load them into five vehicles, parked fifteen feet away from the ammunitions shed. Ishmael joined the men in their work, Amir and Samir watching carefully.

"When is he scheduled to arrive with the American?"

Samir looked down at his watch.

"Not for a few hours."

"Good, we will travel to Jerusalem and watch them ourselves. I imagine few will expect us to be present. Once we make contact with him, we will be able to handle any location issues."

Amir approached the men, shouting instructions as they finished loading the last of the ammunitions and machine guns and began to enter their vehicles. Samir looked down at his cell phone and began to review the recent texts he had received from Ali. He opened the most recent message, scanning the text. He reached the last sentence and sighed tensely as he read the Arabic to himself.

"Leaving for Israel now, no resistance. Will contact when we approach Masada."

"I KNOW NOW you were always the love of my life, the person I was meant to be with. I know I let you leave. But I was messed up in the head. I didn't know what I was doing. Just please, come back to me. I can change; I will change."

Frenchy sat waiting for his wife's response. Turbulence on the flight caused him to grip the arm rests. Maggie sat across from him, her head in her hands, a faint sound of sobbing coming from her. Frenchy reached across, placing his hand on her knee.

She was dressed in the pair of jeans she wore the day they met. Her beat-up black sneakers made him smile despite her sobbing. He stood up and took a seat next to her. He had always found it amazing that her perfume, her shampoo, and her natural smell gave him somewhat of a natural high that seemed to calm him no matter what the situation.

He leaned towards her and kissed her shoulder. She turned away, keeping her hands over her face.

"I know you still love me; just give me another chance. I'm on my way to finding the Sword of Goliath. I'm finally going to be free of shame and depression. Once I find the Sword, I won't need to drink. I won't even want to. It will be the two of us for the rest of our lives. I'll even quit smoking; I know how you're allergic. It will be the way things should have been. Just believe in me."

Maggie removed her hands from her face, but remained with her back to Frenchy.

"I gave you so many chances to change. I can't be hurt anymore. I won't let you hurt me anymore."

Despite his confidence in his words, he was cognizant of all the chances she had given him to change his habits. He looked over at the half consumed six pack of beer resting at the base of his former seat. He stood up and grabbed the six pack.

"Look, these will be the last drinks I ever have. I'll finish this six pack and that will be it."

The anxiety of speaking to Maggie after so many months twinged his brain to reach for a beer.

"You see, you haven't changed. If you meant what you said, you would throw the beer out. But you still need to finish it. You can't just stop. It's always something."

Frenchy knew she was right and, for a moment, he realized he was hurting her once again. After months of crying and cursing himself about who he was, he finally had his chance to get her back and he could not stop himself from grasping one more drink. He set the beers on the adjacent seat and returned to his pleading.

"You're right. Look, I put them off to the side. I don't need them. Just please, give me one more chance."

Maggie wiped her face, still refusing to look at him. She sighed, attempting to compose herself.

"Francis, I cannot go back to you. I have met someone else. Someone who won't hurt me. Someone who cares about me and all the things I love and all the things I find important. He cares for me; he comes to my family's house and doesn't get drunk at my sister's birthday party. He likes to go to movies; he doesn't worry about when he can get a drink afterwards. He doesn't hide from life. He is everything you once were before you let alcohol consume your life."

Frenchy gritted his teeth. Her words instigated simultaneous feelings of anxiety and anger. He gasped for breath, in disbelief at what he was hearing. His hand began to tremble and he gasped again for air.

"You found someone already? Who is he? He is not me; he is not who you love. You're not supposed to be with him; you're supposed to be with me. Look at me and tell me who he is. He is not your future; I am. Tell me, who is he? I'll move to Pennsylvania. I'll move anywhere for you. He won't."

Frenchy clenched his fists, fearing that it was someone he knew. His jealousy began to overwhelm him. He grabbed a beer from the pack and forced the cap off with his hand, slicing his finger. He slammed the beer back down, becoming increasingly angry with Maggie's revelation.

"God dammit, who is it?"

Maggie turned slowly, pausing as she looked over at where Frenchy had been sitting. She sighed and looked at him.

"He's you when we first met."

She lunged at him and grabbed him by the neck. Frenchy fell from his seat, Maggie positioned above him.

"He's you before you threw our life away!"

Frenchy lay motionless, Maggie applying more pressure to his neck.

"I'm sorry," he mouthed, gasping for air.

"You lost me."

Maggie let go of his neck, sitting upright and still positioned on top of Frenchy.

"Fortunately, I'll make sure you never hurt anyone again."

She reached behind her and produced a small gun. Frenchy stared up at her face, stunned that it was no longer Maggie sitting on top of him. She cocked the gun and fired once directly into his chest.

Frenchy felt a strong pressure on his chest where he had been shot. He looked up at his killer, realizing that the woman sitting on top of him was Sarah.

"Now you can't hurt anyone anymore," Sarah said, standing up and dropping the gun on Frenchy's chest.

His chest burned as the pressure pushed down on him. He closed his eyes slowly as he reached up and clenched his chest. He felt darkness seep into his mind and he suddenly realized that he was seconds from nothingness. His mind raced through all the words that he had heard about death, realizing none of them were true.

He suddenly gasped and his body spasmed, quickly awakening from his nightmare. Sarah and Ali stood over him, a look of concern on their faces.

"Frenchy! Frenchy, are you alright?"

His eyes darted around the plane, suddenly realizing he had experienced a recurring nightmare that he so frequently had in the past. He stared at Sarah and Ali, seeing Jacob running up with a red bag.

"Francis, are you alright?"

He collected himself and sat up in the seat.

"Yeah, I'm okay. I just . . . had a bad dream."

Ali inspected his friend, aware that a heart attack at his young age was not implausible given his lifestyle.

Jacob removed a small oxygen inhaler and moved towards Frenchy, his hand blocking the inhaler's path.

"I'm fine, I really am. I have these nightmares all the time. They just happen; I don't know where it comes from. But seriously, I'm fine."

Jacob withdrew the inhaler and returned it to the bag, accepting Frenchy's resistance. Ali sat back in his chair, still concerned at what had happened.

"You were twitching and shaking. It didn't look good."

Sarah sat down next to him.

"What were you dreaming about?"

"I was nightmaring about . . . nothing. It doesn't matter. These episodes happen pretty frequently ever since I got my ass kicked a few years ago. I was beat up with bottles and shit. Messed my face and head up pretty bad. Broke a bunch of bones in my face and I had to get staples and stitches. Ever since then, I have nightmares about being defenseless or being attacked."

Frenchy chose to leave the part out about his ex-wife morphing into Sarah and trying to kill him.

"I'm sorry. Did they catch the guys who beat you up?"

"Actually, they did and they were convicted of assault. But when the prosecutor called and asked if I wanted to oppose the sentence of probation and try to petition for jail time, I said no. So they got probation."

Sarah stared at Frenchy, shocked at his leniency.

"Why didn't you object? It sounds like this wasn't just any old assault."

Frenchy wiped his face with his hands, still a bit dazed from the recent events.

"I don't know. I mean it's not like jail or prison changes a person for the better. Quite the opposite, actually. Besides, I think the guys were eighteen or nineteen. I don't know. Everybody deserves a second chance. They made a mistake, it shouldn't ruin their lives."

Frenchy reached down and picked up the last of the beers in the six pack, opening it and taking a drink.

Sarah stared at Frenchy, her view of him adjusted again at that moment, seeing that, at heart, he was a good person.

"I suppose you're right. Either way, that is definitely a selfless choice."

Frenchy chuckled.

"Very true. In truth, there was nothing I wanted more than to make sure they were punished, that they suffered. There was no better thought than thinking about them becoming some Mike Tyson inmate's bitch in prison. So I guess I'm not all that good of a guy. But nobody's perfect."

Sarah nudged him with her shoulder playfully, appreciating the return of a more genuine part of his personality.

"Well, we're about an hour out and we have begun to make the descent. Pretty soon, your chance to be a real life Indiana Jones will come true."

"Since, apparently, I'm on my period and being honest, I'm somewhat nervous. It was great when we were in the planning stages and even in the escaping-from-the-law stages. But the closer we get to actually doing this, well, I begin to lose faith in my ability."

Frenchy took another gulp of his beer, wiping his mouth and staring down at the ground. He remembered how long it took him to actually write his book, excited about the prospect of its success, but fearful about actually submitting it to be judged by others. This prevented him from actually sitting down and writing. He preferred the dream to the reality of possibly failing.

"Like I said, my father believed in you; I believe in you. Ricky looks up to you. Omitting allowing underage drinking, in this case with your own student, he has every reason to look up to you."

Frenchy looked up from hanging his head and gazed at Sarah. Despite their bickering back and forth, just a few words from her could lift his spirits.

He smiled bashfully, appreciating her beauty.

"So after we meet this Mr. Botvinnik and the Prime Minister, what then, Dr. Degnan?"

Frenchy picked up his tweed Irish cap, securing it on his head.

"My dear Sarah, we are off to Masada."

Sarah's expression changed, confused by his response.

"I thought you said it's not there? You said that's where you thought it was before you read the letter from my father?"

"I know, but since I have no idea what he meant, we may as well start where at least I had a clue. Besides, I have never been to Masada and I really want to go. Didn't we talk about this over champagne?"

Sarah smiled at his rising excitement.

"Okay. But I've got to tell you. You look more like an Irish dock worker than Indiana Jones."

"True and truer. But you can't be exactly like your hero; you need some Frenchy flavor to spice things up."

Frenchy began making clawing gestures towards Sarah while attempting to replicate the hiss of a tiger.

"You know, and I am being genuine, how many times must I say this? Just when I am starting to like you, you start acting like an idiot. I was even going to apologize for smacking you in the balls. But never mind."

Frenchy continued to joke until Sarah's words sunk in and he quickly changed his demeanor.

"Wait, I'm sorry. It's just I love to joke. I don't understand people. It's good to joke about stuff. Even the worst joke still provides a little laughter for someone."

Sarah sighed, unwilling to engage him on this debate.

"Hey, Doc, we are almost there! Get your motherfuckin' game face on."

Ricky pumped his hands in the air as the plane continued its descent.

A wave of anxiety attacked Frenchy's stomach as he realized the time for gloating had passed and the time for action was quickly approaching.

The passengers sat patiently as the plane approached the runway.

Frenchy gripped the arm rest, harboring an equal amount of dislike for both landing and taking off. The pilot slammed on the brakes the moment the wheels touched the runway. Sarah looked over and smiled at Frenchy, his eyes closed and body tense. The plane slowed enough for Frenchy to open his eyes, his entire body becoming relaxed upon his realization that they were driving no more than twenty miles an hour.

"Now, that wasn't so bad now, was it?" Sarah said, smiling and unbuckling her seat belt.

"What are you doing? We have not come to a complete stop. Get that belt back on."

He stared in disapproval as the plane came to a full stop, the clicks of the other belt buckles chiming in.

"You worry too much or not enough. I'm not sure. Either way, you have shown yourself to be a poor judge of when to worry and when to not."

Frenchy mocked Sarah to himself, undoing his own seat belt. Jacob walked up and signaled to the group to move towards the left-side exit. The pilot opened the exit door, signaling to someone outside. The group waited, Ricky smiling eagerly and dancing in place. The pilot waved the group towards him as he exited the plane, walking down the small portable staircase. Frenchy moved carefully towards the exit and looked out.

On the runway stood Eli Botvinnik in front of a black vehicle, flanked by two Israeli military vehicles. Frenchy hesitantly waved to the man. He shook hands with the pilot, as Mr. Botvinnik approached.

"Dr. Degnan, I presume?"

Frenchy smiled, appreciating the reference.

"You must be Mister . . ."

Frenchy mumbled a few syllables, attempting to fake recalling his new employer's name. Mr. Botvinnik looked curiously at Frenchy, not understanding his statement. Sarah extended her hand and began to speak to him in Modern Hebrew. She gestured to introduce Ricky and Ali to him. Ricky extended his hand.

"Nice to meet you, sir."

He looked over at Frenchy, widening his eyes, alluding to the proper way to greet someone whose name you may have forgotten.

Ali nodded at Mr. Botvinnik, cautiously looking at him and at the armed soldiers. Botvinnik mirrored Ali's suspicion, pausing for a moment before returning his attention to Frenchy.

"Welcome to Israel, Dr. Degnan, and to all of you. I hope you were comfortable during your journey?"

"Very. It's a nice plane. Very spacious, very clean."

"Well, I appreciate you coming on such short notice. I wanted to make sure I was the first to employ your services."

Frenchy nodded.

"Of course, not a problem. We were not really keen on spending too much time in Nova Scotia, anyway. I mean, let's face it: it's Canada, am I right?"

He looked over to Sarah for confirmation, his joking smile quickly retreating to a look of shame after seeing Sarah's expression.

"Please, if you would enter my car, we will travel to the Prime Minister's house. He is expecting you. He would like to extend his own appreciation for your willingness to help."

Frenchy bowed in agreement and encouraged his companions to enter the car ahead of him.

"Let's get moving before I say something else that's stupid," he said, muttering to Sarah as she entered the car.

"Now you're learning. See, look at that; I didn't even have to tell you that you were acting like a jackass. You did it yourself. I'm very proud of you."

Sarah looked up and smiled at Frenchy.

"I'm just a bit nervous and tired from the flight. Give me time; I'll get my flow back and you can get back to doing that yourself."

He entered the car, looking back at the military vehicle.

"What's with the soldiers?" Frenchy asked, who had forgotten to inquire earlier when he first took note of them.

"They are here for your protection. They will accompany you on your search. They are a precaution. You do not have to worry."

Frenchy shrugged, indifferent to the response. He looked out of the window, seeing Jensen standing near the plane.

"Shit, I didn't even get to say goodbye to that guy."

He lowered the window and stuck his head out.

"Hey, nice talking to you, however brief."

Jensen put his hand up.

"Best of luck to you on your quest. I'm sure our paths will cross in the future."

Frenchy saluted Jensen as the vehicles began to move.

"So where does the Prime Minister live anyway?" Frenchy asked, buckling his seatbelt.

"He lives in Beit Aghion in Jerusalem. It should not be a long ride," Jacob responded, remaining fixed on the military vehicle leading the caravan.

"Good, because I've got to pee."

Sarah quickly hit Frenchy, shaking her head in disapproval.

"Sorry Miss Lady, but I got to agree with the Doc. I need to pee as well."

Ricky nodded with slight discomfort.

"It doesn't stop with the two of you. Can't you just take a break from the crudeness and attempts at comedy?"

Frenchy nodded, understanding her frustration.

"I'm sorry. Would it have been better if I also mentioned that I have to shit?"

37

JENSEN SIGNALED FOR HIS TWO AGENTS to emerge from the plane. Espinoza and Forester slowly made their way down the stairs, exaggeratingly stretching from their long trip in the cramped attendant's section. Two cars pulled up to Jensen and a tall man stepped out of the passenger side of the second vehicle. He approached Jensen as Espinoza and Forester finally arrived from their slow saunter from the plane.

"Agent Jensen. My name is Isser Zamir. I am with the HaMossad leModi'in uleTafkidim Meyuchadim, or just Mossad—the Israeli . . . intelligence agency. We have arranged a car for you during your time in Israel."

Jensen shook hands with Isser and nodded in appreciation.

"These are my agents, Forester and Espinoza. They will be assisting me during my time here."

"I also have arranged a guide for you. He is very knowledgeable about Israel and the surrounding areas."

Isser gestured to a man sitting in the driver's seat of the first vehicle. The man looked up at Jensen, his demeanor stern.

"Does he smile?" Espinoza asked, taking note that their tour guide seemed frozen.

"I assure you that Ephraim is one of the best." Isser stood firmly, defending his colleague.

"I'm sure he is. I meant no disrespect." Espinoza quickly backtracked, not expecting Isser to take his comment to heart.

"Yes, well. He will take you to a hotel near the Prime Minister's home. My understanding is that they will not be traveling today as the night is upon us. They will be leaving in the morning towards the east at seven o'clock. Ephraim will return by six fifteen a.m. to bring you to Beit Aghion." Isser opened the passenger door, signaling the end to the conversation. Espinoza and Forester entered the back of the vehicle as Jensen shook hands with Isser and entered the front seat. The trio settled themselves and Jensen removed his Blackberry and began to dial. "We have arrived in Israel, and are on our way to Jerusalem."

Jensen paused, listening intently. Espinoza leaned forward and offered his hand to Ephraim.

"Thank you for assistance."

Ephraim looked back and slowly shook Espinoza's hand.

"I'm agent Espinoza and this is Agent Forester. Our director is the gentleman sitting next to you."

"It is nice to meet you. I have heard that you are monitoring another American?" Espinoza seemed shocked at Efraim's flawless English.

"Correct. Just monitoring him though. Our interest is to ensure his safety during his time in Israel."

Espinoza's explanation drew no response from Efraim.

Jensen ended his conversation and turned to face his agents.

"Things have changed once again."

Espinoza and Forester leaned forward, eager to hear what new wrinkle had developed.

"It seems that, provided that Dr. Degnan is successful, we are to apprehend him and his companions and bring them to our office in New York City."

Espinoza sat back scratching his head in confusion.

"I gotta tell you, this is bordering on the ridiculous."

Forester who had never wavered in his allegiance to his mission, nodded in agreement.

"I mean, this is really ridiculous. None of this has made sense; I have no idea who is calling the shots. It's coming from high up but, in truth, how could it? This whole thing is one big waste of time. Not to mention we are FBI agents in a foreign country. This isn't even our fuckin' jurisdiction, to say nothing about the fact that the more we learn about this stupid case, the dumber this whole thing seems. And, oh yeah, let's not forget the fact that we are following a high school teacher who, based on his apartment and our interactions with him, is hardly worth our time."

Espinoza attempted to quell his frustration, aware that no matter how he felt, Jensen was still his boss. Jensen remained still, contemplating a response to what he felt to be a fair assessment of the situation.

"Perhaps . . . maybe we use our own discretion on this one. If we are being told to follow this crew of misfits, we do exactly that. But it might be time we listen to the other side of the story."

Espinoza looked over at Forester, unsure as to what their boss meant.

"I don't really see what you are getting at . . ."

Jensen raised his hand signaling Espinoza to stop.

"We can discuss at another time."

Jensen turned and stared at his two agents, hoping to convey his desire to end the conversation with a piercing stare.

Forester signaled to Espinoza by looking over at Efraim. The silence was broken by the ring from Jensen's phone. He viewed the number before answering.

"What is it?"

Efraim, who had been driving quietly throughout Espinoza's rant, nonchalantly looked over at Jensen.

"We'll keep an eye out."

Jensen ended his conversation and returned the phone to his inside jacket pocket.

"Another one of ye old wrinkles, boss?" Forester asked.

"A wrinkle? Not sure. But you know how it is; what shirt is ever perfectly pressed?" Forester rolled his eyes at the poorly placed metaphor. Espinoza leaned forward and spoke quietly to Jensen.

"Maybe this shirt is too wrinkled and might not be a good fit for us."

Jensen looked over at Efraim.

"Maybe."

"AW, HELL YEAH, now that's what I'm talking about," Ricky said, looking up at the front of the Prime Minister's home.

"I like the arches."

Frenchy joined his student in observing their destination.

"I could take it or leave it. But the arches are pretty badass. Either way, it beats my apartment in my grandmother's house."

Ali shifted uncomfortably.

"I'm sure they do not entertain people like me everyday."

"Would you relax? You're with me. I got this, no problem. Besides, they are not going to do anything to you when they need my help. I would refuse to help them. Trust me."

Frenchy patted Ali on the back and returned to his inspection.

"Holy shit! Are those bars on one of the windows? Ah yes, reminds me of home." Frenchy smiled, reminiscing about his domestic fortress.

"Bars on windows. That's good. Bars on windows make you nostalgic for Jersey City. You Jersey boys are an odd breed," Sarah said

Ricky looked over at Frenchy, the two simultaneously smiling and nodding in approval. The car stopped in front of the entrance door, Assaf awaiting their arrival with two attendants.

"Time is money," Frenchy said, as the car door opened.

He stepped out and stretched, taking in his surroundings. Assaf approached quickly and greeted him.

"Prime Minister, I presume?"

"I apologize, sir. My name is Assaf. I am an advisor to the Prime Minister. Welcome to Beit Aghion."

Assaf greeted Sarah and Ricky, stopping short when his eyes fell upon Ali. The two stared at one another, aware of their familiarity. Assaf broke the standoff and nodded, Ali returning the small gesture of respect.

Assaf turned to one of the attendants and spoke quietly to him.

"Mr. Botvinnik, I am sure you will be pleased to recover such a valuable artifact. It would seem you have the right man."

Botvinnik walked over to Frenchy and placed his hand on his shoulder.

"I am sure all of Israel will rejoice, thanks to our American friend."

Frenchy put his arm around Botvinnik.

"Sure thing, Mr. B. Is there a bathroom around here?"

"I must apologize, how rude of me. This way. Please, let us get your bags."

Frenchy's eyes widened.

"Turns out we don't have any. Been in the same outfit for over forty hours now. We, uh, left in a hurry; we were just so excited to start our journey."

Frenchy forced a laugh and pointed to his pants. Assaf smiled at Frenchy's babbling.

"Well, please, we will make sure to get you some new clothes and clean what you have. The Prime Minister has been awaiting your arrival. Let me take you to your rooms so you may prepare for dinner."

Assaf turned and walked towards the front entrance, the group following. Ricky leaned in and whispered to Frenchy.

"Doc, what does he mean prepare for dinner?"

Frenchy shrugged his shoulders.

"I don't know. Maybe that's his way of saying that we smell. Just go with it. We can get some new clothes and a shower."

The group entered the main hallway. Directly in front of them was a large staircase with a decorative metal railing. Frenchy scrunched his face in disapproval.

"Art Deco, gross."

Sarah gave him a nudge as Assaf led the group up the staircase.

"Ms. Tannen will stay in this room; the gentlemen's rooms will be down to the right. We will arrange for some clothes to be brought to you as you . . . freshen up, as you might say."

"Much obliged, sir. Thank you. Do you need to know our sizes or anything or do you need a credit card? How about an IOU?"

Frenchy reached for his wallet in his attempt to be polite.

"That won't be necessary, and I am sure we will be able to find something that will be suitable for dinner. By that time, your clothes will be clean."

Assaf gestured to one of the attendants and they quickly walked down the staircase. Frenchy turned to his companions.

"Alright, let's get clean, wait for the clothes, and then we can have dinner with the big man himself."

Ali looked down at his watch.

"I assume we will not be going on our search tonight."

"I guess not, but that might be a good thing. I think we are all a bit tired and worn. Let's relax and we can start in the morning. If Bot—whatever his name is—doesn't mind, then we shouldn't. So let's try to enjoy ourselves. It's not every day that we get a chance to be hunted and then pampered in no time at all."

Ali looked suspiciously into his room.

"I guess you're correct."

"Alright, until later, gentlemen," Sarah said, walking into her room and closing the door. Ricky quickly darted for his room and let out a joyful yell. The continuation and improvement of this journey gave him a jolt of excitement. Frenchy tipped his hat to Ali as they both entered their rooms. Ali slowly turned his head, watching Frenchy close the door. He immediately looked around, assessing his surroundings. He moved quietly towards the staircase and peered down towards the entrance door. He crept down into the hallway, peering out through the small window in the door. The military vehicles had moved on from the front entrance and there remained a single attendant.

Ali opened the door slowly and stepped outside, walking briskly upon realizing his departure could be made without notice.

In the window to the left of the main entrance stood Assaf, watching Ali's escape. He moved away from the window, walking into the adjacent room.

"Did he leave?" the Prime Minister asked, sitting in a burgundy arm chair in the corner.

"He did. If I recall correctly, he had minor involvement in the planning of the Binyamina train station bombing. He is not Hamas; I believe he is Palestinian Islamic Jihad. We did not have knowledge of his location."

"I suppose it does not matter. He obviously will fade away. He has no way of returning to the U.S. so he is of little importance right now."

Gershom stood slowly, approaching his advisor.

"A bit strange that he would be the man Degnan would go to for help. Perhaps there is more to his presence than we are aware of."

Gershom waved at Assaf, dismissing his concern.

"You worry so, Assaf. Regardless of who he is, it does not affect our plans. Degnan will travel with military protection. Any fear of our treasure being possessed by a Muslim is unrealistic."

Despite Gershom's confidence, Assaf's apprehension prevented him from shrugging off the threat.

"Please make sure the attendants provide our guests with the clothes they need."

"It is already being completed."

"Very good. Then let us enjoy a drink while we wait. We have much to celebrate. The good Doctor has finally arrived."

"I WILL RETURN IN THE MORNING. SIX FIFTEEN A.M."

Efraim closed his door and drove away from the FBI agents.

"What a pleasant chap, he is," Espinoza said sarcastically. Jensen turned to him and put his hand on Espinoza's shoulder.

"Never divulge any information in front of anyone you don't know. We have no idea who he is. And, moreover, who he is talking to. Pull yourself together."

Jensen walked briskly into the front door of the Alcasann Hotel. Forester turned to Espinoza, hoping to support his partner.

"He's right, but I know how you feel. Let's just get on with it."

The two agents followed Jensen's path, joining him at the reception desk.

"Here are your room keys. Drop your things off and come to my room, 413, and *then* we will discuss our mutual concerns."

The trio walked over to the elevator bay as one arrived.

"Wait, we are sharing a room?" Espinoza said, startled by the same room number on Forester's key.

"Budget cutbacks. Wars cost money. Besides, just put an ironing board in the middle of the bed. That way you two girls don't end up spooning each other."

Despite disliking sexist remarks, Jensen could not resist jabbing at his agents.

"That shit's not funny and there better be a second bed."

Jensen smirked and opened his room; Espinoza and Forester apprehensively opening theirs, praying to see a second bed. They both sighed in relief and entered their room. They dropped their bags, Forester utilizing the bathroom. They emerged quickly.

They walked down to Jensen's open door and entered, joining him at the circular mahogany table next to the TV console. Jensen opened the small minibar and removed two beers and two nips of Jack Daniels. He encouraged his agents to help themselves. The three opened respective drinks, Espinoza and Forester cautiously taking their first sips. Jensen opened one of the whiskey nips pouring it into a small glass, immediately drinking the contents in one gulp.

"So, I think we're in agreement that everything that has taken place over the past forty-eight hours has been or has become bullshit."

Espinoza and Forester looked hesitantly over at each other, unsure how to respond.

"Well, yes, like I said before, and you were right that I should have used better judgment. But let's just look at this whole thing. I assume you were given this assignment to ensure the delivery of a small bomb to Degnan. For, as we were told, he was a threat to national security and needed to be eliminated immediately. Yes, we failed and, for whatever reason, nothing happened. Whether it was tampered with, whatever, but it ends up killing a rabbi. We then are told not to hurt Degnan; simply bring him in. He believes completely that we need him to help his government. I mean, he completely buys into it. Then he ends up running from us. After a bunch of shit that I consider lucky on his part, he gets away. You get bashed over the head while in the dead rabbi's apartment and the government suddenly rescinds everything; no problem with Degnan, one big misunderstanding. But we need to follow him. So we do. And now, we are told we must detain him after he discovers what will boil down to some stupid museum trinket. Did I leave anything out? And, yes, bullshit."

Espinoza looked around, hoping for any response.

"You forgot to mention I got cracked in the head."

Forester seemed slightly offended by his partner's omission.

"Sorry, that's right. Forester gets bashed as well. Anything else?"

Jensen opened the second nip.

"No, that is a fair and accurate recounting of the events from our point of view."

"Well then, I stand by the statement that this is a waste of time, ridiculous and—I'm sorry—but that drunk Irishman, a threat? Go visit his apartment. From the looks of the place, he's a fuckin' deadbeat."

"He's right. The guy is an idiot."

Forester concurred with his partner.

"What I know is, this has to do with a treaty between the U.S. and Israel. For what? Who cares. But this may be more than just a silly mission. This may be a vendetta. In said deadbeat's book, he argued strongly for a free Palestinian state and strongly criticized the Israeli government, chastising the UN for their inaction. Now, his book was ridiculed for lacking hard evidence. But that had nothing to do with his opinions. The book may have been the butt of historians' jokes, but people did cite his reasoning for a free Palestine. I imagine that's how he ended up with the Muslim as a companion. If we remove ourselves from this and examine the entire sequence of events, I think we can find one truth. It seems no matter what, we or Israel want to discredit and embarrass him. Dead or alive seems to depend on the moment."

"But, if that's true, then it's for his opinions, not him as a threat, that they have placed a price on his head. As much as I don't particularly care for him, what we're doing is not right."

Forester leaned back in his chair and looked at Jensen, subconsciously trying to distance himself from Espinoza's comment.

"And that is why we execute our mission, but we use our own judgment as we go. I'm sure we will find out more when we finally apprehend him. Either way, it seems that he is oblivious to what is happening. Still, in the end, we will follow through on our charge. I defer to our government officials. If this came from the top, and it seems it did, then we will trust them, not as you said, a 'drunk Irishman.'"

Despite their boss's return to somewhat absolute obedience, they understood the importance of following their orders and completing their assignment.

"I agree. Let's stay the course. Shit, I'm not getting fired for going soft on this guy."

Espinoza reluctantly agreed, knowing it was the correct course of action, yet still unsure.

"So let's relax for the night; we have an early morning. Meet out front tomorrow at six fifteen and we will proceed."

Jensen finished his last sip of whiskey and stood up, signaling the end of their meeting. Forester and Espinoza finished their drinks and stood up to leave.

"And Carl . . ."

Espinoza turned, as Forester continued out of the room.

"I really do understand how you are feeling. I have had assignments such as this in the past. I get it. And since we are well out of our jurisdiction, let's take that into consideration."

"Thanks boss," he said, leaving Jensen's room.

RICKY EMERGED FROM HIS ROOM and knocked on Frenchy's door.

"Doc, you ready?" he yelled through the door.

Frenchy opened the door and stared at Ricky, each evaluating the other's new clothing selection.

"You've gotta be shittin' me. We look like goddamn twins," Frenchy said in disgust, observing Ricky sporting the same green button down shirt and beige pants. If Ali is wearing the same thing, then I have a new complaint against Jews."

Frenchy closed his door and walked over to Ali's, knocking loudly.

"If you have beige pants and a green shirt on, you're sure as shit not invited to dinner. I'll bring you up a matzo ball later. So come out."

Sarah's door opened and she emerged, wearing a cream colored dress with a subtle floral pattern delicately woven throughout. Frenchy stared, enamored by Sarah's beauty. Her long black hair gently rested on her shoulders. Sarah stared into Frenchy's eyes, aware that he seemed consumed by her presence. She dropped her head and smiled shyly, his stare making her slightly self-conscious.

She looked up and back at Frenchy, producing a confused look momentarily before bursting into laughter, exchanging the previous tender moment for the hilarity of her companions' outfits.

"Don't start. Your people did this," Frenchy said, knocking again on Ali's door.

"The outfits look good; it's the fact that they gave the two of you the same outfit."

"No? Really? Whatever. I want my clothes back. There is no shot in hell I am wearing this tomorrow. Look like I should be going to a country club."

Sarah arched her left eyebrow in disagreement with Frenchy's statement.

"I wouldn't go that far. You are still wearing a wool driving cap and beat-up maroon Doc Marten boots. Like you said, there is some Frenchy flavor in the generic outfit."

Frenchy resumed to his banging on Ali's door.

"What the hell?" He turned the doorknob and entered the room slowly. "You better not be butt-ass naked."

Frenchy looked around the room and listened carefully. He emerged from Ali's quarters and shrugged.

"He's not in here."

"He must be downstairs already. Let's roll. We don't want to be late."

Ricky's comment encouraged the group to make their way down the front staircase. An attendant awaited them at the bottom, directing them to the dining room to his right. They walked into the dining room and were greeted by Assaf, Eli Botvinnik, Gershom, and two other gentleman standing with them. They eyed the dining table arranged to seat nine people. Assaf walked over to them and assessed their new outfits.

"Good evening. It seems everything fits. My apologies for the repeat, but we put this together quickly. May I introduce you to the Prime Minister Yitzach Gershom."

Frenchy shook the Prime Minister's hand.

"An honor to meet you, sir. This is one of my students, Ricky Badaracco, and my . . . um . . . special lady friend, Sarah."

He winked at her, hoping she would understand his movie reference.

"Very pleased to meet you both. These are two of my advisors, Saul and Tovla. They will be joining us for dinner as well. And, of course you know Mr. Botvinnik, who is responsible for all this. Please sit. You must be hungry and exhausted from your trip."

Frenchy sat down next to the head, with Sarah and Ricky taking seats to his right. Gershom sat at the head of the table, his advisors sitting directly to his left.

"I feel like we're about to play fancy flip cup," Frenchy joked, as they all seemed to sit lined up across from the other. "You're the judge," Frenchy said to the confused Prime Minister. Frenchy looked down towards Ricky and Sarah, realizing that Ali was not with them.

"Oh yeah, have you seen my friend Ali? I completely forgot that he wasn't up in his room. We thought he would be down here already but obviously he's not."

Assaf stared at Frenchy, his eyes not wavering.

"I am sorry, but I have not seen him. Perhaps he had other matters to attend to."

Frenchy shook his head at the vague and seemingly illogical answer.

"What business? He wasn't planning to come here; he was with me. I'm pretty sure he doesn't have any appointments."

"Well, I'm sorry, but no one has seen him."

Frenchy shrugged, realizing there was no point in the conversation.

"I don't know. He can be strange sometimes. I'll call him later."

Attendants began to bring various dishes and place them in front of each guest.

"What the hell is that?" Frenchy said, in disgust, at a dish placed near him.

Sarah kicked him under the table, warranting a squeal from Frenchy.

"Is there something wrong?" Gershom asked, aware that Frenchy's question was not positive in nature.

"Everything's fine, Prime Minister. Francis is not very cultured and so new foods sometimes scare him."

She patted his belly and continued.

"But as you can see, he will certainly eat it."

Frenchy's mouth opened in shock at the sharp insult thrown at him. Ricky snorted to himself, attempting to keep his composure. Frenchy leaned into Sarah.

"You think I'm fat?"

"You commented on your weight earlier; it's wrong if I do?"

"Well, yeah, just because I think I'm fat doesn't mean I am. That was cold as ice."

Frenchy frowned, attempting to garner attention from her.

"Anyway, seriously, what's that?"

He realized he was not receiving the attention he wanted so he returned to his original query.

"They are stuffed vine leaves. Seriously, please don't embarrass me."

"Stuffed with what? Looks like a couple of lily pads from the pond in Lincoln Park, and I don't need to tell you what people do in that pond."

Sarah shook her head at his comments.

"No disrespect to your food, Prime Minister, it's been a while since I ate fancy foods. My dad always used to make exotic dishes that often made me cry as a kid. This is bringing back all kinds of memories."

The Prime Minister smiled at Frenchy's attempt to humor him.

"I understand. I have not had a dinner guest such as you in a long time. Well, unless my grandchildren visit."

"Thank you; I know how they feel. They're wise individuals," Frenchy said, reaching for a piece of pita bread.

"Yes, well, ten-year-olds can be very picky." The table began to chuckle, appreciating the Prime Minister's jab at Frenchy. "Still, I assure you the tilapia is the best you will ever have."

Frenchy's disdain for fish was exacerbated when a full fish was placed in front of him, a small portion of Israeli couscous next to it.

"Hell no, who prepared this?" Frenchy looked towards the kitchen, exaggerating his question.

"Hey lady, the fish is lookin' at me; shouldn't you have defaced him or something. I don't really like to get too familiar with my food, you know; eye contact is strictly forbidden."

The rest of the dinner party seemed satisfied with Frenchy's jokes for the evening and resumed eating and chatting.

"I'm serious, the freaking thing is looking at me. I can't eat that," Frenchy whispered to Sarah.

"Eat it and shut up. Your act has run its course; this isn't funny anymore."

Sarah returned to her plate, ignoring Frenchy's look of disbelief.

"So, Dr. Degnan, thank you again for your willingness to help Eli with the recovery of this artifact. Israel has a rich history, its people and the things they have left behind. Eli has told me that he has a small fragment that may help you in your search."

Botvinnik removed a small folder from his bag and pulled the aged fragment and passed it to Frenchy.

"Perfect, I can focus on this and not the creepy fish," he said, muttering to himself. He studied the piece of paper, sighing.

"Dear, would you be a doll and translate this for me?"

Frenchy passed it over to Sarah, forcing a smile.

"Sure, snookems."

She studied it for a moment and finally began to read aloud.

"Ninety meters south of snake path gate at the base of the . . . old marker that helped locate the . . . two miles southwest of the old . . . near the entrance to the . . . marked by a large . . . find the . . ."

Frenchy rolled his eyes at Sarah's translating skills.

"So anyway, this won't help at all because it's not even half a description, it's sliced down so the more you need the information, the less it says. I'm pretty sure it's referring to Masada because of Snake Path Gate. Don't know what marker would be there but, knowing your father, he had a propensity for fantasy and adventure."

The Prime Minister cocked his head; Frenchy's reference to Sarah's father made him pause.

"This whole description is written like it's directions to some lost treasure. I have a feeling the whole map could have been summed up by saying, 'at the base of Masada near Snake Gate Path, find sword.' But please, I am not complaining about the theatrical way he described it. Very cool. I would have done the same thing. But who's half is this, Judah's or Tannen's? Where is the other half?"

Assaf stopped eating and looked sternly at Frenchy, apparently missing his earlier reference. His sharp gaze was interrupted by the Prime Minister's look of concern, subconsciously poking Assaf. The Prime Minister returned to his plate and looked down at his food.

"It seems you are quite familiar with this artifact and its recent history. Tell me, how did you know they had mapped the location?"

Frenchy smiled and raised his glass of red wine, pausing to look at it before taking a sip.

"Is there something wrong with that? After all, wouldn't you want the man who will find this treasure to be knowledgeable about all aspects of said artifact."

Assaf's piercing look faded as he assumed Frenchy knew little more than the existence of the map.

"Anyway, it doesn't matter about the map. If you have the time and the man power, I'll find it. We should start at Snake Gate Path and go from there. We won't stop until we have it. Agreed?"

The Prime Minister looked over at Assaf and nodded a few times, satisfied with Frenchy's resolve.

"You will have what you need," Assaf said, bowing his head slightly to Frenchy.

"I like these eastern countries; everybody nods seriously to say 'yes.' Amazing!"

He raised his glass of wine, holding it near the center of the table, his fellow dinner guests joining him.

"To Goliath and David: if they hadn't tussled, his sword would mean nothing. I've been waiting my whole life for this. And to Mr. B, our patron on this adventure, for making this possible."

Frenchy's behavior seemed to comfort his hosts. He looked over at Sarah and winked. She smiled, impressed again that his silly, adolescent jokes could give way to a sharp charismatic alter ego.

Frenchy glanced down at his food and winced in disgust; he looked over at an attendant and signaled quietly for more wine.

"So, Dr. Degnan, you travel with interesting company."

"Not necessarily on purpose. Truthfully, because of an unfortunate misunderstanding, I had to leave New Jersey quite quickly."

Sarah nudged Frenchy under the table, hoping to disrupt him from divulging anymore details from her father's letter and their escape.

"In truth, Doctor, I am not referring to your present company. I was just curious how you ended up with . . . was it, Ali?"

Frenchy smiled, understanding possible suspicion from his Israeli hosts.

"He's an old friend who helped me on some of my interfaith work at Saint Ignatius. You know, trying to bridge the gap between various faiths through the understanding of history. But no worries, he's a good man. And not what you think. He's no extremist."

"Well, it is interesting you should be focused on interfaith work. In your book, you spoke quite critically of Israel and their treatment of the Palestinians. I'm sure your friend helped you arrive at that view. And that appears less like an unbiased viewpoint."

Assaf saw his opportunity to breech the subject of Frenchy's political views. Frenchy took a gulp from his glass, glancing at Sarah, surprised by Assaf's bold question.

"Well, in truth, Ali had nothing to do with the formation of my opinions regarding the Israel and Palestine conflict. Much of that comes from my father's work at the United Nations and my years of studying history."

"Then your studying of history, I am sure, has highlighted the repeated attacks on the Jewish people as well as our rightful claim to our land?"

"Certainly, Jews or Israelis have been oppressed but, in truth, many people have been oppressed, attacked, killed. Shit, most people have been oppressed at some point. But that does not give anyone a free pass to do the same to others. Particularly given the fact that Israel has violated UN Resolution 181 stating that there must be a free Israel and a free Palestinian state. From what I understand, there is no Palestinian state. Israel is not completely at fault and responsibility must fall on the UN, thus the world, but Israel's actions over the past sixty years certainly have not looked like a peaceful resolution of this issue."

Sarah smiled to herself. Despite not agreeing with Frenchy, she was impressed by how well he articulated his points.

"You look to be Irish, Dr. Degnan. Am I correct?" Assaf said, glaring at Frenchy.

"Half-Irish; the other half might surprise you."

Frenchy grabbed his glass, fearing the discussion was moving away from a cordial back and forth.

"Well, based on your cap, your reddish hair, and your propensity for the drink, let's assume you identify with that side. The last time I was in the U.S., I saw a sticker on a vehicle that said, 26+6= 1. I had to ask an associate what it meant. It seems it refers to the Republic of Ireland's attempt to regain the six northern counties that remain part of Great Britain. For years, both sides have spilled blood, fighting for what they believe to be their land. I suppose you would say that Ireland has no right to take back *their* land?"

Frenchy sighed, knowing the debate over Northern Ireland might be an argument point.

"Honestly, I know how you feel. I really do. You may not believe that but I know, as a student of history, the injustices that followers of Judaism have had to face. I'm Irish; I get it. I have, in my home, a framed 1889 cover of the New York newspaper, the *Puck*. The cover has a normally drawn nativist "white" next to an Irishman who was drawn to look like a monkey."

Assaf raised his hand, hoping interject.

"No, I know, it's not the same. I agree. But here's the thing: The Irish have been shit on for hundreds of years. The famine of 1847 affected the potatoes. Problem is, there were other crops that were unaffected but they were exported out of Ireland. Millions left their homeland or were starved."

Frenchy shook his head, realizing he was losing his focus.

"But never mind that. The Irish were "colonized out" in the six northern counties. Yes, when the Republic was established, it was natural to believe that they should reunite the entire island. But today, the people who live in Northern Ireland are not responsible for what happened to the "native" Irish. And they weren't even the original Irish either. I don't know who is indigenous anymore. But the Protestants in Northern Ireland? They didn't colonize these counties. Those counties *are* their homes. They aren't the people who took the land in the first place. They are what's left when time has passed. Should their claim be less significant than those who believe the land should be under the Republic of Ireland? And truthfully, I don't think either side is right, and no issue is so black and white as I am saying. But no one is willing to listen to the other side. That is the greatest problem in all conflicts. No one will hear, and I mean hear, the other side and value their opinions and views. Instead, we are deaf. We hear nothing but our own agendas. In Ireland, they fought for years, killing in the name of their "own" claim. Yet, only now are they realizing they can coexist without one side winning. But how long will it last? It is the leaders that can change that. Leaders, and the average person, who can't live out political views. They have to learn to coexist. So you ask me: does the Republic of Ireland deserve the six northern counties? No. Because the injustice of the past cannot be made right by retaliatory action in the present. Israel had their promised land and it was taken from them. But again, you cannot make up for past wrongs by wronging in the present."

Frenchy looked around the table, realizing that he had drifted into the negative realm he had so vehemently opposed.

"I'm sorry. I just did everything I just said was wrong. I am truly sorry. I should not be so quick to think I know your experience."

Frenchy looked down, embarrassed at his response. Sarah gently smiled and placed her hand on his.

Assaf sat motionless, shocked at Frenchy's zeal as well as his self-awareness. He rubbed his hands together and sternly spoke.

"I must admit. While in no way do I agree with you on the Israel and Palestine conflict, I respect what you said."

The Prime Minister raised his eyebrows in shock at Assaf's response.

"Few men ever receive such a compliment from Assaf," Gershom said, smiling at his close advisor.

"It seems I was wrong about you, Dr. Degnan. You are a bit of a . . . wild card."

Assaf's lip elevated for a moment, his best attempt at a smile for his verbal opponent.

"That means a lot considering it looked like you might knife me at any moment," Frenchy smiled, hoping his joke would be positively received. "But, again, I am speaking on issues I have no personal connection to. I'm sure there is a lot more to it. So I am sorry. You should talk to my mother. Every time my dad and I go off on this subject at the dinner table, out comes my grandfather's yamakka and her 'how dare you oppose your own heritage.'"

Frenchy's dinner guests slowly processed his minor admission.

"Doc, you're a Jew?"

Sarah glared at Ricky, yet appreciating his blunt question.

"I thought you said you were Irish?" Assaf said, firm in his belief that there were few Irish Jews.

"Irish, only half; my grandfather was a Romanian Jew. Samuel Berkowitz. And yes, my mom was and still is Jewish. I was raised Catholic by both my mom and dad. There was no disagreement between them. But my mom took my siblings and me to temple with her every now and again. My dad would go, too."

The Prime Minister leaned forward, intrigued by Frenchy's confession.

"So Ricky, no, I am not a Jew, but being raised in an interfaith household led to many of my present beliefs on religious intolerance."

Frenchy noticed the positive surprised look on Sarah's face.

"That's right, baby, I can *Baruch atah Adonai Eloheinu Melech* all night long."

Frenchy winked, as Sarah let out a disgusted grunt.

"That's offensive, gross, and bigoted."

"Gotta agree, Doc, very gross, and thankfully, I have no idea what any of that meant." Sarah nodded in appreciation of Ricky's support.

"Well, Dr. Degnan, you are most certainly a wild card. I did not anticipate learning that small piece of information. And while, based on the response from your companions, I can assume that the spirit of prayer was not with your words, your pronunciation was quite good."

"Well, thank you, Prime Minister. I heard that so many times. I better not botch the pronunciation, or my mother and grandmother would both beat me. Well, not really beat me, but you know, get mad and stuff."

The Prime Minister smiled, appreciating Frenchy's awkward amendment.

"Still, you feel no connection to the plight of the Jews? After all, your mother is Jewish and it is passed through the mother. You are Jewish."

The Prime Minister awaited Frenchy's response.

"See, you are a Jew," Ricky said, lamenting his chastisement for his earlier accurate question.

"I am aware of that, but I like to think of myself as a person of faith and also of doubt. I do not necessarily see the need to label myself. Think about it: Judaism, Christianity, and Islam all share a common founder in Abraham. Aside from that shared ancestor, we as religions act like a dysfunctional family. The grandfather doesn't approve of his son and grandson. Believes they are way off. The father thinks his old man is outdated but his son is wild and off the grid. The son thinking his patriarchs never fully got it. I mean, shit. Our disagreements have caused wars for centuries. And you know what? I have read the Quran, the Bible, Old and New Testament, in its entirety. I find it harder to believe in religion than I do in God. Whoever the hell said 'religion divides us' deserves a beer. He or she was right on point. Maybe we should focus less on our differences and more on our similarities, less on our label and more on who we are as people."

Frenchy removed a cigarette and lit it quickly, his hand shaking slightly from the table conversation. Sarah reached over and put her hand on his. Frenchy looked up at her, shocked at the second act of kindness. Her hand seemed to calm him momentarily. He stared into her eyes, his nervousness replaced by his heart fluttering from her touch. He looked down quickly and took a pull on his cigarette, his eyes searching the table for an ashtray. He looked up at his dinner guests, realizing he failed to ask if his cigarette fix was acceptable.

"I'm sorry, I didn't even ask if this was alright."

The Prime Minister smiled and signaled to an attendant who placed a crystal ashtray in front of Frenchy. Assaf looked over at the Prime Minister, the two nodding at one another, signaling an agreement that their discussion on Degnan's genealogy was complete, both not wanting to rile up their guest.

"Well, Doctor Degnan, we are very excited for you to begin your work tomorrow. We have arranged transportation, security, and the appropriate tools for your work. Is there anything specific you will need from us?"

Frenchy stamped out his cigarette, his eyes widened as he scrambled to respond.

"What do you mean 'tools?'"

Assaf cocked his head slightly, confused by Frenchy's question.

"Well, we assumed you would need at least the basic tools for digging."

Assaf's firm demeanor returned as Degnan's charm vanished with his obvious question.

"Oh yes, right, I wasn't sure what you meant by 'tools.' Great, that will be perfect. The basics should be sufficient; after all, Rabbi Tannen and Judah could not have left it buried too deep. That should be fine for us."

Frenchy shifted in his chair, reminded that the time for him to follow through on his confidence approached.

"This may sound like a crazy question but, when we get to Masada, are you relying on me solely?"

"Of course. That is why we have retained your services. I was told by many that you were the best for this job."

Botvinnik quickly entered the conversation, aware that Frenchy's self-confidence was dwindling.

"You will have plenty of help for the labor. We need you to show us where to begin."

Ricky leaned forward from his silent position.

"May I ask a question? What if Doc can't find it immediately? How much time are you willing to give him? I only ask because I've seen movies where the guys who hired the guy to find something begin to get impatient."

Ricky looked over at Frenchy and winked, mouthing "*National Treasure*, at the beginning."

Sarah smiled, for once appreciating their incessant movie references.

"No one expects Dr. Degnan to be successful on the first attempt. But we believe he is capable of locating the Sword. That is all that is important."

Ricky reclined, proud of the response he coaxed from Botvinnik.

"So, what time tomorrow?" Sarah said, recognizing Frenchy's continued depleting spirit.

"We will be leaving at six thirty. Your clothes have been cleaned and returned to your rooms. I suggest you end early tonight so we may have a full day tomorrow."

Assaf responded, hoping to drive home Frenchy's need to be moderate with the wine.

"Sounds like a good idea," Frenchy quickly blurted out, as he put his napkin over his plate and slammed back the last bit of his wine.

"We will be ready to go. Let's get some shut-eye, okay?" he said nervously, standing and gesturing to his companions to do the same.

"So, thank you for a pleasant evening and don't worry, you can count on us to find the Sword for you. And sorry again for my ranting. Sometimes I . . . well, I often act like an idiot so I am sorry about that. Tell the chef thank you for the creepy fish thing that stared at me the whole night."

The Prime Minister looked over at his companions, confused by Degnan's nervous behavior.

"Would you like some dessert before you leave?" the Prime Minister asked, attempting to quell the abrupt end to the evening.

"No, please, I couldn't. Believe me, I've had my share of desserts to last a lifetime," Frenchy said, grabbing his belly fat and shaking it. He shook his head upon realizing the crudeness of his gesture. "See, there I go again."

"Good night, Dr. Degnan. If you need anything, please let us know. We have attendants available all night, if needed."

Frenchy waved awkwardly in recognition of the offer and ushered Sarah and Ricky towards the attendant waiting near the arched doorway. The three moved quickly behind the server, Sarah looking inconspicuously at Frenchy. She bit her lip, trying to refrain from addressing Frenchy's strange behavior. The attendant gestured to the staircase and the three quickly made their way to their rooms.

"What the hell just happened? I wanted some motherfuckin' dessert," Ricky whispered, leaning towards his mentor. Frenchy walked quickly towards his room, turning abruptly.

"So let's get some sleep, I'll see you tomorrow."

He entered his room and closed the door quickly. Sarah and Ricky stared at his door, hoping this was another one of Frenchy's jokes. They stood in silence, awaiting Frenchy's reappearance. Sarah looked over at Ricky.

"I think this shit is fuckin' with Doc's mind. He's not very comfortable with being relied on. I shoudn't mention it because he said it on a retreat and we're not suppose to share what we hear, but he said he hates any pressure. Not a lot of pressure, any pressure. I think that has always been a problem for him: self-esteem with a hint of accepting himself, limitations and all."

Sarah smiled.

"Not bad for such a young man. You obviously care for him."

"We all do. Something real about him . . . even through his facades, goofy behavior, and bad jokes. You can tell he is a good man."

"Yeah, I think I'm getting that. I wonder if his room is locked."

Ricky nodded, happy to see Sarah willing to reach out to Frenchy.

Sarah walked over to the door and gripped the knob firmly, slowing turning it. She opened the door and looked into the room. Frenchy was seated at a table a few feet from a window, a small bit of light coming from the wall fixture above the bed. She stood quietly, aware Frenchy did not hear her enter. Frenchy leaned on the table, his head in his hand, raising a bottle of beer to his lips, before returning to his position.

"Francis."

Frenchy didn't move from his position, prompting Sarah to speak slightly louder. Frenchy moved in recognition of her presence, slowly returning to drinking his beer. Ricky had made his way quietly behind Sarah. She turned and waved him away.

"I'll take care of him."

Despite Ricky's instinctive desire to make a myriad of jokes from her statement, he nodded and closed the door quietly. Frenchy sat up and looked over at Sarah.

"Hey, what's up?"

Sarah walked over to the table, sitting down next to him. She looked down at a twelve pack of beer at his feet. She smiled, shaking her head.

"You are 6,000 miles away from your home and a possible fugitive and somehow you have Budweiser at your feet."

Frenchy uncharacteristically grunted, shaking his head in agreement.

"Well, you know me. They didn't have Guinness; I had to deal."

He reached down and removed a beer from the case and opened it, passing it to Sarah. She took the beer, wiping some condensation from the bottle.

"How do you have it cold?" she asked, smiling.

"I had one of the attendants snag some during dinner. I figured it couldn't hurt to be prepared in case this was a dry dinner."

Sarah placed her beer on the table and leaned towards him.

"So, stating the obvious, something is wrong. Would you tell me what's going on?"

Frenchy reached for another beer returning his empty to the case.

"I know, sorry about the dinner; I can be a real ass sometimes. I'm sorry if I embarrassed you."

"I have been with you on this ridiculous exile for almost two days. You have embarrassed me every step of the way. You know that's not what I am talking about."

Frenchy gulped his beer, aware of Sarah's concern. They sat in silence for a few moments, Sarah leaning further towards Frenchy, hoping to convey her anticipation of his response.

"You know, I don't really know you that well, but what I do know is not the man that ended that dinner. Please, you can trust me. I will not judge. I just need to know."

Frenchy took a long drink from his beer and inhaled loudly as though he could not breathe.

"You said earlier you believe in me. Why'd you say that? I know you said you are basing it on your father's trust, but do you really believe that?"

"Of course, I do. I don't understand. Why are you focusing on that?"

"You see, you said you believe in me. You said you believe I will find this stupid fuckin' sword, despite some not so great research. But how could anyone believe in me? I spent over a year with a man who knew all the research and all the writings I was doing were wrong. He didn't believe in me and he was right not to. He appeased me. And the fact of the matter is, I don't believe in myself. I don't. I talk a big game. I know what this scenario looks like in my fantasy, but I know the truth. It struck me at dinner. I am sitting at a dinner table with the Prime Minister of Israel and some guy who will pay me to find this awful freaking thing. Everything I could have dreamt of. And then I realize, I can't do this. I've gone between excited and terrified for the last forty-eight hours. One minute confident, next, shitting my pants and wanting to hug my pillow. I've got nothing. I don't know what I'm doing. I've never even been to Israel. Every criticism of my book was correct. I didn't research enough; I just ran with an idea. And they're right. That's always my problem. I get excited and spend more time dreaming about the result than actually thinking about how to make it happen. You know I self-published? Couldn't take the criticism from the editors so I did it myself. Sadly, I was better at marketing than writing. My horrid book spread and it spread to everyone."

Frenchy drank quickly.

"But to get back to my original point: the worst part is, the closer I get to actually doing the shit I need to make my dream come true or doing the work to find the thing, I get scared because I know the truth. Fantasy is better than reality. In fantasy, you decide the setting, the scenes, the plot, et cetera. In real life, you are limited by things like a lack of self-confidence and intelligence, anxiety, and, of course, following through. So that's what happened. I came back to earth and realized that I have bullshitted my way to this point and now I can't finish."

He rubbed his face and quickly reached for his pack of cigarettes. Sarah looked down at her hands, unsure how to respond to his substantial confession.

"I don't know what to say. You covered so many things that I'm not sure I could respond."

Sarah sipped her beer. Her consistent criticism of him had been based on her assumption that he had a modicum of the confidence he had exhibited during their odyssey.

"You know, I really, really don't know what to say about everything you said. I can only listen and sympathize. But either way, tomorrow we leave to do everything you have fantasized about. So it doesn't matter what I say, except that your chance is here and whether you are a fraud or not, get ready for it. It's here. So let's try to do something that isn't focused on the inadequacies you claim to have. Let's try to go beyond your exhortation at the Mosque. Let's talk this through and let's stop doing what you said, 'fantasizing.' Let's just do this and put our best foot forward."

Sarah sat back and sipped her beer, staring at him.

"You're not getting it. I can't do this. I am not just saying this; I really can't. As great as the prospect of success may be, I'm afraid to do it. You know what I do every day? I hide from my life. I try and I try to convince myself to get over it, but I can't. It takes so much for me to do anything. Why? Because not doing something is easier. It took me years to write that book. Unfortunately, it had nothing to do with a need for more time to research. I couldn't do it. The first hundred pages were so easy. Then I began to near the end. I couldn't do it. If I finished, I had to be judged. When I was, I got pissed and ignored my friends and family. And look how that turned out. Teaching? I'd rather give busy work. Why, you ask? Because I can't bring myself to stand up and teach. It's the expectation that scares me. Why do something and leave yourself to be judged when you can put it off for another day, or just not do it?"

Sarah shook her head in confusion.

"That can't be true. Look at all the students who love you. They can't love you because you're a bad teacher, not even an easy teacher. Students don't look up to bad teachers or easy teachers; they look up to good teachers and good people. You're telling me you never gave a good lecture or good lesson?"

Frenchy waved his hands, dismissing her question. He picked up his beer and drank for a moment.

"Sure, when I first started out. But now people expect me to be a good teacher. But again, it's the expectation. I can pump myself up to give a good lesson. But how do you follow through? You never want to be the last to leave a party; you leave right after you do a keg stand or tell a great story or catch the eye of a beautiful lady. Then you leave. Then you have people wanting more."

"I have no idea how that makes any sense. So, to you, you do something well and then stop, retire in your prime?"

Frenchy happily gestured towards Sarah's conclusion.

"Yes, you retire on top. I once gave a speech at a school assembly. I had students, faculty, and administrators on their feet in awe at my talk. Since then, I have turned down any offers to speak again. I gave a toast at my sister's wedding that had people rushing up to me saying it was the best they had ever heard. I'll never do it again. If my brother gets married, he's shit out of luck."

"Fine, I get it, leave on top, but what kind of life is that? And why can't you do it again? Why can't you say 'this one will be better?' Or why can't you recognize that no one is perfect? That no one can be on their game perfectly, every time?"

Frenchy seemed to ignore her questions, quite familiar with them as he posed them to himself on a daily basis.

"And, if you can't do it as you have kept saying, how did you do it in the first place?"

French pounded his beer and picked up another.

"Well, booze helps. It's a natural anti-anxiety medication."

"You've got to be kidding me. You are saying alcohol is the key to living? And you are saying that you drink before you teach children?"

Sarah's disdain for his response increased as she processed the implications of his statement.

"No. Well, no, I have never drank before work, but if I could legally do it, I would. And they are not children, per se. You should see the perverted shit they know and discuss. But I drank eight glasses of champagne during the cocktail hour at my sister's wedding, walked into the main room, and was called up. I belted a 500-foot home run with my toast, and then I walked out of the ballroom and into the bathroom and fell over drunk. I didn't have a single drink after that. The old drink had done all I needed."

Sarah set her beer down on the table and stood up, standing across from Frenchy. His description of his alcohol boost turned her off from finishing her drink.

"Well, alcoholism aside and based on your behavior, I think there is no need to question the likelihood that you suffer from it; everything you have said is wrong. If you are so focused on 'leaving them wanting more,' wouldn't this be the number one moment to do that?"

"I just explained to you why this isn't . . ."

"No, you didn't. You said 'I leave the people wanting more.' Who wants more from you in this present situation? No one wants another book from you. You want to talk about expectation? No one expects anything from you. No one thinks you can do this. In terms of your book and your quest for this 'treasure,' well, you were kicked out of the party, drunk, annoying, and embarrassing. You certainly would not be invited back."

Frenchy stared blankly at her, his left eye slightly twitching. Sarah inhaled deeply, aware of what she said. She sat down and picked up her beer, drinking the remainder. She reached for a second beer, opening it aggressively. Frenchy sat motionless. Though uncertain as to what he hoped her response would be to the confession of his life's struggles, her clear and pointed words left him speechless.

"I'm sorry. I didn't mean that. I just got caught up in everything. I don't think you are an embarrassment."

He winced at her attempt at redaction, her words sounding worse when she spoke calmly. He dropped back in his chair, his spirit visibly finished by their exchange.

"Francis?"

Sarah moved her chair closer to him, a panicked sense in her voice.

"Please, Francis, I'm sorry. That is not what I meant. I got caught up in the metaphor or whatever. Please, we need you. I need you. My father could have trusted anyone else, but he chose you."

Frenchy limply removed a second cigarette from his pack, barely mustering the strength to draw the ember from his previous cigarette.

"I think that had more to do with C4 than my ability."

His hand shook slightly as he took another pull from his cigarette.

"I think we better get to bed."

Frenchy stood up and walked over to the door, opening it. Sarah put her hand over her mouth and stared at Frenchy, hoping her look could encourage him to return to his seat.

"I'm not mad at you, and I am not kicking you out, I'm just tired. It's been a long couple of days. And as much as you just apologized, your words are true and may be what I needed to motivate myself."

Sarah stood up and approached him standing in front of him. She stared at him, his eyes looking down. She touched his face and gently moved his gaze towards her. They locked eyes for a moment, Frenchy's cigarette breaking the moment.

"I'll see you in the morning, bright and early for our quest?" she asked, waving her hand to fan the smoke away.

"You got it. I'll see you in the morning."

Sarah cautiously smiled and put her hand on his shoulder awkwardly. The emotions of the entire trip had her confused and unsure what her feelings were for him. She slid her hand from his shoulder to his hand. Despite their banter throughout the trip, she presently felt consumed by his presence and his willingness to share his fears with her. She momentarily leaned in towards him, hoping he would reciprocate her action. Frenchy looked down. Sarah self-consciously returned to her stance slowly.

"So, tomorrow. I appreciate you listening to me tonight. Sorry again for my antics and bad jokes."

Sarah nodded, feeling a sense of rejection.

"Okay, see you then."

She left the room quickly, Frenchy closing the door behind her.

He stood for a moment at the door. His eyes quickly welled up with tears, his feelings overwhelming him. He walked over tiredly to his chair and sat down, picking up his beer, and lit another cigarette. He stared blankly, returning to his thoughts of self-deprecation. He shook his head in despair, adding his failure to kiss Sarah to his list of life disappointments. He looked over at his newly cleaned outfit. He stared at his leather jacket, a hand me down almost as old as he.

He took a pull on his cigarette, returning to his blank gaze. His mind slowed, the alcohol calming him. He recalled Sarah's words. His mind echoed the negative comments he had heard during his lifetime. He began to feel the unpleasant comfort of defeat. His statements to Sarah had been truer than she could have imagined. Sitting in his room, he realized that he could not be anything he had dreamt. While this thought fed his depression, it satisfied his desire to retreat from any further judgment. If he didn't try, he couldn't be faulted. If he had kissed Sarah, then she could criticize. If he didn't, she couldn't. If he failed to find the Sword of Goliath, then his critics would be validated. If he never tried to, his fate was left open. He slowly nodded, realizing that the Sword of Goliath would be found, just not by him. Either way, he would be somewhat vindicated. More importantly, he would be free of the pressure, the burden of possible failure. He slouched in his seat, allowing himself to mull over the opposing argument.

He suddenly stood and grabbed his beer. His internal debate was solved, aided by his slip into warm inebriation. He walked over to the door, anxious to resign his position as a treasure hunter.

He opened the door, two notes falling to the floor. He picked them up, recognizing the writing on the first:

> I'm mad excited about tomorrow, Doc. This is your time now. We're gonna find this thing and you're gonna be able to slap those pecker heads who laughed at you. Can't wait. Don't know what was buggin' you tonight at dinner, but don't worry, we are so close to your dream, and mine, now. See you tomorrow.

Frenchy's expression changed dramatically, remembering Ricky was with him.

"You suck," he said aloud, realizing that the option of running away from his fears had been blocked. He opened the second note:

> Just want you to know that you're my Indiana Jones, and I'm very happy to be here with you. I want to not find this sword tomorrow with you. I don't care. And then maybe we can go back home together and see what happens. Either way, I will be by your side tomorrow. P.S. You said I never say anything nice about you. So here: I think you have beautiful eyes.

"God dammit. How the fuck did they write this shit so quick?"

Frenchy's heart fluttered. The two-note combo had knocked him from his self-defeating haze. He reread the note, savoring Sarah's words. He stared at the last line. It had been so long since he heard a compliment other than "Doc, you the man." He looked up, his mood visibly altered. He closed the door quietly, placing the notes on the table.

"Whatever, fuck my life," he said aloud.

He picked up a pencil and piece of paper on the dresser and sat down at the table. He placed his beer down on the table and stared at it.

"If I'm gonna do this, I better chill on the booze."

He lifted the beer to his lips and drank down the remaining half of the beer, placing the empty bottle into the twelve pack. He picked up his pencil and wrote, "Masada," at the top of the paper. He stopped and stared at the blank sheet.

His eyes wandered down to the twelve pack, noticing six unopened Budweiser bottles. He moved his head back and forth nervously.

"Whatever, shit, it can only help. So I'll quit soon."

He picked up a bottle and placed it on the table. The sight of the beer seemed to prompt his memory as he began to write frantically. He twisted the beer open and drank looking down at his paper and back to the bottle.

"Unbelievable. How can you be bad for the body, when you are so amazingly good for the mind?"

41

A LONE VEHICLE DROVE ACROSS the dusty terrain, moonlight gently shining on the Dead Sea. Ali shifted gears driving towards a faint light in the darkness. He removed his cell phone and pressed the send button.

"I am approaching," he said, in Arabic.

The light grew brighter as he sped towards it. The faint outline of men appeared. He drove directly towards them, the men moving into his path. Ali stopped as two of the men approached, armed with antiquated machine guns. They stared at Ali, waving to the other men to step aside. Ali drove a bit more before stopping and exiting his car, the lights another hundred yards away. He surveyed the dark scene, catching the slight glimmer in the eyes of armed men surrounding the area. A figure approach him.

"How many men are in the darkness?"

Samir brushed his beard and looked back towards the lights.

"About a hundred in the shadows. The rest are working at the base of the fortress. Where are the Americans?"

Samir shined his flashlight into the vehicle.

"That will be explained in time."

Ali looked back in the direction he had come.

"I can see the light from six kilometers out. Move vehicles into the path of the light, and limit the light."

Samir nodded in agreement, shouting in anger towards the light. As a militant man, he prided himself on being thorough. A quality he felt exceptionally important as his brother Amir failed to excel in this area. Amir's focus had always been the intelligence aspect. Still, Amir's similar suggestion to Ali's had been ignored by his brother, causing Samir anger at its reintroduction.

"Have we progressed in our work?"

Ali began to walk towards the lights with Samir.

"It is quite difficult given we are searching without a direction. Please, where is the American friend of yours? Without some guidance, we could be searching for days."

Samir stared at Ali, irritated that he had not answered his original question.

"Where is your brother? We will discuss the problem together."

"So you are agreeing that there is a problem?"

Ali looked forward, ignoring the question.

"We began the excavation believing he would be capable of directing the men. Yet, you are here and I do not see our guide."

"I wouldn't worry too much, Samir. Our new situation requires military action and something I am sure you are capable of completing."

Ali's subtle compliment eased Samir's building ire. Ali's pace quickened as he approached the lights, the shadow of the natural fortress emerged. Amir saw the men approaching and left the base, where men continued to dig.

"We have found nothing," he said, as he met Ali.

"This is where you said the American believes it to be located. In the rebel dwellings on the northeast base."

Ali looked beyond Amir at the men working.

"Please stop with this 'American' label. His name is Francis Degnan, Ph.D."

Amir nodded in accord, aware of Ali's relationship with Degnan.

"Well then, it seems Dr. Degnan was incorrect. There was a possibility that this would have happened," Ali said, continuing to survey the scene.

"Then where is he? We cannot set up camp here for days. If this is not the place, then where is?"

Samir pushed his earlier inquiry.

"I had to leave Dr. Degnan. My identity was compromised when we arrived at the Prime Minister's residence."

Samir's eyes widened, unaware of that aspect.

"We should abandon the digging now. If Israel is aware of our participation, then they will come with forces."

Ali gestured to Samir, hoping to quell his momentary panic.

"We do not have to abandon anything yet, although we will for the next few hours. Degnan and his military escort will be arriving tomorrow. So we must intercept them. I do not imagine a large convoy. We will use Masada as an advantage. Then, when we have overpowered the convoy, we will be able to take Degnan and he will be able to lead us to our object. But this will require planning. So let us gather together and formulate our plan to take the group. Still, the most important aspect, and I will say it now and many times more: our success must be precise. We cannot lose Degnan and we cannot allow any communication back to Israel. Samir, with your expertise, I hope this is possible."

The brothers looked at one another. Despite the setback, Ali's suggestion seemed to rebut any further complaints.

"Do you not think the whole Israeli government will allow time to go by without communication from their group?"

Samir quickly turned towards Ali, following his brother's question.

"No, I do not. But I do know that the object is most likely nowhere near the present location. We will be long gone when they become aware of what has transpired. They will not be able to track us."

"I disagree. We should take one of their men alive so we can continue communications with Jerusalem. But how do we know who will be accompanying them?"

Amir seemed unhappy about the plan and its large amount of uncertainty.

"If it makes you content, then take one. I have an idea about who you should take. We will know who is with them when Balsam contacts us. I asked him to monitor their movements."

The brothers seemed satisfied by Ali's response, unaware of Balsam's amended assignment.

"But listen to me. I do not care what happens tomorrow, only that Dr. Degnan and his companions are not to be harmed. He is my friend and a friend to all of us. I care that he is safe. He has been nothing but supportive to Muslims in the United States and to our claim to Palestine. If he succeeds in recovering it, he must be compensated. If he fails, he will be returned to the United States safely. If I hear tomorrow from you that he has been harmed, I will blame you and I promise I will kill you."

Samir squinted at Ali, angry that he was singled out for a threat. Amir watched the two men stare sternly at one another. He wiped his brow, slightly concerned by Ali's anger.

"That is agreeable. However, why such an impassioned protectiveness of this man? I am aware you are friends. But where does this rage come from?"

Ali's gaze broke and he looked at Amir.

"He is a good man, a smart man. More importantly, he has trusted me. In no way will I betray that trust."

Amir stretched his hand towards Ali in agreement with his terms.

"He will be safe. Samir's skills go beyond simply combating the enemy. But please, Ali, recognize that, no matter what your friendship is with this American, you have already betrayed his trust. Do not allow yourself to forget that he may no longer be your friend."

42

JENSEN SHIFTED IN THE FRONT PASSENGER SEAT, reaching for his coffee in the cup holder. Espinoza and Forester looked through binoculars, observing the Prime Minister's residence.

"We should have slept longer, Degnan's a drunk. Drunks usually avoid early mornings."

Espinoza ignored Forester's comment, searching for movement in Beit Gurion.

"A convoy has assembled. I don't see the good doctor, but there is a reasonable military presence."

"No doubt, if they are traveling outside Israel, they will need some protection. My most recent message from headquarters says they will be moving east towards the Dead Sea. Not necessarily outside of Israel, but never hurts to travel with protection."

Jensen resumed his work on his Blackberry. A figure walked past the passenger side of the vehicle, surprising both young agents.

"Holy shit. It's him."

Forester remained reclined, avoiding visibility. The three watched as Degnan crossed the street towards the residence.

"I suppose you were wrong, Forester," Jensen said, observing Degnan entering the front entrance.

"As if you didn't all agree with me when I said it," Forester said, resuming his surveillance.

"Agreed," Forester's partner said, recognizing his superior's unfair comment.

Ephraim remained silent, observing the scene. Degnan emerged from the residence, lighting a cigarette and looking over multiple sheets of paper.

"Looks like he's taking this shit seriously. I'm somewhat impressed," Jensen said, commenting on Degnan's early arrival and seemingly serious analysis of possible notes.

"Look, no disrespect boss, but I know you and Espinoza have some sort of weird respect for this guy, but let's not give too much credit. You're impressed that he is awake and that he might be able to read."

Jensen chuckled at Forester's comment.

"Sometimes it's all about the little things," Espinoza said, tapping Forester to resume his surveillance.

"So that's Degnan's lady friend, Tannen's daughter, and his student. Where's the Muslim?"

The three gazed at the emerging party.

"Who cares? He's off doin' a goat."

Ephraim flinched at Forester's crude comment. Jensen noticed the response.

"I trust this convoy is aware of our presence?"

Ephraim reached down and put the car into gear.

"Yes, sir, they are aware of your presence. We will be behind the last vehicle to remain out of sight. We will have contact with the military convoy throughout the duration of the trip."

"Is Tannen's daughter blushing at Degnan? I've seen a lot of shit in my day, but if she is giving it up to that ass, I believe the world will end in 2012."

Forester's comment intrigued his colleagues, even Ephraim squinting his eyes to better see the scene.

"Stranger things have happened. But not many."

Ephraim seemed amused by Espinoza's comment.

"Women do not only gravitate towards the most successful and handsome. Even dogs have their day, correct?"

Jensen and his agents smiled timidly, amazed at Ephraim's participation.

"Did you think I was not listening to everything you have said?"

Ephraim shook his head as he looked at the perturbed looks on their faces. He reached down and took an unopened pack of cigarettes, packing them against his palm. He muttered in Hebrew as he looked back at the front entrance.

"Americans . . ."

"I HAVE TO BE HONEST. I didn't expect you to be up and about before me, or even still here for that matter," Sarah said, as she emerged from the front door of Beit Gurion.

"Doc, we went to your door and you weren't there." Ricky approached, hugging Frenchy. "No homo. But I am so glad to see you. I was worried."

"Well, in truth I was done with this last night. But I got your notes. I may be afraid of many things and may run away from a lot in life, but I couldn't leave you guys. Plus, I felt guilty as shit."

Frenchy winked at them, raising his eyebrows and smiling.

Assaf emerged with the Prime Minister and a group of men.

"Well, Dr. Degnan, I see you are ready for the day?"

Frenchy raised his right hand, clutching his papers.

"I've got my notes and am ready to do my best."

Frenchy's stomach turned, their presence reminding him of the actuality of the venture. "So, I assume all of you are not going with us. What's the plan?"

"You will have the military convoys in the front and rear. These vehicles have materials, equipment, and workers. You will ride behind Mr. Botvinnik and his guards."

Assaf gestured towards the various vehicles assembled.

"Sorry to ask, or I will be sorry to ask, but why such the military guarding presence?" Frenchy's anxiety gave way to a reasonable fear for his safety.

"It's simply procedure. We want to make sure you are safe and do not run into any problems."

Despite Assaf's realistic statement, Frenchy did not feel consoled.

"Trust me, Dr. Degnan, we will be fine. This will be the day you become known to the whole world."

Frenchy turned away from Botvinnik, shrugging towards Sarah. She took Frenchy's hand and smiled at him.

"I told you I will be here with you. Let's not waste too much time before you change your mind and run screaming."

Ricky put his arms around Sarah and Frenchy, pushing his head between theirs.

"I agree. But one of you has to tell me what happened last night. Did you guys bump uglies?"

Sarah broke from the group embrace, rolling her eyes. Ricky watched her walk towards their vehicle, turning back to his mentor.

"I knew it, Doc. You two smooshed! I saw it coming when she mouthed 'I'll take care of him.'"

Ricky made an exaggerated attempt at sounding sensual. Frenchy pushed his student's arms away, quickly rejoining Sarah. Ricky looked back at Assaf and the Prime Minister, shaking his head in disappointment.

"You know, this is bullshit. I'm in a foreign country risking my life while trying to play cupid to set these two up, and what happens when it works? I can't even confirm that they wiggled the light fixture."

Assaf remained stern, the Prime Minister smiling in confused politeness. Assaf's eyes looked towards the convoy, pushing Ricky towards the cars. Ricky's casual demeanor changed quickly.

"So, anyway, I'm gonna go over there instead of here."

He quickly moved away, joining Frenchy and Sarah in the vehicle.

"That guy is a douche. He just stares in anger. I mean, like, lighten up. And if you guys had just given me the details, I wouldn't have been left with those dickish buzz kills."

Frenchy looked down at his papers, unaware of Ricky's complaint. The convoy began to move slowly, the Prime Minister nodding solemnly towards the moving vehicles.

Sarah looked out at the neighborhood, her thoughts returning to her father. She smiled sadly, as she envisioned him as a younger man on the original quest that discovered the ancient relic. Her eyes welled up with tears. Frenchy placed his hand on hers, aware of her present emotions.

"You okay?" he asked, gently moving her hair with his left hand, exposing her face. She smiled, rubbing her cheek on his hand, eventually resting her head on his hand.

"I assume you're thinking about your father."

Frenchy wiped the tears from her cheek and gently rubbed her cheek. Ricky slowly moved forward, pretending to look ahead. He stared blankly, attempting to assess his mentor's actions inconspicuously.

"I have been thinking a lot about him, too. I've been trying to understand what he wants me to do. Why he sent you to me. Why I'm even on this weird mission. It's almost like he orchestrated the whole thing to satisfy my dreams. Maybe he sent you to me so I could finally know what love is."

"Gay," Ricky blurted out, disrupting the moment.

Frenchy looked over at him with his disappointed teacher's scowl.

"Oh, come on, that was so gay. But anyway, so you two are definitely . . ."

"God dammit Ricky, yes, I like her. I really like her and I hope she likes me too. Okay? Giggity, that's what she said, no homo, handlebars? Get it out now so we can move forward without your constant 'I'm not listening to your conversation, I'm not looking at you through my peripherals.' I like her. Okay? No more."

Frenchy's exasperation caused the driver and passenger to turn around and stare momentarily.

Ricky's stunned look quickly left as he smiled. He looked up at Frenchy and Sarah, returning to his mentor. He lunged forward and hugged Frenchy.

"That's all I wanted to hear! This is freakin' sweet, Doc! I am so happy for you guys. But what the fuck are 'handlebars?'"

Sarah wiped her eyes, laughing at Ricky's response. Frenchy patted Ricky's back with his hand as Ricky reached over to pull Sarah into the embrace.

"Okay, okay, great, good. I'm glad you're happy."

"Now, no matter what, this was all worth it."

Ricky returned to sitting, content at the recent happenings.

"So what, that's it, you're done?"

Ricky looked at Frenchy, confused.

"Yeah. What else do you expect? I can lead you to the water, but you got to drink on your own."

Frenchy glanced over to Sarah for an explanation. Sarah shook her head, ignoring the comment.

"So what about these papers?"

"Well, after you left last night I decided to quit. But as I left to tell the Prime Minister I was out, I stumbled upon your notes. After reading them, and, by the way, thank you to both of you for the notes, I decided if I was actually going on this trip, I needed to be prepared, so I sat down and wrote out notes-slash-ideas on what to do. Doesn't mean they are correct but . . ."

"Would you stop giving us a disclaimer? We are both here and we both get it."

Frenchy nodded in agreement, looking over at Ricky.

"Hey listen, your girlfriend has a point."

Ricky winked and smiled, exaggeratedly.

"Well, I thought about everything and I decided you guys were right. I probably was off. And I bet your dad knew I was off in my writing. But it can't be that far off because he said so. Thus, I tried to start from scratch, so to speak, and look at everything. Now, that fragment of your dad's original map said something about Snake Path. But it also mentioned a marker. I have no idea what that is about but I figure if the marker is near Snake Path, then we find that thing and go on from there."

"Any idea where the marker will send us?"

"To be honest, I don't know if the marker will send us anywhere. My reasoning is his map doesn't have enough info to lead us anywhere else. I figure it has to be somewhere on the fortress. I had originally told your father I thought it would be in the Sicarii dwellings. But the directions refer to 'at the base.' So, maybe I was right after all; just the wrong section of the fortress. We work at the base of the big rock and maybe we find what we want."

Ricky patted Frenchy on the back, leaning forward.

"All it took to get you on point was two notes from us? You're a totally different guy now . . ."

Frenchy shot his hand up, stopping Ricky's statement.

"Easy, I'm just nervous so I'm focused. Soon and very soon I will be back to my lame jokes and annoying behavior."

He grinned at Sarah as Ricky seemed consoled by Frenchy's words.

"For the sake of my interest in you, I hope it takes a while to find this thing otherwise I may not have enough time with the wonderful Francis to fall in love and thus be forced to put up with your bullshit alter ego," Sarah said.

Ricky smacked his knee, laughing at Sarah's forwardness. Frenchy gave a dirty look to his laughing sidekick.

"I get no respect. And where are you from—the 50s? Smackin' your leg? How long until we're at Masada?"

The passenger turned, looking at his watch.

"Perhaps an hour. Masada is about a hundred kilometers from Jerusalem. We will be leaving the more populated area soon."

Frenchy nodded and leaned back, pulling his hat over his face.

"I got about two hours of sleep last night. I'm gonna knock out."

"You can sleep at a time like this?"

Ricky stared, confused at Frenchy's posture.

"You would, too, if you were exhausted as well as terrified. Wake me up when we are close."

Ricky looked over at Sarah, realizing his mentor would no longer be a source of entertainment.

"Wanna play *Never Have I Ever*?"

THE JEEP HIT A DEEP HOLE, Frenchy flinching out of sleep.

"Doc, check it out. There's nothing here."

Ricky gestured towards the window. Frenchy stared out into dry desolate land, his gaze shifting to Sarah's window. The dusty landscape was a sharp contrast to their earlier surroundings.

"Well, I guess that's why the Essenes thought the end of the world was coming. I'd believe it too if I was stuck in a cave around here."

"Who the hell are the Essenes?"

"They were a Jewish sect in the first century. They were the Dead Sea Scrolls people. They were preparing for the end of days, and, yes, same as the movie with Schwarzennegger."

The convoy slowed slightly.

"Are we here?" Frenchy asked, assuming the decrease in speed meant arrival.

"No, but very close. The military vehicle ahead is stopping."

"Did you sleep?" Sarah asked, smiling at his slightly dazed look.

"A little. Your 'Never Have I Ever' game with Ricky made it difficult. I couldn't help but play passively. Thank God it was kept somewhat PG."

Sarah laughed, looking down at her hands.

"Here you go. Better get ready."

She handed him his notes, leaning in and kissing his cheek.

"One for good luck."

She blushed, returning to his gaze as the vehicle stopped completely.

"Gay," Ricky blurted out, attempting to hide his comment through a fabricated cough.

"Oh my God, shut the hell up. Like you never have said or heard such a comment?"

Ricky stared unintelligibly at Frenchy, exaggerating his dumb look.

"Forget it. When you get older, you will find that it is comments like this that can make your heart stop, start, flutter, whatever."

"I know. It would do the same to me if I heard something like that and I have heard and said such things to girls. But that doesn't change the fact that when it's not me, I have to recognize the gayness and comment on it. It's an unspoken rule."

The muffled sound of glass cracking paused Ricky in his explanation. He looked over at Frenchy.

"What?"

He reached towards Frenchy's face, using his finger to rub his forehead. They looked down at his finger, Sarah joining, realizing the mood had changed.

"Did my pimple pop?"

Loud gunshots suddenly rang out. Sarah and Ricky ducked down, as Frenchy looked out the back window.

"Holy fuck."

Frenchy ducked down, as the back window shattered.

"What do we do?" Frenchy yelled, putting his arms over Sarah and Ricky. Neither answered as the gunfire continued. The loud voices of men could be heard as they ran past the vehicles. Sarah gripped Frenchy's hand, Ricky burying his head into Frenchy's stomach. The gunshots triggered Frenchy's memory, as he recalled a shooting near his house two years earlier. He began to shake, remembering how he ducked from his living room window, unsure what to do when he heard the gunfire. He clutched Sarah's hand, pulling Ricky closer to him. The shots suddenly stopped, the three remaining huddled.

"Don't move," Frenchy whispered.

He listened terrified as the crunch of footsteps on the dry soil grew louder. Ricky's door opened. Frenchy shuddered as the sensation of dying in his earlier dream returned. He closed his eyes tightly and gripped his companions, accepting his inability to stop the inevitable. The door suddenly closed. The three flinched at the slam of the door. They began to hear the muffled voices of men, moving around the vehicle. Frenchy opened his eyes, looking down at Ricky and Sarah, their heads pressed against his stomach. He began to lift his head as he heard the handle of the door creak.

"Dr. Degnan?"

Frenchy looked up slowly, recognizing the figure in front of him.

"Sir?" Frenchy said, trembling, unable to remember the man's name.

"Are you alright?"

Frenchy sat up, gently tapping his companions. Sarah looked up, somewhat relieved to see Mr. Botvinnik at the door.

"Mr. Botvinnik, what happened?"

Ricky sat up, quickly looking around.

"Our convoy was attacked by a militia."

Frenchy attempted to sigh, his breathing interrupted by his shaking. He reached into his pocket and removed a cigarette. The transmitter in the vehicle went off, Botvinnik looking over.

"You okay?"

Frenchy looked over at Sarah and she began to cry, her face returning to his shoulder.

"Holy shit, Doc, they're dead."

Frenchy followed Ricky's gaze to the driver and passenger in their vehicle. Blood splatters covered the windshield; the two men sitting motionless. The transmitter went off again. Botvinnik opened the front passenger side door, reaching for it. He spoke as he checked the passenger's pulse. Sarah listened carefully as he spoke in Hebrew.

"What the hell do you mean everything is fine? We're sitting in a car with two dead bodies!"

Botvinnik returned the transmitter and closed the front door, quickly opening the back door.

"Please step outside. I can explain."

Botvinnik encouraged them to exit the vehicle. Frenchy looked at Sarah, unsure about her outburst. Ricky hesitated to exit, hoping for Frenchy's approval.

"Why did you say everything was okay? I'm no expert but our convoy just got fucking shot up and our driver is dead."

Frenchy's hands shook as he took a drag of his cigarette, his expression remaining serious. Botvinnik turned around as a man spoke quietly to him.

"What the fuck is going on and where have you been?"

Ricky's eyes widened as he viewed Ali, replacing Botvinnik at the door.

"Please remain calm, Francis. This was done to save you."

Frenchy smoked his cigarette, his mind trying to digest the situation.

"Please, Francis, trust me; I would never harm you. Please come outside."

"Hell no, you know what? I am not moving until you tell me what's going on."

Ali shouted towards the back of the vehicle. The front doors opening as two men removed the dead driver and passenger.

"That is fair. I was trying to help you avoid watching the men being removed. Mr. Botvinnik and I orchestrated this to save you from men who are using you and who would have killed you after you found the artifact. The Israeli government has no care for your welfare and neither does the U.S. government. What do you think this has been all about? While I value you as person, this seems to be bigger than an Iron Age sword and a teacher from Jersey City."

Frenchy remained dazed, still trying to sort through the cluster of events that had blitzed his mind.

"Alright, you're right. If this is not about me, then what the hell is this all about? There is no way I am worth any of this so what is this about?"

Ali returned to shouting directions. Botvinnik emerged, entering the passenger seat.

"We have about twenty minutes to Masada. I will explain on the way."

Ali closed the door, walking to the driver seat and entering. Men raced around the Jeep, the sound of engines being started caused Ricky to slouch down in his seat. Ali started the Jeep and began driving.

"Francis, none of this has to do with you. You are a side note in a larger issue. In truth, it would seem your involvement is the product of an overly meticulous advisor to the Israeli Prime Minister, and a chance connection to the man who actually found this . . . symbol."

"That's all well and fine but that doesn't explain what the hell has been going on, and why I am hearing this from you now, and not . . . oh, I don't know, a thousand other opportunities when we were traveling here."

Sarah gently pushed Frenchy back.

"What is the truth, Ali? No more hints or alluding to the truth. Just, what is the problem?"

"First, if I could have told you, Francis, I would have but that would not have made things any better. Perhaps it would have made things worse. And second, I only fully understood your participation when I left you last night. To be brief, the U.S. and Israel are involved in a treaty to allow U.S. military bases in the region. Based on the current U.S. administration, I do not believe the bases are peacekeeping measures. Your involvement? It would seem Israel wanted the recovery of this Goliath's Sword as a national symbol, showing their triumph over the original Palestinians, the Philistines. Rabbi Judah disclosed his and Tannen's discovery to the Prime Minister. Tannen seemed to let slip that he felt you should be the one to recover the Sword. Apparently that displeased the Israelis. Assaf Greene, the Prime Minister's advisor, did not trust Tannen and thus decided to guarantee he would not compromise the search by ensuring you would be eliminated. Whether he had Tannen killed, I don't know. When I saw him yesterday, he knew who I was and so I couldn't take the chance of staying. I left."

"My father did the right thing and he was not killed; he was dying," Sarah shouted fiercely, her anger lingering as the group sat quietly.

"I am sorry, Ms. Tannen. I am not saying that your father did anything wrong. In fact, he showed his honor by opposing their request. It seems, inevitably, that he was convinced by his friend, Judah. But he never trusted them and it would seem that's how he was able to save Francis. After that, your existence on the run presented a problem and so their plan changed. I imagine they realized that Tannen's idea of having you find it turned out to be a wise suggestion, and thus why we were brought here."

Ricky nudged Frenchy, trying to show his distrust through his stare. Frenchy shrugged, unaware of any alternative to their current situation. He turned forward and spoke directly to Botvinnik.

"Where the hell do you come in Mr. B? If I recall, you were with the Prime Minister and Assaf on this whole thing."

Botvinnik turned around, looking at Frenchy sharply.

"Dr. Degnan, I do not appreciate that attack on me. I am a loyal Israeli. However, the U.S. military in the Promised Land is not acceptable. I have made arrangements to ensure that this will never take place."

"Then what the fuck are we doing here? If this stupid agreement will be stopped, then why aren't we blowing the whistle on this whole thing and why aren't we on our way home?"

Botvinnik smiled at Frenchy, who glanced over at Ali.

"I made an agreement with your friend here. We have agreed that we will work together to defeat the U.S.-Israeli agreement. His and my condition is the recovery of the Sword."

Frenchy snapped his gaze over towards Ali. Ali shifted in his seat, aware of Frenchy's obvious attention.

"So you are doing exactly what the Israelis did, just . . . it's okay, right? Because your cause is better, right? I don't know much but I'm pretty sure that this is some hard-core hypocritical bullshit. And you know I don't play any of that shit. I come from Jersey City. We don't get used, we use others."

Frenchy's voice changed to a strong ghetto voice.

"Doc, what do you mean you use others?"

"Shut up, Ricky!" Frenchy snapped, aware of Ricky's valid question.

"You are telling me, Dr. Degnan, that you would refuse to find this artifact, an artifact that has been your focus for the last twelve to thirteen years?"

"I see Ali has told you a bit about me."

Frenchy removed another cigarette, visibly resentful of Botvinnik's knowledge.

"Francis, please just cooperate. I promise that you will be returned safely home and you will be compensated for your work. I am asking you to help us. My colleagues, they do not ask. I would prefer to have your cooperation, not forced by them."

Frenchy's tough guy attitude retreated as the blood stains in the car reminded him of the capabilities of Ali's friends. He turned to Sarah, hoping she would provide some counsel.

"I don't think you have a choice. Let's just do this and get out of here."

Sarah leaned in and hugged Frenchy, Ricky joining them to Frenchy's discomfort.

"How do I know you are not just saying that like everyone else we have encountered on this journey? The Feds, the Israeli government? It seems no one is telling the truth."

"There is a difference between them and us. They care only about money. They do not try to understand issues; they simply focus on their own self-preservation and what is most profitable to them. I care about a fair and just solution. A solution you know has been unjustly and illegally withheld from Palestinians. This artifact? This is simply a means to rally our people. To make them rise up and force the world to fulfill the promise made sixty years ago. For Israelis, it is just another notch in their belts of supremacy and injustice. For us, it will remind us that we cannot allow the world to hide behind fear as a means to oppress. It will help us take the steps to reclaim what was lost."

"I don't know, brother, sounds a lot like the same shit Israel is spewing. Violence is not the way to achieve what you do deserve. I agree with that viewpoint, but you are doing exactly what the world expects: violence to achieve your ends. It will only invalidate your rightful claim and countries will continue to ignore your plight because how can you deal with people who are killing civilians every day? Do you think blacks in the U.S. would have achieved any rights if they used violence to achieve their aims? I don't think so. You would have heard people saying that they're savages, that they don't deserve to be treated as equals. It would have played into the country's fear. Just like you will, if you use violence."

"I don't disagree that non-violence is a better method, except when violence is what your opponent is using. And, if I remember correctly, Thomas Jefferson said, 'the tree of liberty must be refreshed from time to time with the blood of patriots and tyrants.' Violence is necessary, particularly because nothing has changed since the founding of Israel."

Botvinnik raised his hand, hoping to halt the political discussion.

"Regardless, we are approaching Masada. Are we agreed that in exchange for safe passage and monetary compensation, you will locate the Sword?"

Frenchy looked down at his notes. Despite all that had transpired, he recognized the futility of opposing their request.

"I'll try. And then we are returned home. Agreed?"

Ali smiled, appreciating Frenchy's agreement. The jeep stopped at the base of the immense fortress.

"Then I believe we have an accord."

ESPINOZA AND FORESTER observed the convoy through their binoculars, their position a few hundred yards away from Masada.

"I can't believe what just happened. What the hell is going on, sir?"

Jensen paced behind them furiously, dust emerging from his footsteps.

"Sir?"

"I'm not sure. There's nothing we could have done. We are not even supposed to be here."

"What the hell was that? Do you think Degnan was killed?"

Jensen looked back at Ephraim, sitting calmly in their vehicle. Jensen gritted his teeth and turned back to his agents.

"He doesn't seem too surprised, does he?" Jensen said, quietly.

His agents remained fixed on the movement at the base of the fortress.

"You think he knew this was going to happen?"

Jensen nonchalantly brought his binoculars up to his eyes and stared off into the distance.

"Not sure. But I am not sure this is the appropriate response. As it took place, he didn't even flinch. He simply watched, stone-faced."

Espinoza rose to his feet and stood next to his boss.

"He was on the radio. Do you think he reported what happened?"

"Let's find out. Do you have a recorder?"

Espinoza nodded, the two returning to the car. They entered the back seats.

"Have you radioed to your people to let them know of the attack?"

Ephraim remained still.

"I did. They have asked us to monitor the situation. Military reinforcements have been deployed."

Jensen looked over at Espinoza, surprised at the unexpected response.

"If you are concerned with my response, I apologize. This does not shock me. These people are barbarians. They are not civilized. They will kill anyone. My eyes have witnessed many a similar attack. It is difficult to muster the ability to be surprised when such a scene has become commonplace."

Ephraim turned around and looked at Jensen.

"We could not do anything. Our best course of action was to observe. Justice will be done."

Jensen nodded in agreement, gesturing to Espinoza to exit.

"So much for that. Although that puts my heart at ease a bit," Espinoza said, looking to his boss.

Jensen surveyed the surrounding areas.

"We can't stay here. We need to get closer without being seen."

Forester stood up and pointed towards an area to the north of the fortress.

"Doesn't that look like a good spot? Near that row of palm trees. I think I even see some vehicles there."

"We can scout it out, but we have to decide what we're going to do."

Espinoza looked confused.

"I thought we were going to stick to the original mission, monitor? Besides, if there are military units on the way, I think we should defer to them."

"I agree, if there were military units on the way."

The two young agents looked at each other, unsure how to respond.

"He didn't call in reinforcements. He didn't call at all. Little trick of the trade. A recently used transmitter will cause interference with say, a recorder. There was none. He hasn't used that since we left Jerusalem."

Forester, an expert in electronic devices, looked skeptically at his boss.

"I've never heard of that trick."

Jensen looked sternly at him.

"Of course, you haven't. Most radios are not outdated like his. Regardless, we are going to make our way over to that area and try to move in on the convoy. If we get the chance, we will take Degnan and his traveling companions and get the hell out of here. Agreed?"

Espinoza wiped the sweat from his forehead, looking over at his partner.

"You're the boss. I'm in," Forester said.

Espinoza raised his hands in acquiescence. Jensen looked back at Ephraim and gestured for him to join them.

"Good, grab your stuff. Let's get away from this guy. The more we're around him, the worst off we will be."

FRENCHY AND SARAH slowly sauntered towards a group of men standing near the base of Masada, Frenchy eyeing a path behind them as diggers removed dirt from the base. Botvinnik gestured towards them, encouraging them to step closer. Ali walked over to the men and greeted them. Other men from the convoy quickly joined the group. Frenchy surveyed the massive structure, momentarily losing himself in the chance to finally stand before it.

"Mr. Degnan, my friend has put much faith in your abilities. I pray for you and your friends that you can fulfill our expectations," Samir said, clenching his fists.

Amir quickly approached, speaking in Arabic to his brother.

"My apologies, Dr. Degnan. We appreciate your help," Amir said, with Samir shaking his head in opposition.

Frenchy eyed Samir. Despite being fearful, his temper flared at the lightly veiled threat.

"Well, you know me, always happy to accommodate a request, especially when it's at gunpoint."

Frenchy smiled defiantly at the brothers. Sarah kicked the dirt, hoping to draw Frenchy's attention.

"Anyway, sorry about that. As much as I look forward to skin cancer, perhaps we could get moving on the finding of this thing so I don't return home a shriveled tomato?"

Amir laughed, appreciating Frenchy's directness.

"I couldn't agree more. Please let me show you what we have been working on."

The group walked over towards the main area of the digging. Frenchy observed a small pile of pottery fragments, their presence increasing his excitement. He was unaware of the attention his presence had drawn from the diggers. He spotted a stone tablet and immediately walked quickly towards it.

"Holy mother! It's a marker," he said, turning back to Sarah and Ricky.

Ricky ran up next to Frenchy, mimicking his excitement.

"Well, kiss my ass. Doc, this is what that half-map thing said. A marker."

Frenchy grabbed a small brush and cleaned the front of the small stone slab.

"Yes, as I was going to explain, we uncovered this in this area," Amir said skeptically, concerned by Frenchy's enthusiasm.

"Latin inscription. Can you translate it, Ricky?"

Frenchy smiled, challenging his student.

"Doc, stop this shit. Really, just translate the freakin' thing. No lessons."

Frenchy grinned, returning to the inscription. Sarah joined the two, holding Frenchy's arm.

"May Jupiter strike down the man who removes the plague from this cavern, the blood money spent."

Ricky raised an eyebrow.

"Are you sure you are translating this correctly?"

Frenchy muttered to himself, repeatedly translating the phrase.

"I mean, I don't know, Jupiter striking us dead? Sounds a bit like that movie *The Mummy*."

Frenchy slowly raised his head, displaying his displeasure at Ricky's comment.

"You know what I'm talking about. We watched that in your World Civ class. Don't tell me you don't find this inscription a wee bit creepy?"

Frenchy rolled his eyes.

"First, I showed that because I was hung over from the night before. Second, I have a hard time getting spooked by any movie with Brendan Fraser as the lead, at least since his work in *Encino Man*. Third, Jupiter as a god went out long ago. So suck it up and stop being so scared."

Sarah observed Frenchy's confused expression as he returned to the marker. Frenchy placed the stone down and stood up, looking around at the excavations. He turned towards Amir.

"Where was this found?"

"It was found there," Samir said, pointing to a large area that had been excavated.

Sarah joined Frenchy as he surveyed the empty area. He carefully lowered himself into the trench. He ran his hand over the subterranean section of rock, stopping at a cutaway section. He signaled to Ricky to bring the stone slab. Ricky handed the marker down to Frenchy. He placed it into the empty area, the slab roughly fitting. He removed the slab and scrutinized the opening, reaching into the area and pulling his hand out filled with dirt and rock shards.

"What do you think?" Sarah asked, kneeling down to get closer to Frenchy's eye level.

"There's a hole in the middle, goes back about a foot but that's it. Nothing in it." Frenchy searched the area at his feet, returning consistently to the opening, reaching in repeatedly, and feeling around in the hole.

"What's the word, Doc, you look confused?"

"It's exactly where I thought it would be. It's exactly the way I said it would be, minus the marker. And it's not here. I mean, granted, I didn't know it would be exactly like this, but still. And the marker doesn't say anything else. It's just where I said it would be. I don't know. I'm not sure where we go from here. It ain't like we have another clue. It says it should be here. But nothing."

He lit a cigarette, remaining in the hole, continuing to search. Ali and Samir approached Frenchy.

"So obviously, it is not here, maybe it once was but no more. What is the next step? Where is the artifact?"

Frenchy snapped in irritation.

"Stop calling it 'the artifact,' for Christ's sake; it's annoying."

Ali and Samir stood motionless, ignoring his aggravation, and awaiting a response to their question.

"Look, I'm sorry. I don't know; I need to think. Is that okay? Just give me a little bit of time. I'm not an archaeologist. I'm from Jersey; I can't suddenly have epiphanies on the spot."

Amir shouted over to his brother in Arabic, Samir responding sharply.

"Take the time you need. We will continue digging."

Samir walked back to his brother, Ali lingering momentarily.

"Just relax. You do not handle pressure well. Sit and think."

Frenchy mocked Ali's statement, pulling himself out of the hole.

"I'm going to sit and think in the shade."

Frenchy began to walk.

"But Doc there is no . . ."

"Shut up, Ricky, just shut up; I know there is no shade."

Frenchy walked over to one of the military vehicles, plopping down against the back tire. Ricky looked down, hurt by Frenchy's anger. Sarah put her hand on his shoulder.

"Let's go sit with him, not say anything, but just sit with him in silent support."

Ricky nodded sadly, the seesaw of emotions beginning to take its toll. The two walked over and sat a few feet away from Frenchy leaning against the vehicle. Frenchy removed his notes staring wearily. Ali walked over handing him a bottle of water.

"Hydrate yourself. The sun can kill you in other ways than melanoma."

Frenchy stood slowly, opening the bottle for a sip.

"You know, Ali, I really don't know if I am going to help. This is what I worked my life for, this moment here at the base. I'm not certain I will be able to figure this out."

Ali smiled, drinking from his own bottle.

"Just do your best. Either way, in two days you will be back in Jersey City, safe. Do not allow Samir to worry you. I made you a promise. Just please, make your best effort."

Frenchy looked around, shielding his eyes from the sun.

"You know, I always wanted to visit here. Any chance I can take a walk up a little? Call it my reflection constitutional."

"Of course. Just know that, if you run, Samir will kill you."

"That's comforting; thank you. May I take my sidekicks? Like you said, if I try to run, I'll be dead."

Ali looked over at Ricky and Sarah.

"Sure, but to make Samir happy, I will send a body guard with you." Ali called over to a man standing near the other military vehicle. The heavily cloaked man walked over to Ali, his machine gun hanging from his right arm. Frenchy smiled awkwardly.

"Terrific, a bodyguard. Is he carrying that to protect me or to, um . . ."

"Relax, this isn't Jersey City. Here you need someone with a machine gun."

"Great. Well, let's take our stroll."

Frenchy gestured to his companions to join him as he walked towards a roughly marked path.

"What a nice day for a walk, isn't it?" Sarah joked, as she took Frenchy's arm. "Perhaps we can consider this our first date."

Frenchy looked back at Ricky following, the armed man a few feet behind.

"Sure, let's. I love dates that include a student and an armed Bedouin."

They walked casually, looking around at the surrounding area.

"I assume you're frustrated?"

Frenchy looked at Sarah and down at her arm in his.

"You know, this is a bad precedent to be setting. When I'm honest and tell you my feelings, you like me more, and you become affectionate. By tomorrow, I will have shared my innermost feelings and the last time I wet the bed."

Sarah rolled her eyes.

"No, seriously, just think about it; less than twenty-four hours ago, you hit me in the balls, and now look at us, out on a date, arm-in-arm, touring a magnificent fortress."

"You're ignoring my question."

Frenchy broke away and picked up a rock.

"Yeah, well, we are just buying some time. I don't really have a clue what to do next so I figured how often do we get to tour such a natural wonder? And yes, I am frustrated. But not too much. I actually feel somewhat better, knowing that I was kind of right."

"Bullshit. You feel good. Don't lie. I could only imagine what you are feeling, having done everything right, only to be disappointed. Believe me, I'm actually pretty upset. You were right all along and my dad let you write your thoughts and feelings and be ridiculed when all along he knew you were right."

"Easy on your dad. What was he supposed to say? 'Hey Frenchy, great book and, by the way, you're absolutely right, but I can't tell you why.'"

Frenchy threw the rock up the path.

"I love my father, but this is not right."

"Hey, you know I'm not thrilled, but he was a good man, I hold no anger towards him. Hope he's at peace, whatever the hell that means."

Sarah stopped walking putting her hand over her eyes.

"What's the matter, dust in the eye?"

Sarah removed her hands from her face, revealing tears in her eyes.

"I keep forgetting he's gone. Everything happened so quickly. I left his burial."

Frenchy put his arm around her, attempting to console her.

"Hey, I'm glad you left and I am sure he is too; it's because of him that we are here together and I'm still breathing."

"Yeah, but Doc, the rabbi made sure you would not be hurt. Once he did that, why send you on a mission he knew you would fail at, no disrespect. But seriously, once you got his letter, you could have gone to the authorities and they would have protected you. Why save your life and then send you when he knew it wasn't here?" Ricky asked.

"I don't know. Maybe he wanted me to find it."

Ricky walked quickly to catch up to Frenchy.

"No, think about it: if he wanted you to find it, he could have given you the location. You don't save someone's life and say, 'I destroyed the map but don't worry, follow your gut.' You tell them where it is so you have leverage, not just the hope that they can find it."

Sarah looked back at Ricky, his words going beyond her simple disagreement with her father.

"Are you saying my father was playing him?"

Ricky stopped, attempting to backtrack physically as well as verbally. Frenchy stepped into a constructed section of Masada.

"This is one of the rebel dwellings."

Sarah continued to glare at Ricky, looking over at Frenchy, angry that he did not defend her father. Frenchy looked back, feeling Sarah's stare.

"I don't think your father played me. But Ricky's point has made me wonder something. If your father found the Sword and now it's gone from the original site, either he had it or he knew where it is now, or he never found it. I don't know. Can we all just chill out for a moment and cool down, figuratively?"

He walked over to Sarah, standing in front of her crossed arms.

"Please? No one is blaming anyone. We need to relax and keep it together."

Sarah nodded, somewhat defiantly. Frenchy looked around at the surroundings, observing the faint remains of man-made walls.

"It's amazing, this could have been where the whole thing took place."

"What whole thing?" Ricky asked, joining Frenchy.

"The mass suicide of the Sicarii. This is where it may have happened. The men killing their wives and children and then choosing lots to decide who would kill everyone else. It's no wonder Silva left the sword here. I wouldn't want anything to do with the Jews after seeing that. Well, probably not. Odds are at the top. But think about it."

Ricky picked through some rocks and small shards of pottery near the base of the wall.

"Pretty fucked up."

Frenchy dropped his head in exhaustion.

"I know I have said it the whole time but can we limit the usage of the f-word."

Ricky shrugged, resuming his light rummaging.

"Hey, Doc, how do you know all the stuff you just said?"

"What do you mean?"

"I mean all the stuff you just said about the women and children being killed by the father slash husband, and then drawing lots? I thought everybody was dead when the Romans finally showed up?"

"Yeah, how did they know what happened?" Sarah chimed in with Ricky, following his logic.

"The only record that exists is the historian Josephus, and he got his info from two women who escaped."

"Are they the ones who said the sword was buried here?"

Frenchy paused from his inspection of the room, muttering to himself.

"Maybe. I suppose that could be it. Of course it was . . ."

Ricky and Sarah walked over to him, hoping to keep the discussion away from their escort.

"What?"

Frenchy grabbed Ricky and hugged him, turning to Sarah and kissing her passionately.

"Get some, Doc . . ."

"Not now. That's it. The only people aside from Roman soldiers who would have known that the Sword was here was the two women. And if they told Josephus, that means they probably took it after it was buried by Silva. And if they took it, then your father followed the same logic. If it was buried here, but now gone, the women had it. And there's only one place you take something like that after a mass suicide of the Sicarii."

"Of course! You bring it to the Wailing Wall."

Frenchy exhaled loudly as the unfortunate alternate possibility emerged. He stuttered, trying to accept his conclusion's uniqueness.

"Well, um, yes, maybe, but no, you take it to the burial place of the first Sicarii, the founder. And the founder of the Sicarii is someone you know quite well. He's just not known for it. The founder is . . . oh shit."

Frenchy flinched, his face panic stricken. The armed escort stood behind Sarah and Ricky, his gun pointed at Frenchy.

"I'm not going to run, sir. Please tell me you speak English. I am not going to run. I was about to return to the base to tell your friends. Please don't kill us. It just took a walk to figure things out."

Sarah slowly walked forward and gripped Frenchy, Ricky turning and standing next to Frenchy, his hands held high above his head.

"In the future, I wouldn't ever move unless the guy tells you to."

Frenchy held Sarah tightly. The man stepped closer, the muzzle of the gun closer to Frenchy's face.

"Of course, after all that, I finally get a clue and now I'm dead."

ESPINOZA AND FORESTER carefully made their way towards the tourist center. They carefully searched their surroundings, aware of how quick the attack on the convoy had come. They cautiously checked the building doors, unsure if a worker would be a welcomed or dreaded encounter.

"Where the hell is Jensen?" Espinoza asked, frustrated at his absence. "We're supposed to cover him and now he's gone."

"Well, he must have moved in closer so we should do the same."

Forester pushed forward, a sense of panic filling his body. They moved towards the convoy one hundred yards away, dropping to a crawl.

"It's hot as balls out here. We should have brought some water from the car."

Espinoza nodded in agreement, scraping his body along the dust and rock-filled terrain. They begin their ascent up the path, moving closer to Snake Gate Path. Forester paused, removing his binoculars.

"I don't see Degnan or his friends. Just some armed men and I think I see some diggers at the base. No sign of Jensen."

"Well, I hope not; otherwise then, they can see him as well. We need to get out of sight. There's a cutaway section up on the left about forty feet. Let's settle there."

Forester nodded and the two quickened their crawl towards the indentation in the left spine of the fortress. The two agents surveyed their surroundings, dissecting the camp. The armed men stood motionless, Ali and Samir standing near the excavation. Forester looked back at the tourist center.

"Not sure why it's closed."

Espinoza joined Forester's gaze, eventually looking up to a cable connecting the top of Masada to the base.

"I'm sure there is a reason. Whether that reason is legitimate or bullshit, who knows."

Espinoza's phone vibrated in his pocket, causing Forester to draw his weapon. Espinoza removed the phone, reading a text message.

"Unbelievable, we're in shit-ass nowhere and still got service. Jensen says he is close to the convoy. Says we need to pull back to the tourist area."

Forester fell back against the rock, annoyed at the futility of their assent.

"He says we should go now; one of us has to go get Ephraim."

The two looked down, pondering the meaning behind Jensen's text. Espinoza looked back at their previous location, suddenly frustrated by how far they had come in trying to protect Jensen.

"Let's go, let's just do it. I'm feeling sick from this heat. Let's take this route. It's out of sight so we don't have to crawl."

Forester pointed to an outlet leading to the south side of the small rock causeway. Espinoza followed him, looking back at the convoy once more before following Forester. They briskly walked down the uncut path.

"I'll go to Ephraim. You good to stay around here?" Espinoza asked, hoping Forester would agree.

"No problem, I'll stay here. Any chance it's a crime to break in and take a bottle of water?"

Espinoza chuckled, wiping sweat from his lip.

"Not if you get me three. Shit, we aren't even suppose to be here. If we get arrested, I'd welcome it."

FRENCHY BEGAN TO TREMBLE as the man moved the gun closer to his face.

"I didn't mean anything by that last comment. I was just commenting on my shitty luck. In no way am I speaking ill of you."

The armed guard gestured with his gun, moving the three towards a corner of the decayed room.

"I'm sorry guys, I shouldn't have taken us away from Ali; he was the only protection we had and now he's down there."

Sarah eyed the man as she moved with Frenchy's body. He cornered them, unexpectedly backing away and keeping the gun on them. He looked down the path where they had come, quickly returning to his close position to them. Frenchy jumped back, moving Sarah behind him, assuming an attack. The man slowly lowered his gun and removed his face garb.

"Shit, Doc, these guys are as white as you," Ricky said quietly, as he studied the man's face.

"They're so well-covered, it wouldn't surprise me," Frenchy said, mimicking Ricky's low tone.

"I'm not one of them, you idiot. I'm an FBI agent, Al Jensen." Frenchy cocked his head to the left, staring at the man's face.

"No, you're not; you're what's-his-face from the plane."

Frenchy became suspicious, worried more about the man's sudden revelation than the diminished threat to his life.

"I lied about who I was because I've been tracking you."

Frenchy nodded, seemingly complacent with Jensen's response.

"Help! Ali, help . . . help . . ."

Jensen raised the gun, Frenchy ceasing his cries.

"Stop, you idiot, I'm not going to hurt you; I am here to tell you simply that we are watching you and will protect you. If you have the chance to break away, we will be watching and we will pick the three of you up. That's all. We are here for your protection."

Sarah emerged from behind Frenchy.

"The FBI has already shown that they do not care about us."

"You said us; that's so nice," Frenchy said, caught up in Sarah's statement of solidarity.

She glared at him, returning to Jensen.

"I don't care anymore about what happened in the past. I have followed my orders and done what I was told. And that led me here. And I have seen enough to believe this is not right. We will follow you and protect you. I'm calling the shots, no one else."

"Who's we?" Ricky snapped, looking around for his colleagues.

"I have two agents with me. You may be familiar with them, I believe. Ms. Tannen, you clubbed one of them."

Sarah scanned her memory, hoping to retrieve the reference.

"That does not help your credibility. If I'm not mistaken, your agents were the ones that first mislead me. Why should I believe you?"

Frenchy grabbed for his cigarettes. Sarah, sadly shaking her head, recognizing Frenchy's anxiety from his habits.

"Tell you what, if you scream to your Muslim friends when we get to the bottom, then I will leave with my agents and we will not follow or protect. But if you want to take a chance and believe me, then you shut up and tell them your epiphany. Either way, I'll be fine getting away. I'm a fucking FBI agent, not some dipshit Jersey asshole."

The three looked at each other. Frenchy smiled.

"Let's see what happens when we get to the bottom, you'll have my response then."

Jensen took his cloak and covered his face, hanging his gun from his shoulder.

"You really don't get it. Our escort is in on this whole thing as well as your friends down there. This is bigger than your little fucking quest. But you believe what you want to."

Jensen gestured to them to move towards the path for their descent. Sarah nodded, hoping to get Frenchy to move. He lit his cigarette and entered the path. The three quickened their pace to separate themselves from Jensen.

"So do I scream bloody hell or no?"

Ricky shook his head at Sarah, not interested in participating in the discussion.

"I don't know. But if we let him go, it might not hurt to have someone watching."

"Any reason why you didn't help us when our convoy was ambushed?"

"If you mean when a calculated attack was launched with inside support—if you are referring to that one—well, let me see. We were a couple hundred yards away with hand guns and a stoic Israeli driver. Did we think we should have? Yes, but it turns out it was a wise decision that we didn't. Now that is enough, no more questions."

The three walked for a few minutes, not talking. Frenchy looked around as they descended from the fortress.

"You know, I didn't get to tell you where I think this awful artifact is."

"Should we mention it with Captain America behind us?" Sarah said, sarcastically.

"Well, dear, our new location is Machaerus Herodium."

Ricky seemed confused by what sounded false.

"That's the first of the Sicarii?"

Frenchy shook his head at his sidekick.

"No, not him; it's Herod's castle, supposedly the place where John the Baptist was executed. John the Baptist was the first Sicarii. The first assassin."

Frenchy turned and glanced at Jensen.

"I've heard of such place. Not a bad place to escape from. Too bad John couldn't," Jensen muttered, lifting his gun.

Despite the veiled communications from Frenchy, he feared the possible ambush below. The group emerged from the last bend of the path. Ali and Samir looked up the path. Frenchy waved happily to the awaiting group.

"Ali, I may have it. I think I know where it is."

Ali shouted in Arabic to his men, the group surrounding Frenchy in anticipation.

"When I was in what I thought was the rebel dwellings, I suddenly realized it was the synagogue. If the Sword had been taken from here, the logical place would be Herod's fortress, Machaerus Herodium—where John the Baptist was executed. John the Baptist was originally considered to be a messianic figure and linked to the House of King David."

Ali stood still, attempting to process Frenchy's revelation.

"But Francis, why and who would bring the sword to John the Baptist's tomb? And moreover, why him? Why not bring it to Jesus' tomb? He, too, was a descendant of the House of David."

Frenchy paused, pretending to contemplate the question.

"Who would take it? The women who escaped from here. They probably took it and brought it to John's tomb because at that time the Jesus movement was small and somewhat alienated. Plus, John rebelled against the norm, the status quo, like Jesus, but on a much higher level. John was not afraid to rebel. The Sicarii were known for valuing John's approach. Plus, why take a sword and bring it to an empty tomb? You bring it to the first Sicarii: John the Baptist. Who knows why they took it. I don't freakin' know, but it's not here and it makes sense for it to be a place connected by history and close in location."

Frenchy removed a cigarette, his hands shaking to light it.

"You have any water?" Frenchy asked. One of the men handed him a canteen.

Ali and Samir began to speak to one another in Arabic, Amir joining the exchange. Frenchy stood, his hands trembling slightly. He looked around cautiously, searching for Jensen. In the distance, he saw a figure walking quickly down the path towards the tourist center.

"Well, Francis, let us continue this journey. Herodium is in Jordan so we will have no difficulty entering the country and we will have as much time as we need to excavate."

Frenchy smiled and embraced Ali. Ali broke from the embrace, yelling to the diggers. They began to assemble their tools and load them into the vehicles.

Frenchy walked over to the original trench, picking up the marker. Samir grabbed his arm as he lifted the stone slab.

"You can take your hand off me, cousin. I sure as hell don't think you should be touching me. And if you want this marker, well, you can kiss my ass. This is part of my compensation."

Samir strengthened his grip on Frenchy's arm, staring defiantly into his eyes. Ali took notice of the confrontation.

"Ali, tell your camel-humping friend to take his filthy, skanky hands off of me. This is part of the deal. I take this. This is mine or I walk."

Amir joined the conversation.

"I do not have a problem with Dr. Degnan taking the marker. But please, Doctor, do not threaten us. You have told us where the artifact is located. Your leverage was given away when you excitedly shared your, what was it, epiphany."

Frenchy recognized his mistake, avoiding responding to Amir by staring at Samir's grip on his arm. Samir reluctantly released Frenchy's arm.

"Are you a movie lover?" Frenchy asked, walking towards Amir.

"I am quite sure we do not share the same taste in film."

"No doubt, my brother, but there is a must-see film with Nicholas Cage, called *National Treasure*. In the final scenes, Cage's character gives the location of a vast treasure to guys holding him hostage for his help."

"I am not sure I follow."

"Well, it turns out, that clever Nick Cage gave false info. And they end up screwed. So before you go thinking you have me figured out, remember that I have watched every adventure, treasure-seeking movie ever made. I know the game."

Amir smiled and extended his hand to Frenchy.

"I am sorry Dr. Degnan. I underestimated you once again."

Frenchy winked, shaking Amir's hand. He pulled him in for an embrace.

"Just remember, Ali and I are the only friends you have here. If we looked the other way, my brother would cut your throat without pause and the same for your young student. Your lovely Sarah, well, he doesn't seem to have much respect for Israelis, particularly their women."

Frenchy stood still, his expression serious. His stomach turned as he recognized he had no control in his present situation.

"I certainly appreciate your protection. And I promise to deliver on this search."

Amir bowed his head and slowly released Frenchy's hand. Sarah approached, smiling towards Amir as he walked away. She grabbed Frenchy's arm and leaned towards him, resting her head on his shoulder.

"I know it doesn't change anything, but could the next search site not be in a hostile Islamic state? And I am not so sure our FBI detail will be able to enter."

Frenchy brushed her hair from her face, staring cautiously at the armed men near the vehicles.

"Well, you know me, can't ever make anything easy. It wouldn't be fun. And I have a feeling our friends will do fine in following us. Let's just go do this, find the Sword, and then get the hell out of here."

Sarah looked up at him, pulling away to stand in front of him.

"You mean you would let them have the Sword? After all this?"

Frenchy wiped his forehead, lighting another cigarette.

"To be honest, while an adventure was what I always wanted, I don't want this. If there are people who are willing to kill others over this or sign treaties for monetary interests, then let them have it. It's not worth it. As far as I'm concerned, if I can get you and Ricky home safe, then I've succeeded in my quest. Besides, FBI, Muslim extremists, Israeli officials and military, and private collectors? I want no part of this anymore."

"But we are a part of it and we cannot ignore the fact that those in power abuse their power, and it is the average person that suffers. The Israeli government, Palestinian extremists . . . I don't know, I agree with you but I just think we can't go home and pretend none of this happened, or that we are not responsible."

Frenchy exhaled smoke through his nose, a sharp look emerged as Sarah's comment triggered the sudden change.

"What's wrong?"

"Nothing. You know, I have been educated in either Catholic schools or Jesuit Catholic schools for almost my entire education. I've worked in their schools for eight years. The one consistent message has always been what are you doing for the betterment of others? Are you caring for the whole person?

Are you being a man for others? Do you root out injustice? All these questions have plagued me. Yet, in my classes I often pose questions similar to what you just said. Who is responsible for injustice? My answer is always the same: everyone. We are responsible. I guess when injustice is thrown in your lap, I do what everyone does, ignore and run away."

The two stood silently.

"Alright, we'll do something. Don't know what yet, but we will do something to stop things like this. But I don't care about the sword. As far as I'm concerned, the greatest treasure on this quest was you. If I can return home and maybe take you out on a second date, a date that doesn't involve armed militants and a student, then I'm okay with everything."

"Gay."

"Motherfucker," Sarah said, biting her lip, her mild euphoria interrupted by the dependable, juvenile comment. Ricky held his finger up, hoping to stem the onslaught of anger.

"First of all, you need to be more vigilant; I just crept up without you two lovebirds knowing. If I had been an assassin, I could have killed you. Second, really? The two of you go from seventh grade fighting to love-struck Shakespearean bullshit. What's next, you gonna call each other by pet names? Hi, Frenchy Wenchy. Oh, hi, Schnoopy. Get it together! There are guns around us and we need to find this stupid thing. I'm officially using my sidekick card and saying that we need to get the hell out of here soon so I don't end up a lime in their fucking non-alcoholic Corona."

Frenchy seemed impressed by Ricky's assertive statement.

"I'm impressed, Ricky. Shakespearean? Not bad. I don't understand the lime in the Corona reference though."

"Let's just say I will not be the flavor that is pushed into the bottom of the bottle."

Ali yelled to Frenchy, encouraging him to move towards their original transportation.

"I still don't get it, is that a sex reference?"

Ricky gestured indiscriminately with his fingers, hoping to convey his metaphor through gestures.

"I think that made it worse, and I am pretty sure that I do not want to continue this." Frenchy raised his hand, halting Ricky's attempt at charades. "Just get in the car, please. This has moved towards the weird, and stop saying 'gay' every time I say something nice to Sarah and vice versa. We will never get the chance for that movie-like kiss if you mutter 'gay' after every comment."

Ricky shook his head in subtle disagreement, walking towards the jeep.

"I'd thank you for reprimanding him, but that was fairly delicate."

Sarah walked ahead of Frenchy, entering the vehicle, Ali holding the door.

"Let us continue the journey. We should still have some time to excavate."

Frenchy entered the vehicle, grinning at Ali's statement.

"Yeah, that's fine. Just remember: now that we are entering Jordan, I don't want you to say, 'Oh, I'm sorry, our agreement only applied in Israel.'"

Frenchy gripped the marker as Ali shut the door. He looked over at Sarah and Ricky, observing the blood spatters on the sides of the interior.

"Well, *that* makes me feel comfortable to be back in this vehicle. A little blood spatter from the assassination—how quaint."

The three sat back, simultaneously sliding down into their seats. Ali entered the driver's seat, looking back at his passengers.

"Why are you sitting that way?" he asked, looking over at Botvinnik as he took the passenger seat.

"Oh, don't worry; we're just preparing for the future."

"That is fine, just be prepared for a longer journey. We have to go around the Dead Sea to make it to Machaerus."

Frenchy gave a positive gesture to Ali.

"Fine with us. I just hope for a safe, attack-free trip."

FORESTER DREW HIS FIREARM as he saw a man in the distance running towards the tourist center. Jensen waved his hands as he approached. Forester dropped his gun, recognizing his boss. Forester clenched his fists as Jensen slowed to a casual walk.

"You know, boss, us as a backup only works if we can see where you're going. When you go off running and disappear, that makes it difficult for us to follow. And yes, if you are noticing my anger, it's because I'm very angry."

Jensen looked past Forester, his attention drawn to a vending machine. He removed his gun and shot at the lock, the door violently popping ajar. Jensen grabbed the door, trying to force it open. Forester held a bottle of water in his hand, extending it to Jensen.

"You know, I'm not incompetent; I opened that without a single shot fired. Now, what the hell is going on?"

Jensen snatched the bottle of water, consuming the entire bottle.

"First, we will not talk in front of Ephraim. I assume Carl has gone to get him?"

"Yes, he has. Then tell me now before they show up—what the hell happened?"

Jensen threw the bottle to the ground and grabbed Forester's satchel, removing a second bottle.

"You better watch your tone. I appreciate your concern and upsetment, but watch your goddamn tone."

Forester sneered, lowering his head as a mock-submissive gesture.

"I met our friend, Dr. Degnan. He and his two companions are fine, but they are being held by Islamic extremists. One of them is his Muslim friend from Jersey City; the other, I believe was part of the convoy from Israel. Actually, I believe he was the man who brought them to the Prime Minister's residence and when they left, he was in one of the rear cars."

"So what, Degnan's friend was playing him the whole time? And this Jew was too? He must be with the Palestinians."

Jensen walked away from the tourist center, the sound of a car's engine drawing him away.

"Yes, but he's safe, so long as his Muslim friend is alive. It seems to be a very militant group. Well-armed, and based on what we saw, well-acquainted with military tactics."

Forester joined Jensen, watching their vehicle approaching.

"How did you get to Degnan?"

"I nabbed one of the guards. Used his garb and took his place. I was lucky to be called to accompany them on a walk. I was just hoping to hear what was going on. Instead, I end up with our friends. Degnan knows what he's doing. And he agreed to come with us at the first chance they get to escape."

Forester secured his gun, seemingly relieved by his boss's words.

"Well, good, we nab him and we go home and turn him in. Maybe we get a vacation out of this bullshit."

Jensen waved as the jeep approached.

"No way. I am not turning him in to anyone; not until we know he won't be touched."

"You gone soft boss, your last communication said we bring him back and turn him in."

"Tell you what. You look me in the eye and tell me you believe he deserves to be in the custody of any law enforcement agency here or at home. You do that and I will nab him right now. But there is no way you believe that. We may think he is a loser, but I will not follow through on bullshit orders. Now shut up and follow my lead when we get into the car. I don't trust Ephraim and I know I'm right about that; despite your disagreement on my electronic experiment, he is wrong. Now look happy but dehydrated."

Forester changed his posture. In spite of his disdain, he valued his boss's opinion. The car stopped abruptly, Espinoza opening the door.

"What the hell is going on?" he said in exasperation.

"Everything's fine, I think I have a bead on where they're headed. Can you get us to Machaerus in Jordan?"

Ephraim showed no emotion.

"Of course. I will radio back to headquarters to make sure they know our destination."

"Please do, we will need all the help we can get."

"THIS REMINDS ME OF KANSAS. Except instead of seeing corn fields for the last ninety minutes, I've only seen dusty rocks and water I can't drink."

Ali chuckled at Frenchy's observation.

"You know, Francis, I've given much thought to your helping us on this search. I do believe you will achieve the scholarly exoneration you deserve. After you find this for us, you will be paid handsomely and will receive the credit for the find. But I worry you may not be loved by your fellow Americans. They may not appreciate your cooperation with an Islamic militant group."

"Ali, I have been wanted for murder and arson in the last two days by my fellow Americans. And based on what you said, they don't seem to care about me so my fellow Americans can suck a nut."

Sarah instinctively hit Frenchy, giving him a look of disapproval.

"Sorry, sorry—I need to learn to use more appropriate words to be crude."

"On a different topic, one of our guards claimed to have been attacked at Masada. He said he was knocked unconscious and when he was awoken by a fellow guard, his tunic was returned. He was the guard I sent with you on your walk."

Sarah calmly squeezed Frenchy's thigh.

"Is that right? Is that heat stroke? Can that make you pass out and hallucinate? I feel his pain; I feel exhausted and still the day is young."

Ali carefully scrutinized Frenchy's behavior, attempting to gauge his truthfulness.

"Well, whatever it is, you certainly have a way of scaring my men. They say you cannot be trusted."

"Ali, come on, you know me! I can't lie to save my life. Maybe if they properly hydrated themselves, they wouldn't be passing out and then waking up the same way but claiming they had been knocked out. Besides, I don't know if you've surveyed the land, but I don't see anyone who could blend in and sneak up. Unless you're a goat or a rock . . . well, maybe not a goat, haven't seen them either."

Botvinnik looked over at Ali, his glance interrupted by his cell phone ringing. He spoke for a few moments, Sarah leaning forward to listen. He ended his phone call and placed his phone on the center console. Frenchy casually looked at Sarah for a discreet synopsis. Sarah shook her head, dismissing Frenchy's interest.

"We are coming up on Machaerus. Where should we begin?"

Botvinnik turned and awaited Frenchy's response. Frenchy looked down at his notes, trying to buy some time in search of an answer.

"Well, before we take the trek up the mountain, we should check the hermit caves at the base. Because of the importance of the fortress being John the Baptist's place of execution, I would imagine two women who escaped from Masada might have decided to spend the rest of their days as hermits at the place of the founder of political execution."

"What do you mean?"

Botvinnik shifted his body facing Frenchy fully.

"The first Sicarii was John the Baptist. The Sicarii are named for the daggers they used. They practically invented the art of political assassination. Sneak up on a dude and knife him, then scream for help. They were pretty badass. And John the Baptist was their founder."

Botvinnik looked skeptically at Frenchy's explanation.

"Forgive me, but I was under the impression that John the Baptist was nonviolent. If I recall, he prepared the way for Jesus, baptizing him."

Frenchy smiled.

"I like the way you said 'prepared the way.' You got that from *Godspell* didn't you? I know you did, I bet you love show tunes."

Botvinnik raised his left eyebrow, failing to understand the reference.

"Anyway, no. JTB, John the Baptist, straight gangster. He ate locusts and didn't take shit from anyone except, of course, Herod, who in fact had him killed. But John was crazy. He didn't tell people to repent, he was nasty about it; he made people repent, whether they liked it or not."

Sarah and Ricky joined Botvinnik in his skeptical stare. Frenchy recognized their looks.

"There are tons the bible doesn't tell, like the Gnostic gospels that were suppressed. Did anyone think Mary Magdalene would be characterized as Jesus' 'favorite disciple?' No. Same for John the Baptist. He was not a passive preacher. He got in your face with the remnants of locusts stuck in his teeth and he made you repent . . . Alright, well, the locusts in the teeth is probably not true but, trust me, he was no pacifist. Why do you think he garnered so much attention?"

Ali put his hand up, hoping to stem Frenchy's ranting.

"We are here. And enough with this conversation. We will search the caves first."

The jeep slowly made its way up a twisting road, the convoy stopping at one of the curves. Frenchy looked out of Sarah's window, seeing the faint openings of caves in the distance.

"Please tell me we are not walking there. And that terrain looks a bit rough and we certainly are not on level ground. The diggers can go, right? I can stay here in the van and supervise?"

Ali turned off the jeep's ignition and stepped out of the vehicle. Botvinnik followed, with the two of them opening the rear passenger doors. Ricky and Sarah exited. Frenchy remained, nervously seated.

"I didn't hear if that was a 'no' to my supervision. So I can stay here, right? After all, I am no archaeologist. The guys with shovels are much better at digging than I am."

Ali stared blankly at Frenchy, waiting for him to get out of the vehicle. Frenchy sneered, reluctantly sliding out of the car.

"Let's go. There is no need in bringing the diggers yet. Let's survey the scene."

Frenchy carefully stepped over the stones that bound the road way and began to walk up a small hill towards the caves in the base of the mountain. He observed stones protruding from the grass.

"Hey, check it out. I think this was the aqueduct that brought the water up. Very cool."

Sarah smiled at Frenchy's reemerging eagerness.

"So you are a classicist."

"Yup. My dad told me after I kept changing majors to find the one thing I loved and major in it; worry about money and whether I could get a job, later. Found two professors I loved, Samons and Kleiner. Took a bunch of their classes and fell in love with the classics. The glory of Greece, the grandeur of Rome, the majesty of Egypt . . . and the rest of the ancient peoples. Loved it ever since. I'll teach any history, but get me on classical civilizations and all those fears that I told you about are gone."

"So why don't you teach the classics?"

"Well, to be honest, World Civ is as close as I've come. And no college or university would accept me because they think I'm a crackpot. Can't blame them."

"Well, maybe now you will have that chance. Find this and all their insults will be changed into servings of humble pie for them."

Frenchy smiled, as he viewed the caves a few feet ahead.

"Maybe they will. But whether we find it or not, I've gotten to see stuff I never would have been able to. Teachers don't exactly rake in the big bucks."

Frenchy walked behind Ali towards the first cave. They entered slowly, the crackling of small rocks under their feet. Ricky followed quickly behind, Sarah waiting at the mouth of the cave.

"So Doc, what do you think? Is it just going to be laying about?"

"Doubt it, unless today is my fuckin' lucky day, which history has proven it probably won't be."

Ali paused, observing a fragment of a bowl. Ricky moved closer to Frenchy.

"So, when are we ditching these niggas? I'd prefer to hang with, you know, someone who isn't Muslim."

Frenchy stopped, halting Ricky in his tracks.

"I'm okay with just about anything you guys say, but your talk about Muslims has always bothered me. You think white FBI agents are any better? And as I have told you so many times, imagine the tables were turned. You think not being Muslim makes us better, or being Muslim makes you a bad, bloodthirsty terrorist?"

Ricky backed off, recognizing his mentor's point. Frenchy waved his hand and the two continued to move.

"And don't forget, one man's terrorism is another man's freedom . . ."

A loud cracking noise halted Frenchy's lesson. He looked back at Ali. Ali looked up, aware of the noise. He stared back at Frenchy, raising his hands, uncertain what their next move should be. Suddenly, the rocks below Frenchy and Ricky gave out, the two dropping with the floor. Sarah raced into the cave, hearing Frenchy's girlish scream. She approached Ali, dust filling the air.

The sound of cracking rock ceased after a few moments. Ali and Sarah slowly approached the hole and heard subtle moans emerging from the floor. Ali stopped, putting his hand up to keep Sarah from continuing.

"The ground may be volatile. Francis!" Ali called, repeatedly.

"Yeah, it sure as shit was, over here. Ricky seems to be okay."

"How far did you fall? I don't want to approach and cause anymore breaks."

Frenchy did not respond. Sarah pushed past Ali and walked over to the hole.

"Frenchy, are you okay?"

Her eyes scanned the dust-filled hole.

"I'm fine. I think we hit it. This is not a random break. Looks like this was cut as a passage way. Hold the hell on."

Sarah and Ali lingered, listening to the movement of rocks below.

"Damn right. This is awesome. I fell into something like they do in the movies. Well, and in real life, that's how we got some of history's treasures, but whatever, there is a passage down. Got to crawl through."

The dust slowly settled, revealing Frenchy and Ricky ten feet below the floor of the cave. Sarah and Ali stared down as Frenchy took his lighter and illuminated a small opening into a crawl space.

"Can I get a flashlight? I don't want to waste my fluid."

Ali yelled towards the mouth of the cave; a man came running in with a small flashlight.

"I'll come down and give it to you."

"No, just throw it to me. I'll go with my sidekick. We're good. Plus, the drop isn't that easy."

Ali held the flashlight, thinking about Frenchy's request.

"Come on, Ali, let me do this. I want to do this and emerge with the thing. Give me my moment. And get a camera."

Ali reluctantly dropped the flashlight down to him. Frenchy looked up at Sarah and smiled, giving her a wink.

"Not bad, huh, Miss Lady?"

Frenchy tipped his Irish cap, Sarah smiling at the sudden possibility.

"Let's go Buck Nasty, time to go exploring . . . wait. Are there scorpions in this region?"

Ali looked confused, glancing over at Sarah as she subtly shook her head.

"No, not in this region."

Frenchy accepted the response, crawling into the passageway. Ricky pumped his fist at his observers and followed into the hole.

The two snaked their way through the primitive tunnel.

"Hey, Doc, not to second guess but remember when you wanted the diggers to handle this? I'm starting to think that may have been a good idea."

Frenchy continued his forward movement. Despite his momentary excitement, he too, began to feel the symptoms of claustrophobia.

"Yeah, well, backing out might be even worse since we can't turn around. Since I just made up that whole, stupid 'let me do it' line, let's just get to the opening."

Frenchy's acute awareness of his present situation triggered his anxiety. One of his biggest fears had always been being confined in tight spaces. As he surveyed the rock a few inches above him and to his sides, panic began to set in. He flinched, his panic manifesting itself physically.

"Ahhh. What the hell, man? You just kicked me in the eye."

Ricky stopped from proceeding, rubbing his eye. Sweat began to bead up on Frenchy's forehead. His eyes darted erratically, searching for space.

"Ricky, I'm freakin' out. Seriously, I'm gonna fuckin' lose it."

"Chill, chill. Don't kick anymore. Seriously, where the fuck is the end? How close are we?"

Frenchy shined his flashlight hoping to see an exit at the end.

"Shit, shit, shit! I see rock ahead of me. There is no fuckin' exit."

Frenchy began to spasm, pushing against the walls of the tunnel.

"Okay, okay, just get to it, there is no way you cut a fuckin' tunnel like this and then have it lead to nowhere."

Frenchy suddenly let out a strange yelp. Ricky tried to back away, afraid of a second blow to his ocular region.

"What happened—what? Just move, Doc; now I'm freakin' out."

Frenchy screamed in fear.

"You're freakin' out? I . . . I am . . . my brain is feeling weird. It's the way I felt on the swings with the Marshmallow people."

Despite the panicked situation and the fear of being stomped, Ricky's mind attempted to process the unexplained mention of Marshmallow people.

"Dammit, Doc, move your nigga ass and go forward, you little bitch, and get to the fuckin' end before I beat you."

Frenchy's panic attack was momentarily halted by the onslaught of inappropriate language.

"Hell no, motherfucker, you don't talk to me like that, you punk bitch; I'll bite your nose off."

Frenchy looked forward, breathing heavily, waiting for Ricky's response.

"Yes, sir," Ricky said, timidly.

Frenchy began moving forward. His physical anxiety remained but his anger clouded his ability to acknowledge it. He reached the end of the tunnel and began striking it with his fist. The rock began to crumble as the strength and pace of his onslaught increased, at last clearing a passage wide enough to pull himself through. He turned sharply as Ricky fell into the opening.

"What the hell was that? I don't give a damn what you think we have been through; you don't ever speak to me like that ever . . . ever. And the n-word again?"

Ricky remained on the ground, trying to regain his balance.

"I'm sorry. I was just trying to . . . I'm sorry! I will never speak to you like that again. I was panicking."

"Well, so was I but I didn't call you the n-word or bitch."

Ricky dropped his head, timidly looking at his hands.

"I know, but hey, at least we're through."

Frenchy exhaled violently, realizing he no longer felt the panic. His eye twitched and his lip quivered as he realized Ricky's reason for the outburst. Frenchy's shoulders dropped, realizing his response was as inappropriate as his student's verbal attack. He put his hand on Ricky's shoulder, a small cloud of dust puffing up from the contact point.

"Well-played, young man. Well-played. I certainly owe you . . ."

"Don't worry about it, Doc. To be honest, that was pretty gangster. I never thought I would hear that part of Jersey City come out of you."

Ricky sighed nervously, overwhelmed by the last two minutes. Frenchy looked back at the tunnel.

"Let's just enjoy having space while we can before we go back."

The two smiled at one another.

Frenchy waved at the dust particles illuminated by the beam of his flashlight, wiping sweat from his face. He surveyed the large room, the high rock ceiling providing added comfort. He shined his light across the cave's ground; rocks covered much of the area. The light hit a stone structure. The two approached slowly, observing its tomb-like features.

"You think it's the Sword?"

Frenchy knelt at the base, rubbing his hand over the side.

"Doubt it, unless Goliath's sword was the size of a man. If this is what it took to house his sword, I give props to David. Goliath was supposed to be six-foot-four-ish. This case would house a sword for a twenty-foot-tall man."

Frenchy felt around the cover, pushing to move it. He looked at Ricky, gesturing for him to help. The two of them each took a deep breath before pushing forcefully, the lid moving slightly. Breathing heavily after their efforts, Frenchy leaned on his knees. They resumed their push, moving the lid a foot.

"What'd you say about diggers?" Frenchy said, gasping for air.

As they propelled their bodies into motion, the lid gave way and fell suddenly to the ground, cracking. They fell forward on the tomb, regaining their composure and looking in.

"That doesn't look like a sword."

Ricky's view seemed to deflate his spirit as he leaned wearily, staring into the tomb.

"And that's not a body either."

Frenchy wiped his hand across his cheek, his sweat and the thick dust on his face combining to create a mud-like residue.

"Yes, thank you, Ricky, I can see." Ricky reached in and grabbed a decaying paper roll.

"Any chance this is worth something?"

Frenchy examined a second scroll before placing it back into the tomb. He raised another, flinching monetarily.

"There's your body, Ricky. And scrolls like this are great for nerds to look at."

Ricky ignored the last comment, looking at the scroll's vacant spot.

"Creepy, the dude was buried in paperwork . . . Get it? Like what would be said by a guy . . ."

Frenchy's stare halted Ricky's comical explanation. Frenchy looked around the room, in disbelief, at his surroundings.

"Well, whatever, I guess this stuff is important. You know what? It is. I'm sorry I am getting caught up in treasure hunting. That's not right. This could be very important; like the Dead Sea Scrolls or the Nag Hammadi stuff."

Frenchy continued his inspection of the room.

"Doc, check it out, his head isn't connected."

Frenchy gasped, moving away from Ricky's playful exhibition.

"What the hell is wrong with you? Put it down. Where do you get the courage to touch a dead body?"

"Doc, Kris Kearny's mom owns a funeral parlor. What the hell do you think we grew up around?"

"Just put it down. Of course, it's not connected; you just ripped it off the body."

Ricky pointed at the tomb.

"No, look, the skull was severed from the spine."

Frenchy sneered in disgust.

"What, like you wouldn't listen to discussions about dead bodies if you could."

"Actually, I wouldn't. I lived across from a funeral home when I lived in Boston. I didn't even want to watch them wheel them in."

Ricky rolled his eyes, returning the detached head to its original position.

"So what now? There's nothing here but a dead dude and a bunch of scrolls."

"Just grab what we can carry and let's get out of here. We can sort this out later."

Frenchy grabbed a scroll carefully and turned, stopping as he looked at the narrow passageway. Ricky took his scroll and moved past Frenchy.

"Wait. You said the head was severed? You thinking what I'm thinking? Could this be John the Baptist's skeleton?"

Ricky paused, a bewildered look on his face.

"Not what I was thinking. I don't know! You should know. Besides, if it is, we can have the diggers deal with it."

Frenchy returned to the stone sarcophagus, looking hesitantly. Ricky followed trying to read his mentor's stare.

"You think this is him?"

"Hell, if I know. When I was on my Indiana Jones kick as a kid, I did shitloads of research on things that I could discover as an adventurer. I remember reading that old Johnny's noggin was in a church in Damascus. So I lost interest as it couldn't help me further my delusions of grandeur."

Frenchy looked around the room, searching for some sort of clue.

"But you know what? Now that I think about it, I did read that the church where his head was supposed to be, in a nice gold thingy, became a mosque after Muslims conquered the area. It's not totally crazy to imagine that those people considered him a prophet, taking his head, and hiding it so it wasn't in a mosque. And this would make sense as a place to hide it."

"Doc, if this is old Johnny, what does it matter; you can't prove anything. Unless you have his relatives around to match his DNA. Let's bring these sample scrolls back and see if they're worth anything. Otherwise, we'll let the digging dudes work in here and we can go search the other caves. If there was a passage leading here, maybe there are some in the other ones, too."

Frenchy lingered for a moment. Despite being a lapsed Catholic, the possibility of being in the presence of such a religious figure, filled him with awe. Ricky stood at the entrance to the passageway.

"Come on, Doc, it doesn't matter. No way to prove it and that ain't the Sword of Goliath. By the way, I'm going first. When I freak out, I'll kick you in the face this time."

"No problem. I can handle it this time; it was not knowing how much further that made me freak out. If I know there's an end in sight, I'm good."

The two began to make their way through the passage, the scrolls slowing their progression.

"This sure has been a strange adventure. I mean, like we just found a dead dude at the end of a passageway. Shit, old man, we are actually finding stuff! It may not be what we are looking for, but the marker and now this. Not bad for our first adventure."

Frenchy coughed as he inhaled the dust from Ricky's rough movements.

"What do you mean 'first adventure?' I'm retiring after this and so are you. No way in hell I'm doing this again! Dust, sunburn, blood splatter from fuckin' dead bodies being killed. Indiana Jones moves on, no problem; me, I'll have nightmares for years. My shrink will be able to retire on my therapy alone."

"Whatever, I'm almost out."

Frenchy grabbed Ali's hand as another man relieved him of the scroll. They helped him to his feet, Frenchy patting Ali on the back in appreciation. Frenchy smiled over at Sarah, her visage remaining serious. Frenchy looked beyond her, a familiar face staring back at him. The man's identity sunk in. Samir walked over to Frenchy, a cold look on his face. Frenchy smiled, trying to avoid divulging any recognition of the man.

"How did you find three white guys in this place? I thought I had the market cornered for sunscreen."

Frenchy's comment elicited no response from any member of the group. Samir waved, his men violently moving the three men forward.

"If you know these men, I suggest you tell me. Otherwise, they will be killed immediately in front of you."

Frenchy laughed nervously, looking frantically at the faces of the entire group, hoping for aid in this tense situation. Samir snapped his fingers, drawing Frenchy back.

"These men die now unless you tell me that you know them."

Frenchy rubbed his hand together, his palms sweating. He quickly lit a cigarette, looking up at Jensen. Jensen's expression remained firm, showing no hints of any emotion.

"Last chance, Dr. Degnan," Samir said, mocking Frenchy's title.

"Okay, I know them. They're my insurance, my backup. But they were never going to do anything. I just asked them to follow me; you know, make sure you follow through on your agreement. I'm . . . you know, connected."

Those of the group who spoke English looked confusedly at Frenchy's statement.

"You understand or not? I'm connected. La Cosa Nostra."

Jensen seemed to slightly wince at Frenchy's verbal gambit.

"You didn't think I would go anywhere without having a little insurance?"

Samir stepped in front of Frenchy, staring eye-to-eye with him.

"You better get your fuckin' camel breath outta my personal space, son."

Frenchy's return to a ghetto lingo seemed not to affect Samir's position. Ali walked over and separated the two.

"Please, Francis, you are telling me that you are connected to the Mafia? And you decide now to use their help? Not, for example, the many times we had nowhere to turn?"

"Yeah, Doc, and I thought you were Irish Jew?"

Frenchy stood defiantly.

"Ask them? And I couldn't trust Americans until I knew they were not involved."

"I don't think we need to ask these men. Let us ask their tour guide."

Samir signaled to men at the mouth of the cave. Ephraim appeared at the entrance and made his way towards the group, a gun pointed at his back. Jensen clenched his fists at Ephraim's emergence. Samir began to speak to Ephraim in Arabic. The two conversed, Ali and Amir joining the conversation. Frenchy puffed nervously on his cigarette. He looked over at Sarah.

"Hey, I think we found John the Baptist's head," he whispered. Sarah quickly dismissed his attempt at introducing a new subject.

The four men stopped talking, walking over towards Frenchy.

"He says these men are your bodyguards. He says he was paid to bring them around to make sure you were safe."

Frenchy casually flicked his cigarette, his confidence returning.

"No apology needed, my friends. I understand."

Frenchy walked over to Jensen, patting his face, attempting to mimic a scene from *The Godfather*.

"If you are going to protect me, please make sure you do that. How can you protect me if I have to save you?"

The armed men released the three agents, helping them to their feet.

"Now, if we have finished the pissing contest, can we get back to work?"

FRENCHY SAT ON A ROCK near the entrance of the cave, smoking a cigarette. Sarah sat next to him, poring over a section of the scroll. Jensen and his agents stood in the shade of the cave. Botvinnik had another scroll laid across the hood of the jeep.

"So I assume this is in Hebrew? Otherwise, it looks like you are just pretending to read," Frenchy said, winking.

"It is, but it's just a segment of one of the Gospels."

Sarah rolled the scroll up.

"Even if we could read these scrolls immediately, it would take forever. Anything else we can go on?"

"Well, the diggers are working in this cave; the other caves have nothing. I had Ricky jumping up and down, trying to get the floor to break like this one did, but nothing. It's just a bunch of rocks."

Frenchy eyed the men moving about. He began to look around nervously. He stood and walked over near Jensen, bringing Sarah with him.

"I'm going to talk and look forward. Every now and again laugh as if I am telling jokes."

Forester rolled his eyes at Frenchy's attempt at covert behavior.

"The Sword is not here. It's in Jerusalem. It was never here, but I hoped this would give us a chance to escape."

Frenchy's eyes widened, encouraging the forced laughter of the group.

"I think we need to give them the slip."

Jensen smiled, patting him on the back.

"I would, too, as our driver would never have agreed to that bullshit story, nor would your captors. They know exactly what is going on. When I give you the signal, you say it is time to search the top."

Frenchy belted out a hearty laugh.

"Sounds like a dipshit move as then we can be surrounded."

Jensen waved playfully at Frenchy, pretending to hug his ribs at Frenchy's hilarity.

"Shut the fuck up and do it. I have a feeling you couldn't navigate an IKEA store let alone know how to get out of here."

Sarah hugged Frenchy.

"Just do what he says. I think he may be right."

"Fine, I'll do it."

The group slowly stopped their theatrical performance, returning to a serious tone. Shouting came from the center of the cave, Ricky running out in excitement."

"Doc, it is old Johnny! We got an inscription below his body. It is him! We did it motherfucker!"

Frenchy's eyes widened, running towards his student. Ali walked behind, a slight smile on his face.

"It is true, Francis; below the skeleton is a small inscription praising the sarcophagus as John's resting place."

Frenchy's excitement visibly began to build.

"And check it out, Doc, look."

Ricky held up an intact ceramic vase.

"Can I keep it? I certainly deserve it. I found it messing around in this place."

Frenchy smiled at Ricky's search.

"You know, I think you are better at this than I am."

Ricky smiled eagerly at the compliment from his mentor.

"So what do we do?"

"Well, I think this is as equal a find as the Sword of Goliath. We should focus our work on this. Do you have any ideas on where to go next?"

Ali waited, hoping for a new epiphany from his friend.

Frenchy's excitement clouded his remembrance of Jensen's advice.

"Well, I'm not sure. We have to exhaust all our possibilities here and make sure we check every cave and crevice at the base, where the hermits would have camped."

Sarah joined the conversation.

"What about the top? Any chance Herod's stronghold would hold it?"

"Probably not; it was a Roman garrison when the Sword would have been hidden. I doubt they would be so stupid as to hide the thing when the Romans still occupied the top."

Frenchy high-fived Ricky, returning to exultation about their new find.

"I still think it's worth looking."

Sarah casually smiled at Frenchy. He looked up blankly, remembering what his words should have been.

"You know, it doesn't hurt to check. I truly believe it is here. We'll go up. After all, I always wanted to climb this thing. I mean this is my only chance."

Ali nodded in agreement.

"Come on, men. Me, my lady, and my apprentice are going up and you need to protect us."

Frenchy's group stood, prepared to make their ascent. Amir had been observing the exchange. He approached quickly, grabbing water to hand to Frenchy.

"You'll need this. But I really could use Ricky's eyes to help search this area. As you can see from his vase, he has a knack for archaeology."

Ricky flexed his muscles, enjoying his praise.

"I agree, Doc, I think I need to keep working down here. Let me know what you find. Anything I find, I will split with you seventy-thirty."

"I'd prefer if he stayed with us. We have worked as a group; we need to stay as a group."

Sarah put her arm around Ricky, bringing him back into the group. Amir called over to his brother.

"You see, I don't think we can do that. Having three FBI agents with you may facilitate your escape. And while this find is quite remarkable, this is not what we agreed on. So you choose. Either you go without your student, or you don't go at all. As you said, Doctor, there is little chance they would have buried it within a Roman occupied area."

Samir physically entered the conversation, joining his brother. Frenchy looked to Jensen.

"So you knew the truth but played like you didn't know. What the fuck? I'm not a professional. Don't get my hopes up."

Amir cocked his head to the side, confused by Frenchy's blank statement.

"I believe that is obvious, Dr. Degnan. I would have hoped that, by now, you would have gained some sort of respect for our abilities. Unlike the Israelis, we have to be thorough. We knew of the FBI agents. We ensured that a man recommended by Botvinnik would be their guide. You see, if we are not meticulous, we are giving the Israelis even more of an advantage than they currently possess. But fear not, we plan on honoring our agreement with you. However, my brother expects you to be honest and candid during the duration of our time together. While this trip to Machaerus has yielded a find worth exploring in the future, our desired artifact has not been recovered . . . excuse me, our Sword has not *yet* been recovered."

Amir's diverse response left Frenchy and his companions stumped. Frenchy looked over at the agents. He scratched his head, lighting another cigarette.

"Alright, but fuck it—new amendment to the deal. They are part of the deal now, too. They get returned with us, safely."

Frenchy's attempt at negotiation seemed to amuse Amir.

"You know, Dr. Degnan, our goal is to ensure the defeat of this U.S.-Israeli treaty. Having three FBI agents as added insurance to our current measures certainly could not hurt our position."

Jensen's disdain suddenly emerged as the negotiation continued.

"How about this? No payment; I'll find it and then you let us go. Nothing, just let us all go."

Jensen gently shook his head at Frenchy's offer, unable to hide his disapproval.

"What? If we get home safe, who gives a shit."

Jensen stared back at Frenchy, remaining silent. Amir observed Jensen's attempt at nonverbal communication.

"Perhaps you should discuss as a group and then we can resume?"

Jensen stared sharply at Samir.

"Fine, go over there and we'll discuss."

Frenchy walked over to the agents, Sarah and Ricky quickly joining.

"Dude, what's with the cold stare? I'm just trying to save your ass."

Jensen violently grabbed Frenchy's shirt, pulling him up to his face.

"They are not going to honor any agreement. So stop with this idiotic negotiation. Just find the damn sword. Your usefulness has long since expired. Find the thing and that is it."

Frenchy pushed away from Jensen, angrily attempting to process his point. Amir walked over, recognizing a roadblock in their deliberations.

"Here is our last offer. We will ensure the safety of the entire group. And you will still receive compensation. But I hope you come up with a new idea for its location."

Frenchy dropped his cigarette, removing his hat and brushing back his hair in anxiety.

"Okay, okay. I know where it is, but it's not an easy location and you can't excavate. It's in Jerusalem at Akeldama, the death place of the first Sicarii, and it won't be easy to get into because there is a monastery built on the thing but if we get in and your guys do their tough guy shit, we should be able to find it."

The group seemed shocked at the quick change in search location. Samir spat at the ground in anger. He pulled a gun from his side and pointed it at Frenchy. Ali looked to Amir who seemed in agreement with his brother's response.

"That is a very quick change from our present location. Did you have a change of heart after speaking with your bodyguards?"

Samir gestured towards his men, the armed guards surrounding the law enforcement trio. He moved forward pressing the gun against Frenchy's forehead. Frenchy's body began to shake. His heart raced. He became acutely aware of his trembling; his attempt to stop the tremors only made them worsen. He looked up at Samir, his mind flashing to the last time he had a gun in his face. He closed his eyes, attempting to move forward beyond his memory. He placed his hands over his crotch, his memory reminding him of his response to the previous situation.

"That's enough, Samir. Let him be," Ali interjected, his comrade ignoring his request.

"Give me a reason why I should not kill you now. You have not been honest in upholding your part of the agreement. Why should we?"

Frenchy suddenly gasped for air, his eyes rolling to the back of his head, his body slowly falling backwards hitting the ground heavily. Samir stared down at Frenchy, his expression skeptical at the validity of the fall. Sarah ran over to Frenchy, but Samir stopped her with the barrel of his gun.

Ricky stepped forward, angered by the present scene.

"You know what, you dickhole, I'm not okay with you bullying people. You're a scared little bitch who doesn't know how to interact with people so you scare and intimidate them. Well, no nigga does that to my mentor, nobody . . ."

Samir's gun went off, Ricky dropping to the ground. Samir swung his aim back towards Sarah and Frenchy. Ali made an initial move towards Ricky, halting his instinctive response.

"Wake him up!" Samir yelled, angrily.

Sarah slowly knelt next to Frenchy, staring at Samir's pistol. She looked over at Ricky, somewhat consoled as she recognized that he had been hit in the leg.

"Francis, please. Francis, wake up."

She gently shook him, becoming more forceful as her efforts failed to revive him. He opened his eyes, smiling when he saw Sarah's face above his. Her scared expression soon brought him back to reality. He slowly sat up, blankly staring at the armed men. His stare fell upon his student, clutching his leg. He quickly raced over on his hands and knees to Ricky.

"Shit, shit, shit! Where is the shot?"

Ricky did not speak, removing his hand to expose blood from his calf. Frenchy slowly stood, his fury removing his earlier fear. He turned towards Samir, a sneered expression searing towards the shooter. He gritted his teeth, attempting to suppress his temper. He walked away from Ricky, approaching Samir. He lifted his gun, slightly happy at Frenchy's response. Frenchy put his hands up in response to the weapon, showing he was no threat. His trembling resumed. Samir gripped his gun, stabilizing his feet. Frenchy's second bout of trembling seemed to concern Samir more than the first. Frenchy deliberately put his right hand towards Samir, cautiously approaching him. Samir took his hand, scoffing at the unexpected peaceful gesture. Frenchy leaned in slowly.

"After I find this fucking thing, and this is all over, perhaps you would give me a minute of your time. Without your big bad gun, and your big bad soldiers protecting you? After I . . . I find it."

Frenchy aggressively pointed towards himself. His sudden confident mood seemed to lessen Samir's momentary concern.

"I will give you all the time you would like. But you have not answered me. Why should I not kill you, given you seem to be an accomplished liar."

Frenchy put his hands up again, pumping them, exaggeratedly.

"Don't go shooting me as I reach in my pocket. I'm just retrieving something."

Samir strengthened his arm, pointing the gun closer to Frenchy. He removed a coin from his pocket, flipping it in the air and catching it, offering it to his opponent.

"Please pass that to your brother; I am not convinced you can read." Samir took the coin, cracking a smile at the insult. Amir took the coin and examined it.

"Let me help you. That's a piece of silver from the reign of Tiberius, the Roman emperor. It could be one of the thirty pieces of silver, Judas Iscariot, the first Sicarii received for betraying Jesus, or not. Too fast for you, or can you keep up with me? I found the coin at Masada in the hole where you found the tablet. But your diggers must have missed it because it was laying there lodged in the rock. Tiberius was emperor when Jesus was executed. The marker was left before the women would have taken the sword. But it mentioned, the 'blood money' Judas took. But those women were smart enough to leave a little clue behind it. Not bad for two broads who probably had almost no education and were returning to the place of a mass suicide that took the lives of their families."

Ali joined Amir in looking over the coin.

"And it's not Julius Caesar. Tiberius was a Caesar as well. So don't get confused by the inscription, you ignorant pieces of shit."

Frenchy focused on Samir.

"Then what was the point of our trip here?"

Ali took the coin and handed it back to Frenchy, convinced of his story.

"Well, at the time, this was a rational place to search that I knew wouldn't yield the discovery; it would give me time to try and escape with the agents. And don't give me that look. You're telling me that, if you were abducted, you would just blindly follow and not try to escape? Bullshit. You would have booked it, too. Oh, and if you want the exact location, and I mean the *exact* location, they are to be let go when we get to Jerusalem. Besides, we cannot be walking into a monastery with armed gunmen and a party of twenty, for Christ's sake. And that is the offer; otherwise, you can kill us now. I have a feeling you were going to do that anyway based on your inability to act in a civilized manner."

Frenchy deliberately pointed at Samir as he finished his statement, removing a cigarette from his pocket.

"Oh shit, I almost forgot: Amir, Ali and I go in, not GI Mohammad over there. I don't want him getting angry and shooting Brother Seamus in the goddamn monastery."

Ali shook off Frenchy's insult, walking over to the brothers, speaking in Arabic for a few moments. Samir turned away angrily, staring Frenchy down before moving away from the group.

"You certainly are not the same nervous, self-conscious man you have been this entire trip. You waver between two different Francises."

"Well, my mother says I'm depressed and suffer from anxiety, who's to say I'm not bi-polar and a schizo?"

"Against my brother's counsel, we agree to your proposal. Our workers will remain at this dig site as your attempt to avoid the search has led to an interesting find. If you are so confident that you have the exact location, then we certainly will not need them. However, given the fact that you will not reveal the exact location, we would be foolish to walk into a monastery with you without some insurance. Therefore, our amendment to your proposal is the young lady remains in our custody until you have found the sword. And Samir comes with us."

"Hell no. You must be outta your goddamn mind if you think I am going to leave my lady with your men who I doubt treat women properly, ever. And no apology for that statement."

Sarah smiled at Frenchy's casual reference to her as "his lady."

"I can understand a Westerner's opinion on male-female interactions in the Middle East, mostly because you do not understand. But now is not the time to discuss. And whether you apologize for that insult or not, I would advise you to remember who you are speaking to."

Amir's calm threat filled Frenchy with fear equal to Samir's militant approach.

"I am sorry. But I will not agree to that, nor to your men holding my student who has already been shot and needs immediate medical attention."

Frenchy inhaled from his cigarette, nervous about the back and forth negotiations.

"I guess this is why Palestinians and Israelis can't get along. When they get close to an agreement, there is always something neither will budge on."

Ali and Amir smiled at Frenchy's observation.

"Well, both sides usually resume killing each other. That may not bode well for you as we have the weapons. I would suggest you make the effort."

Frenchy looked over at Jensen who had remained quiet during the entire exchange.

"Okay, how about this? They all go free and Samir comes with us. He can either kill me, if I fail, or give me my minutes with him. Either way, you know I'll do everything I can to find the sword since he'll have a gun in my back the entire time. Now, is that good enough? If we leave now, we can make it to Akeldama before it's too late."

"Fair enough, I am sure Samir will enjoy that scenario. However, your friends will be monitored. We do not want them getting any crazy ideas like trying to rescue you."

"Good, fine. That's fine. Glad we could settle that. Now let's go. No militants. And get Botvinnik; he has to come because he seems to have pull in ol' Jerusalem and he is in contact with the other crazies who want this freakin' artifact."

Amir nodded in agreement, walking into the cave. Frenchy returned to Ricky with Sarah joining him.

"Hang in there, brother. I know it hurts but we are going to get you help soon."

Frenchy handed him some water from a crinkled water bottle. He drank quickly, leaning forward to speak.

"Okay, Doc, but no lie: I am never sticking up for you again."

SENATOR MAINI SAT AT HIS LARGE ORNATE DESK sifting through papers. His secretary knocked and entered, followed by a well-dressed man carrying a briefcase. The senator eyed the two as they walked in, returning to his paper shuffling. He gestured towards a chair situated in front of his desk. The elderly man bowed his head and sat, placing his briefcase at his side. The secretary exited the room. The senator leaned back, reclining slightly in his chair.

"I am sure you are aware of how busy a time it is here in Washington, given the escalation of armed forces to the Middle East announced by the President."

The Senator's guest sat comfortably, not responding to Maini's hint about his hectic schedule.

"Nevertheless, my secretary said you requested this meeting because you had sensitive information regarding a resident of Jersey City. No doubt you know it is my hometown and I have an affinity for everything Jersey City, which is why you received this meeting. That and any constituent of mine is always important. So, Mr. Nasser, what is it that you have?"

Nasser folded his legs smiling, at the sad uniqueness of the senator's concern.

"Are you familiar with Dr. Francis Degnan?"

The Senator scoffed, smiling warmly.

"That kid. He's not his father; I went to high school with his father. Brilliant man, amazing writer. His son, not so much. The kid has good intentions, but not the follow-through. As a writer, well, how to put this? He should have used a ghost writer."

"Then you are aware of the accusations against him . . ."

"Of course, but thankfully they were redacted, though that probably didn't make his family feel any better. Why do you ask? Is he in trouble?"

Nasser put his hand up attempting to quell the Senator's protective instinct.

"He is fine. He is off in search of his coveted artifact."

The Senator stared, assuming there was more to the current reason for their exchange.

"You don't like your president, do you?"

Maini rolled his eyes, dismissing the question.

"Well, it is because of your outspoken criticism of your Commander-in-Chief that I deliver this to you."

Nasser reached for his briefcase and placed it in front of the Senator. Maini leaned back, suspicious of both Nasser's statement and gift. Nasser recognized the Senator's apprehension, taking the briefcase back and opening it.

"Please, we are on the same side. This is what I want you to have."

He removed a bundle of manila folders and handed them to the Senator.

"I will not explain as you should spend some time reviewing the documents yourself. Still, I suggest you make this your priority. I have enclosed my number where I can be reached. After you review the files, please let me know if you are interested in making this your . . . crusade. You have two hours to review. After that, some of my associates will be delivering the same information to other senators and representatives."

The strange turn in conversational direction left the Senator confused. Nasser closed his briefcase and stood up, preparing to leave. Maini also rose, signaling to Nasser to remain.

"I cannot remain while you review these. There are other things I must attend to. Please call me immediately with your answer."

"Wait, why did you come to me with this? And I probably should have asked this earlier but who are you?"

"I came to you with this because you were recommended to me by a friend. He said you were an honest man. And as I told your secretary, I am Ahmed Nasser, a concerned citizen."

The stunned senator watched as Nasser exited the room. He looked down at the manila folders. His assumption of Nasser's nationality made him panic suddenly, wondering if the files were laced with anthrax. He paused, considering such a possibility, but quickly dismissed it as he reasoned that Nasser was able to get through security without issues. He sat down and opened the first folder, removing several papers. He began to read the top page. His expression changed as he read, abruptly opening the other folders and finding pictures and a flash drive. He paused, looking at the folders. He hit a button on his phone, calling a number on speakerphone.

"Kris, get Eric and come into my office now. There is something we need to deal with."

BOTVINNIK CLOSED HIS CELL PHONE, looking at his watch. Frenchy leaned forward.

"You know your cell phone has a clock, right?"

Botvinnik ignored Frenchy's comment.

"I have arranged for entrance to the monastery."

Frenchy shook his head, suspiciously.

"Who in hell are you? How do you make a call and get a private admission to a Christian monastery?"

Frenchy mocked Botvinnik, making exaggerated gestures of his prestige.

"I am a private collector, but I am also a member of the historical society of Israel."

"Yeah, well, I'm a Devils season ticket holder but I sure as hell don't get private access. Hell, I still have to pay nine dollars for a fuckin' beer."

Botvinnik smirked, turning to address Frenchy.

"I am a little bit more than just a member."

Frenchy exposed his upper row of teeth. Sarah poked him, hoping to disrupt his intentionally hideous expression. Frenchy looked perturbed at Sarah and shrugged while removing a cigarette from his pack.

"You know, Dr. Degnan, if you keep smoking like that, you may not live through this adventure."

Frenchy stared sharply as he thumbed his lighter.

"Yeah, well, Mr. B, given Samir's penchant for violence, I wouldn't want him to have the satisfaction of personally killing me."

Frenchy looked over at Ricky.

"You okay, brother? Soon as we get into town, we'll get you to the hospital."

Ricky struggled to laugh.

"I don't know if you can find the sword without me. Remember, I found the vase and helped find the inscription on ol' Johnny's tomb."

"Very true. But I have some really good motivation, you know: find it or I get killed by a nutjob. I may be able to pull this one through."

Ali looked in his mirror observing the exchange.

"Francis, I strongly advise you to just find the artifact and turn it over to Amir. Samir is an extremist. He is very valuable but in times like this . . . his, as you said, penchant for violence can often be a detriment to our work."

"Look, I'll find it. But if it's not at the monastery, I have nothing else. And it will be pointless trying to ask for more time."

Ali stared back at Frenchy as the cigarette in his hand began to shake. He looked over at Sarah as she noticed his trembling.

"What? Just because I recognize I will be screwed doesn't mean I'm not terrified. I call bullshit on all movies that show a guy saying some crap about being okay with dying. Hollywood distorts that shit. You know what happens if I fail tonight? My ass is running out of there. It's bullshit, people accepting death. In the real world, if you know you're about to die, you either book it or, if there is a lady around, you know, do the hibidity dibity."

Ricky began to laugh, shaking his head.

"The hibity dibity, Doc?"

Frenchy took a long pull on his cigarette.

"You know, this is like having my mother and grandmother on this trip."

"Well, Francis, good luck on the hibity dibity with three Arab men; one who wants to kill you. If that time comes, I would suggest running."

Frenchy smiled at Sarah's witty comment.

"Damn, you're right. I should have told them you would come with us."

Frenchy winked, making Sarah blush momentarily.

"So, since I suck at this and should have discussed this before, where are you dropping them off and when?"

Botvinnik turned, observing Ricky.

"They will be dropped off at a hospital on our way to our location. It does not matter the name. In truth, whichever one is the easiest as we approach the monastery."

"And I assume the people you were originally working for still think we are out near Masada?"

"Actually, no, I let them know before we left that there had been an ambush and we were hiding out in the caves around Masada. Assaf was very angry. His temper, it can cloud his judgment."

"What are you, the Godfather now?" Frenchy said, pausing suddenly with a realization. "You're gonna kill him. You are pulling a Sonny on them."

Botvinnik looked over at Ali, the two smiling.

"I am sure I do not know the reference, but I believe you have the heart of the plan. Knowing Assaf, he is incapable of controlling his temper. With him out of the way, the Prime Minister will lose the one man that has pushed him for this treaty with the U.S. The Prime Minister is weak. He will not follow through."

"Is that what you meant when you said you were dealing with the treaty or whatever you said?"

"Dr. Degnan, you really have little faith. He is one part of the equation. Only one part."

Frenchy unbuckled his seatbelt and leaned forward fully.

"Look, I am on your side for everything. If this treaty stuff is true then it is absolutely wrong, as is the denial of Palestine as a free state. But I'm not on board with fuckin' killing anyone."

"Killing can be a necessary part of life. Think about it, Doctor. You were being chased by your own country and they did not want to chat. They were willing to have you killed for this treaty, for the greater good of the U.S. One person killed to benefit others. You are honestly saying that you believe this does not take place? You would be dead, the cost of gasoline would drop, and your fellow Americans would applaud the leaders who had you killed. Even if it were released and you were killed for that, most would view it as 'for the greater good.' Killing is part of our world."

Frenchy fidgeted in his seat, the discussion of his murder disturbing him.

"While I am glad I was not killed, I am saying no one should be killed. Killing is not necessary. There are other ways to deal with conflict besides shooting someone or blowing yourself up in a market or firing missiles. It's not right and will never be right. Look at us. There is a Christian, a Jew, and a Muslim in this car right now. Aside from that being the start of many bad jokes, can't we all agree that, in our religious traditions, it is very clear that we should not kill? No exceptions: just we, thou—, whatever, shall not kill. You can disagree with people. You can believe that people are unjust, but nothing is solved by killing. Or my favorite: the no-guilt killing using bombs, missiles, et cetera. Because in the end, the idea of 'an eye for an eye' still exists. It can only be broken by someone who is willing to step up and say, 'someone close to me was killed and I mourn that person, but I will not retaliate. Instead, I will try to understand why that person killed my friend, family member, whatever.' Every Islamic suicide bomber is pissed about something, just like every Israeli is pissed about something, but nothing is solved by seesaw murders. Someone has to stop and say, 'I am willing to hear why you did that and maybe, what I have done to cause your anger.' I mean shit, what the fuck?"

Frenchy sat back and exhaled, shaking his head at his failure to end his rant with a thought-provoking conclusion.

"You live in a world that is not ours, Dr. Degnan. I appreciate your passion, however misguided."

Botvinnik removed his phone and began typing. Frenchy sat frustrated.

"Fuck it. I'll prove you're wrong. Somehow, I will do it. I won't let your viewpoint be accepted."

Botvinnik ignored the comment. Sarah put her hand on Frenchy's, valuing his fanatical protection of life.

"The world needs more Francis Degnans," she said, kissing his cheek. "Who would have thought I'd be saying that after the start we had?"

"Very true. You slammed me up against the wall of my office. Who'd thought I liked a dominant woman."

Ricky winced in disgust at the progressively personal conversation he was hearing.

"Are we there yet? I can't listen to my teacher and his dominatrix woman reminiscing."

"It's dominant," Frenchy said.

"Dominant or dominatrix, it is irrelevant," Ali butted in, bringing a close to the bizarre back-and-forth.

"We will be arriving at the hospital in a few minutes."

Frenchy's nervousness returned as he heard Botvinnik speaking on the phone.

"Please take care of Ricky. And please be careful."

Sarah nodded in agreement. She looked cautiously at Ali and Botvinnik, making sure they were not listening.

"You be careful and, whatever you do, if you have the chance to run, run."

Sarah stared into his eyes, quickly grabbing and kissing him. The two remained in their embrace, Ricky slowly inching over to see.

"I'll be okay. I have said this about a hundred times on this trip, but it is time to do my thing. I'm serious this time."

The vehicle came to a stop. Ricky looked out at the well-lit entrance to the hospital. His door opened and he was greeted by Amir.

"You are free to go."

Amir waved at Jensen to assist Ricky as he tried to exit the car. Jensen was visibly irritated at Amir's beckoning, walking over slowly and staring at Amir as he helped Ricky. Sarah joined them as Espinoza and Forester were escorted over. Amir began to enter the vehicle, Jensen grabbing his arm firmly.

"Where are our phones and firearms?"

Amir looked at Jensen's hand on his arm, glancing over at three of his guards. Jensen's grip tightened momentarily before finally releasing.

"You will receive all of those things when Dr. Degnan completes his job. If he fails, I would suggest reporting them stolen to Verizon."

Amir smiled and sat down next to Frenchy, closing the door. Samir opened the opposite door, taking his seat to Frenchy's left. Frenchy looked back and forth to his sides in disbelief.

"You have got to be shittin' me."

Frenchy waved exaggeratedly to Sarah and the rest of the group as Ali drove off. Jensen looked back at the three remaining guards who returned to their two vehicles.

"Let's get him inside."

Jensen signaled for the group to move towards the exit. He stopped Forester and Espinoza.

"Stay out here and watch the area. Something is not right. In about an hour, come in and stand by the door and survey from inside. We can shake this 'tail.'"

The two agents nodded, surveying their surroundings without moving their gaze from Jensen. Jensen followed Sarah and Ricky into the hospital. Espinoza and Forester turned towards each other, nodding.

THE SENATOR STOOD BEHIND HIS DESK, his speaker phone ringing with a dialed number. Senator Heller sat across from him, staring at photos.

"Thank you for being early, Senator Maini; I trust you have reviewed my proposal and documentation."

"To say we're a bit put off by this information would not be conveying our true feelings."

"Good. I assumed you would reach out to your trusted colleagues. I assume Senator Heller and Representative Sullivan have joined you. The three of you may be the only honest politicians in Washington, and from New Jersey, no less. Not exactly the beacon of honesty and honor. Nevertheless, I must apologize for leaving, but I had to ensure the safety of a friend. I will return to your office in a few minutes."

Maini looked confused at Nasser's proximity to the office building.

"Then why . . ."

The call ended abruptly, the three congressmen remaining in silence.

"Are you sure we shouldn't be concerned about this, Nasser? After all, he drops a bombshell and then leaves only to return a few moments after you call him?"

Heller nodded at Sullivan's comment.

"If a shred of this stuff is true . . . no, if a sliver is true, we are all screwed. How do we proceed?"

Heller stood up, dropping the photos on the desk.

"Please, don't be so melodramatic. We move on just like we have from any other scandal. My primary concern is why this guy has given this to you and, as he said, he assumed you would show us."

The buzzer on Maini's desk from his secretary broke their group contemplation.

"Send him in."

Maini returned to his colleagues.

"What I want to know is what this Nasser wants. It is not always prudent to flood information to the public."

The door opened and Nasser entered, extending his hand to Heller and Sullivan.

"Sit, please, I think we can abandon politeness and just focus on this."

Nasser sat as Sullivan brought a third chair over.

"Of course. I am sure you have many questions, but in truth I am sure you understand that time is a factor so let me see if I can preempt any such queries. That information has been collected by a series of individuals scattered throughout your government. You can question the authenticity and whether it is true or not, but I will be taking this to the media in roughly three hours. You must be the face behind the information, you must guarantee that you will take the appropriate course of action to ensure that those guilty of these crimes are dealt with in the appropriate manner—"

Maini held his hand up, stopping Nasser.

"I appreciate your concern but I am not sure any crime has been committed here. Sleazy and dishonest, yes, but that does not always translate into indictments. But, more importantly, what do you mean this information came from people within our own government? What people?"

Nasser smiled tentatively.

"Who they are is unimportant, and why they leaked this information . . . well, let's say they were performing their civic duty."

The congressmen sat motionless, concerned by the vague response.

"Please make this your priority. When the media receives this, they will expect swift action. I am asking that you drive that action. What you have is proof of much more than sleazy actions. Whether the U.S. justice system deems it criminal will not change the world's reaction. And that is why you must track this to show that actions such as these will be vigorously pursued as will the men who acted. Given these actions, it is not about what the citizens of the U.S. will think; it is about the world's response, which will not be pleasant."

"What about Degnan? There are pictures of him with the Prime Minister of Israel, and then with Islamic militants. How does he fit in?"

"As I stated before, he is safe. He has merely been the victim. I will ensure that he and his companions are returned safely to the United States. Please, you focus on how you will handle this situation. Now, have I eliminated your questions?"

The congressmen chuckled.

"Not even close."

"Well, I will be sure to return and help you with your investigation. But as I said before, my goal now is to secure Dr. Degnan's safety."

Senator Maini shook his head in disbelief.

"Do you have ADHD? You can't seem to stay in one place for long."

Nasser stood and nodded.

"When completing a job such as this, it is important to never stay in one place for too long. Too much to do, too much risk."

Nasser smiled and started walking over to the door. The three men stood quietly. Sullivan looked to the senior Senators. Maini turned to the table behind his desk, removing a bottle of Jameson whiskey and pouring it into three glasses. He turned and handed a glass to each man. He picked up his own glass and held it up.

"Well, if it is true—if the president, VP, Secretary of Defense, and the FBI are all in on this operation—we may not be too popular after this. So here's to doing something, whether it's wise or not."

The other two glasses joined Maini's. He drank the full glass and placed it on his desk. He grabbed his phone and quickly dialed.

"If this Nasser is arranging transportation for Degnan, I want you to be there to make sure he's safe."

Congressman Sullivan's eyes widened, unsure of the task he had just been given. "I'm not so sure I am the right . . ."

Maini held a finger up.

"Nasser. Change of plans. Congressman Sullivan will meet Degnan with your men. I want him to feel assured."

Maini listened carefully, nodding and then placing the phone down.

"You will be fine. I need you on this."

Sullivan reluctantly nodded. Maini picked up a photo of Frenchy, standing near the base of Masada.

"Thank you. And let's be honest: if this Nasser is lying, then we are all fucked. But for now, let's hope for his father's sake, and for ours, that Nasser knows what he is talking about."

"SO, ANYBODY CATCH THE DEVILS GAME the other night? Brodeur is my man; he is the greatest goaltender in the history of the NHL."

Frenchy's eyes widened as he stared at Samir.

"Sorry, that's right; you guys only play dodgeball with human heads. My mistake."

His companions remained silent, ignoring his goading.

"So, Samir, what do you do when you're not shooting innocent teenagers? I bet you play the cello, hmm? Maybe a little Pachelbel's Canon in D to get you pumped up to kill innocent people?"

"Francis, that is enough. Remember what I said to you."

Ali stared back desperately. Frenchy removed his last cigarette.

"Are there any 7-Elevens around here? I need cigarettes and a Big Gulp right now. Or booze, if they got it."

No one responded to his comment.

"No, seriously, I need cigarettes. I am not doing this without cigarettes."

Ali sighed, reaching into the pocket of the driver's side door, throwing a pack at Frenchy. He picked up the opened pack and examined it.

"I can't smoke these. These are Camels."

"When we arrive at the monastery, please refrain from your usual commentary. Our visit is a special favor. While I enjoy your remarks, I would hate to miss this chance."

Botvinnik's thinly veiled threat seemed to deflate Frenchy's spunk. The jeep continued to climb the steep road. The last bit of light remained in the sky, as they approached the monastery of Saint Onuphrius. The lights of the jeep illuminated a large, red door topped by a series of inscriptions. Frenchy sighed deeply, his anxiety returning. His companions exited the vehicle, staring back at Frenchy as he remained seated, smoking. Amir extended his hand. Frenchy sat motionless. The kind gestured filled him with panic. He made his way out and stood, stretching, exhaling smoke, and dropping his cigarette to the ground.

"Nice red door."

Samir nodded his head, gesturing for Frenchy to move. Botvinnik approached the door, knocking loudly. The sound of the large door knob twisting caused Frenchy to flinch. A gray bearded man in a black cassock opened the door, looking at the group before stepping aside to allow entry. Frenchy smiled and nodded, foolishly. They entered a stone-floored room which opened out to the back section of the monastery.

"Nice plants," Frenchy said, pointing to the right corner of the room. Frenchy smiled uneasily, walking over to the archway and looking out over rocky sections of the hill. He stood and smiled as he gazed out at the lights of Jerusalem below.

"Now, this is a view." He paused after his comment, observing the rocky terrain connected to the monastery. "There, that's where it is. This was a cemetery, the potter's field. If there is a place where you would put the Sword, it would be down there."

Botvinnik turned to the monk and spoke to him in Greek.

"He will take us down."

Frenchy raised his eyebrows in excitement as they followed the monk through an adjacent room and down the staircase.

"I know we can never be friends again, Ali, but this is awesome. Look at this place. A monastery on the location where Judas killed himself."

Ali patted Frenchy on the back in agreement. The monk led them out onto a cement platform, rock formations leading out into the hillside. The group evaluated the possible paths. Frenchy stared at one path, squinting as he stood thinking.

"This may sound silly, but my gut says we go that way and drop down to that entrance."

His companions stood silent, awaiting objections. Frenchy shook his head, stepped up on the rock, and carefully balanced himself, cautiously jumping from one section of the rock to another. His companions followed his lead. He made his way to the entrance of the first crypt, grabbing at the gate blocking his way.

"Hey, Father, the door is locked."

Botvinnik turned, recognizing the monk would not understand. The monk raised his hand, holding a large key ring. Botvinnik looked back at Frenchy, expecting him to return for it.

"What the hell? You're closer. Just get the damn key and let's go, Ol' Man River."

Botvinnik carefully turned and crawled back to the monk, slowly returning with the keys to Frenchy. Frenchy grabbed the keys from Botvinnik, as he gasped for breath.

"And I'm the smoker?" Frenchy quipped, as he opened the gate.

They entered, Frenchy's thoughts returning to the last time he entered a rock formation. He crept softly, walking past skeletons in carved tombs within the rock. He turned and winked at Ali in excitement.

"If I didn't have my possible death looming over this task, I'd be pretty excited."

Frenchy continued, stopping as he realized the light was gone.

"We need flashlights."

Samir sighed in irritation. Botvinnik regained his composure joining the group.

"Francis, you go back. If you didn't spend your whole time in awe of how this parallels your favorite movies, you would remember the essentials to finding treasure."

Frenchy recognized Ali's point, hoisting himself up onto the rock and returning to the monk.

"We need flashlights. Lights. Flashy lights."

Frenchy amplified his voice, attempting to convey his request through hand signals. Botvinnik shouted from the tombs. The monk smiled, walking back towards the staircase. Frenchy followed as the monk opened a door near the base of the staircase. He handed him two DeWalt flashlights.

"You have got to be shittin' me, DeWalt? Fuckin' Americans. And we curse the Chinese."

The monk nodded, staring blankly. Frenchy turned back toward the rocky formation, quickly moving to the gate. He handed one flashlight to Ali, taking the other and illuminating the path ahead of him.

"Let's go see more dead guys, my future murderers."

He moved slowly, briefly shifting the light onto each skeleton as he made his way deeper into the ground. His light returned to a large segment of the stone wall, situated between the rockier sections with cutaways for corpses.

"What is it?" Ali asked.

Frenchy rubbed his hand against the rock, brushing dirt away from the wall. His efforts revealed an oval-shaped marking on the center of the stone.

"What is it?" Amir asked, moving in to inspect.

"It's the Ichthys."

Amir turned to Frenchy awaiting further explanation.

"Iesos Christos Theou Huios Soter. It means 'Jesus Christ, God's son our Savior.' It's an early Christian symbol. If I remember correctly, it was a way of telling each other where to meet or some stupid shit like that. I saw it on Jeopardy."

"Why would there be a Christian symbol here?"

Frenchy stood up and lit a cigarette.

"Because this was a cemetery for non-Jews. Other than that, who knows? Let's take the wall down and see if we are wasting time. But we need some tools."

His companions froze in anger. Samir stepped forward, screwing a silencer on his gun. He fired repeatedly at the wall, stopping and reloading, and emptying a second clip. Samir moved forward and pushed at the wall, budging it slightly. He looked up at Frenchy and winked. He stepped back and kicked the wall, the lower part of it soon falling away in large chunks.

"Sure, what do I know? Let's shoot the thing. Let's ruin the wall and hit whatever is behind this. Oh, and thanks, dick, for saving the ichthys though. That would have been worthless, right? Oh, and I hope you wasted your bullets so we can really tangle later."

Frenchy muttered to himself as he followed Samir through the hole in the rock. They stepped into a small enclosure.

"I am not comfortable being in a room with you alone."

Frenchy looked back waiting for Ali and Amir to follow. Samir stared back at Frenchy, smiling. The awkward staring was interrupted by Amir and Ali, emerging from the hole. Ali and Frenchy illuminated the room with their flashlights, roughly a twelve-by-twelve-foot room. The group observed a single sarcophagus near the far wall.

"You know what? It just occurred to me why this trip has been so productive in the archaeological sense. There is a reason why other people don't break walls down or go in caves they shouldn't be in. Because we are not archaeologists. We are tomb robbers. We should not be doing this shit. Excavations? Maybe, okay. But we sure as hell are not doing that. Look, what a surprise, a sarcophagus. How lucky? No, not luck, it's because we're doing the wrong thing. We're not innovative seekers, we are irresponsible brutes."

Frenchy rubbed at his eyes, oddly frustrated by a possible discovery.

"Francis, without our actions, things remain lost. We are not wrong, far from that. We are doing what archaeologists wouldn't think of doing. We knock walls down and break through because, if we don't, we do not find that which we have been searching for."

Ali smiled as he finished, gesturing for Frenchy to proceed to the tomb.

"I'm just sayin', there is a reason why we've been so lucky. Because you don't do it this way."

Frenchy walked slowly forward, dropping his cigarette butt and stamping it out. The other three followed. Frenchy looked at the lid of the sarcophagus. He observed an engraving of a small dagger.

"That's the Sicarius, the dagger of the Sicarii, where they get their name from. This might be it."

Ali nodded in reserved excitement. Samir moved to take the lid off before Frenchy grabbed his arm.

"Please, just give me a minute, please!"

Amir nodded his head, his brother stepping back. Frenchy removed a Camel from his pocket and lit it, gazing at the room.

"Another cigarette?"

Frenchy mocked Ali's chastisement.

"You know, whatever we find in this coffin, look at where we are. Despite the horrid way in which we search and excavate. We made it to the end. Whether we like each other or not, we may have found John the Baptist's skeleton. We found a piece of silver; whether it's Judas's or not, we still found *stuff*. I guess I always thought I could never find anything because everything of note had been found."

Ali walked over and put his hand on Frenchy's shoulder.

"Very true, regardless of how we have found them, we have found them. Let us finish this."

Frenchy inhaled deeply, dropping his cigarette. He walked over to the sarcophagus, grabbing at the stone slab and pushing forcefully; the others quickly joined in helping to move it. A small opening emerged as they pushed the slab onto the ground. His eyes widening as he took in the contents. Ali, Samir, and Amir joined him, all staring down in awe. Frenchy reached down slowly, removing a three foot sword lying on the chest of the skeleton. Ali and Amir looked on in excitement as Frenchy examined it.

"Shit . . ." Frenchy said, examining further, fingering the blade. "I think, maybe, this is it."

Samir approached, looking carefully at the sword.

"I thought Goliath was a giant? This looks like the sword of a regular man."

Frenchy held the curved blade up.

"Goliath was a giant to Jews. He probably was my height or maybe two inches taller. Definitely not Andre the Giant tall. Everybody was shorter back then. A guy six feet two would have been a monster. This is something. It looks like authentic Iron Age gear, but again, I'm no archaeologist."

Amir took the sword from Frenchy, admiring it. Frenchy leaned in and looked at the skeleton. He turned his head, eyeing the bones. He reach into the sarcophagus, removing two scrolls from the hands of the skeleton. He smelled the scrolls, breathing in deeply. He carefully unfurled a scroll, scanning it with a sense of urgency.

"Not sure but I think this is Greek. Where's Mr. B?"

Amir looked over, unaware of Frenchy's find. He signaled to Samir to call for Botvinnik, who slowly crawled through the opening, breathing heavily. Frenchy walked over to him aggressively.

"Is this Greek and, if so, what is it?"

Botvinnik sighed and looked at the scroll. Frenchy held the light as Botvinnik read.

"Very interesting."

Frenchy flashed the light in Botvinnik's eyes, responding to his statement.

"Sorry, didn't mean that. What's so interesting? No stalling, just blurt it out."

"Could be the Gospel of Judas, but it's in Greek."

Frenchy stood, pondering the statement.

"What does that matter? What makes it very interesting? They already found the Gospel of Judas."

Frenchy looked back into the sarcophagus.

"It matters because the only copy of the Gospel of Judas that exists is in Coptic and is from two hundred years after Jesus died. It was speculated that the Coptic version came from an original Greek copy, but no copy has ever been found. Please, Dr. Degnan, you of all people. You do not watch the History Channel?"

The group paused, recognizing the value of the find.

"It also means that there is a good chance these are the remains of Judas. His followers, the Gnostics, must have buried him here and the sword placed here with him."

Samir shook his head in confusion.

"I thought you said the two women who escaped from Masada took the sword and brought it back to the original Sicarii?"

Frenchy shook his hands, dismissing the reasonable question.

"I can't keep track of what I've said in the past because my theories change as I go."

Ali chuckled at Frenchy's admittance of his wavering ideas.

"Look, the Gospel of Judas portrays Judas as a good apostle. In fact, the only apostle who understood Jesus' message. It makes him not a traitor, but the number one apostle, and Jesus' liberator. Who knows who put the Sword here, but it's here and we found it, along with the world's most famous traitor. Who cares what I've said! My blabbering and inability to be firm on anything has paid off. Because of my insecurity and lack of self-confidence, I adapted as I went along. We could still be at Masada digging. Instead we're here with the Sword, and with a major find in these scrolls, not to mention the possibility that we found Judas's body. Either way, cut me some freakin' slack. We did it. And I get to live—booyah."

Frenchy took the sword from Amir and held it up.

"I feel like He-Man."

His companions ignored the outdated reference and smiled at him. Samir removed his gun, the silencer still on it.

"Whoa, hold on a fuckin' second. We agreed; we had a deal."

Samir held the gun up to Frenchy.

"Well, this is a familiar sight. Should have known you would screw me. Thanks, Ali, so much for being my protector."

Samir quickly shifted the gun away from Frenchy, firing. Botvinnik dropped to the ground, shot directly in his forehead. Frenchy looked down in astonishment. Ali and Amir quickly seized the scrolls and sword, walking passed Botvinnik's body, and crawling through the hole. Samir secured his gun in his waist.

"Hopefully, we will still be given the opportunity for those few minutes to settle our dispute," Samir said, winking at Frenchy, turning and crawling through the hole.

Frenchy stood stunned. He stared down at Botvinnik's corpse. He stumbled backwards towards the sarcophagus, dropping down and leaning against it. He grabbed his chest, his heart palpably thumping through his shirt. He stared at a small stream of crimson blood flowing away from Botvinnik's head. Frenchy began to heave, vomiting to his left. He crawled to the other side of the stone coffin, gagging. His hands trembled as he held his head, trying to compose himself.

"Please, God, help me."

The absence of Botvinnik's body from Frenchy's peripheral vision helped him to slow his heart rate. He retrieved a cigarette, the light shaking in his hand. He exhaled slowly, watching the smoke rise into the beam of his dropped flashlight. He listened for any sounds in the catacomb. Despite the sudden murder, Frenchy hoped his captors would return for him. He sighed deeply, aware that he had to leave the room. He peered back towards the makeshift entrance, attempting to avoid glimpsing the corpse again. He lodged the cigarette in his mouth and closed his eyes. He quickly ran over to the hole, lunging through it, and hitting his head on the jagged rock at the top of the opening. He grabbed his forehead in pain. He looked down the entrance passage, seeing a small glimmer of light from the moon. He walked towards the night sky reaching the edge of the cave, still hoping to find Ali.

He stared down at the lights of the city below, over the rock wall. His panic returned as he remembered Botvinnik's body. He awkwardly made his way over the wall, dropping down onto the hill. A small trickle of blood ran down his cheek from the new gash above his right temple. He threw his cigarette and began to run down the hill. The fear of being alone and the unfortunate ending to his search propelled him faster. His mind raced for the name of the hospital where Ricky and Sarah had been left. He jumped over a rock, not realizing the large drop below. He landed awkwardly, falling down and rolling over repeatedly. His body flew over a six foot wall onto a terracotta patio, crashing against the ground. He tried to push himself up from the tile but his arms gave out, dropping his body back down. The patio light came on as a man emerged quickly, rushing cautiously over to Frenchy. He shifted his body and put his hand under Frenchy's head. Frenchy cracked his eyes open, blood dripping from the added wounds from his latest tumble.

"Are you alright?" the man asked, with a heavy accent. Frenchy mumbled. The man leaned in to hear. Frenchy swallowed trying to repeat himself.

"I don't want . . . to play anymore."

"ARE WE DEAD? Or maybe not both dead, but am I dead? Or maybe you are visiting me in a dream. I'm not sure; either way, is there a chance that we are . . ."

Maggie held her finger up to his lips, as she had done so many times during their relationship, when Frenchy would babble uncontrollably. Frenchy smiled. He viewed the familiar surroundings, and he was flooded with a warm feeling. His eyes surveyed Maggie's childhood living room.

"So, not to push my query, but are either of us dead?"

Maggie shook her head.

"I'm pretty sure we are not dead. Well, I'm definitely not. You? Maybe, after running like an idiot down that sizable hill."

"That's comforting," Frenchy said, squirming at the thought of his own death. "Well, if I'm dead then I assume this is my last chance to talk to you."

Maggie's head moved slightly, expressing interest, shifting her bangs to the left. Frenchy's heart fluttered, remembering how much he enjoyed every movement or gesture she made.

"Well, before you kill me or beat me, or remind me of how terrible I am as a person—like what usually happens when we meet like this—I just want to emphatically, and without any agenda, say . . . well, I get it now. I really do. And I'm sorry."

Maggie reached out and took his hand.

"What do you mean 'you get it?'"

Frenchy rolled his eyes.

"Now I know I'm dead and this is my penance for my sins. Fine, you want me to say it: yes, I took you for granted; yes, I repeatedly hurt you; yes, my drinking, my depression, it ruined what we had, and yes, I let you go too easily."

Frenchy grabbed his head. His irritation at hearing the words he had heard in his mind for years pushed his limits.

"Look, it may seem like I am mad, but I'm not. It's just so hard to admit what terrifies me. It's easier to either wallow in self-pity or shun responsibility away from me."

"As late and as strange as your delivery is, I accept and do appreciate you saying that. It doesn't change anything. Things can never be the same between us."

Frenchy pumped his hands, acknowledging her statement.

"No, no. I get it now, more than ever. You said once that you learned to appreciate what we had without longing for any rekindling. I just needed to recognize what I had done. Not to try to get you back, just to make sure you knew and thus, I can now finally move forward. And maybe stop having these ridiculous dreams where you or someone kills me. I'm serious. The other day you were one of Stalin's men and you shot me in the heart. Come to think of it, you always stabbed or shot me in the heart in my dreams. Fuckin' weird. Anyway, hopefully I have made you feel better and at least I finally owned up for myself."

Maggie smiled and looked down, reaching into her pocket and removing a small stone.

"My worry stone! Holy shit, I thought I lost it."

"You did, I found it in the couch of my parents' house. Couldn't bring myself to throw it out."

Frenchy nodded awkwardly, realizing he had hastily barbecued most of the things she had given him after she left.

"I couldn't agree more."

Maggie placed it in his hand. Frenchy looked down in appreciation, remembering how much he used it in his life.

"I think you need it now more than ever, and it helped me through the tougher times so I return it to you."

"Thank you, seriously, thank you."

The two smiled at each other. Frenchy looked around, feeling exonerated and renewed.

"So this must not be a dream, because we now have an awkward moment. So thus, I'm going to leave."

Maggie continued smiling, appreciating his humor. Frenchy turned towards a large window, remembering the door to be on the left.

"One more thing."

Frenchy turned and anxiously glanced back at Maggie, fear of an attack returning.

"I know you burned all my things. You never could lie."

Frenchy sorrowfully nodded. Maggie walked over to him and kissed his lips. Frenchy breathed deeply.

"I'll see you soon."

Maggie walked past him towards the door. Frenchy grinned, feeling free from his guilt. He sighed, realizing his heart now longed for Sarah. He turned, suddenly feeling a burning sensation in his chest. He looked down, shocked to see a knife sticking out of his chest. He grabbed the knife, trying to remove it. His chest felt heavy. He looked towards the door for Maggie. Her sudden absence seemed to increase the pressure on his chest. A feeling of darkness rushed into his mind. He dropped to his knees as he sees a framed picture of Maggie and her new boyfriend hanging on the wall. He stared at the man, suddenly realizing it to be himself. He gasped as he fell to the ground.

"Goddamnit, I said I was sorry . . ."

57

"I'M SO PROUD OF YOU," Sarah whispered, as she stroked Frenchy's bruised face. Frenchy looked around, fearful of a second death-filled dream.

"Relax, don't move. You got pretty beat up from the fall. Luckily, you survived with only a bunch of nasty cuts, a sprained knee, four broken ribs, and a concussion."

Sarah's recount of his injuries suddenly heightened the pain from the mentioned areas.

"Luckily? I feel like shit. Wait, where's Ricky?"

Sarah smiled, looking over at the neighboring bed. Ricky sat happily, busily tapping on his iPhone. He hopped out of bed and gave Frenchy a bear hug. Frenchy gasped in pain, smiling through the aching embrace, knowing his student was okay.

"How's the leg?"

"Great, it wasn't as bad as it felt. Turned out he missed the bone. Did cause a lot of blood loss and I don't think I'll be playing rugby this spring."

Frenchy recognized that that would be a disappointment to Ricky as well as his teammates.

"I'm sorry, brother. I didn't want this . . ."

"Don't apologize, Doc. I will forever be known as the student who went on an adventure with the Doc, and took a bullet for said man. That's not a bad consolation prize, eh?"

Frenchy smiled and took Ricky's hand, attempting some type of handshake.

Frenchy looked over at Sarah. Her new outfit and happy demeanor caused him to tear up.

"Are you crying?"

Frenchy gulped trying to respond.

"I've got to tell you, seeing the two of you healthy and happy is more than enough to make me cry. This was not the adventure I expected or envisioned. Wanted by my own government, being on the run, terrified at every turn, watching people get shot and killed, getting my ass kicked by some Jew hill, betrayed, falling in love, depression . . ."

"What was that last one before depression?"

Sarah leaned in, goading Frenchy to repeat.

"Oh, falling in love with the Middle East and it's beautiful historical sites, its lovely sun-scorched terrain, and its quaint, murderous governments and militias. God, who could not make the Middle East number one on their vacation list? After this, I'm heading to Cambodia. God I love the holidays there."

Sarah followed through on her lean, kissing Frenchy.

"Yeaaaaaah buddy," Ricky said, winking, and pretending to kiss the air in an inappropriate manner.

"Fuck off, young man. And yes, I can curse because I feel like shit. When do I get out?"

"Tomorrow, but tell us all about the monastery at Akeldama. What happened when you found the Sword?"

Sarah pulled her chair over, sitting and holding Frenchy's hand.

"Where's Jensen and the other two skanks?"

"They left a day ago. Returned home. They were apparently wanted for questioning."

Frenchy shook his head with confusion.

"Pretend that the last time I knew what the fuck was going on, I was a human snowball crashing down a hill. A steep hill. How long was I out and what is going on?"

Ricky and Sarah recognized Frenchy's frustration as warranted.

"You were brought into the hospital about four days ago. Unbelievably lucky that you would end up in the same hospital. You've been out since then, kind of like a coma, but nothing to get worried about. The doctor said the pain meds and your previous seventy hours may have aided it."

"What the hell is 'kind of like a coma?' How hard did I hit my head? Whatever."

Frenchy refocused, waving his hand in impatience.

"Then what?"

"So then, well, as you crude Jersey boys would say, the shit hit the fan. The U.S. government and the public got information on the U.S.-Israel treaty and corruption, et cetera, and, of course, the attempt to kill you."

"So they *were* trying to kill me. I knew that Jensen was full of shit."

Frenchy snarled in anger.

"Francis, they returned to testify against their superiors and they admitted their culpability. In the end, they tried to make it right. Still, this whole mess has created a tense environment. Relations between Israelis and Palestinians are volatile, to say the least. The Prime Minister of Israel resigned."

"What about Assaf? And what do you mean 'volatile?' And give me more about the U.S. shit."

"Assaf is dead; killed in a battle with the same militia that graced our presence. Volatile? Well, let's just say Palestinians are none too happy about what Israel was planning, and Israelis, I imagine, are upset at what was planned, or failed, depending on the Israeli. And at home, well, two senators from New Jersey have pushed for emergency meetings in Congress. A representative from Massachusetts has called for a full investigation. Impeachment was mentioned as well. It seems you Jersey boys and apparently Mass boys are crude but also very productive."

Frenchy smiled, raising his fist to Ricky's outstretched one for a bump.

"Well, that will take forever and nothing will come of it, but at least they are doing something. How'd you know I found the Sword?"

Sarah leaned in and kissed his forehead.

"That's what I asked. We just know that everything we did has been reported and the media is all over it. I mean everything. Machaerus, Masada, you at the monastery, everything. And they have given you and your 'team' the credit for various discoveries, particularly the alleged Sword of Goliath."

Sarah's talk of credit seemed to alleviate Frenchy's pain. He tried to sit up a bit, Sarah adjusting the bed.

"So, what happened when you found it, Doc?"

Frenchy pondered Sarah's news for a moment.

"Well . . . I don't know. Actually, it was pretty freakin' awesome aside from the company I was keeping at the time. We found an ichthys carved into the wall and only I knew its meaning. Then dickhole Samir blasted the wall to create a passage where we ended up finding a sword, possibly on the remains of Judas. And we found scrolls—possibly of the Gospel of Judas with the Gnostic text—but in Greek, older than any copy ever found. Or at least I hope so. And then . . ."

"What? And then what? What kind of story is that?" Ricky blasted, unappreciative of Frenchy's pause.

"I'm not finished. And then Ali and the two bash brothers shot Botvinnik, took the sword and scrolls, and left. They didn't even touch me. Then I freaked out and ran."

Frenchy paused. His perturbed look halting the conversation.

"How the fuck could anyone but Ali, Samir, and Amir, know about that. They just left. Samir, that douchebag, winked at me. Then they were gone."

"Maybe they weren't that bad after all," Ricky shrugged, injecting his thought as a possibility.

"You believe that? They're not that bad? They commit multiple murders and shoot you in the goddamn leg, but no, you're right; they're not that bad."

"Who cares now? They gave you credit. The news has you as the man who found everything—the possible remains of Judas and John the Baptist, the scrolls, the Sword—everything. It wasn't front page because of everything else, but there was a lot of coverage."

Sarah smiled, trying to highlight the positive.

"In truth, now that my adrenaline is gone, I see things a bit differently. Credit is nice, but most of what we found is probably nothing. The chances of finding or, better yet, verifying, the bodies of John the Baptist or Judas are slim. We found the Sword as your father hoped. But just because he believed it was Goliath's sword, and I pray it is, doesn't make it fact.

"Maybe worse is, after all this shit, I have no idea what side anyone was on. People promised shit, then bailed, then kind of followed through. Agents tried to kill me, now dumbass government shit, and for God's sake, we're in Israel without passports."

His scattered thoughts and fragmented complaints frustrated him. Sarah placed her hand on his chest.

"Let's simply say this: who knows what side anyone was on? We *are* all alive. That's all that matters."

Sarah's focus on their safety caused Frenchy to sigh with minor relief. He looked at his companions. Their beckoning faces helped him move forward.

"And, we have an escort home."

"What do you mean, like a hooker?" Ricky laughed heartily, stopping when his mentor seemed serious.

"I'm not addressing that. And our *escort* was sent by your Jersey boy, Senator Maini. He has us returning to New York, arriving in Newark."

Frenchy gritted his teeth.

"Um, no, we are arriving in New Jersey. Newark is not New York and will never be New York. That shit pisses me off so much. You know when they broadcast Giants and Jets games on TV, they show aerial footage of Manhattan? The fuckin' teams play in Jersey. Not New York. What the fuck is wrong with people?"

Sarah allowed Frenchy to rant, patiently waiting for him to run out of steam.

"Yes, well, we will be arriving in New Jersey tomorrow after you get out in the morning. We will have protection during the whole investigation process. So don't worry about getting home. And don't worry about everything else. It is not our problem or our responsibility. The right people will be brought to justice. And regardless of why Ali, Samir, and Amir did what they did. You *have* been given credit. Let the scientists and historians battle over the scrolls and bodies. We don't have to worry about any of it. We are safe and will be okay."

Frenchy stared into Sarah's eyes. Despite his foul mood, her main point could not be ignored.

"You're right. I still don't like this but you're right. Just one more question: why did the news believe that we found that stuff without the stuff?"

Sarah walked over to a table near the door. She picked up two newspapers and brought them over.

"See for yourself." She turned to a later page and handed Frenchy the paper. He looked up at the top of the paper.

"*New York Times.*" He squinted, trying to analyze the picture. The headline read, "Alleged Biblical Discoveries Connected to U.S.-Israel Alliance."

"Son of a bitch. Those bastards did turn it in."

Frenchy scanned the article.

"Well, at least it's in the right hands. Says here, teams are preparing to analyze the remains. How the hell do people work so fast?"

"Well, you missed three days. However, I wouldn't expect anything for months, maybe years."

"I know. You're right. It will take years for this to get sorted out."

"So, all you've talked about this whole time was redeeming your name. I'm pretty sure you've been redeemed. We don't need the reward money you were promised. You'll be fine without it; you work. Though you may need to smooth things over with your boss after setting the building on fire."

"Hahaha, very funny. Speaking of work, and since I clearly spent this entire trip talking about myself, I may be a little late in asking, but what do you do? Then again, maybe it's that you never opened up the way I did."

Sarah patted Frenchy's hand.

"No, the former was correct. You never stopped talking long enough for me to open up."

"Bitch slapped." Ricky snapped his fingers and made a shooting gesture.

"You're a moron. So, what do you do?"

"I'm a social worker."

Frenchy chuckled.

"I could see that. I knew I liked you from the beginning."

"What are you talking about? You wouldn't stop bitching when we met."

He rolled his eyes, aware of her point.

"Anyway, I did like you; I just wasn't a fan of your pattern of repeated assault against me. Either way, I agree. We are safe and I have been redeemed and the sons of bitches who orchestrated this shit will get what they deserve. If we're going back to the dirty Jerse' tomorrow, all that's left to figure out is how to explain to Ricky's father the bullet hole in his leg. Aside from that, we are all good."

FRENCHY LIMPED OUT OF THE ENTRANCE to the hospital. Camera lights began to flash as he emerged.

"What the shit? Why are there camera people here?"

Frenchy winced in pain as he grabbed Sarah's arm.

"I assume word got out that we were here."

Ricky jumped in front of Frenchy, pushing a cameraman back.

"Back the hell up, nigga, before I drop you. I ain't playin'."

A well-dressed man pushed the photographer back, clearing a path towards a black Mercedes-Benz. Another man stepped forward and opened the back door.

"Well, gee whiz, this looks awfully familiar."

Frenchy looked over the crowd, hoping for an alternate route. Sarah pulled on Frenchy's arm, trying to lead him to the vehicle.

"Are you out of your fuckin' mind? I'm not getting into anymore vehicles. I'm not even getting into a cab. Call it learning from history, bad history, something we as people do not do. So I will start the trend."

Sullivan stepped out from the back seat. Frenchy stared skeptically, aware of the man's familiarity. Sullivan approached and extended his hand.

"Dr. Degnan, I presume. Congressman Sullivan. I have been sent by Senators Heller and Maini to accompany you back to the States."

Frenchy reluctantly shook his hand.

"Sullivan, huh, any relation to Patty Sullivan? I heard a lot about him when I was up in Boston."

Sullivan smiled and nodded with pride.

"That man was a hero to everyone in Boston, not just Southie. He's my father. He was the hardest working man I've ever met and also the most honorable man."

Sullivan's response seemed to calm Frenchy's suspicions.

"You know, I was working for a guy from Southie when he passed. My boss, Jim, was in awe of Patty Sullivan. He told some amazing stories about him, about how much he cared about people, not just his constituents."

"What was your boss's name?"

"Jim Hughes. He worked at Boston University most recently."

Sullivan laughed.

"Big Jim? Of course. Like my father, that man could tell a good story. He should've been in politics."

The two laughed together, enjoying the momentary reminiscence. Sarah stepped forward, hoping to gently interrupt their venture down memory lane.

"Maybe, since you are comfortable with the Congressman, we can head home?"

Sarah's question drew Frenchy back to reality. He leaned forward and kissed her cheek.

"Absolutely. Plenty of time to bullshit later."

Frenchy entered the vehicle awkwardly with Ricky trying to help him. Sarah and Ricky quickly ran to the other side to enter. The vehicle began to speed ahead, the media quickly moving out of the way.

"Now, that's the way to drive; you bring this guy from Boston, too? Only Massholes drive like that."

Sullivan laughed.

"Easy there, Dr. Jersey, you don't have the highest insurance rate for no reason."

"Well-played, Sullivan. Now, what the hell is going on at home?"

Frenchy's jump changed Sullivan's mood.

"Not sure what's going to happen."

"But it was you, Maini, and Heller who reported this?"

"Well, it's not that simple. A man named Nasser delivered the information to Senator Maini. It was all a bit strange because the man was acting very peculiar. But he provided information, pictures, emails, wiretaps, and other records that essentially proved the existence of the treaty between the U.S. and Israel. But it also showed some incredibly shady dealings, including money transfers of massive amounts between individuals and our elected leaders, among other questionable shit. And, of course, the FBI's attempt to assassinate you—"

"Oh yeah, that ol' chestnut," quipped Frenchy.

"—and since I've left Washington, the senators informed me that boxes of information have been delivered to Maini's office, all related to this fiasco. Amazing that the government still uses paper files. But perhaps the strangest part is—all the information came from within our government itself—but no one can trace any of it to any specific person. Despite being in this post-9/11 world of widespread mass surveillance and high-tech intelligence gathering protocols, we couldn't find out who leaked the information, or who produced it to be leaked . . . I'm sure we will, in time, but just a bit strange."

Frenchy shook his head in disbelief.

"'Strange' just doesn't seem to be a strong enough description. All I wanted was a little redemption. What happens? I end up connected to this corrupt government shit."

"Well, I wouldn't be so upset. I'm sure you are aware, given the cameras from the hospital, that you have been given credit for whatever it is you found. In fact, you may have found nothing of value, but people are aware of it because of the said connection to 'corrupt government shit.' You are quite the popular name at the moment."

Ricky grinned, hoping to capitalize on the positive comment from the Congressman.

"My man does have a point, Doc. Tell you what. If you get nothing from all this, I'll go halves on whatever this bad boy fetches."

Ricky pulled the vase he had found at Machaerus from a hospital towel. Frenchy rolled his eyes at the kind gesture.

"I think, given the bullet wound, you can keep my cut."

Frenchy peered out at the lights from the airport. He sighed, his concern for their safety slowly returning.

"You sure we won't have any problems on our way home?"

Sullivan wiped his forehead.

"I hope not. I was sent here to make sure you felt comfortable. I am out of the planning aspect of this."

"What the hell does that mean? Who's planning this?"

"I thought I told you; Nasser is planning your return. He was very clear that he would ensure that you came home safely."

Frenchy grabbed for his cigarettes.

"What happened to my . . ."

Sarah handed him the pack Ali had given him.

"I don't condone it but here."

"You know, not to harp on this, but Nasser is not exactly a . . . good ol' boys name. Is there a chance this guy is connected to the negative aspect of this whole catastrophe? I'd feel much more comfortable if we weren't taking a terrorist-associated aircraft."

Sullivan chuckled at Frenchy's awkwardly stated comment.

"Ordinarily, I would be concerned, but I pulled a fast one. A little insurance: our driver is an Air Force pilot and his colleague is a special ops soldier."

Frenchy looked skeptically at the two men. Sarah raised her arms in frustration.

"Honestly, Francis, if we die on the flight home, it's not like we would be able to prevent it. If they want us dead, then we will probably die. Suck it up, it's in God's hands now."

Frenchy winced at the generic statement. He leaned into Sullivan.

"You got any booze on the plane?"

Sullivan winked and sat back, looking out at the airport. Frenchy raised an eyebrow, not satisfied with the response.

"While I take that to be a positive, I need to be sure. I'm sure as hell not flying eleven hours without a little liquid relief."

"Worry not, my Irish brother. It's been taken care of."

SENATOR MAINI WALKED PAST a cluster of his aides busily moving around his office. He opened his door, surprised to see Nasser sitting in the lobby.

"I didn't want to disturb your staff so I waited."

"For a man who seems to always be moving, I'm surprised you could stand the pause."

Nasser rubbed his hands together, staring at the senator.

"I suppose that is a fair assessment. But then again, my work for now is almost complete. I stopped by to let you know that Dr. Degnan and his party will be arriving in Newark, tomorrow at four p.m. It might be nice to alert his family and his companions so that they can meet them."

Maini nodded in appreciation.

"I wonder if I may pose a simple yet important question?" Maini asked, eyeing his guest.

He walked over and sat in the leather chair adjacent to Nasser.

"Of course. I am happy to help in any way. I certainly am impressed with your resolve and your willingness to pursue justice, particularly given the unfortunate circumstance of being in opposition to our government."

"Well, let's be honest. I hardly had a choice, given your clear intention to release the information anyway. Still, my question may sound harsh and please excuse my words, but who the hell are you? I am sure you are not Mr. Nasser as you introduced yourself."

Nasser chuckled subtly.

"I mean, you have provided quite a large amount of information yet the names that would help us know who leaked this information have been redacted. And like I said, I have no idea what you even do or what your connection to all this is. As far as I know, you are the world's greatest investigator for collecting all of this."

"Do you believe that you are a good man, Senator? A moral man, just in his actions?"

Maini seemed indifferent to the question. He sat up in the chair, preparing to answer.

"I make mistakes just like everyone else. But I'd like to believe that I do what is right and I believe I am a good man."

Nasser leaned forward.

"You believe that, if you witnessed injustice, you would do something to rectify said injustice?"

"I do. Injustice is everywhere. As an elected official, I have to do what is right. Whether my constituents or not, I was taught to be the voice for the voiceless."

Nasser seemed pleased with the response. He patted Maini's knee.

"Well, you don't think you are the only one who believes that, do you? The names missing are people who think just like you. But unlike you, witnessing injustice is not . . . how would you say it . . . easy to report. You are fighting now, against this injustice, because most likely you will be admired for doing this. It does not change the fact that you are doing it. But there are many people who, if caught fighting injustices, may be fired, ostracized, or even killed. So they remain anonymous, as I do. But people still act. And we look to people like you who can reveal injustice without suffering greatly."

Maini sat still, attempting to draw from Nasser's response his identity.

"So, what you are is a person who delivers evidence of injustice?"

"Sometimes. Still, I cannot answer your question because I prefer to remain anonymous. Otherwise, I'll end up a target. Of what, who knows, but certainly a target. Now that I have made things even more confusing, I must go. But know that what you do is exactly what you said. You are the voice for the voiceless. And a voice not just for the victims of injustice, but also for people who wish to enact positive change but find themselves in scenarios that prevent them from practically or safely doing so."

Maini stood and shook Nasser's hand. Despite the lack of information, Nasser's principles gave him comfort.

"I suppose I'll see you the next time injustice surfaces," the Senator blurted out, curiously awaiting his guest's response. Nasser smiled and walked towards the door, stopping and looking back at the senator. "Not likely."

FRENCHY GRIPPED THE ARMREST as the plane touched down; the sound of the brakes engaging forced his eyes closed. The plane slowed drastically, moving into a slow cruise, signaling the end of the landing process. Sarah unhooked her belt and smiled giddily at Frenchy.

"We made it—we're home!"

Frenchy searched for wood to knock on.

"I'm not content until we are out of the plane . . . actually, till I'm home . . . better yet, back to work, and I know no one is coming to kill me."

Sarah leaned forward and kissed Frenchy on his lips, stopping his babbling. He looked shocked at her boldness.

"What's wrong?"

Frenchy shook his head.

"Nothing, I'm fine. Just still scared, that's all; your history of violence towards me forces me to keep a wary eye."

The plane came to a stop and Ricky popped out of his seat.

"I love you, Doc, and enjoyed our trip, but I'm not waiting for you. I'm gettin' the fuck out of here."

Frenchy unbuckled his seatbelt and stood slowly. Ricky pushed past Frenchy towards the exit. He hobbled forward, stopping to shake Sullivan's hand. The attendant opened the door.

"Move, lady, I'm outta here."

Ricky looked out and flinched, as a roar from the crowd gathered outside on the tarmac hit him. Ricky turned and grabbed Frenchy, bringing him to the doorway. The crowd bellowed louder when they saw Frenchy. He mimicked Ricky's reaction, the two hoping to push the other into the spotlight. Frenchy paused, realizing the futility of the act. He squinted quickly, wondering if this was an angry mob and not just a spirited group of welcomers. He turned and pulled Sarah up with him. A section of the crowd cheered, the rest uncertain about who she was. Someone in the crowd whistled.

The three stood paralyzed at the top of the moveable staircase. Sullivan put his hands on Frenchy's shoulders.

"Not bad, huh? I told you, you were famous."

Frenchy stared at the crowd, speechless. A lone voice echoed from below.

"For God's sake, would you get off the damn plane!"

Frenchy winced at the familiar voice of his grandmother. Despite her abrasive comment, her voice helped push his first foot forward. The group descended from the plane. As they made their way down the staircase, the faces of the crowd became clear. Each of them smiled at seeing the familiar faces. Frenchy's parents and siblings stood quietly, simply smiling as he made his way down. Ricky gestured colloquially at many of his classmates, returning the strange greeting.

Sarah began to sob as she saw her sisters crying in happiness. The assembled students rushed to the group, hugging and high-fiving Frenchy and Ricky. Frenchy continued beyond with Sarah to their families. Frenchy's father extended his hand, shaking Frenchy's momentarily before pulling him in for an embrace. His mother rushed in and dragged Frenchy's siblings in.

"Family hug, the way we used to," Frenchy's mother shouted.

They embraced, suddenly being interrupted by the jabbing of a wooden cane. Frenchy shook his head and walked over to his grandmother, who was seated on a folding chair.

"How do you have a folding chair on a runway? What the hell is wrong with a wheel chair?"

She swung her cane, nearly clipping Frenchy's left eye.

"I'm no cripple. I don't need it. By the way, yesterday was the first of the month; don't forget the rent."

Frenchy's family muttered various exasperated words in unison.

"I will never miss that phrase, no matter how close I recently came to being killed. And of course, Grandma, I'll write the check when we get home. Would you like my kidney or a few pints of my blood with it?"

"What the hell does that have to do with it? I said 'don't forget the rent.'"

Frenchy was preparing to argue with his grandmother when he was pushed by his sister towards Sarah. He walked over to her and extended his hand to her sisters. He greeted them politely and then waved his family over.

"This is Francis, the man of the hour."

Frenchy's eyes lit up and he nodded in agreement, turning to his family.

"And this is Sarah, my love interest on my adventure. And guess what, Grandma? She's a Jew."

His family responded in embarrassment at his blunt comment, aware of what was coming next.

"A Jew? Well, Jesus was a Jew."

Frenchy's mother swiftly moved in front of her mother, shaking the hands of Sarah's sisters.

"Do you have to provoke her every time?" Frenchy's mother asked.

"Well, for once, my provocation is actually relevant. But anyway, now that we've all met and exchanged pleasantries, I really want to go home."

Sullivan joined the group.

"Go home and rest. We'll handle everything else. We're just glad you're back safe and unharmed."

Frenchy looked over at Ricky. He caught a glimpse of Ricky's father, his arm around his son.

"Ohhhh shit."

Frenchy slowly hobbled over towards the father-son duo. He scanned his surroundings, aware that the father's Italian heritage might have associated him with the sort of men Frenchy would prefer to avoid.

"Sir, I don't know how to convey how sorry—"

"You know, the moment you guys left with my boy, I realized I had made an enormous mistake."

Frenchy nodded humbly, wondering if this was the opening line to a verbal and eventual physical thrashing.

"Yeah, I figured that would have happened. I'm so sorry about everything that happened and, yes, he kind of got shot in the leg. But he was so brave and he stood up for me."

Mr. Badaracco chuckled.

"He's home safe. That's enough. His 'kind of shot' leg will heal. All that matters now is that he's back. I may change my mind once everything sinks in, but you have plenty of time to run before I come and kill you."

Frenchy smiled awkwardly.

"Oh, you and your jokes . . . right? Or should I really be planning a quick exit right about now . . ."

Sarah grabbed Frenchy from behind and kissed him.

"Well, I see she's a keeper, Francis. She knows just when to pull your plug."

Frenchy's mother walked over and hugged Sarah.

"Pull my plug? That can be taken in so many . . ."

Sarah repeated her silencer.

Frenchy opened his eyes from Sarah's kiss and looked to Ricky for commentary.

"I ain't got anything to say now that my father is next to me."

Frenchy laughed, winking at his sidekick.

"Thank you again for letting your son come with me. I don't think I would have succeeded without him, and certainly would not have stayed alive without him."

Mr. Badaracco shook Frenchy's hand firmly.

"Like I said. My feelings may change. Keep a travel bag ready in case I change my mind."

Frenchy giggled exaggeratedly, hoping to make light of a second direct threat.

Ricky stepped forward and hugged Frenchy. The two held on, aware of what they had been through together and the change in their relationship.

"Not sure if I can call you my mentee anymore. I think I learned as much from you through this whole mess as you may have from me. It was an honor to work with you on this."

Ricky nodded proudly, aware of the compliment Frenchy had given.

"Thanks, Doc. You don't have to dream of being Indiana Jones anymore. You got enough credit to be your own character in a movie . . . minus the uncertainty, of course. I told you. Be confident. You got whatever you want."

"Not grammatically correct but I appreciate the sentiment." Frenchy patted Ricky on the cheek. As the young man walked towards his family and friends, Frenchy returned his gaze to Sarah.

"Hey, Junior!"

Frenchy turned and smiled, appreciating the reference.

"It was an honor, Doc. Next adventure, instead of the Middle East, maybe our quest takes us to Weehawken."

"That is absolutely agreed."

Frenchy watched Ricky and his father walk away. He shook his head, enjoying his student's final comment again. He hobbled slowly over to Sarah.

"You know, you should come to my house to relax. It's on the way to the city so I can drive you home after. Terrible traffic, if you go now. Terrible."

Sarah blushed slightly.

"I could do that."

"Sweet! Hey, Grandma, I'd have you come back with us, but I figured you wanted to have dinner at my mom's house."

"Oh well, it's been a long day. I'm sure Grandma wants to get home."

Frenchy and his mother locked eyes in a responsibility standoff.

"I'm pretty sure Grandma would like to have dinner at your house. Plus don't you remember, Grandma? You left your sweater at my parent's house last week. And it *is* your favorite sweater."

Frenchy's grandmother sat pondering her options. She picked at her teeth with a plastic toothpick.

"Okay, dinner it is," she said, leaning on her cane to stand.

"I'd say it's good to have you back safe, but after that little move to avoid driving her home, it just wouldn't be true." Frenchy's mother smiled as she patted her son on the head, ending with a strong smack.

"I deserved that. I'll take G-ma out tomorrow to the Pathmark."

"You're damn right, you will," Frenchy's mother said, sneering at him as she bid Sarah farewell.

The remaining people in the welcoming party began to disperse. Congressman Sullivan gestured to a few cars near the group.

"Go relax. We'll be in touch. Senator Maini will be happy to know you are okay.

Frenchy paused, remembering the Senator's connection to his father.

"Tell him it is much appreciated."

Frenchy's father overheard his classmate's name.

"You know, we were the two top students in our class from Saint Ignatius. One ended up in civil service, the other politics."

"Who was number one, you or Maini?"

Mr. Degnan winked at Frenchy and ushered him to a waiting car.

"Enjoy the long journey home."

Frenchy laughed. He opened the door for Sarah, entering after her. The car slowly pulled away, the few lingering students ran behind the car jokingly.

"Well, I assume we're in for another long car ride. You may hate planes but I am sick of being in these government vehicles."

Frenchy turned to her, his demeanor changing.

"Hey, I really want you to know that I don't care about anything from this trip, except that I met you . . . again."

He looked down nervously.

"Anyway, I guess I want to say 'thank you' and a unilateral apology for all offensive comments I made and will make moving forward."

Frenchy's nervousness made Sarah appreciate what seemed to be such a confusing statement.

"But I am trying not to be offensive. It's just so hard. When you meet my best friend, Joe, you will understand why. We've said such inappropriate things for so many years—God, I don't even know how to start to change. It's like learning to shit all over again."

"I suppose as long as you are trying. But just remember, I still have the right to put you down."

Frenchy winked strangely, his thoughts veering towards a sexual interpretation of her comments.

"Yes, I suppose it is only fair that you . . . put me down."

His smirk made Sarah push him playfully.

"No, but seriously, can I wax that ass or what?"

Sarah's shock at his crude statement paralyzed her usual violent reaction. Despite the raunchy question, she smiled.

"We are almost there, Dr. Degnan."

The driver's interjection distracted Sarah.

"Wait, what? I thought this would be a long trip."

Frenchy rolled his window down and inhaled.

"Smell that methane? Now that's Jersey, baby. And it's fifteen minutes, tops, from my house to Newark airport. Cut that in half with fancy secret service flashy lights."

Frenchy eyed the familiar sites of his neighborhood. The barber shop where he had his hair cut; unfortunately, by a man who didn't speak English. Thus, Frenchy's hairstyle varied based on what his barber thought he understood.

They made a left turn up Boyd Avenue, accelerating towards the top.

"Right up there," Frenchy said, excited.

Sarah looked skeptically, eyeing a dice game taking place in a driveway across from where they stopped.

"You live across the street from . . . that?"

Sarah pointed towards the raucous group illegally gambling.

"Yeah, of course, I do. They're good people. If they want to play dice, let them play. They're respectful. If it's too loud, I ask them to quiet down and they always do. Neighborhoods may look shitty, but there are good people who live in them. Even people who play dice in a driveway. We only see or hear the negative aspects of communities. But if you look closely, you find that most people are caring, hard-working people. This place may have the occasional problem, but it's my home, and I love everyone in it . . ."

Frenchy eyed a stumbling man, gliding awkwardly down the block.

"Except him. He took a shit in my driveway. I know it was him. He even wiped and left the toilet paper. Who carries toilet paper with them for spontaneous shitting?"

"Well, that's comforting. You had me going with that speech, until you highlighted human excrement as a side story."

"Good note. Good note."

Frenchy stood up and stared longingly at his grandmother's house. Sarah's expression lacked the same appreciation for the two-family home.

"And you do. You have bars on your windows."

"Only to keep me inside when I turn into the Hulk at night."

His futile comment failed to comfort Sarah or satisfactorily explain the fortress that was his home.

"Come on."

He grabbed her hand and slowly pulled her up the limestone steps. He unlocked the front door and entered the hallway. He closed the door and commenced the usual ritual of multiple locks. Frenchy took Sarah's hand and kissed it, aware of her apprehension.

"Please trust me about my neighborhood. This is an amazing place and . . . holy shit. My dog."

"What?"

"Pray to your God that my parents took care of her. Otherwise, there may be an excess amount of doo doo and piss all over."

He walked towards the door, hearing the aggressive scratching of Cleo at his door. He opened the door slightly, Cleo wedging her snout into the crack and slamming the door open.

"Nipples!"

Frenchy painfully lunged down and began hugging and kissing her.

"Her name is Nipples?"

Frenchy's address to his dog worried Sarah.

"No, her name is Cleo, but she has saggy nipples from when she had puppies so sometimes I call her Nips, Nipples, Nippies, or any other variation. Who the fuck names their dog Nipples?"

Sarah smiled at Frenchy's seemingly logical response.

"Let's go, this bitch needs to relieve herself. We're good, no shit anywhere I can see, thus far."

She smiled, watching Frenchy limp hurriedly through the small dining room and into the kitchen. She stopped, observing the decor of his apartment.

The dog quickly doubled back, running at full speed and plunging her snout into Sarah's crotch. She jumped back, pushing Cleo away.

"Yeah, so I meant to tell you that she was abused. And for some reason, she has responded to the abuse by being a bit of a pervert. Sadly, I'm being serious. She acts totally inappropriately."

Sarah seemed unamused, pushing Cleo's head away again.

"I am sure she will be much more of a proper lady once she has pissed in the backyard greenery."

Sarah followed Frenchy to the back hall, looking out the windows, as Cleo rampaged into the small yard.

"Greenery? It's bricks with dog shit everywhere."

"Very true, but I've not had a chance to clean lately. And the key words you said are canine feces. As I've told you, I've had humans shit on this property." Frenchy placed his hand on her hips pulling her close to his body. She shook her head bashfully.

"Come on. A yard full of poop is not exactly romantic."

Frenchy pulled her away from the small hallway, backing her through his kitchen and towards a more horizontal placement in his living room. He stopped suddenly.

He gently moved Sarah behind him. She laughed, assuming it was one of his antics. She took his hand, noticing it shaking slightly. She looked up and peered over his shoulder. Two men sat quietly in the living room. Her heart fluttered, fearing the same end as Frenchy.

She grabbed his shoulders and stared, the two men remaining in Frenchy's arm chairs.

She confusingly felt relief as she realized she knew one of the men. She looked down, searching for identification. She stepped forward, Frenchy immediately pressing her behind him. Her firm grip on his hand tried to convey stability.

Unfortunately, he took it as fear. He lunged towards his closet, a few feet away from them, grabbing a metal bat.

"Francis, no! It's—"

The two men remained seated, unmoved by his weapon. Sarah recognized Frenchy's paranoia and rushed forward.

"Stop! Dr. El Deri, what are you doing here?"

Sarah's knowledge of the man spurred panicked conspiracy thoughts in Frenchy's mind.

"What are you doin' here? Fuck, are you with them?" Frenchy demanded.

Frenchy's happiness with Sarah had not come without questions about whether her feelings were authentic.

"What?"

"I mean, are you like everyone else? Double agents or whatever the fuck they are?"

Sarah shoved Frenchy in anger.

"What the fuck does that mean? Is that a 'stop it silly,' or an 'oh shit, you found me out?'" Frenchy eyed Sarah, trying to decipher the meaning of her shove. She grimaced in disappointment.

"Perhaps you could put the bat away, Dr. Degnan? I certainly mean you no harm. Actually, we arranged your safe transportation home. I would much rather explain everything in a calm atmosphere."

Frenchy's hands kept gripping the bat. His eyes darted from person to person.

"Oh, nice. The usual 'we' statement. Comforting. I'm sick of this cryptic bullshit. And what's in the fuckin' bag? You got a bomb in that bitch?"

"I assure you there is no bomb. While you may not believe me now, I assure you, if you give me a few minutes, you will believe my intentions are peaceful."

Sarah put her hand on Frenchy's shoulder. He flinched in fear.

"I'll put the bat down once you explain how you know him. And you called him Doctor . . ."

"Allow me to explain. My name is Nabin El Deri. I am a doctor, but more related to our situation, I was Rabbi Tannen's doctor. My colleagues and I have been monitoring your progress over these past few days. Will you now sit down so I may continue in a violence-free atmosphere?"

Frenchy sighed and lowered the bat, sitting down and placing it on his lap.

"What do you mean you've been monitoring us?"

Sarah stepped forward, joining Frenchy's suspicion.

"Well, after your father died, I had to make sure I followed through on his requests. He knew what his good friend Rabbi Judah was doing, so he made sure his last acts before he died leveled the playing field. The C4 without a detonator to Dr. Degnan, the C4 with the detonator to Judah, the disappearance of the second half of the map, which I should give to you before I forget." El Deri handed an envelope to Sarah with the second half of the map.

"You had her father's half of the map? Why didn't you give it to me? That would have made things so freakin' easy. And how did you get it? I thought the bad Rabbi had it."

"He did have it. Rabbi Tannen had to give Judah his half. Then, we reclaimed it."

Frenchy lit a cigarette, shaking his head in disgust.

"I don't think I want to hear anymore. All this is pissing me off."

"Please, let me continue. We could not stop all of these events so we made sure to help in every way we could . . ."

"What events? You mean all that awful shit that has happened to us in the last week? And if you tried to help, you guys suck ass at helping. We spent our time on the run only to be helped out by the bad guys, only to be taken by more bad guys, oh and with my friend . . ."

"May I finish? I am happy to answer any questions afterwards."

Frenchy picked up the bat from his lap.

"Our ability to help was limited. We could not stop what Israel did. We could not stop your own government from chasing you. But we were able to wrest you from Israel's hold. We freed you from that caravan to Masada. Yes, in a violent manner. But sometimes, force is necessary."

"You're telling me that Ali and the douche brothers were with you? They're part of this 'we?' Because, if so, you need to think about what your membership looks like. Your boy shot my student and I was ready to fuckin' kill him, and I'm a goddamn pacifist."

"They were out of line and we have dealt with them, but Assaf and his men would have killed you immediately once you found the sword. So, while uncivilized, we did what we had to."

Frenchy mocked El Deri's last statement.

"Still, we knew you would find the sword. The other finds, well, sometimes good things happen to bad people . . . or good people, depending on whom we are talking about."

"That's not funny, for starters, and two, stop saying 'we,' I hate hearing that shit. You're not 'we'—you're full of shit!"

"Of course. I understand your feelings. But let me continue. So once we secured the Sword, regardless of the manner in which we did, we moved forward towards the completion and original goal of the operation."

"Wait, before you finish, what was the deal with Botvinnik? Your murderers killed him."

El Deri, nodded remorsefully.

"Again, it was wrong to kill him, but his betrayal of his own country made him an untrustworthy individual. Still, we needed his help to follow through and find the sword. But again, murder is not what we are about, and the men have been dealt with. Nonetheless, once we had what we needed, and I met with the senators and exposed the governments' unethical, if not illegal actions, we were able to ensure your safety home. The rest is out of our hands. We have presented everything we can to expose the injustices of both Israel and the United States. Our job is done, and in the end, a little retribution for you, Dr. Degnan. After all, you found your sword, and possibly found some very famous skeletons, not forgetting the scrolls."

Frenchy sat waiting.

"So, that's it? And who knows if it's authentic. You see what this week has done to me? When I read Tannen's letter, I was a believer that the Sword existed. Now I'm a doubter and generally irritated at the world."

He inhaled from his cigarette waiting for a response.

"Well?" Frenchy asked. "Is that it?"

El Deri looked over at his silent friend and smiled.

"So, now that you have given us absolutely no information and sufficiently raised my blood pressure, may I start my questions that I am sure you won't answer?"

El Deri nodded, crossing his legs.

Frenchy removed the map from the envelope as he glared at El Deri. He took his half and placed them together, reading the full description.

"This doesn't bring you to the actual location. These directions keep you at Masada. This would have been worthless. I thought he found the goddamn thing. These directions suck."

"Thankfully for Rabbi Tannen, his friend trusted him completely. Tannen never had any intention of creating a map to its location. Fortunately, Judah never looked at the map. He trusted his old friend to make an accurate account of their finding. If he had checked, he would have realized his good friend had ensured no map would have led anyone near the actual location.

Frenchy scratched his head in confusion.

"But Judah knew where they found the sword. He could have found it without the map?

"Yes, he could have. But he was killed. Tragic, but necessary."

"I like how we moved right past the murder of the guy, but whatever. I guess I'm old fashioned, I guess murder is commonplace these days."

Frenchy squirmed in his chair.

"So, the map was a waste. How did Tannen expect me to find it then?"

"I believe he knew you could. And it would seem his faith in you was not misguided. Though the first section of the map did help a bit. Still, he ensured it would not be found by Israel. I would consider his work to have been well-accomplished."

Sarah nudged Frenchy, hoping to push him beyond his interrogation.

"Fine, I'll accept what I think is bullshit, but whatever. I'll move on. First main question, who is 'we?' Fuck it—better yet—who are you, and then who is 'we?'"

"I am a doctor . . ."

"No shit, slick, but Sullivan said the guy who arranged our safe return was named Nasser."

"My name is Nabin El Deri, but sometimes I use an alias. Nasser is one I use."

"Great, love the name. Very cute. So, next: who is 'we?'"

"We? 'We' is a group of people who, when they come across injustice, act. 'We' does our best to live out the values that span all three great Abrahamic religions and all others, that embrace agreed upon values in countries all across the world. Certainly you, a Jesuit educated man, would agree."

"First, kiss my ass with that comment, like you know me. And my education taught me to not kill. Something you and your bullshit group seem to forget. But I'm sorry, I digress. To get back to your explanation of 'we,' I call absolute supreme bullshit on this one. You are not the League of Superheroes. No . . . the Justice League, that's what I was looking for."

El Deri's companion chuckled at Frenchy's reference.

"And what the fuck is with this guy? He hasn't said a word. He's just sitting there like an ass-clown."

"You will have to excuse my friend. He enjoys observing. Let me ask you a simple question, Dr. Degnan. Is it so hard to believe that there would be a group of people who want to oppose injustice? How often do we hear conspiracy theories about the 'Skull and Bones,' or the 'Illuminati,' Freemasons, or whoever else we name, claiming that they run the world with greed and exploitation as their modus operandi. But you are mistaken; we are no league of heroes. We are ordinary people. You pass 'we' on the streets every day. You buy coffee from 'we,' you ask 'we' to 'supersize it' when you pass through a drive-through. You yell at 'we' when it takes forever at the DMV. We . . . are far from extraordinary."

"Oh my God, you dickhole! I do not believe that the high school kid at McDonald's is a soldier for justice, nor do I believe the hipster at Starbucks is either."

"Let me clarify. This is no league. Nor do 99.9% of 'we' even know they are part of anything. Most people want resist injustice but they just can't—why? Because most would lose their jobs, be ostracized, et cetera. My colleagues and I provide a way to do the right thing without facing any persecution."

Frenchy waved El Deri off, convinced he had found a gaping hole in his explanation.

"But then how do you fight injustice? If none of your members are willing to speak up, and even know they are in some stupid league, then how do 'we' do anything? I certainly have never heard of the league of ordinary gentleman defeating anything."

"Fair point. Allow me to better explain. If you are a low-level employee and you know your company is oppressing, say, a group of people in some Third World country. Do you go to your boss and say, 'I disagree with what our company is doing?' Do you believe said employee would still have a job come Monday? Of course not. But say you could prove said injustice. But again, what would you do with it? So you complain to your friends about it by email, or Facebook, or to your family. Still, you cannot do anything but whine. Now imagine you are contacted by someone who says they can take what you know and use it, to ultimately do what you wanted to do before you stopped, fearing the ramifications. Suddenly, what you wanted to do can be done without any penalties. Your desire for justice is now taken over by people who know how to execute. 'Joe Employee' returns to work unaffected. But the direction sought by said 'Joe Employee' now ensures justice. That's where my colleagues and I enter the situation. We call ourselves 'The Milites.'"

Frenchy laughed quietly, appreciating the use of Latin.

"I knew you would like it. We are the warriors for the average person. Does it always work? No. But we have a better chance of succeeding than a first year employee working a menial position, and we make sure nothing is ever traced back to our people."

"It's very charming, but I have never heard of any successful jobs your group has completed. In truth, if you kids do expose injustice then you suck. Injustice exists everywhere, in every part of our world. You may want to get on that; maybe offer some sort of incentive, so things get done. Because for every single injustice you claim to expose, a hundred others go unnoticed."

"I don't disagree that injustice occurs each day all over the world. But we can only do what we can. Again, you are missing what we are. We are not miracle workers. Certainly not 'superheroes.' Still, there must be an attempt at balance, even if we are unable to reach it. Is it better to say there is no point and give up? I do not think so, and I believe you disagree with that sentiment as well. What have we done you ask? To be honest, the internet has made our work possible. So our work has only begun in the last decade. Why should I list our successes? I'm sure that would not satisfy you. I would only ask you to think about how many unjust actions have been exposed since we started our work? In your heart, you believe all were done simply by ordinary people willing to face the consequences of opposing their employer, their family, their government? I would very much enjoy that belief. Still, I do know many people who have selflessly stood up against injustice. But for those who cannot risk unemployment in this economy, we seek to help them with their professional dilemma."

"Hold up. You said, 'and tell their families.' I got the internet as your in. But do you spy on people? Are you bugging phones, you piece of shit? Is that how you know me?"

Frenchy stood in anger winding up his bat swing. El Deri stood, holding his hands up in surrender

"Please, Dr. Degnan. We do not use anything to hurt anyone. But do not try to convince me that our own government does not record and monitor what we do and say. They do! Fortunately for us, we have the best tech support, and the government remains a few steps behind us in software updates. We use what we hear for good. The government uses their surveillance to oppress. We are not alike. How else would we be able to access all documents for evidence? Our hackers are the true superheroes. They find the voiceless crying out for help. They are the ones who find the evidence. I would say that positive far outweighs the negative of being spied on."

"Are you a Muslim group? If so, I'd diversify your membership. Muslim groups are not exactly the 'cool group' these days."

"Not all. Our 'founder' is a Frenchman. A very smart man. He was appalled by the actions of many governments and their people. He believed that governments and their officials were corrupt, but the average person was not. He used his skills to . . . 'listen.' He found that, like him, most people were against much that their own governments, companies, et cetera, did. He slowly reached out to those who were 'protesting' most adamantly. The original 'Milites' came from that first outreach. And we continue to recruit. But back to your question: no, not a Muslim group. And my religious and ethnic affiliation just happened to fit with this situation. But I doubt I would be of service if the next injustice to fight were in Ireland."

Frenchy sat slowly, mulling over El Deri's words.

"The 'Ireland' comment was actually funny. I still don't buy any of this shit. But fine, whatever. Another pleasant yet completely shady explanation. But you know what? While I appreciate your rhetoric and gift for making light of rights violations, I return to my original comment. I call horse and bullshit. And again, seriously? You guys are some justice warrior group? Jerking off to recorded conversations of normal Americans? Do you spank each other as initiation? You are exactly what's wrong with the government and the world."

"Do not demean who we are by questioning our courage and resolve. We are no cult; we have no rituals and there is no initiation. We are ordinary people. You, of all people, should understand. You are very involved in the community service program at Saint Ignatius Prep. And if I am not mistaken, you have attended the Pax Christi Peace Walk every year since your senior year of high school. You gave a reflection at one of the Stations of the Cross, 'Veronica wipes the face of Jesus' again, if I am not mistaken. You spoke about the preferential option for the poor, and the need for individual as well as government action to aid the voiceless and oppressed."

Frenchy shifted uncomfortably. He stopped, thinking about El Deri's words.

"Is that true?"

Frenchy's past actions reinforced Sarah's respect for him.

"Yes, it's true. I'm more concerned that this perv knew what I was doing as a seventeen-year-old."

"You see, Doctor. You were made for 'we.' You know why 'we' do what 'we' do. I would even venture to say that you have imagined yourself creating such a group. But like I said, we are no secret society. Perhaps closer to a social network. Perhaps our name should be the National Association of Justice Seekers. But NAOJS simply does not have a nice ring to it."

Sarah laughed, taking Frenchy's hand.

"So what, great, you have this group. I assume you're here to ask me to join?"

El Deri smiled.

"Well, to be honest, no. As a scholar of history, I believe you are aware of many injustices in the world, but you are a teacher. Sadly, you are of no use to us. However, if that is an inaccurate assessment, we will find you. We will be monitoring. Still, the reason why we came here was to explain everything so you understood, and particularly to tell Sarah that her father did what was right, and she should be proud of him."

The mention of her father made Sarah tear up again.

"He always knew what I did as a 'hobby' and always helped whenever he could. When he realized what was happening, he asked me to help him. Unfortunately, as Dr. Degnan mentioned, we did commit murder, and do other things that were certainly not in our fictitious mission statement. But in the end, we did what we knew was just. Your father begged that we ensure no one was hurt, not even those willing to kill an innocent man. Sadly, we could not avoid it. But I want you to know that he knew nothing of what we did. I sent the bomb to Rabbi Judah. Your father never would have allowed it. But he is like you, Dr. Degnan, pure of heart."

"I still don't agree with anyone being killed."

"I know you do not, hence the pure heart. But as long as you now know what was going on, and Sarah knows her father helped but knew nothing of how we acted, I believe our job is done. Lastly, I do have a parting gift."

El Deri's companion reached down and pulled a large hard shelled suitcase.

"If that's the Stanley Cup, I'll kiss you."

El Deri missed the reference, smiling awkwardly at Frenchy's statement. He opened the case and removed the historical blade Frenchy had found.

"No shit."

"Please, Dr. Degnan. I admire you . . . but not enough to give you the artifact. We had a replica made. It was our top priority if that affirms our appreciation for you. And extremely difficult to complete before you returned from Israel. It is not that easy to make a copy of something like a sword, so please be flattered that we did this for you."

Frenchy took the sword, smiling at El Deri's honesty. He grinned, his eyes widening. Sarah hugged his shoulder, looking at the sword.

"Everything happened so fast and I was shitting my pants at intervals when we found it so I didn't get a chance to appreciate it. I don't care if this is a replica; this is the replica of something I found. I'll take that."

"And of course, this."

El Deri handed him a leather folder. Frenchy handed it to Sarah as he rubbed the sword, too enamored to focus. She opened the folder.

"I don't understand."

"Those are the papers for the scrolls. The scrolls are yours . . . for now. The skeletons, no, but the scrolls are. Those are the papers when they were submitted to Cairo. They know you found them. Whether you own them, I cannot say, but that is, I suppose, the equivalent of a title to a vehicle for them. As I have said, the rest is in your hands. Now, I must bid you farewell."

El Deri and his companion stood. Frenchy fumbled with the sword, still in awe at the parting gift.

"If it is acceptable to you, I would like to exit through your backyard. Two Muslims leaving your house may cause your bodyguards to panic."

Frenchy shook their hands. Sarah smiled at El Deri and hugged him. He rubbed her cheek gently.

"Hey, easy there, old man. That's my lady."

"Perhaps I may be invited to the wedding."

The two men walked towards the back.

"Hey, Doc, watch it back there. My dog is out and she shits like crazy."

"I appreciate the warning. But I have already journeyed through your 'minefield of feces.' I will leave the door open so she may enter. Perhaps a diaper for your canine. It may help the smell in your city."

Frenchy snorted, slowly catching the insult to his hometown. He turned to Sarah, holding the sword. Her cheeks still glistened from her earlier tears. He put the sword down carefully and put his head to hers. He pulled her towards the couch.

"You okay?"

She sighed and kissed him strongly.

"This has been an emotional roller coaster of a week. I lose my father. Leave him to save you . . . and perhaps . . . and just perhaps, fall for a strange man from Jersey City."

"Well, I can't disagree, I *am* from Jersey City."

The two embraced. The galloping from Frenchy's dog broke their focus. Cleo jumped up between them, situating herself.

"So this one is a bit of a brute. And her lunge into my crouch certainly was not appropriate. You certainly know how to pick them."

"Yes, I do."

Frenchy smiled, kissing Sarah's cheek. He removed a cigarette from his pack and lit it. He rubbed his eyes, Sarah recognizing his frustration.

"I was just kidding about Cleo. She's fine; a pervert, definitely, but she's fine.

"It's not that. And in truth, you are being kind to Cleo. When she pins a dog, it looks like a violent rape. Really, it's embarrassing. I'm banned from the South Orange dog park."

Sarah chuckled at his revelation.

"No, I'm tired, confused, overwhelmed, and more than all of that, I really don't know what this was all about let alone how we actually found . . . stuff. No map, winging everything, and yet somehow it worked. What we found, I still have no clue but we did find shit. I don't know. I feel like there's something missing. People do not get so lucky. The whole secret society bullshit all around just weirds me out, but the worst is I hate not knowing what's really going on. Your father's doctor can explain, but it just seems beyond strange and none of this really makes sense. We can pretend that it sounds plausible but if you think about it, this shit doesn't add up."

"Do you believe in God or at least fate?"

Frenchy rolled his eyes and took a pull on his cigarette.

"Please, I hate it when things are confusing or don't make sense, people bring God or fate into it. I know plenty about God and, no, I do not believe God is behind this."

"Fair enough, and clearly a sore spot for you so I'm sorry that I asked. But how about you view it this way. Whether it's God, fate, or perhaps you would prefer, luck, we are alive so that is success to me. I still have questions as well. But I would rather enjoy our success than stress about everything being consequential or logical."

"I know, it's just tough. I wish I could do something where it's just me, start to finish. No unanswered questions. It was me who made it happen and I could explain every step . . ."

Frenchy leaned back and looked at Cleo. Her tail thumped under her body as she basked in the attention. He tapped his cigarette over the ashtray.

"But you mentioned luck? That's what I believe this was. I watched a documentary a few weeks ago that talked about the most recent ancient discoveries and the artifacts still 'out there.' One of the commentators said the only future discoveries will be ones of pure luck. He even mentioned people falling into rooms with treasure. I suppose I should just be happy that it was us who fell into these discoveries. God or fate, no. But luck ain't bad. Just feels weird."

Sarah took Frenchy's cigarette from his hand and placed it to her lips, breathing smoke out through her nose. She stamped it out and smiled.

"I don't think things like this end with an amazing feeling. But I'd rather say I had a bumpy adventure with you, ending with a weird feeling, than a smooth, perfect journey with no questions left with anyone else. And the weird feeling will leave."

"You smo . . ."

Sarah pushed Cleo off the couch, kissing Frenchy and climbing onto his lap. Frenchy looked up at Sarah, slowly unbuttoning her dress. He peeled the straps gently. He moved to kiss her neck when she suddenly shrieked. Frenchy sat up, holding Sarah on his lap, hoping he had not been too aggressive.

"What? I'm sorry. What did I do, I thought you . . ."

Sarah looked behind her holding her dress up with her hands. She swung around and glared at Frenchy. He looked beyond her and down at his leg.

"Oh, yeah . . . that *would* kill the mood."

Frenchy shook his leg and yelled in chastisement, trying to dislodge Cleo. She continued gyrating on his leg, her nails touching Sarah's back. She screamed again, flopping on the couch and putting her feet up to defend herself. Frenchy finally disentangled Cleo from his leg as she continued to thrust at the air, scraping her paws against the carpet.

"I'm sorry."

"It's okay. Just . . . can we put her back outside?"

Frenchy nodded. He winked at Sarah, aroused by her current position. He leaned in and kissed her, moving down to her neck. She moaned playfully.

"Hurry up and put her outside and come back."

Frenchy slowly popped up and riled Cleo to run to the back. He winked and ran after her.

Sarah rubbed her face, still shocked at Cleo's boldness. Frenchy came running back, quickly jumping towards Sarah. She squealed happily, as he suddenly slowed and gently helped her recline on the couch. He gently positioned himself above her. He caressed her lip with his thumb to her delight. He moved in to kiss her, pausing to speak.

"But just so I'm clear before we continue. Based on your reaction to Cleo's advance, threesomes will be a no-no, right?"

ABOUT THE AUTHOR

ERICH BERKOWITZ SEKEL is a proud resident of Jersey City, New Jersey, and currently the Associate Director of Campus Ministry for Community Service at Saint Peter's University. He is on the Board of Directors of Rebuilding Together, Jersey City.

CPSIA information can be obtained
at www.ICGtesting.com
Printed in the USA
LVOW11s2208180117
521454LV00003B/292/P